The Spy Within

Dottie Manderson mysteries: book 6

Caron Allan

The Spy Within: Dottie Manderson mysteries: book 6

Dedication

To Angy and Emma, thanks for keeping me sane. Ish.

Chapter One

Saturday 31ˢᵗ March 1934

Mrs Sedgworth was still panting after her desperate sprint along the dark lane to the farmhouse. She had rapped on the front door, and now she was waiting for someone to open the door. She leaned on a railing and tried to calm herself. It would be no help at all to be puffing and panting as she tried to explain what she needed. Above all, she had to preserve an air of calm dignity. No one must know what she had done.

The door was opened by a young boy. He peered at her curiously but said nothing.

'Is your mother at home, dear?' Mrs Sedgworth asked, smiling kindly at the boy as if this was purely a social call. He still didn't speak, but left the door standing wide and scampered off along the corridor. Somewhere at the back of the house Mrs Sedgworth could hear voices.

A woman approached, her hands covered in flour.

'I'm so sorry to bother you,' Mrs Sedgworth said. 'I've had a slight accident with my car and need to telephone for—er—assistance. Do you by any chance have a

telephone I could use? I'll pay for the call, of course. Mrs—er?'

'McRae. *The phone is just here, ma'am, please help yourself,' the woman said. She stepped back and indicated the instrument on the wall near the door. The little boy clung to her apron.*

'Thank you, you're very kind.' *Mrs Sedgworth waited, smiling. But the woman continued to hover. Mrs Sedgworth's call was not the kind of conversation to be overheard. She said, 'I'm so sorry to have disturbed you when you're busy. Don't let me keep you from your cooking. I'll only be a moment, and I'll wait outside. I suppose your husband isn't at home?'*

'No, but I expect him any time now,' *Mrs McRae said. With a nod and a smile, she returned to her kitchen, taking her son with her. Mrs Sedgworth seized the phone and rang the operator.*

'Put me through to Gervase Parfitt of Westhorpe Dale, please.'

She prayed he would be there. It felt like forever before the operator said, 'Putting you through now, caller.' Then there was Parfitt himself answering the phone.

'Oh Mr Parfitt. It's Mrs Sedgworth here. We met at the charity auction just before Christmas. Look I'm terribly sorry to bother you, but I've had rather a mishap. I wouldn't usually trouble you but my husband is away and I just didn't know who else to ask. You see, I'm in something of a fix.'

At the other end of the line, Parfitt, already a busy man, nevertheless scented possibilities. He expressed concern and Mrs Sedgworth knew she had called the right person. She looked over her shoulder to make sure she was alone, and dropping her voice, she said, 'Please help me, Mr Parfitt. I've had an accident with my car. I-I've hit someone. I rather think he may be dead.'

Mrs Sedgworth remained outside the farmhouse, having thanked the woman for her kindness and pressed a ten-shilling note into her hand. She waited. She wrapped her coat closely about her, wishing she wore stouter shoes; her feet were numb with cold. Her breath clouded the air before her face. She couldn't go any closer to the car. She could just make out the dark shape of it along the lane, but venture closer, she couldn't bear to do. To see the man lying there...

Parfitt was with her in less than fifteen minutes. His calm manner and gentle understanding soothed her. Guiltily, she realised that in the past she had rather snubbed him, but in a crisis, he was clearly admirable. She made a mental note, when this awful evening was over, to make sure to invite him to her next dinner party.

'Oh, Mr Parfitt, is it—too late? Is it awful? He came out of nowhere, I just didn't know what to do, or where to turn.'

He smiled gravely at her. 'There, there, Mrs Sedgworth,' he said, immediately scenting the alcohol on her. 'Don't distress yourself, ma'am. Unfortunately these things do happen from time to time, nobody's fault, a dark lane, late at night. Only to be expected.'

'And is he really...?'

'Just leave it to me, my dear Mrs Sedgworth. Try not to think about it.'

'Oh it's just terrible! What on earth will I tell my husband when he comes home next week? What about the police?' That sudden thought alarmed her. She clutched at Gervase's jacket. 'I can't go to prison! I just can't!' Her voice was rising in panic.

He fought down the urge to slap her, and said with another of his grave smiles, 'My dear Mrs Sedgworth, just you leave it all to me. I am the police, after all. And I know you didn't mean it to happen. Just leave everything to me, and I promise, no one will ever hear a word of it from me. There's nothing to worry about.'

'Oh Mr Parfitt, you're so kind,' she said, and began to cry.

Repressing a shudder, he handed her a handkerchief. 'There, there, my dear. Now let me get on. I'll take you home presently. But first I need to speak with the farmer, to use his phone.'

'*Oh he's not at home,*' *Mrs Sedgworth said.* '*Just his wife and son.*'

'*I believe I saw him go in the back door a moment ago. Never you mind about that, anyway, come along and sit in my car and keep warm, and I'll be back in moment.*'

'*Oh Mr Parfitt!*' *she said again. She felt so grateful. She was so relieved she had called him. He was the perfect person to help her out of this awful mess. He was after all, the assistant chief constable.*

Tuesday 29th January 1935.

'I can't help it, Gervase. My father won't have you in the house. In any case, I don't want to see you... After the disgraceful way you acted? No I don't agree it was... Of course I care about your... No, *of course* I don't expect you to wreck your career by... Yes, I know your reputation is very... There's really no need to use that kind of language, Gervase! Really I... No, I...'

Dottie stared at the telephone receiver. Even holding the instrument three feet from her ear she could still hear every furious word he uttered. Suddenly, she thought, why bother? She replaced the receiver and went to join her parents in the drawing room.

'Gervase again?' her father asked, a rare crease of displeasure between his eyebrows.

She nodded. 'I hung up on him.'

'I hope he remained civil,' her mother said without looking up from her embroidery.

'No, Mother. He was not in the least civil.'

Her mother frowned as she stabbed the needle into a patch of pale blue. 'Horrid man. I can't think what I ever saw in him.'

Dottie was torn between a desire to laugh and cry. 'Me either. I must have been blind. Or deaf. Or both. In any case, it's all right because I'm never going to see him again. What a good thing we didn't announce our engagement.'

'Oh definitely.'

There was a short silence. Dottie knew her parents were

desperate to know if she'd seen anything more of Detective Inspector William Hardy since she'd returned to London a little over two weeks earlier. He had helped her so wonderfully in Sussex recently, when she had been in serious difficulties through no fault of her own. He had been... Well, *wonderful* was the only word she could think of to describe what he'd done. Dottie had hoped he might contact her but he hadn't.

A possible reason for that was indelibly seared into her brain: as she and her mother had said goodbye to him and thanked him for his help, he had been collected by someone in a car. That someone had been a woman. A blonde. And she had kissed him in such a way that it was perfectly clear the relationship was neither platonic nor new. Dottie had tortured herself with the memory of it, longing—yet dreading—to know more.

The phone began to ring again. Dottie tensed. If it was Gervase ringing back...

Presently the door opened and Sally, the new maid came in. But instead of coming to Dottie with a message, she spoke to Mrs Manderson.

'Excuse me, ma'am. It's Miss Flora on the telephone for you. She told me to say it's important.'

Mrs Manderson lay aside her embroidery hoop and hurried out. Dottie sat on the edge of her seat. What could it be? What could be an important reason for her sister to telephone?

After a few minutes, Mrs Manderson returned. She looked grave, Dottie thought. And hard on that, with a sudden sense of fear she thought, surely the babies are all right?

She said, 'Mother, what is it?'

'Dorothy dear, Herbert. Flora was telephoning to let us know that George's mother died this afternoon.'

Dottie felt guilty at the sense of relief that washed over her. 'Oh dear,' she said. 'Poor George. I know it was half-expected but even so. I hope he's all right?'

'Flora said he's upset, understandably, but yes, I think he's just glad she didn't suffer for a long time. He would have found that harder to bear. And Piers of course. Flora will let us know about funeral arrangements.' She sat down and took up her embroidery. 'Poor Cynthia. Losing Diana undermined her health terribly, I'm quite certain. One wouldn't recover from losing one's daughter like that.'

The funeral was a week later.

A maid relieved Dottie of her coat and veiled black hat and carried it away to the cloakroom. Everyone was gathering in the vast chilly space of the entrance hall. Another maid was doing the rounds of the mourners with a tray of sandwiches, and behind her, a young footman was offering the mourners sherry. Even in these circumstances Dottie spared a thought to wonder if so many staff were strictly necessary. It was a huge house, to be sure, but now that there was only one occupant...

The solemn murmur of voices began to grow in volume, and the temperature in the hall rose as the number of bodies increased. Soon it began to feel more like a party than a short respite from the cold weather that attended the funeral. Only the family still seemed to be grieving.

'George, I'm so sorry about your mother,' Dottie said gently. 'I think the funeral went off as well as anyone could have hoped.' She swept her much-loved brother-in-law into a tight, fierce hug.

The funeral had exhausted him, she could tell. His wife, Dottie's sister Flora, hovered protectively, anxious to ensure that no one upset him or taxed the last of his reserves of composure. Relieved to see it was Dottie who was talking to him, Flora turned away to attend to the infant twins in the care of their nanny. Diana was, as always, quiet and cherubic, but Freddie was squalling again, his cheeks crimson and shiny. Certainly he was teething, Dottie thought as she glanced that way.

She led George a little further apart as a gaggle of ladies armed with advice surrounded Flora, the nanny and the two babies.

'Thanks,' George said. 'I'm just glad it's over. Father will be relieved too.' He half-turned to look across the room to where his father was standing, ostensibly part of a group deep in sombre conversation, but in fact Piers Gascoigne was staring at the floor, lost in thought. The hand which held his glass had tilted and the sherry was in danger of spilling. Dottie noted that he was excessively pale, his lack of colour exaggerated by the severity of his black suit. He looked easily twenty years older than his actual age of fifty-nine.

She shook her head sadly, and turning back to George, asked, 'Is anyone staying with him tonight?'

'Yes, my mother's younger sister, my Aunt Sarah has come to stay for a few days. Frankly I'm worried about how he will cope on his own once she leaves.' He gave a deep sigh. 'We shall see, I suppose. I know I ought to have arranged to stay myself, but I just couldn't face it. Things have been rather strained between us.'

'Another sherry?' Dottie knew of the strained relations between father and son, and the cause of them.

He shook his head, wrinkling his nose. 'Not really my drink.'

'How about a whisky? I'm sure Overton could rustle you one up.'

He brightened. 'Good idea.'

Dottie went in search of Overton and explained that Mr George needed picking up a bit. Overton, like all butlers good at their job, immediately procured what was required and Dottie rejoined George a minute later, handing him the glass. He disposed of its contents in one gulp.

'That's better.' He set the glass aside. 'Dottie, I've got something to give you. It's from my mother. She asked me to give it to you. When she knew she wasn't, you know...'

Dottie nodded. But she was puzzled. She and her parents had always got on all right with George's parents, but they had only seen them once or twice a year. Certainly they had never been on gift-giving terms, except for a traditional bottle of wine at Christmas.

George dug in his pocket and drew out a small envelope, slightly bulging. He gave it to her. 'I've put a little note inside, it explains things a bit better. At least, I hope it does.'

Dottie took it from him. She was about to open it, but he put his hand over hers. 'Not here, Dottie. Can you wait until you get home?'

She nodded, definitely intrigued now. She put the envelope in her little black clutch bag. Her mind was still busy on what it might contain as George said, softly, 'Heard from Parfitt?'

She shook her head. 'No. That's over. I told him in no uncertain terms what I thought of his lack of support when I was in Sussex. He rang me last week, but he got quite heated, and... well I'm afraid I hung up on him.'

'Quite right too, the idiot deserves it.'

'He was already furious, so I'm not surprised he hasn't been in touch since. I'm rather glad, actually.' She shrugged, replaying the horrid conversation in her head. 'But finally, it's finished. I wouldn't mind if he'd apologised, or even if he'd just lied to me and simply said he believed I was innocent, but that he couldn't help me because of his professional position. If just once he'd said that he'd been desperate to support me. For some reason he managed to make me feel as though I was the one in the wrong. Again.' She gave George a crooked little smile. 'Now I'm beginning to think I never even loved him in the first place. Perhaps it's all for the best. I can't spend my life with someone like that. I need someone I can trust, someone who will support me. I know that sounds silly, but...'

'Not at all. I think that's the least one can ask of the person one plans to spend one's life with.' George looked across at the group centred about his wife and baby.

Babies, Dottie corrected her thoughts. As far as the world was concerned, the two babies were twins, both of them the children of Flora and George, although the close family knew the truth: that baby Diana was in fact the illegitimate daughter of George's sister Diana who had died upon giving birth to her child just eight months earlier. George and Flora had adopted baby Diana as their own, and their own child, Freddie, had been born a little more than three weeks later.

The loss of Diana had driven a wedge between George Gascoigne and his father Piers, and between Piers and his wife Cynthia who had passed away a week ago leaving a devastated Piers with more guilt than he knew how to handle. Dottie glanced across the room at the man. He looked completely stunned by his bereavement. If anyone ever doubted a heart could break, they had only to look at Piers Gascoigne de la Gascoigne: a wealthy landowner from a very old family, and yet all alone now in this great barrack of a place except for his staff.

George, still gazing at his little family, smiled, the careworn creases between his brows and around his mouth smoothing away. 'I'd be lost without Flora.'

Dottie kissed his cheek and went to join her parents. If only I could find a man who inspires the kind of love that George and Flora share, she thought, not for the first time.

Back in London, on the following evening Dottie knocked on the front door of a large townhouse. If she'd let herself think about what she was doing, she would have turned and hurried away again, nervous of facing the man she'd come to see.

As she waited for the door to open, her thoughts conjured anxious alternatives. What if he was out? Or just didn't want to see her? The lights were on, so he was likely to be at home. Or was he?

Added to those thoughts was the desire to run. It wasn't yet too late, she told herself, still not too late to quickly run back down the steps, along the street and around the corner. He need never know she had been there... She hopped from one foot to the other.

Then suddenly it was too late to run: the door opened, light spilling out onto the damp stone steps. William Hardy stood there.

He was wearing old boots, old paint-smudged trousers. His shirtsleeves were rolled back, the old shirt open-necked with no singlet underneath. Her eyes took in the smooth skin of his neck and the little patch of light-coloured hair on his chest. She forced herself to keep her eyes on his face. His eyes were very blue, his fair hair rumpled, white paint streaked his chin. His eyebrows, the cheekbones... The breath in her throat choked her. Such a beautiful man. Clearly, he was taken aback to see her there. He stepped back—wordless—to let her in. For several seconds she stood there before reminding her feet to move and go inside.

He shut the door, taking a long time to do so. He was composing himself, she knew. She stared at the breadth of his shoulders, his slim waist, his lean hips, and wondered yet again how she had ever thought Gervase anything like him.

William turned and said, with a half-smile, 'So, you've obviously heard about your friend Mrs Carmichael leaving me this place in her will last year.'

'Yes,' she said, and ran out of words. He was staring at her still. Should she simply state her business then leave? Perhaps he really wanted her to go. Perhaps...

'Come through to the kitchen. The sitting room's a mess at the moment.'

'Decorating?' It was a safe, normal thing to ask.

'Yes, I've almost finished downstairs. I've been here eight months already.'

'The hall is much nicer now that horrid brown paper has gone. It looks bigger and brighter.'

'And the draughts have gone too. I repointed the brickwork and replaced the glass in the door.' There was a gentle ring of pride in his voice: the man from a wealthy family who had come down in the world only to discover he could learn new skills. 'Now then...'

He pushed open the door at the end of the hall, then stepped back to allow her to go first. He bumped into her. She had expected to follow him through the doorway and was too close, already taking a step forward. The physical contact was a jolt in the limited space and caused them both to take a rather theatrically large step apart, with stammered apologies on both sides. Dottie was certain she'd seen exactly that in a farce at a West End theatre recently.

The kitchen was bright and warm, and very fresh-looking with the new paint, new lino, and the new stove. Everything was so neat and clean. A table with four chairs had been set in the centre of the room. It was perfect, thought Dottie, and said so.

He set the kettle on the stove to boil. Dottie pulled off her coat and scarf, draping them over the back of the nearest chair, then she pulled off her gloves, one finger at a time, added them to the coat and scarf, and put her bright red hat on top of the heap like a cherry on a cake. She took a seat and waited.

He was fussing with the crockery, cutlery, tea, milk. He's trying to decide what to say, she thought. In the end, he just ran out of things to do and stood with his hands resting on the edge of the sink, staring out into the darkness that hid the little garden.

'William,' she said. His head went up but he didn't turn. 'William.'

This time he had to respond. He turned, leaned back against the sink, arms folded across his chest. He looked on the defensive, like a man backed into a corner. While she was still planning what to say, he spoke:

'Why are you here, Dottie? I mean, I'm glad to see you, but...why? Does Parfitt know? Would he approve of you calling on a single man in his home?'

His mention of Gervase induced her to snap at him, 'You can leave Gervase out of it. As far as anyone else is concerned, you are a trusted family friend.' Irritation made her add, heedlessly, 'Goodness knows why.'

There was a prolonged, somewhat frosty silence. William didn't move from the sink, and eventually it was left to Dottie to rescue the boiling kettle, pouring a little hot water into the teapot and leaving it to warm, and placing the kettle back on the stove. She felt exasperated by the situation, by herself, and him too, of course. Clearly the recent renewal of their friendliness in Sussex had died an immediate death. She didn't know whether to slap him, scream at him, kiss him, storm out, or what to do... Her mind played through various scenarios, none of which ended happily.

She opted for calmly coming to the point. 'I'm here because I have something to give you.'

She bent to open her bag and took out the tiny package from George's mother. She held it out to him, not wanting to cross the room to him. He didn't move. She shook her head. If possible, she felt still more exasperated. They were behaving like schoolchildren. Especially him. She put the package on the table, and only when she turned to see to the teapot did he come away from the sink and pick it up. She emptied the water out of the teapot, spooned in tea leaves then poured in the fresh boiling water and replaced the lid.

She watched him, part policeman, part angry ex-lover, as he first looked then finally began to unwrap the parcel. His fingers trembled a little. That hurt her. That they had done this to one another. That she—*she* had done this to them, to him. After all the help he had given her in Sussex a mere two or so weeks ago. And where had Gervase been then, just when she had needed him most? Sitting safely behind his desk polishing his reputation, that's where, she reminded herself furiously. She poured the tea into two cups.

As the paper opened in his hands, she said softly, 'George's mother died last week. He gave this to me after the funeral yesterday. Just before she died, she had told him she wanted me to have it. She wanted it to be reunited with the rest of the mantle. I—I thought you might be able to see to that.'

Finally the thing, soft, faded and warm, fell out of its trappings and into William's palm. He stared. As realisation hit, he looked up at Dottie, but dipped his head again almost immediately.

'The final piece...' His voice was barely above a whisper. He carefully unfolded the uneven rectangle the size of a woman's headscarf.

'Yes.'

'The Gascoignes had it all this time?'

'Yes,' she said again.

He drew a long, shaky breath. 'They are an old Norman family, so I suppose it's not much of a surprise.' He looked down at the tiny piece of ancient fabric. 'Even on its own, it's still...'

'Wonderful? Beautiful?'

'I was about to say, sacred. I know that sounds rather melodramatic, but...' He turned it over in his hands, his touch gentle. 'Impossible to believe that this fabric is, what? Six hundred years old? More?'

Dottie came closer to get a better look.

'Easily seven hundred years old. Possibly as much as eight hundred. And yet the colour is still so rich here and here.' She pointed with a neatly manicured fingernail, taking care not to touch the ancient emerald-coloured fabric. 'There's even a tiny hole there, look, where someone put in a stitch. Perhaps in the wrong place, and it had to be removed? Perhaps an apprentice, still learning the broderer's craft? We'll never know for sure.'

He turned the fabric to catch the light, saw the tiny hole and nodded. There was a glorious starburst worked in gold and silver threads in the centre at the top of the rectangle, and beneath that, a tiny manger, the straw inside it also consisting of gold threads and tiny pearls...

He fixed his eyes on her, intense yet veiled. She felt as though he saw all her thoughts but kept his own well-hidden. Softly he said, 'I know it's not for me, but all the same, thank you.'

She bit her lip. She could not cry. How her emotions dipped and soared these days, untrustworthy, flighty. She couldn't seem to keep them in check. If he touched her now, if he spoke even one syllable of kindness...

He stepped back, turning to grab the paper from the table, and placed the fabric in it once more. Then having wrapped it and slipped it back inside the envelope, he put it in a drawer in the dresser.

'I'll make sure it's delivered to the museum. The rest of the mantle is still with the restorer, but they expect to have it finished by Easter.'

'Wonderful.' She took a breath and on it, she took a step towards him. This could not go on. She had to fix this. It was now or never.

There was a sound behind her in the hall. The front door had just banged shut. Dottie sent him a questioning look.

William looked towards the door, clearly knowing who had just arrived. His expression was impossible to read. Dottie felt troubled. She heard the clattering of a woman's heels. His sister? But surely Eleanor was still in Matlock? A woman's voice, coming nearer, called, 'Bill, Darling, it's only me!'

It was the woman from the car two weeks earlier. Dottie and her mother had seen him get into the car with her, had seen her lean over and really kiss him. The woman halted in the doorway. A blonde. Big blue eyes, lots of glittery eyeshadow and deep red lipstick. Petite but curvy. Very curvy. She glanced from William to Dottie and back again, her perfect eyebrows raised in dainty enquiry.

William crossed the room to her side and kissed her full on the lips before helping her out of her fur coat. 'I've just made a pot of tea,' he said.

His look was guarded, secret, as he looked back at Dottie and said, 'May I present Miss Moira Hansom, my f-fiancée.'

William leaned against the wall by the front door for a moment before returning to the kitchen. He knew Moira would not be fooled for a second. She was an astute woman at least, regardless of her other failings.

'So that's her,' she said as soon as he came back.

'What do you mean?' As far as he was aware, he'd been careful to never mention Dottie. But Moira would just *know*, of course.

'Well when I came back in August, I could tell you were stewing over someone. And the fact that you never said anything, well, that just made me more suspicious.'

'Ridiculous.' He turned to the sink, tipped away Dottie's

untouched tea, then began to wash the two cups. He was angry with himself. He'd given himself away, and it was too late to change that.

'If you say so,' she said in that arch, teasing tone with the hint of a giggle that he found so annoying. 'Though I think that just proves how serious you were about her. You *were* serious, weren't you?

He said nothing, but scrubbed furiously at a teaspoon. She came up behind him, but he was so busy with his thoughts, he didn't know she was there until her hand was on his shoulder, making him jolt in surprise.

'Is it still serious?' she asked softly.

He still said nothing. He felt her move away from him, and she began drifting about the room, picking up this and that, and sending him little laughing looks as she allowed her voice—a constant babble like a stream over stones—to ripple on and on. She had learned the trick of it years ago from close observance of some of the women she'd met at functions; it wasn't really the kind of thing they taught girls at finishing school. It was yet another thing he detested about her, how false she was, keeping her voice high and light and girlish even though she was thirty, and her smile never fading whilst her words were laced with the pure malice that burned inside her.

'I suppose her figure's not too bad, though that thin boyish look is so very twenties. Men like something to hold on to, don't they? Well you certainly do, at any rate. And that hair! But then again, with a new style and a proper cut from a decent salon, it mightn't be too bad. A bit more make-up too, to hide how pale she looks. She probably doesn't understand how to use it properly, she struck me as being a bit gauche. Yet she surely can't be as young as all that? Still, perhaps it works for her, that fragile, helpless, wide-eyed fawn look. What was her name again?'

'Dottie Manderson.' He said it through gritted teeth. The few dishes were done. He was just standing there with his hands in the empty bowl. He fixed his eyes on the darkness beyond the window, beyond his own reflection, looking back a year to the time he thought everything would be wonderful.

'Dottie? What's that short for? Dorothy? How terribly old-fashioned! And why was she here, exactly, this Dottie girl?'

This last bit was said with an underlying edge. Now we've come to the crux, he thought. This is what she really wants to know. He was tempted to yell at her, 'None of your damned business!' but in the end he controlled his temper and said calmly, 'Something to do with a case of mine last year.'

Whatever she had been expecting, it wasn't that. A long half-minute ticked by before she said, in a more normal voice, 'Well, I think it's a bit forward of her to come to your home like that. She probably thought she could throw herself at you. It's a good thing I came in when I did. The little idiot didn't realise the position she could be putting you in, the trouble that could make for you. Perhaps I should phone her and tell her not to do it again.'

Not trusting himself to reply to that, he said simply, 'I'm going up for a bath.'

He was in the hall when she quickly put on her seductive voice, and called, 'If you like, I could come up and scrub your back for you.'

He'd have laughed if he hadn't been so angry. He ignored her, and when he reached the bathroom, he locked the door.

Moira Hansom frowned when she heard the bolt go across. So that was how it was, was it?

*

Chapter Two

That Monday morning William was summoned.

He stared at the chief superintendent now and said, bluntly, 'I'm afraid I don't think that will work.'

But polite disagreement never got you anywhere with the chief super. The older man frowned over his spectacles at Hardy and said waspishly, 'Well you must make it work, laddie. That is what I want you to do, and you will do it. Unless you've decided to pursue a career elsewhere, of course.'

'No sir. I'm sorry, I didn't mean...'

'If nothing else, you surely want to save your friends from making a terrible mistake? I thought the Mandersons *were* friends of your family? Good friends, I thought, although their private concerns are not exactly the Met's priority.'

'Oh yes, indeed, sir, but...' Hardy thought desperately. There was only one thing he could say. He said it. 'It's just that I expect to be on my honeymoon shortly.'

That surprised the old boy. One greying bushy eyebrow raised. 'Honeymoon, eh? Well, well. What a dark horse you are. I assume the lady has been given approval by your chief inspector? Nothing's come across my desk. I think I'd remember.'

Hardy hesitated. He had a definite sense of the rug being pulled out from underneath him. He was forced to admit, 'It's still going through, but Chief Inspector Barrie didn't seem to think there was anything to worry about.'

William Smithers huffed. 'Not for him to say, though I'm sure there will be no objections to the lady. Known her long, have you?'

'Six or seven years,' Hardy said, as if that clinched it.

The chief super nodded. But if Hardy thought the mere matter of a honeymoon would get him out of his predicament, he was sadly mistaken. The chief super picked up a sheaf of papers, then peering over his spectacles once more, he said, 'You'd better get it done before the wedding, then, hadn't you? Or explain to your intended that police work will always come before your personal life, and the sooner she comes round to that, the better. That's all.'

'Yes sir.' Hardy left feeling heavy-hearted. What on earth was he going to say to Dottie?

On the back of that came the thought that he'd better talk things out with Moira too. He didn't see her as the kind of woman to let a bit of police work get in the way of her bridge parties or soirees. He didn't waste time wondering why his first thought was about Dottie, and Moira was very much in second place. He already knew the answer to that.

At his desk, the chief super set down the papers he'd picked up to serve as a signal to Hardy that the conversation was over. He turned his chair to look out of the window. Odd, he was thinking. I shall never understand that young fellow. The rumours said Hardy was madly in love with this pretty little thing, Miss Manderson, yet now, when he'd half-expected to be asked to approve the match, a completely different woman was, so to speak, on the table as Hardy's future wife. The chief super shook his head sorrowfully. He'd never seen a young chap less enthused about the prospect of a honeymoon with the girl of his dreams. He reached for his phone.

'Tell Barrie to call me as soon as he can, would you, Miss Payne?'

Ten minutes later, the chief inspector rang through. 'You wanted to speak to me, sir?'

'Barrie, what's young Hardy up to? Why is he marrying the wrong girl?'

There was a sigh at the other end. Then, 'No idea, sir. It's lost me ten bob.'

'You had a bet on it?'

'Sir, I confess I did. Thought it was a dead cert too. That Dottie Manderson. She used to work as a mannequin, now she owns the company. Nice family, very sweet girl, just what we'd approve for the lad in the normal run of things. Then out of the blue, he comes into my office looking like a wet Wednesday, saying he's going to marry this other woman.'

'Been playing around and got her into trouble, has he?'

'I don't know, sir, to be honest. I asked a few questions, delicate-like, but didn't find out anything.'

He didn't hear his superior stifle a laugh at that. Chief Superintendent Smithers's opinion was that Chief Inspector Barrie was not overly gifted with a sense of delicacy.

Barrie said, 'She's not so good, from our point of view. There are things I'm pretty certain he doesn't know about her. Nice family, again, for the most part. But she hobnobs with some of the less salubrious of our well-heeled classes. Her first cousin's that Armstrong fellow we've been watching for a while now in connection with the dope-ring across the Midlands.'

The chief super was staring out of his window once more. He didn't like the sound of it. 'Well, drag your heels over the approval, will you. Tell him it's got buried under some more important reports you're doing for me. If he enquires. Though I doubt he will. I've just given him that new matter you and I talked about last week. Should keep him busy for a while.'

'Of course, sir, whatever you say.'

One of the apprentice seamstresses came to tell Dottie she had a visitor.

'It's a *gentleman*, miss,' she said, her eyes as round as saucers.

Dottie was already on her feet and heading for the front of the building. Without knowing who it was, of course, she couldn't just ask the girl to send him through to the back office. Yet who could it be? It wouldn't be her father. Or George, who had been to the warehouse several times with Flora. Everyone knew them by sight. Her heart was sinking as she thought perhaps Gervase might be in London and have decided to come and have it out with her. She did not look forward to being shouted at and intimidated.

But it wasn't him. The man was standing in the middle of the hallway, peering in at the cutting room door, and looking very interested in everything he saw.

'William!'

She'd said his name, her tone warm and pleased, before her brain reminded her he was now engaged.

He transferred his hat to his other hand and just briefly touched her hand in greeting.

'Good morning.'

'Hello.'

He waved his hat at the cutting room, and in the opposite direction at the open door of the storeroom where the senior seamstress was going through the rails checking the finished garments against her list. 'This is all very impressive. And a lot bigger than I imagined.'

'I'm very pleased with how things are coming along. The new styles are very popular. Do you want me? I mean, do you want to *see* me?' She blushed like a schoolgirl over the slip.

He pretended not to notice. 'Yes, please. I'd appreciate it if you could spare me a little while. I thought you might like to go to lunch?'

She couldn't help herself, she said, 'And just what would Miss Hansom think about that?'

It was the wrong thing to say, of course, she had known that right away, but she couldn't seem to stop herself from saying it. His expression immediately became remote, his manner formal.

'Or perhaps I can just discuss a police matter with you here? It'll only take a few minutes of your time. Do you have an office or somewhere?'

Now she was annoyed—with him as well as herself. To make matters worse, she'd done herself out of having lunch with him. She put out a hand to touch his arm.

'William, I'm sorry...'

He jerked away from her and hit his elbow on the door jamb. His curse brought raised eyebrows and laughing looks from the three women at work in the cutting room.

Dottie turned on her heel and led the way back to her office without saying another word. She took her usual seat at the desk, leaving him to perch on the hard chair. She arched an eyebrow at him and waited.

He glared at her.

After another minute's silence, she said, 'This is completely ridiculous. Either you want to talk to me or you don't. Stop wasting my time and tell me what you want.'

The silence continued whilst he debated telling her what he really wanted. In the end he just said, 'Come out to lunch. You've got to eat, surely? If you stop mentioning Moira, I'll try to keep my temper, and we'll get along perfectly well.'

'All right. Lyons?'

'Or there's a little restaurant a bit further on? The Silver Moon?'

'On a policeman's salary?' She said it gently, with a teasing look. 'Thank you, that would be lovely. I usually forget about lunch altogether.' She was on her feet and reaching for her coat. He took it and held it for her as she slipped her arms in.

'I can believe that. You girls are all skin and bone these days,' he grumbled.

'Oh shush, grandpa! Come on then. I'll just let everyone know I'm going out.'

It was a wonderful feeling to walk along the road with him. She would have liked to hold his arm, but he didn't offer it. Still they were—more or less—out together. To her delight, he did take her arm at the crossing on the corner, and once they were over, he didn't drop his hand away.

The restaurant wasn't too busy, and within a few minutes they had been shown to a table and had given their orders to the waiter. He poured their wine and left.

Dottie looked at William. He looked at her. It was difficult to know what to say.

Fortunately their food arrived quickly. It gave them something to be busy with, as well as a topic for conversation. They both began to relax.

She asked after his sisters and brother. He asked after her family. That took them to the end of the soup. Their main course arrived. They ate quickly and more or less in silence. Once the plates had been cleared, and Dottie had, unusually, declined dessert, the waiter brought them coffee then retreated.

William got out his notebook. This was it, then, she thought. Down to business. She noticed he was nervous.

'What is it you want me to help you with?'

He hesitated. 'This is a real police investigation,' he said. 'I want you to know that. It's not just me being angry and wanting to lash out and hurt you.'

Dottie felt cold inside. What on earth did he mean? She said nothing. Her eyes, huge and anxious, stared at him.

'It's about Gervase Parfitt. I'm investigating him for illegal activity. It's come from high up, and it's highly confidential. I assume you visit him from time to time at his home, and I wanted to ask—or rather, I *didn't* want to ask, but I've been told I have to—ask for your assistance. Next time you visit him, I'd like you to try to find out anything you can that we might be able to use as evidence, or to help me to get more evidence. He might keep records of some sort. I can offer some suggestions.'

'Oh.' She was completely dumbfounded. There was a protracted silence. Just when he was on the point of suggesting that they leave, she said, 'I've never been to see him in his home, he always comes here. But in any case, I've broken things off with him. I don't really see how I can help you.' She thought for a second then added, 'What on earth do you think he's done? This is insane.'

She was tense. He wanted to reach out to take her hand, but decided against it. He didn't want her to feel he was trying to manipulate her. Somewhere in the back of his brain, another little bit of his consciousness was hearing her words over again: *I've broken things off with him.* He wanted to rejoice at that.

Outwardly calm, he said, 'I tried to get taken off the case, but I was told to get on with it. And yes, perhaps I was a bit angry. But I'm not trying to hurt you, Dottie. This isn't about you and I. As I say, it's a real case, a real investigation.'

'And as *I* said, Gervase and I are not together anymore. Tell me exactly what it is you have against him.' Her chin came up defiantly.

He stirred his coffee and drank some. 'Do we want something else to eat? I think they have cake.'

'No, William, we want you to get to the point.'

'Right, er, well. There are several quite serious cases that we are building against Parfitt. I've decided to concentrate on one or two cases in particular; that way I believe I have a better chance of getting a conviction.'

Dottie thought about this. The cold sense of dread had returned in the pit of her stomach, and about her shoulders like a pall. 'Actual criminal cases? Are you quite serious? Do you actually *know* anything, or only suspect? If you're right, will he lose his job? Will there be a scandal?'

William gave her a straight look. 'Yes, he will lose his job. There will most definitely be a scandal. He is likely to go to prison for a very long time.'

She gasped at the word 'prison', but then William said:

'Or, he could very well be hanged.'

He watched in dismay as her face registered shock, her lovely hazel eyes filling with tears. He could have kicked himself. She might no longer love Parfitt—or did she, a devious imp in his brain challenged—but even so she wouldn't want to see any harm come to the man.

He reached out to take her hands. For once she didn't snatch them away.

'I'm so sorry. I shouldn't have said it like that. Please, Dottie, don't...'

She extracted her hands to rummage in her bag for a handkerchief. Even without looking he knew it was one of his. He felt exasperated with himself. Why had he ever doubted? A woman who carried around one of your handkerchiefs in her handbag at all times—that was a connection that would never go away. Despite all evidence to the contrary over these last few months, he was still there in her heart.

She was more composed now, but horrified at the possible outcome of assisting him. She leaned towards him now, keeping her voice low.

'William, I can't help you if it's going to come to a death sentence. Oh William, I just can't.'

He nodded, watching her face as she thought about it a little more.

'Tell me truthfully. Has Gervase really done anything so terrible? If it's just a matter of cutting a few corners or, well I don't know, a breach of procedure or something like that... Has he actually hurt people? Have people genuinely suffered because of anything he's done?'

He couldn't meet her eyes, didn't want to see how she cared for his rival, because that's what Parfitt was after all. He looked at the table. 'I believe he really has. I just can't prove it at the moment. At least, I can prove parts of it, but it's not enough to take to court.'

'But bad enough to *hang* him?' Her voice was urgent now. 'What has he done? William? You have to tell me everything.'

He sighed. Now that he thought about it, his plan would never have worked. Because of course she wouldn't just accept what he told her without proof. Which he didn't have with him. Nor was this a conversation to have in a public place.

'Not here, Dottie. I can't tell you anything in detail here, it's too crowded. I should have realised you'd need more information. Of course you do. Can you—would you—come to the house this evening? Or I could come to yours?'

She debated with herself. Then said, 'I can't make it tonight. And I know I'm not allowed to mention the M-word, but would your fiancée be happy to have me in her home?'

He frowned. 'It's not her home. It's mine. She was just visiting me the other evening.'

'She has a key.'

He gave a slight nod. He said, 'Yes all right. She has a key, and yes, as you've no doubt guessed, she has stayed with me—overnight—several times.'

He felt ashamed. He watched for her reaction.

She wouldn't meet his eyes. She bit the inside of her lip, determined not to show any emotion at the thought of another woman with him. Any woman. Let alone that bottle-blonde, ample-bosomed woman. With him. In his arms. All night. Tears prickled her eyelids. She would not let them fall, she wouldn't. She took a firm grip on her emotions and forbade her tears to fall. She said nothing, afraid to trust her voice. In the end it was he who spoke again.

'Dottie, I told you, she doesn't live with me. She has her own flat. In any case, she's visiting relations in Bournemouth for a couple of weeks. So if you don't mind, you could perhaps come to the house. If not—and believe me, I do realise it's a lot to ask—I could come to your parents' house and bring my notes with me. It's entirely up to you.'

'I don't want my parents to know about Gervase's crimes. They already utterly despise him for letting me down in Sussex. If they knew about this too...'

'Thank you for helping me. I know it's not...'

'I need to think about it. I haven't said yes yet. I still have no idea how I can be of the slightest use. He never talks to me about his work. And even if I do help you, it won't be to hang him, William. I can't do that. If that's what you're trying to do, I won't help you.'

He nodded. 'I understand. Again, I want you to know, this is not merely some vendetta on my part. If I don't do it, they'll just get someone else. It's vital that he is called to account for the things he's done.'

She waited a beat, then said, 'Well, I must get back to work. Thank you for lunch.' She was on her feet, gathering her things. He took her coat from her and held it for her. He fought the urge to kiss her neck, or even allow himself to breathe in her soft scent.

'Let me walk you back,' he said, getting out the garish new wallet and taking out some money. He left it on the table with a nod at the waiter who was already coming over. William received his change, left a tip, pocketed the rest, and saw now Dottie was halfway out of the door. He hurried after her. Outside on the pavement they halted. She still wouldn't look at him properly. He felt like a traitor.

'Don't come back with me, William. I want to be on my own. I need to think.'

'When will...?'

'You'd better phone me. I might be able to do next Monday. I can't come tonight, I'm working late. And tomorrow is out for the same reason. In fact most of this week... I'm at Flora's on Friday evening. There's Janet's wedding on Saturday. Then I have a cocktail party at the warehouse for my clients on Sunday evening. After that, there's nothing much until next Thursday night, when I'm going out with Flora and George and a few friends.'

He groaned. 'Good Lord, I'd completely forgotten. The Valentine's ball. They've invited me too, a-and Moira.' He shot her a worried look.

'Perfect,' she said in a furious tone. 'That's absolutely bloody perfect.'

Without another word or look, she marched off, fury in her straight back, rigid shoulders and rapid steps.

William sighed again and went back to his office.

That Saturday, the Mandersons attended the wedding of

their former maid, Janet Butler. For Dottie, it was as moving as when her own sister had got married. Janet was radiant in the lovely white dress. She walked down the aisle of the little church on the arm of her father, who looked old for a man with five daughters in their teens and early twenties. His shock of thick white hair was the only robust thing about him.

Janet's mother, half smiling, half weeping, sat in the front row with the rest of the girls, her younger daughter Sally, now following in her older sister's footsteps in the Manderson household, sat beside her, beaming all over her face. The friends and family of both bride and groom filled the pews behind Mrs Butler and her daughters. Dottie, Flora and George, and Mr and Mrs Manderson sat behind their cook, their other maid Margie, and Flora and George's staff, Cissie, and Mr and Mrs Greeley. On the other side of the aisle behind Sergeant Frank Maple's parents, his widowed sister and her three fidgeting children, there was a large contingent from the police station, including of course, Maple's good friend and work colleague William Hardy. Maple's brother, another George, stood beside Frank as his best man.

The bride came forward to walk to the altar. Various of her little nephews and nieces were doing duty as pageboys and bridesmaids, beaming excitedly at the guests as they walked down the aisle behind her. Janet lifted her veil as she prepared to make her vows, smiling at Frank, who was suddenly emotional. To everyone watching, it was astonishing to see the burly, usually intimidating policeman so vulnerable. His mother wept with joy.

The service was short, unlike the wedding breakfast. The newly married Mr and Mrs Frank Maple came out of the gloomy church into bright sunshine and were already in the pub when the inevitable rain began, the bride still with rose petals in her hair.

Mr and Mrs Manderson left after about an hour, but the younger members of the family stayed on. William too remained, and Dottie was glad that either Moira hadn't been invited or hadn't wanted to attend.

The pub was rowdy, affording little chance of conversation, and no room to dance, but at last the newlyweds were sent off to their wedding night in their new home together. Dottie felt envious of their happiness, though glad of such a joyous conclusion to the sneaking in and out of the house that Frank had been doing for the last year.

It was just after lunch on Sunday that William telephoned Dottie.

'It's me,' he said, unnecessarily as he'd already told her mother who was calling when she'd answered the phone. 'I hope I'm not interrupting anything? I know you said you were busy tonight. I wondered if you could come over tomorrow evening to go through the case, if that's still all right? That is, if you are still willing to help me?'

'Of course,' she said. Her heart was hammering inside her ribs. 'What sort of time?'

'About eight? Or a bit later? I could come and pick you up.'

'About half past would be better. And there's no need to drive over. I'll walk.'

'Sure?'

Trying to catch her breath, Dottie said casually, 'Yes. I assume Moira is going to be out?'

'I told you, she doesn't live here.' His voice held a note of exasperation. 'She's still in Bournemouth.'

'About half past eight, then?'

'That's fine. See you then.'

On Monday evening she got home later than planned. She ate dinner hurriedly, and barely satisfied her curious parents with the information, 'I've got to go and see William about something. I won't be late.'

As she rushed upstairs to get ready, her parents exchanged looks of bewilderment. Her mother remarked, 'I've always liked William.'

'Yes, a decent young fellow,' her husband said, 'And I'm sure he won't be a police inspector forever.'

'After Gervase Parfitt, an inspector seems like a pleasant change,' Mrs Manderson replied.

Dottie did her make-up carefully, spent quite a lot of time trying to get her hair just right, and changed her outfit three times, her final choice being a comfortable, unostentatious but attractive coat and skirt.

She arrived on time, but only just. She was breathless, and somehow her hair had got fluffed up in all the wrong places, and the fresh breeze had whipped too much colour into her cheeks. She tried to tame her hair as she waited for him to open the door.

Unlike last time, he was wearing a proper shirt and tie, a jacket, decent trousers, and polished shoes instead of old work-boots. The jacket had to be new, she thought, having never seen it before. Moira Hansom was certainly making him spend money on himself. The jacket was brown, which was not a colour that suited him, and Dottie didn't like it any more than she liked the shiny new wallet she'd seen at the restaurant. But she said nothing apart from, 'Hello.'

He stood aside to allow her to enter. 'Kitchen or sitting room?'

'Kitchen.' She didn't need to think twice about that.

'Good idea. Well, do go through, you know the way.'

The radio was on, a soft classical piece was murmuring in the background. As before the bright kitchen was warm and welcoming.

He took her overcoat away to hang it up. She lay the little hat and gloves on the dresser with her bag.

'Tea? Or something stronger?'

She shook her head. 'Not just yet.'

'In that case, let's sit down.'

He drew out a chair for her, then took a seat opposite her, pulling a huge file towards him.

Dottie found she was nervous. She licked her lips and waited for him to speak.

It was one of those box type files. Just the size of it filled her with dread. What on earth had Gervase done? William lifted the lid and raised the spring mechanism that held the papers. He took out the stack of papers and closed the box again.

Dottie looked at the pile of papers. There were not even enough to half-fill the box. That reassured her, and she let out a long-held breath and relaxed a little. This had to be a good sign, and no doubt things were not so bad as she'd imagined these last few days. Obviously—and she was annoyed with herself for not realising this sooner, it might have spared her some anxiety—obviously William would take a sterner view than perhaps she herself might. He would be looking for every little breach of procedure, whereas Dottie was only concerned about the possibility that Gervase had hurt someone.

She almost laughed when William, clearly concerned for her, said, 'It's all right if you want to change your mind. I'd quite understand. I know I'm asking an awful lot of you.'

'The thing is,' she said with the air of laying all her cards on the table. 'As I told you, I've broken things off with Gervase. So I'm just not sure I can be much help to you.'

'Let me tell you a little bit about what I already know. It's not really very much, so it won't take long. Then we'll see how you feel about it.'

She nodded. She glanced behind her at the stove. 'Do you mind? I know I said no to tea, but I think...'

'Yes, of course.' He made to rise, but she waved him back.

'I'll do it. You start telling me things.'

She went to the stove. An experimental lift of the kettle told her it was already full enough. She lit the stove and set the kettle to boil.

William cleared his throat, straightened his papers and began. 'Well many of the details are rather hazy. It seems likely that Parfitt's illegal, and also unprofessional or perhaps it's better to call them unethical, activities began quite soon after he joined the force.'

Dottie nodded. She felt anxious again. A cold lump seemed to sit in the pit of her stomach. She wasn't the guilty one, she reminded herself. This was Gervase's guilt, not hers. All the same, that sense of dread seemed to fill her. She busied herself with making the tea.

He was watching her closely. 'Are you all right?'

She passed him his cup. And came back to sit at the table with a cup for herself. She managed a smile. 'Yes, I'm fine. Just—nervous—that's all.'

He regarded her thoughtfully. 'I must admit, I hadn't really thought about what this must be like for you. The man you love...'

That braced her. She folded her arms and glared at him. 'I don't love him, William. I thought I'd made that quite clear. But that doesn't mean I don't care what happens to him. I'm just a bit scared of what I'm going to find out, that's all.'

He couldn't help glancing down at the page in front of him.

'Sorry. He has done some truly awful things, I'm afraid. And those are just the things we already suspect or actually know about.'

She blanched. Her shoulders were tense and rigid. She gripped her hands together in her lap.

He put a hand over hers. Gently he said, 'Look, Dottie, we don't have to do this, you know. I can go back to my chief superintendent and say you can't help us. I did try to tell him it's not fair to ask this of you.'

'No, I want to help. I do. It's just... Can you promise me that the worst thing that can happen is that he'll go to prison? If it's worse than that, I couldn't possibly...'

He considered it. But he couldn't lie to her. 'I can't be sure of the outcome. My job is just to investigate the crimes. When you hear what he's done, you'll see it's very serious. You'll see why I can't make any promises. In the end, it's not me but the court that decides how justice is to be served.'

She was in an agony of indecision. She knew it was her duty to help the police. But what about her own sense of guilt? How could she live with herself if Gervase was condemned to the gallows because of something she said?

There was silence in the little kitchen. Dottie was wondering what to do, and William was waiting patiently.

He wasn't annoyed with her. He was glad she was thinking about things so carefully.

She picked up her cup, cradling it in both hands, her elbows propped on the table in the manner disapproved of by mothers everywhere. In this attitude she fixed her full attention on his face as William began to speak. She had to remind herself to listen to his words and not simply gaze at his face.

Out loud she asked, 'Has he—*killed*—anyone?'

It wasn't the kind of question you should have to ask about anyone, let alone someone you had once contemplated marrying. She expected William immediately to laugh and say, no of course not, don't be silly, he hasn't done anything so terrible as all *that*.

He didn't.

Dottie's eyes widened as she stared at William across the table. 'William!'

Again that slight jerk of the shoulder, not quite a shrug of helplessness, but impossible to ignore. 'I don't have any evidence to prove that he's killed anyone.'

She gaped at him. 'But you believe he has! My goodness, I thought you'd laugh at me for being silly.'

'There's no *definite* proof. I'm still looking into things. But given his other activities, it seems not merely possible but probable. But as I say, I'm still trying to piece it all together and...' He stopped rambling and looked at her. Her hands were over her mouth. Wide, horrified eyes stared at him. 'I'm so sorry,' he added softly.

She dismissed his words with a terse, 'If the experts are to be believed then we all could kill if we had to, if we were cornered with no other way out.'

Her look challenged him. He said, simply, 'You couldn't.'

She glared at him.

His smile came out of nowhere, as his smiles tended to do. 'I can't believe you're angry with me for thinking you could never kill,' he said.

She refused to smile back at him. 'I might,' she said, and didn't even feel any horror at that admission. 'If someone I really cared about was in danger, or if I had to defend myself, I think I might. If I had a child to protect, or a l...'

She had been going to say, lover, but then she looked at him and the word just wouldn't come out.

He grinned again. Then she couldn't help laughing too.

'I don't know why that felt like such an insult,' she said. 'Why was I cross that you thought I couldn't commit murder?'

Silence fell on them. The kitchen was homely and comfortable. She liked it. She liked being there with him. It was horrid to think of Moira being there with him. It was none of her business, of course, but she was glad Moira didn't live here with him.

'We can definitely accuse him of bringing the profession into disrepute,' William said, looking down at his notes.

She nodded, trying to set aside her own feelings. Both for William, and for Gervase. Once again she made herself concentrate on what he was telling her, and not think about the planes of his cheekbones, or his eyes, his eyelashes, or his hands, with the long, slender fingers.

'That doesn't sound very serious,' she said.

He raised his eyebrows and tried to give her a stern look. She flapped a hand at him.

'Oh come on, William darling, compared to murder...'

The word murder paled in comparison with what she'd just called him. He stared at her. She blushed and stared back. Neither of them said a word. He picked up his papers for about the sixth time, and Dottie looked very carefully at the nails on her right hand.

After a moment, he said, 'Er—so—bringing the profession into—er...' and at the same time, Dottie said,

'Does she always call you Bill?'

'Into disre—what? Yes, she does.'

'And so do Flora and George, don't they? And Frank Maple.'

He set the papers down. 'Yes, they do.'

'Does everyone call you Bill except me?'

His eyes were very blue, she thought. He nodded, then said, 'Actually your mother calls me William too.'

Dottie wrinkled her nose. 'She calls everyone by their full name. You've probably heard her call me Dorothy at least a dozen times.'

He nodded again. She was staring at him now as if he was an interesting example of some sort of moss. 'Do you prefer to be called Bill?'

'Yes.' Then he added, 'Though not by you. I like it when you call me William.'

'You don't mind? I'm not sure I could start thinking of you as Bill after all this time.'

'Not so very long,' he murmured softly.

'Fifteen months. Since November 1933.'

'I remember that first time I saw you, I thought how lovely you were. Then the next day I came to see you, to ask more questions.'

'I bet you didn't really need to know anything,' she said with the hint of a smile.

He grinned back. 'No. I just wanted to see you again. You sang for me, remember? The words of that song?'

She nodded slowly and shivered. 'It was awful, actually. You know, finding Archie Dunne like that. I used to love that song, but not anymore. Now every time I hear it, it reminds me of finding him that night.'

'Sorry. I forgot about the horrid associations. At the time I just thought you had a very pretty voice.'

They looked at each other. The clock ticked on. The tea grew cold. After what seemed like an eternity, William gathered up all the papers and replaced them in the file, and closed the lid down with a thump. There was no point trying to do this today, he decided. Again.

'Some other time, perhaps. Are you at the warehouse tomorrow?'

'Yes. It's a busy time.'

He got up. She got up too. Without any discussion he walked her to the door. He was reaching past her to put on the light but his hand stopped on the wall, and with a resigned sigh, he leaned forward and kissed her softly on the cheek.

'You're an engaged man,' she reminded him and took a

step away.

'Hmm.' He said. Then he snapped the hall light on, helped her on with her coat, opened the door, and allowed her to go past him and down the steps.

'Let me walk you home.'

'No, William. Thank you,' she added. 'I'll get a taxi on the corner.'

He didn't speak again. Neither did she. As she went along the road, she glanced back and saw him standing there still, leaning against the door jamb, a silhouetted figure motionless, apparently deep in thought.

Dottie was deep in thought too. On the corner she came out onto the main road and quickly hailed a taxi. She climbed inside, glad to be out of the cold night air. As the taxi carried her home, she stared into the darkness. Gervase was completely forgotten. She was still sitting at the table in William's kitchen.

'What does 'bringing the profession into disrepute' actually mean, anyway? You never did tell me.'

Her question was greeted by a loud bark of laughter from William at the other end of the line. She'd called him almost as soon as she'd arrived home. She hadn't bothered to say who was calling, but he didn't need to be told who was on the line, of course. He knew her voice better than anyone's.

'You distracted me. Well, in layman's terms, the reputation of the police force as a whole should be such that every member of the public has absolute faith and confidence that the force will act with honesty and integrity in every aspect of their role, to guard the safety and well-being of the public.'

'And how specifically has this particular person failed to do that?'

'What do you mean, this particular person?'

'You know perfectly well who I mean. I don't want to say his name on the phone, you don't know who might overhear.'

'Ah, I see. Very good. I don't have all the proof I need

yet, but I do have a statement from a witness who says that *this particular person* got their aunt in such a muddle about her statement that she withdrew her testimony.'

'Oh but surely that's just one batty old lady getting confused?'

'That's exactly what a defence lawyer would have said. That's what our particular person told the old woman, along with how awful it would be for her and her family if she died in prison because she perjured herself in court by saying something she wasn't completely certain about. All right, I take your point. Another thing we have is two different people saying they were paid by Par—er—this person to give testimony that allowed an accused person to go free.'

'Hmm.' The phone line crackled softly, and was silent. William held his breath, trying to catch the sound of her breathing. He couldn't, the line was too fuzzy. He wanted to be with her again. It was less than half an hour since he'd seen her but he was missing her desperately.

'Shall I come over?' he suggested oh-so-casually.

There was a long silence as she debated this, then, 'No, better not to, I think. Can you just tell me a bit more?'

'All right.' He clamped down hard on his disappointment. 'Let me see. Well, I believe he was involved in either taking or delivering bribes to look the other way during criminal activities ranging from illegal gambling to procurement, to theft of goods from warehouses. And I'm pretty sure he was a regular stand-in on identity parades. I can't quite figure out how that worked or why it was useful, I'm still looking into it. As you probably know witnesses, or indeed victims, come into a police station to identify the perpetrator of a crime. The police organise a line-up of individuals, the suspect is placed amongst these, and the witness has to walk along the line looking at each person, then they have to put their hand on the shoulder of the one they recognise in connection with the crime.'

'I see,' said Dottie. 'Or rather, I don't. How would that benefit...?' She was trying to see how that could be of use to anyone. At the other end of the line, to William she sounded as though she were so close by, she was right there with him in the room. His heart ached for it to be that way in reality.

'No, it's an odd one. Basically on several occasions, a witness came to the station for an identity parade and chose the wrong man, so that the accused had to be released and... My God.' Abruptly he fell silent.

'William?'

'I've just worked it out. It's so obvious. How has no one ever realised what was happening?'

'So the witness made a mistake and chose the wrong man? People don't always remember what they saw. Surely that happens all the time?'

'Yes. Exactly. For a long while, that was believed to be the case. But now some bright spark has noticed that on each occasion, the witnesses had chosen not just the wrong man but the *same* wrong man. Again and again. Gervase Parfitt.'

'I thought we weren't mentioning names?' she said. Then, 'I didn't realise that policemen were used in identity parades. I assumed members of the public were dragged in off the streets.'

'They often are, but it's not always possible. Even here in London, we can't always get enough of the right people at short notice. It's fairly common for off-duty or spare staff to help out in this way.'

'And who was this bright spark you said has noticed what had happened?'

She heard the smile in his voice as he said, 'As a matter of fact it was me, about thirty seconds ago.'

On Tuesday evening, Gervase telephoned. Dottie had phoned him the day before, immediately after speaking to William. Gervase was cold and distant, and she had to demean herself to the point of almost begging for his forgiveness, avowing her undying love and pleading for a second chance. He'd told her stiffly that he would need to think about it, and that he'd let her know his decision.

She heard the phone ringing and was already on her feet coming to the door when Sally came into the room.

'If you don't mind, miss, it's that Mr Parfitt on the phone.'

Dottie nodded, and they went out together, Dottie heading to the phone with a sinking feeling, and Sally returning to the kitchen.

'Hello? Gervase?'

'Good evening, Dottie. I thought I would let you know that I shall be coming to London tomorrow. We can talk over dinner at the Exeter. I've made a reservation for seven o'clock. I trust that is suitable.'

'Oh yes. Lovely. Thank you, Gervase.' She injected some enthusiasm into her voice. His tone was polite, his manner formal. Her heart sank. Clearly he was not ready to fully forgive her. That came as no surprise; she imagined he'd like to keep her on tenterhooks as long as possible.

'Very well. I shall see you tomorrow. I shall call for you at a quarter to seven.'

'All right, thank you,' she said again. He said goodnight coldly and hung up the telephone.

She sighed. Oh well, she'd tried her best.

Tomorrow night, she thought as she returned to the drawing room, she would get herself up and make herself as charming as she could, but it might well be that William had to find other means of getting evidence against Gervase. Dottie found she was not at all upset that her relationship with Gervase Parfitt appeared to be incapable of being revived.

'Blast it,' she said, 'I forgot to tell him about Flora and George inviting us to the Valentine's party they are having at the Regency on Thursday night.' The odds were that she'd be going without a partner that evening.

And William would be there—with *her*.

Both her parents were in the drawing room, quietly reading, relaxed. It seemed too good an opportunity to miss.

With Gervase arriving from the Midlands the following day, she had been trying to find the right moment to let them know what was going on. Of course she couldn't tell them everything, just that she and Gervase were seeing one another again, the great man having grudgingly acceded to her request for clemency.

And her parents wouldn't be at all happy about that, even less so if they knew a tenth of what she now knew about that man.

She dithered in the doorway, fiddling with her bracelet and wondering what to say. She practised a few ideas in her head.

'Dorothy, what have I told you about loitering in doorways?' her mother immediately said. It was just the opener Dottie needed.

'Oh yes, sorry, Mother. Er, but seeing that I've got you both here...'

At this her father peered over his newspaper in alarm.

'I just wanted to let you know—er—to tell you...' What was that phrase she'd just thought of? Her brains seemed to have jumbled themselves up. She looked from one to the other of her parents. 'It's just that... It's all back on again with Gervase. At least, I think so. He's coming up tomorrow. We'll be dining out. Anyway, goodnight.'

And she was gone from the room, leaving them to look at each other in bewilderment.

*

Chapter Three

The Regency was packed. The noise was like a wall against which the clientele had to practically hurl themselves if they were to have any conversation at all. Their group had managed to corner a couple of tables and put them together to make one large one. Drinks were ordered, and everyone leaned forward in their seats, trying to make themselves heard above the din.

Dottie was there with Gervase, of course, having virtually prostrated herself over dinner the night before at a vile, pretentious restaurant, the kind he favoured, alternately apologising and admitting she was foolish until he was satisfied enough to graciously deign to consider her once more his 'sweetheart'.

This evening, Valentine's evening, loomed ahead of her, its possibilities for enjoyment severely limited by the man who was her escort. But not just him. On Gervase's right was Moira Hansom, here with William. Moira had gone all out in a slinky dress with a *very* low neckline. Her lipstick was warrior-red, her false eyelashes effectual swords that raised and lowered in a calculatedly seductive fashion whenever she spoke to any man but especially William.

Dottie ignored Moira as best she could but directed covert looks at William, very handsome in his evening suit. As if sensing her gaze, he glanced at her and glanced away again.

She craned forward to hear a joke Alistair was telling them all, but it fell rather flat due to the noise all around drowning out every other word. Everyone smiled politely and nodded. Alistair, realising it was a waste of time, devoted himself to conversation with Charles who was sitting next to him.

Gervase leaned towards Dottie and said, fairly quietly for once, 'Are those two nancy boys? I've never seen them with any women.'

Dottie picked up her drink, needing to gain herself a few moments. She knew full well that Gervase had only met Alistair and Charles twice before tonight, so it was hardly a long acquaintance. She decided she could get away with a lie, because this was not the sort of thing you could be truthful about with someone like Gervase.

When she first met him, he'd appeared to agree with all of her attitudes—modern, liberal, respectful, and generous towards others. Yet over the last few months, as she'd got to know him better, his true self had begun to be revealed. She now knew he had the most vile, rigid views on romance and what constituted a socially acceptable pairing.

'Not at all,' she told him now without even blushing. 'Charles used to be fearfully in love with George's sister. She died last year, remember? But unfortunately, she was already involved in someone else. And Alistair, well, he says he's too young to settle down. He plans to wait until he's thirty before marrying—says a wife will put a stop to all his vices. He and Alistair have known George since they were all at Eton.'

'Hmm.' Gervase clearly felt he knew better, but decided not to contradict her. It annoyed her that he always thought he knew better. Even worse, this time he was actually right. Very few of their friends knew the truth behind Charles and Alistair's 'friendship', and that was the best way.

Dottie sighed inwardly and sipped her drink. She longed for the evening to be over. Or at least for the band to come on—at least if she was dancing, it would take her mind off Gervase and all the things he said that either offended or irritated her. Even though she'd begged him to take her back—for William's investigation, of course— Gervase was making no effort to show any kind of appreciation. Rather he acted as though it was she who needed to work for his forgiveness. He saw himself as the injured party, as always.

Moira Hansom laughed her perfect, ladylike, musical laugh at something George was saying. How Dottie hated that woman. If only George and Flora hadn't felt they had to invite her. Although of course if they hadn't, William would without a doubt have had something to say about that. But it would have helped her story about the 'bachelors' along quite a bit with one more single man in their party. Dottie's eyes followed the perfect line of Moira's perfectly gloved arm to where the hand rested on William's knee. Dottie was consoled by the fact that he looked irritable, and seemed quite unable to disguise the fact.

Moira laughed her perfect laugh again, and Dottie couldn't help exchanging an eye-roll with her sister Flora. Flora hid a grin and turned away to talk to George. Dottie was spared any further suffering as the band now came onto the stage and took their seats.

The compere announced, 'Good evening ladies and gentlemen. Happy Valentine's Day! Welcome to the Regency. Tonight we will begin with a nice little foxtrot, to get all you romantic souls onto the dancefloor. Ladies and gentlemen, I give you, the Regency Eight, with *Heart And Soul* followed by *The Thinking Man's Blues.*'

There was a little ripple of applause. The men at Dottie's table stood politely, and Dottie was relieved to see that George immediately asked Moira to dance. How sweet of him, Dottie thought, immediately hoping William would... but no, he smiled and held out a hand to Flora, who accepted, sending a teasing glance over her shoulder at Dottie as she joined him on the dancefloor. The other couple at their table, Miss Phillippa Belvoir and her 'cousin', Miss Madeleine Smith, cast about them for male partners.

Gervase quickly—and not very gallantly—gripped Dottie's elbow and propelled her towards the floor, leaving Charles and Alistair to partner the two ladies.

It was pleasant to be moving. Gervase could be relied upon to produce a stream of uninteresting conversation, mainly centred about his own experiences or opinions, but at least he rarely required any actual response from her beyond the usual, 'Oh yes,' or 'Really?' For the hundredth time that evening, she asked herself how much longer she could bear it. Predictably his first remarks concerned Phillippa and Madeleine.

'Rum pair, both of them. Old before their time. Clearly not a clue about make-up or fashion. Not a jot of sex-appeal between the two of them. No wonder they're both on the shelf. Good thing they've got each other to give them some companionship in their old age. I bet they sit up half the night knitting and wailing about how unfair men are.'

'Probably,' Dottie said. Privately she was remembering Phillippa's formidable reputation as a bridge player who had won a fortune over the years, and that Madeleine had a keen interest in the stock market. Not to mention their lavish, and to Gervase's mind no doubt louche parties. They also travelled widely, more fortunate than Charles and Alistair in that no one thought it odd when two single ladies chose to share a bedroom or to go everywhere together.

Luckily for Dottie, she didn't have to spend the entire evening dancing with Gervase. She danced next with George, then with Alistair, which she greatly enjoyed as he was graceful and confident on the dancefloor. Then, she turned to find William standing behind her, holding out his hand to her.

'May I?'

'Of course,' she said, and found she was breathless. Moira was already being swept off by Gervase for the second time, Dottie noted. Her imagination gave her a glimpse of Gervase eloping with Moira, and herself in William's arms, happy forever.

Perhaps it would have been better if the back of her dress—her own design, of course—hadn't been cut quite so low.

They moved off together, perfectly in time with the music and one another. But she couldn't relax. All she was aware of was his hand on her back. At least it was warm, she thought, remembering a previous dress, a previous evening, when they hadn't danced, but oh, how she had wanted to dance with him.

The floor was crowded now, and a couple of times they rather got swept along with the flow. She exchanged a smile with Gervase as he went by with Moira in his arms. They seemed to be enjoying their dance together, laughing and talking as if they'd known each other for years. So much the better, thought Dottie. She had no objection to Gervase developing a new interest in another woman, and if that woman should be Moira, well, what could be better than that? It could lead to the perfect conclusion all round.

She stumbled slightly, knocking her knee against William's, and they both apologised. Looking down she saw some gentleman had dropped his pipe on the dancefloor. A waiter darted over to retrieve it: no doubt someone would be looking for that later. She smiled up at William, and began to relax. She could see Gervase and Moira were now safely further away, and she took the opportunity to lean closer to her partner.

His response was immediate. He put his cheek next to hers, closed his eyes for a second and allowed himself to enjoy the moment. The next dance was even slower and the lights dimmed slightly. As if the dancers needed any encouragement. Almost everyone was smooching.

Dottie sent an anxious look around for Gervase, but saw he and Moira were now almost at the other end of the dancefloor. For Dottie it was almost as good as being alone.

They swayed. The skirt of her gown swirled softly about her calves and ankles, and there was his warm hand on the small of her back, his firm grip on her hand. His shoulder was solid under her other hand, his cheek slightly rough against hers. His chest against hers, his hip against hers, his thigh...

'I don't know this tune,' he murmured. 'What did he say it was called? It's a new one to me.'

'The Very Thought Of You,' she said.

After a slight pause, he said, 'How very apt.'

She wondered if she imagined that brief nuzzle against her neck and then his cheek was next to hers again. She relaxed into his arms. For just two or three minutes more, he was hers, and she was his.

Then the music stopped. The lights glared, and the dancers, embarrassed and all too aware of one another, hurriedly stepped apart, and the only thing anyone could do was to smile broadly and applaud the band. Gervase made his unwelcome way back to Dottie's side, and Moira followed close on his heels.

The compere made his next announcement, the music started again, and Moira immediately reclaimed William for the Ladies' Choice, and Dottie found herself stepping out of time with Gervase. He immediately began to complain and criticise, irritated by everything: the way her dress flared out about her, getting in his way; the way her hair tickled his face; the band and their music; the crowded dancefloor. It all annoyed him, his annoyance making the dance a miserable and perfunctory exercise. And his hand was like ice on her back.

Dancing with George, Charles and Alistair lightened her mood. They all danced well, and knew how to make her laugh, lifting her spirits. But just when she'd planned to ask for William's hand for the final dance of the evening, his fiancée got to him first, sending a quite unmistakable look of triumph at Dottie as they went by her. Gervase returned from the bar and came over, about to take her hand, not even troubling to ask, not smiling at her or appearing in any way to enjoy her company. She held back, inventing a twisted ankle. Really it was her heart that had been wrenched and just couldn't take any more that evening.

Gervase collared a waiter and ordered yet another drink. Dottie sighed. Gervase drunk was even worse than Gervase sober. As soon as possible, she got Flora to herself and said, 'Could you invite me back to yours for the night, I can't bear to be with him for a moment longer.'

Her sister needed no explanation. As soon as they began to leave, Flora grabbed Dottie's arm and said in a very clear voice, 'Oh darling, I'd almost forgot you were coming back with us. What a good thing I didn't invite anyone else!' She turned a bright smile on the rest of the group, 'Sorry, we've got to dash, poor old George has an early start in the morning.'

George—used to these sudden revelations—gave everyone a rueful smile. 'Sorry folks! How alarmingly middle-aged we are now. All responsibility and good sense. But it's been grand. Can't wait to see you all again soon. Take care, all.'

They said their goodnights outside and went for their cars. Gervase looked furious, but Dottie practically skipped away, her 'twisted' ankle completely forgotten. She felt only relief at evading Gervase's embraces for an evening. She followed her sister and brother-in-law to their car.

But behind them a debate was starting. Good manners made them halt, Dottie's heart sinking. It transpired that William's car wouldn't start. Several of the men gathered around but couldn't find the source of the problem.

'We can give one of you a lift,' George offered.

William hesitated. Moira turned to smile at Gervase, who immediately said, 'If it helps, I'm more than happy to drop Miss Hansom off at her flat, if Mr Hardy is going with you, George.'

Moira gave every appearance of being embarrassed but grateful, and politely followed Gervase to his car.

Dottie was puzzled, yet relieved. How did he know she

Caron Allan

had a flat? It was a miracle he could even remember her name. She shook her head and forgot about it. They all dispersed. William and George, Dottie and Flora moving away again in the direction of George's car. It was only a short walk. Not far enough for William to contrive to lag behind the others with Dottie. But at the car, with a secret look at Dottie, Flora said, 'William, dear, I hope you don't mind sitting in the back. I'm afraid I feel a little car sick these days if I don't sit in the front.'

'Of course,' he said. He shot Dottie a grin that made her heart sing.

It wasn't far to his home, but for seven minutes, Dottie and William sat in the back of the car together. Dottie peeled off her gloves and lay them in her lap. In the darkness, he reached for her hand and held it tight.

'Flora, did you know he was engaged to that—that woman?'

Dottie had planned to introduce the subject of Moira Hansom much more naturally, subtly, but impatience, coupled with a desperate urge to discuss the previous evening caused her to just blurt it out.

It was the following morning and they were in the nursery. Flora was patting baby Diana dry with the softest of towels. Naturally this involved a great deal of kissing of the tummy and blowing raspberries on the arms and legs and cheeks of the baby, who laughed at each 'attack'. Dottie had charge of the larger, heavier Freddie, always willing to play or giggle at the faces his aunt pulled. He rolled over on his blanket and crawled away at full speed; Dottie only just had time to get hold of him before he helped himself to a piece of coal from the scuttle.

'He's far too quick!' she exclaimed. 'I barely took my eyes off him for a second, and he was gone.'

'No, darling, of course we didn't know. I mean, he rang the day before and asked if he could bring someone. I suppose we guessed it would probably be a woman. But I had absolutely no inkling whatsoever that he was engaged to her. *Watch him!*' Flora added in an urgent tone. She nodded in the direction of her son. Dottie managed to grab the nearest foot, halting him in his progress long enough to get a firm hold around his middle. She hoisted him onto her lap, and extracted the heel of her shoe from his mouth. 'Ugh, Freddie! No darling, that's nasty, you don't want that.' He beamed at her and held out plump little hands for the shoe again. She found him a building block made from soft cotton in red and yellow, and gave that to him. Of course the corner of it immediately went in his mouth. To her sister, she said, 'I don't like her. Though that's hardly going to astonish anyone. Obviously I'm violently jealous.'

'Obviously,' said her sister. 'Remember our nanny used to say, 'handsome is as handsome does'? That's what came to mind every time I looked at her last night. I mean, she's quite decorative, I suppose, but in that very brassy, artificial way. I really wouldn't have thought she was William's type at all.'

Dottie was silent. She cuddled Freddie close, dropping a kiss on his sweetly-scented, curly fair hair. His eyes were drooping closed. In a soft voice, she said, 'What if he actually marries her? What shall I do then?'

Flora came over to sit on the floor beside her, her back propped against the foot of the nursery sofa. Diana, almost asleep, swathed in soft folds of a shawl, nodded against her shoulder. The two sisters sat together, a sleepy baby in each woman's arms.

After a long silence, Flora put out a hand to stroke Dottie's hair back from her temple. She shook her head in sympathy. 'I don't know, darling. I really don't. We shall have to hope for the best.'

'That was my first ever dance with him,' Dottie remarked, blinking away tears. She fidgeted with Freddie's bootee. 'I've known him for over a year now, and that is the only time we've ever danced.'

'Was it nice?' Flora fixed her eyes on her sister's face. A smile lit up Dottie's features, and her eyes half-closed at the memory.

'It was heavenly. I never wanted it to end. And then they

played that wretched Ladies' Choice, and that awful woman came charging back and grabbed him off me.'

A few days later, at the warehouse, Dottie said, 'You do think I'm doing the right thing, don't you? I'm not just doing it to try and get in William's good books.' She was looking at Flora through the steam spiralling up from her cup. The warmth was very welcome. A cold night had led to a world sprinkled with white at dawn, and although it was already gone, the pavements were wet and slippery and the cold air seemed to get right into your bones.

'Of course!' Flora immediately responded. 'Though it's hard to see how you could fail to want to help. My goodness, just imagine if you'd actually married Gervase and then all this—whatever it is—came out.'

Dottie gave an involuntary shudder. 'Awful,' she agreed. 'Though of course, I'd have to stick it out, give him my wifely support and so on.'

'Oh yes, but it would be the most humiliating, disappointing, awful, embarrassing...'

'All right, all right,' Dottie said hastily. 'But all the same I do feel vaguely disloyal.'

'Nonsense,' Flora said, in an admirable copy of their mother. 'Gervase is awful, and I'm so relieved—we're *all* so relieved—you and he are no longer, well, you and he.'

'I am too, yet I've got to go through all this pretence to try to help William.'

'Oh no, not working with William, spending time with William, talking to William. How horrid for you!' Flora said in a mocking tone, her eyebrows arched even more than usual. 'Did he give you any instructions that need to be decoded, like in all the best thrillers?'

Dottie put her tongue out at her, and continued with, 'I've barely spoken to our elusive inspector lately. He rang me briefly yesterday to see if I'd made up my mind to help him. I said I had, and that I'm going up to Gervase's at the weekend. William asked me to try to find papers that show money being paid out or received. 'Or anything useful,' he said. All very vague. And he said he would try, note well, *try* to see me up there. I've no real idea how I'm supposed to find out anything. I mean, Gervase is hardly likely to have incriminating papers just lying about. Am I supposed to rummage through his things? Search his study? What if I get caught? It's all very uncertain.'

'Just pay attention when he waffles on about work,' Flora said. 'They love it when you do that. It makes them feel important.'

'Gervase already feels important,' Dottie said. 'He thinks he's third in line of importance only after the King and the Prime Minister.'

'Encourage him to talk about work, unburden himself. Ask if he's feeling all right, his blood pressure and whatnot. Tell him you're concerned about the impact his very demanding...'

'...and important!'

'...and *important* position is having on his health.'

'How will I slip something like that into our conversation?'

Flora thought for a moment. 'You could say a friend of Father's died as a result of working at a stressful occupation, and that he wasn't even forty and it's made you worry about Gervase. Say you think he looks a bit pale. Or flushed.'

'That might do the trick.' Dottie was impressed. It sounded like the kind of thing she could say.

'And keep telling him how proud you are of his achievements, whatever they are, and that you can't understand why, given all his self-sacrifice etc etc, that he's not already a peer.'

'Oh that's good. I'll write all this down when I get home. Though I'm not sure I can deliver these lines with the same shocking disregard for the truth that you so easily employ.'

There was a tap on the door and it opened.

'Excuse me, Miss Manderson. These are now ready, if you'd like to take a look.'

The tall woman of uncertain years bore the ubiquitous emblems of the seamstress: a measuring tape hanging about her neck, and a small arrangement of pins in her lapel.

Dottie took the pile of garments from her, and with great excitement began to look through them. She held out one little garment to Flora.

'Isn't this adorable? What do you think? Would you put a little girl in one of these? It's for age two, so it's too big for Diana at the moment.'

It was a little dress, in many ways just like all the other little dresses one saw everywhere, with the gathers across the top of the chest and the little capped sleeves, but a lacy petticoat was attached on the inside of the garment, and the fabric used for the dress was the same as that used for one of the afternoon-dresses for women.

'Oh Dottie, it's beautiful. I'd love one of these for Diana if she was old enough. And I love the idea of the mother-daughter look, too. You'd better make a lot of these, they'll be popular. Are you going to do them for the under-twos?'

'Oh yes, eventually.' Dottie was pleased that Flora was so enthusiastic, as it was buying baby clothes with Flora that had given her the idea. 'We're just trying out a couple of sizes, but I'm already thinking of making them for the whole range from six months old to five years. You definitely like it?'

'I adore it! I shall definitely have one when you bring them out.'

After a few more minutes of examining the other items, Dottie handed them back to the seamstress.

'Thank you, Mrs Avers, I'm very happy with these.'

'Thank you, Miss Manderson. And about the new fabric order?'

'Oh it should all be here next Tuesday. They said about two o'clock, but we both know they are not usually on time. In any case, I shall be here, so you don't need to worry about it. And where are we with that skirt suit design we altered? The one in the burgundy wool mix?'

'It'll be fine, I'm sure, miss. And I know you were worried that the shade was deeper than expected, but it looks very good indeed. I'll have it finished by tomorrow to show you.'

'That's lovely, thank you. I was worried about that.' Dottie beamed at the older woman. Flora saw that they respected each other's judgment. Truly, she thought, and not for the first time, Dottie was *good* at this.

They spoke for a few minutes' more, then Mrs Avers left, and Flora said, 'So you decided to just take a risk and go ahead with the children's range?'

Dottie nodded. 'Oh I know it seems silly to try to do too much too soon, but so many clients have been asking, it seemed too good an opportunity to miss. But it's only two outfits for the little boys and four for the little girls at the moment, so just a small range to test the waters, so to speak. If it doesn't take off, well, it won't be too much of a disaster. But orders are already coming in thick and fast for the mother-daughter winter coat and dress, and of course the Christmas Day dress.' She grinned at Flora, 'We did a special mother-daughter dress. Or at least, we had already designed the women's winter cocktail dresses, and so we thought, let's do matching frocks for the little girls. We're all so excited. Everyone loves making the little dresses and other things. It seems more like fun than work at the moment.'

She stretched and yawned. Flora laughed and said, 'Well if you're going to be busy with work, you'd better hurry up and get this thing with Gervase sorted out.'

Dottie exhaled sharply, sending her fringe up into the air then floating back down to softly settle into place. She slumped back in her chair. 'I'm already regretting saying I would go up. I'm catching the train late on Friday morning, then coming back again Sunday afternoon.'

'It's a bit of a nuisance not having your car.'

'True. I'm certainly missing it. But so long as Imogen and Norris are finding it useful, I don't mind. And it's only for another two weeks. Coming back to the weekend at Gervase's, as far I'm aware there's a dinner party or something on Saturday at his parents', so that only leaves Friday evening and Sunday morning to get through. Even so I'm dreading it, but if there's a chance I might be able to help William, I have to go, and try to get in Gervase's good books by being the perfect little woman.'

Flora gave her look that said that might be stretching her talents too far. She said, 'Well for your sake, I hope William turns up. You don't want to go into the dragon's lair all on your own.'

'He said he'd see me up there, but beyond that, he hasn't said what he has planned.' She thought then added, 'I suppose it will be all right? I mean, it's just making myself pleasant to Gervase and some of his cronies, and very likely his horrid mother. At least I think that's all it is.'

'Just so long as Gervase doesn't expect you to make yourself extra pleasant to him, if you know what I mean.'

Dottie sighed. 'Oh I've been wondering about that myself. I'm hoping he'll behave himself. He's usually only just about manageable.'

Flora raised her eyebrows. 'That bad? Oh Dottie, do be firm with him.'

'I shall. The last thing I feel like doing is getting amorous with Gervase 'All Hands' Parfitt.'

*

Chapter Four

Dottie's train journey was uneventful and dull. She had hoped to have a certain detective inspector sitting beside her for the journey to Nottingham. Not that they exactly shared good memories of train travel together. Even so, she'd thought he would want to discuss his case, and she had envisaged them cosily sharing notes and ideas. But she had not heard from him since Monday, and so here she was on her own.

With no policeman to talk to, she was forced to use the time to do some work, spending over an hour just on the task of checking invoices and orders for the warehouse, when she would have far rather spent that time flirting and talking with the man she now knew she loved.

But she had gone over it all so many times in her head, and now was tired of thinking 'if only' and 'how could I?' She hoped that between the two of them they could find time to put things right.

Meanwhile, looking at the page in her hand, she wondered how she had come to spend £47 10 shillings and sixpence on buttons alone? She shook her head as she reluctantly placed a tick in the 'approved for payment' column. Garments had to have buttons, after all. The buttons on the negligee sets were beautiful, like tiny pieces of art. Tiny pieces of expensive art, she admitted. But they finished off the negligees to perfection. She only hoped her customers would think the same, and buy lots and lots of them.

That completed, she spent a happy half hour going through the new orders. There was nothing too demanding there, and most of the clients had made deposits on the work ordered. Things were looking very good. Obviously it was going to be another year or two before they really started to attract clients, and as a result of that, serious orders. Her plans to open up the first floor of the warehouse block to use as workrooms was looking less like an indulgence and more like a necessity.

She had other plans too. She put the notebook and invoices away to stare out of the window at the passing scenery, the cottages, villages, rivers and fields that dashed past almost too quickly to be seen. But she was only partially aware of what was outside the window. Inside, she continued to think about what Flora laughingly, but proudly, referred to as her 'empire'.

She wanted to create a nursery at the back of the warehouse.

A couple of the girls who modelled or sewed for her had 'got into trouble', including poor Gracie, a girl of only seventeen. She had been taken in by a smooth-talking fellow from the docks who'd had no intention whatsoever of marrying her. He had promised her the earth, showering her with gifts, then fled like the proverbial scalded cat the moment her situation had become known. His unconcerned claim of 'Nothing to do with me,' rang all too true of a certain type of man. His scurrilous suggestion that Gracie—young, timid, pretty, and with no father or older brother to back her up—had too many 'suitors' to know who the child's father was had infuriated and disgusted Dottie.

She remembered Mrs Carmichael talking to her about it, sitting in the office that was now Dottie's, pouring

The Spy Within

herself a drink, kicking off her shoes to rest her tired feet, and dumping all her jewellery in a tangled heap on the desk without any regard for the value of the gold or precious stones. Dottie smiled, shaking her head at the memory.

The problem was that there were no adult men in Gracie's family, no one to provide for the family or protect them. Her little brother was only nine years old. Her mother was not strong, and the family had no other choice, Gracie's mother had to look after the new baby whilst Gracie came to do sewing for Dottie four mornings a week. Without that money, the family would have no income, and therefore no roof over their head nor food on the table.

Dottie had discussed her ideas with the few other businesspeople she had met. The men all said she was just being foolish, or sentimental, and that she'd be wasting her money. The women—fewer in number, certainly—said they thought it was an excellent idea. And it was partly selfish, she had to admit. Gracie had been a good mannequin until her 'unfortunate event', but she was an even better sewer—fast, neat, and able to see what needed doing and get on with it. Dottie didn't want to lose her. Nor did she want the family to suffer because they had no income and couldn't keep a roof over their heads or food on the table.

To Dottie it made good business sense that for a relatively small expenditure, she could allocate and furnish a room where the staff's babies or little children could play or sleep under the care of one nurse, and the mothers could spend their lunch hours in the nursery, or take breaks to feed or sit with the children. Having discussed it with Gracie—who had burst into tears and hugged her—and the other two young mothers who worked at *Carmichael's*—she began to feel it could work. Of course, she would need to find a nurse for the children. The thought of a nursery was exciting. She had so many other plans, she hardly knew where to start. The money would come from the sale of various unneeded assets she

57

had inherited from Mrs Carmichael and also from her profits. It was really a really ludicrously small amount, she thought. A little money went quite a long way if you were careful to plan things.

She got out her sketchbook and began to amuse herself with a few preliminary new costume designs, slightly spoiled by the movement of the train jogging her at the wrong moment, and lists of ideas for the next range of ladies' wear. Then she added two more ideas to the children's range.

Eventually the train arrived at the little country station just outside Nottingham, and it was time to get off. Dottie watched an expectant mother fight the elements—it was pouring down with rain now—and the steep steps down from the train, to deposit two irritable toddlers onto the platform. Dottie ran to gather up the woman's basket and bag to hand down to her, whilst the guard of the train wrestled the heavy pram down the ramp from the luggage van, the porter took the shopping from Dottie and got everything safely stowed on the pram, then the two little ones were squeezed inside. Their mother was so grateful, clearly not used to people assisting her.

Dottie gave up her ticket at the barrier, went out to the road, and looked around, hoping to see Gervase in his car.

He wasn't there. That surprised her. She began to head towards the little taxi rank, empty at the moment. It seemed she would have a wait, and she had no umbrella. There was a car parked some way along the road. A woman got out of it now and hurried towards Dottie, clamping her hat on her head as she approached.

When she got nearer, she called, 'Is it Miss Manderson?'

Surprised, Dottie said she was.

'How do you do? My name is Holcombe. I'm Mr Parfitt's secretary. He asked me to come and meet you. I'm afraid he couldn't come in person.'

Still surprised, Dottie nevertheless said, 'Oh how kind. Thank you.'

'May I take your case?'

Dottie felt embarrassed, not wanting to cause further

work for Mrs Holcombe. 'Really, there's no need, I can manage.'

'This way, then.'

Mrs Holcombe went off at a breathless pace; there was no time for conversation. Dottie's luggage was quickly stowed in the back of the car, and as they got in, and set off, Dottie was at last able to say, 'I'm so grateful to you for meeting me. I'm sure you've got quite enough to do as it is. I had expected to take a taxi if Gervase wasn't here to meet me.'

'It's no trouble at all,' Mrs Holcombe said. Dottie thought she seemed surprised at Dottie's gratitude. Her glance sideways was a calculating one. Dottie wondered what Gervase had said about her that made Mrs Holcombe look at her like that. Was Mrs Holcombe one of Gervase's conquests? That would not be in the least surprising, though Mrs Holcombe looked like a woman who had more sense than to be taken in—as I was, Dottie thought ruefully—by some man with an extremely convincing line in flattery.

After a moment, Mrs Holcombe added, 'Have you been to this area before?'

Dottie said, 'Once, last summer. I stayed with a family friend of Gervase's.' She paused, wondering if it was too informal to call him by his first name to his secretary. Perhaps she ought to say Mr Parfitt, as Mrs Holcombe did. Certainly people always said the youth of today had no manners and were too informal, and Mrs Holcombe was at least ten if not twenty years older than herself. 'Although I have visited Mr Parfitt's house, I've never stayed there before.'

'Of course,' said Mrs Holcombe, more for something to say, Dottie guessed.

'Do you come from this area yourself?' Dottie asked.

'Matlock Bath. Over the county border in Derbyshire.'

'What a small world,' Dottie exclaimed. 'I have friends in Matlock itself, though I don't suppose you know them. It's always the same isn't it? When people hear I live in London they ask if I know so-and-so who lives in such-

and-such street, and of course, I never do. Outsiders tend to assume everyone knows everyone.'

'Try me,' Mrs Holcombe said with the ghost of a smile.

'Joseph Allsopp and his family. Their niece is living with them at the moment, Eleanor Hardy. In fact she's been with them for about a year. Her mother died...'

'How sad. Yes, actually I do know them.' But Mrs Holcombe didn't elaborate. Another fleeting sideways glance, then darting away to attend to the road again. Her look was definitely wary.

'I don't know them all that well, but they seem to be nice people.'

'Yes, they are.'

Again there was no elaboration, and Dottie turned to look at the scenery, but the world was greying now as the light faded. She felt weary from the journey, and inside, a renewed sense of dread of the weekend visit began to gnaw at her.

It was fully dark by the time they reached the house, but the lights shining from the windows were cheerful and inviting. Almost as soon as Dottie opened the car door, the front door opened, spilling golden light onto the gravel, and a maid came hurrying out with an umbrella to bring Dottie into the house, as the butler grabbed her luggage.

'Hello Mr Michaels, how are you?' Dottie beamed at the butler as he set her things at the foot of the stairs. He gave her a formal bow, then a wide grin.

'Lovely to see you again, Miss Manderson. You're looking very well. I'm very well myself, good of you to ask. Now come into the drawing room, miss, and get yourself by the fire. It's that chilly this evening.'

Mrs Holcombe stood in the doorway. Michaels nodded to her and smiled.

'Good evening, Mrs Holcombe.'

'Mr Michaels. Not a very nice night.'

'No indeed.'

Michaels helped to load up the maid with Dottie's bits and pieces, who immediately proceeded upstairs.

'Well I'll be off for now. I shall see you later this

evening, Miss Manderson,' Mrs Holcombe said.

'Really?' Dottie hoped her surprise hadn't sounded rude.

'Mr Parfitt probably mentioned that he is having a small dinner party this evening, to introduce you to a few friends. He has very kindly extended an invitation to me.'

'Oh.' Dottie managed not to sound too dismayed. 'I had forgotten. But it will be lovely to see you again later. And thank you once more for meeting me. Bye for now.'

The thought of a dinner party so soon was a depressing one. But on the bright side, she reminded herself, at least if there were guests here all evening, she wouldn't have to be alone with Gervase. That wouldn't be much use to William, of course. Then, she would be able to say goodnight as soon as everyone went home, pleading tiredness—genuine tiredness—from the journey. She felt very happy with this plan.

'Mr Gervase is not yet home, Miss Manderson, so perhaps you'd like some refreshments? Then I'll show you to your room, give you a chance to get settled in. Please come this way.'

Tea was already waiting for her in the drawing room. It was odd to sit there all alone in the large strange house she knew Gervase intended to be their marital home.

But the tea was welcome, as were the hot buttery crumpets.

Half an hour later, Michaels conducted Dottie upstairs.

As they went, she noticed he had a long smudge of whiteish dust on his shoulder, and tiny white specks all down his front.

'You've got something all over yourself, Mr Michaels,' she commented, pointing.

He seemed taken aback, but simply brushed it off and said, 'So I have, miss, thank you.'

He conducted her along the upstairs corridor, chatting all the way about the dreary time of year, how everyone hated the winter, didn't they, and weren't they all longing for the spring. 'Nothing like a warm sunny day to make you feel all's right with the world and the good Lord is in his heaven.'

'Oh absolutely,' Dottie agreed.

Beneath this amiable exterior, Michaels was debating with himself nervously. What if he had misread her, and she actually knew of Mr Gervase's arrangements, perhaps even welcomed them? After all, young people were young people, and she was supposed to be half mad with love for Mr Gervase. Not that he could see it himself, but it wouldn't be the first time he'd misjudged someone. He told himself he ought to have waited until he was sure, but it was too late now.

In any case, the older generation always talked of the low morals of the younger, but thirty years as a butler had shown Michaels that young people had always run in and out of one another's bedrooms in the dead of night when it was generally supposed that no one was around.

Why, on the eve of King Edward's coronation, there had been that awkward incident with the Duchess of Ashbourne and the young fellow who was later the Conservative MP for West Bridgeford. He shook his head, and sent Miss Manderson a sideways glance as they turned the corner and came to the door. She didn't seem the type. Not that you can always tell, he knew that, but she seemed a little on the naïve side. Very sweet. Very young. Too young for Mr Gervase, the old goat. He liked them young. In Michaels' opinion Parfitt liked them a sight too young. Yes, he was fairly sure now she had no idea what Mr Gervase was really like.

He halted beside the door. 'Here we are, miss. This is the room Mr Gervase asked me to prepare for you.'

He could tell she didn't pick up on what he'd said. But he was glad to get that bit in, just so she knew it was Parfitt's own idea. Still, he felt compelled to ensure she had all the facts, so he nodded to the door across the hallway, the only other door at this end of the house.

In a perfectly ordinary tone he said, 'And that's Mr Gervase's room, right there.'

She was looking about her now, her expression one of

someone sizing up a situation. He felt glad about that. He continued his little flow of conversation. 'His room looks out onto the front of the house, whilst your room looks out over the gardens. Much nicer, in my opinion.'

She smiled, automatically polite. 'Oh definitely.'

He turned the handle and pushed the door wide. He stepped back to allow her to precede him, but as soon as she stepped forward, without even looking inside, he threw up a warning hand to stop her, and exclaimed a little too loudly, 'My goodness, what on earth has happened?'

Not that his so-called surprise would have deceived a child, but her attention was on the mess inside the room, and not his words.

'The ceiling's come down,' she said.

And indeed that was the case: plaster hung in chunks from a ceiling that dipped alarmingly in the middle. There was a gaping hole right above the bed. The bed and the carpet were coated in lumps of plaster, and plaster-dust coated the whole room. The light-fitting hung down, dislodged from its place in the centre of the ceiling.

'Oh dear, oh dear, this won't do at all,' Michaels said, shaking his head. 'We'll have to put you somewhere else for the weekend, I'm afraid, miss. I really don't think we'll get all this fixed just in the next day or two.'

'Of course.' Dottie nodded. She no longer looked at the room but at him. Her hazel eyes, very pretty eyes that he had thought so soft, so innocent, regarded him now with knowing amusement.

He backed out of the doorway, appeared to consider for a moment, then said, 'Perhaps we might put you in the little blue room at the end of the corridor, miss. It's true that it's not quite so large, or modern, but it has a pleasing view of the garden, and a private adjoining bathroom. And it's just that little bit warmer on that side of the house, protected from the wind you see. I feel sure that's the best choice, given the circumstances. If you don't mind following me, miss...'

She followed him, a puzzled look on her face. He led her

to the opposite end of the corridor and opened a door. He held back to allow her to enter the room.

'It's lovely,' she said. And it really was. The ceiling was where it should be, the room completely clean and ready for occupation. A fire burned in the grate. He crossed the room to open another door.

'Your bathroom, miss. Nice to have one all to yourself rather than to share Mr Gervase's.'

He saw the momentary alarm in her eyes, then the relief that followed.

'Oh definitely,' she said mildly.

Message received and understood, Michaels told himself with satisfaction.

She turned to the window. Outside, it was completely dark, with no chinks of light spilling out into the darkness.

'Oh yes,' Dottie said with irony, 'a *much* nicer view.'

Michaels transformed a snort of laughter into a coughing fit, pulling a handkerchief from his pocket to cover the sound. Something fell out of the pocket and banged down onto the floorboards, rolling a few yards to halt at the edge of the carpet.

They both watched the thing roll, then Dottie stooped to retrieve it, handing it to him with a straight face.

'Don't forget your screwdriver, Mr Michaels.'

'Thank you, miss.' He kept his countenance admirably, Dottie thought.

'This will be perfect,' she said, looking about her.

'Very well, miss. I'll acquaint Mr Gervase with the change in arrangements. And if you don't mind a short wait, we'll get this room ready for you, and have your luggage brought along here from the other room.'

He could see she was trying not to laugh as she stepped around her suitcase and hat box, and headed to the door of the dust-free, spotlessly clean room, with the fresh linen on the bed, and the flowers in the vase on the little side table.

'I'll wait downstairs in the drawing room whilst that's being done,' she said.

'Very good, miss.'

As she got to the door, he was right behind her. She put a hand on his arm. 'Thank you, Mr Michaels.' Her look was grave.

He felt quite overcome for a second. She was a sweet little thing. Well not so little, she was as tall as he was. He put his hand over hers, not at all the done thing ordinarily. 'You're quite welcome, Miss Manderson.'

As she went into the hall, she said over her shoulder. 'By the way, before you show that room to Gervase, you'd better straighten the counterpane and brush it down. You've left footprints all over it.'

Dottie enjoyed sitting for a while once more in the peace and quiet of the drawing room. The house was silent, or nearly so. Her sharp hearing picked up odd sounds from the back sections of the house. She was puzzled by the incident upstairs. She wondered whether she ought to ask Mr Michaels about it.

Because... What did it mean? Why had he done that? It was perfectly obvious—she had all but accused him, and he hadn't denied it—that he had deliberately pulled down the light fitting and with it half of the ceiling in the bedroom that Gervase had told him Dottie was to use. Clearly Gervase had seen this visit as an opportunity to make a nuisance of himself by trying to pressure her to sleep with him.

What she didn't understand was why Mr Michaels felt the need to make that more difficult for Gervase by removing Dottie and putting her in a room so far away from Gervase's own.

She ought to have asked, but she had been afraid of what he might say. Because surely this meant, didn't it, that she was not the first.

She had never flattered herself that Gervase had 'saved himself' for her and her alone. That was a ludicrous and naïve assumption. To begin with, he was far older than she, a 'man of the world' in the usual sense, meaning sexually experienced.

Perhaps it was the result of some of the things William

had hinted at that she now wondered, for the first time, if Gervase was the kind of man who took—things—by an arrogant sense of right, rather than accepting permission or denial.

Certainly he had been 'difficult' about her continued refusal of his advances, seeming to think that continuing to see her and spend time with her practically amounted to entitlement. He had asked her to stay at hotels with him, to go away with him. He had even, in one particularly incautious moment, ventured so far as to offer to buy her a flat which he would use to visit her whenever he was in town. He had hastily apologised, trying to say that he had only been joking, though she knew he had been perfectly serious.

Well, she would have to be on her guard, that was certain. Surely she could evade him for one weekend? Or make it clear from the outset that she expected him to abide by her wishes, or she would leave.

She got up to move around the room, feeling anxious and longing to return to the railway station to take the next train back to London. How very quiet the house was, she thought again. There were other houses just along the lane, but it felt so remote.

This could have been her life, she thought, if she had accepted it and wanted it. The large, well-furnished home, the staff, the grounds, the status that Gervase himself constantly crowed over. Herself here in this room, day after day after day, waiting for him to come home, or to receive his guests.

She was shaking her head. No, this would never have suited her.

She knew policemen were all too often called from home, did not work office hours, were likely to be called out when you were having a romantic dinner, a family picnic, a celebration, a funeral, if you were on the point of giving birth, or if you were in bed with a fever. Rain or shine, a policeman went where he was needed, when he was needed.

But, Dottie thought, Gervase was not that kind of

policeman. And although it was by no means a mansion, William's house was perfect for a family. Or for two lovers. How much nicer to sit waiting for him, warm and cosy at William's kitchen table, sewing or drawing or reading, than in all this chilly finery. How much better to lie in his loving arms, than to have your heart in your mouth waiting for the awful sound of Gervase's step in the hall, his tap on the door, as he came to insist upon his 'rights'.

Just then a car pulled into the drive. The headlamps bathed the front of the house and died as the car turned along the bends of the drive and halted right outside the front door.

She went to the window and watched as a uniformed constable got out of the driver's seat of the highly polished car, and hurried to open the rear passenger door for Gervase to alight. Gervase snapped irritably at the driver, then without a backward look, strode into the house. The car drove away. The front door slammed.

Dottie's heart sank. Gervase was bad enough, but Gervase in a filthy mood was infinitely worse. She turned to face the door, aware she was presenting herself as the perfect little wife-to-be. She patted her hair and smoothed her dress and wished she'd thought of changing her clothes and freshening her make-up.

In the hall Gervase was clearly being greeted by Mr Michaels. There were the low sounds of an exchange of male voices, then footsteps approaching. Dottie felt so tense, rigid, waiting for the inevitable. It was like waiting for your own execution, she thought.

'Dottie, dearest!' Gervase rushed over and dragged her into a tight close embrace. He smiled. Michaels hasn't told him yet, Dottie realised.

'Hello, Gervase. Have you had a good day at work? How are you?'

'Fine, fine. Nothing to give me any worries. So much the better now I have you beside me, my darling. Pleasant journey up? I know it's a rather tedious one, having done it quite a few times myself now. But not too terrible, I hope?'

'No it was quite pleasant. Would you like some tea? This

is a bit cold now, but I could ring for some more?' She dithered by the little table.

'God, no!' was Gervase's immediate, scathing response. 'No, I always have a whisky when I get home. And take a moment to relax before dinner.' He crossed the room to the little walnut cabinet and helped himself to a drink from a handsome decanter. He lifted it towards her with a querying look.

'Oh no thank you, not just now.'

He drank his whisky down in one gulp then poured another and came to sit beside her. He sat with the hand holding his drink draped across her shoulders, an embrace she hated, always fearing the drink would spill all down her. But she said nothing about that, commenting instead,

'Your Mrs Holcombe told me you are expecting a few people to dinner this evening?'

'Ah yes,' he smirked at her. 'Should have told you, I know, but it slipped my mind. Just a few close friends, and my parents of course.'

'Of course,' she said. 'How lovely.' She ought to have guessed. She'd expected to spend some time with his dreaded parents. She'd just hoped it wouldn't be until the next day. 'And Mrs Holcombe, too, I understand?'

'Yes. Thought she could round out the numbers a bit. She's all right. A bit dowdy, and pushing forty, but she can be useful.' He seemed to notice her appearance for the first time. A slight frown appeared. 'Is that what you're wearing this evening?'

'Goodness, no. This is just the outfit I travelled up in.'

'Oh that's all right then. Good. Well, I'm going up for a bath and to get dressed for dinner. See you in about an hour.' He pulled her into a clinch and kissed her with more force than yearning. 'Jolly good to have you here, Dottie my love.'

At the door he paused and turned back. 'By the way,' and he couldn't hide a self-satisfied smirk, 'How's your room?'

She gave him a beaming smile. 'Oh Gervase, it's lovely. Just perfect, thank you.'

'Good, good.' He turned and ran up the stairs. She heard the rough sound of him rubbing his hands together gleefully as he went.

She waited a few minutes then went up to her room, and began to get ready for the dinner party.

As Dottie came downstairs forty-five minutes later, she saw Michaels hurrying across the hall to the front door. She went into the drawing room, and found Gervase standing in front of the fire, sipping from another crystal tumbler. How much did he drink, she wondered. True, he always drank a good deal when they dined out, but she'd always thought that was because of the occasion, that they were dining out, not because it was as essential to him as the food itself. She would keep an eye on him this weekend to try to fathom whether he had a problem with alcohol or if he was just indulging himself from time to time.

'Ah, there you are. Good.' He set his glass aside and placing his hands on her shoulders, looked her over, nodded approvingly, then kissed her on the cheek, mindful of her carefully applied lipstick. He stepped back from her, smiling with his lips but not his eyes.

It was odd, she thought. His touch, his kiss. Both seemed rushed, perfunctory. His manner was cool towards her for the first time since they'd met. She felt relieved yet puzzled.

'Your guests are arriving,' she said.

'*Our* guests, dearest,' he corrected her gently, again with that smile that stayed firmly on his mouth. 'Now, I shall introduce you. And obviously you will go in to dinner with my father, whilst I shall probably escort Mrs Sedgworth. After dinner, you will lead the ladies from the table back in here for coffee, and we men shall of course join you all after about an hour.'

Dottie nodded and smiled. There was no time to say anything, the door was opening and people began coming in. Gervase went forward to greet them, a broad smile—a genuine one this time—on his face, his hand outstretched to shake that of each gentleman who came in. Dottie straightened her shoulders, lifted her chin and put on her best party smile.

'Sedgworth, my dear fellow! And Christobel, looking lovely as always.' He kissed the elegant older woman's hand in an unnecessarily courtly manner, or so Dottie thought. It was as if he was saying to her, see, it's only you who displeases me.

Dottie began to come forward too, smiling a welcome, ignoring the butterflies inside her. She had done this so many times, she reminded herself. Although never as Gervase Parfitt's intended fiancée.

'Good evening,' Dottie said, first to the woman, then the man.

'Ah,' said Gervase, making her feel as though she'd made a mistake somehow. 'Allow me to present my fiancée, Miss Dorothy Manderson, from London.'

Dottie shot him a look but didn't think it was worth contradicting him openly. She shook the gentleman's hand, and smiled at his wife again as Gervase said, 'Dottie, this is Major Jimmy Sedgworth, and his lovely wife Christobel.'

The door opened again and Michaels said, in a hushed deferential voice, 'The Chief Constable of Nottinghamshire, Mr Edwin Harpur Parfitt, and Mrs Evangeline Parfitt.'

Dottie just had time to think how odd it was that Gervase's own parents were announced by the butler.

'Ah, my parents. You've already met them, Dottie, no need to be scared of them.' Gervase turned to shake his father's hand and kiss his mother on the cheek.

Rather like he kissed me, Dottie thought. She was needled by him saying 'no need to be scared' in front of everyone, making her sound—and feel—childish. But she didn't let the smile fade from her lips, as she greeted his rather intimidating parents.

'Of course. How lovely to see you both again, and looking so well.'

Later she couldn't recall whether either of them actually spoke to her, or if they merely shook her hand and kissed the air near her right cheek. Not that it mattered, hopefully she would never see them again after this.

Almost immediately another couple arrived, younger this time, and Gervase hurried to introduce them as the Honourable Marcus Armstrong and his fiancée, Miss Venita de Paul.

A little trivial conversation followed once the introductions were completed, with the inevitable comments about the weather and how everyone was keeping, health-wise. Dottie's face ached with smiling, and yet again she thought, I could never be part of this world. Who has their own father announced by the butler at a small private dinner party? She couldn't seem to get past that. Gervase was clearly in his element, laughing and joking, oozing good humour and witty conversation. Everyone seemed perfectly at ease, apart from perhaps the older lady, Christobel Sedgworth, who seemed a little tired, or ill at ease. Dottie went to her side and asked her if she gardened. It was a safe bet, most older ladies living in the country did, she had found, even if only in a genteel way of snipping flowers for the drawing room. Christobel Sedgworth seemed delighted to be asked, and chatted away for several minutes about her roses, promising Dottie cuttings in the spring.

Gervase's parents all but ignored her, giving all their attention to Marcus Armstrong and Venita de Paul. Gervase was talking stocks and shares with Major Sedgworth.

Beside her, Mrs Sedgworth fell silent, and watched Gervase and her husband with rather a worried look on her face. Dottie said in a light tone, 'How dull it must be to be a man and have to talk about money all the time.'

Mrs Sedgworth turned to look at her and for the first time Dottie saw a genuine smile.

'Oh it's their field of expertise. Men are used to taking the lead in most things.'

'Definitely,' Dottie said, adding with a little too much candour, 'I wish Gervase had let me know I was now his fiancée.'

Mrs Sedgworth laughed. She put her arm through Dottie's, seeming now to be completely at ease. She led Dottie back to a sofa and they sat down.

'My dear, that's men all over. If they think a thing, to them it has become a reality. Has he even asked you to marry him?'

Dottie thought for a moment. 'Well, we did talk about it, just before Christmas. But I rather blotted my copybook, and it was all off.' She went on to explain briefly about the events in Sussex, telling Mrs Sedgworth how she had been actually arrested for murder and put in jail for several days pending further investigation.

Mrs Sedgworth's eyes were like saucers, as she hung on Dottie's every word, the way people do when they hear such a bizarre story.

'And he didn't support you?' Mrs Sedgworth murmured, glancing across the room to where Gervase was pompously holding forth to both the Major and Marcus Armstrong.

Dottie had hoped she had minimised Gervase's abandonment of her. Clearly not. She had been an idiot to bring up the subject. She said, 'I'm afraid we rather fell out about it. But you know, he couldn't risk his reputation by getting involved. I see that now. At the time I was frightened, I suppose, so I panicked.'

Mrs Sedgworth raised an eyebrow that suggested she cared less than a fig for Gervase's reputation. Dottie began to think she rather liked Mrs Sedgworth.

'I should think you were more than a little put out,' she said to Dottie, putting a hand on Dottie's arm. 'I'd have packed him in, if I'd been in your shoes.'

In for a penny, thought Dottie. She'd definitely been too open with someone she'd only just met. There didn't seem much point in holding back now.

'I have to admit I did, as a matter of fact. My parents were furious with him too. And...' She halted, realising she'd been on the point of divulging a confidence too far. She couldn't mention William Hardy.

'And here you are now,' Mrs Sedgworth said after a pause.

'Yes...' Dottie felt as though she'd run out of things to say. She looked across at Gervase and almost shuddered at the mere sight of him. Mrs Sedgworth was watching her closely, taking it all in.

It was a huge relief when Michaels appeared in the doorway and announced that dinner was served. Dottie and her new friend got up and began to make their way towards the door, but a frown from Gervase halted Dottie in her tracks, and she waited until his father offered her his arm.

It seemed ludicrously formal given there were only eight of them and all friends at that, but she smiled at the man beside her. She waited for Gervase to take Mrs Sedgworth into the dining room as he'd said he would, but Gervase offered Mrs Sedgworth a little bow then went past her to stand beside Venita de Paul with his arm extended in invitation.

Dottie wondered if she had imagined the little frisson of surprise in the air that had accompanied Gervase's action. As she walked in behind Gervase and Miss de Paul, she saw that Mrs Sedgworth was escorted by Marcus Armstrong, and that Gervase's mother accompanied the Major.

Throughout dinner, Dottie felt like a small child permitted to sit with the grown-ups. She sat between Edwin Parfitt and the Honourable Marcus, and found herself talked across and rarely with. Any comment she made was treated with an odd mixture of surprise she had spoken at all, and embarrassment at what she said. In the end she said nothing.

Evangeline Parfitt and Venita de Paul declined any interest in dessert, and it was clear from Gervase's look that he expected Dottie now to rise and lead the ladies away so the men could drink themselves stupid and tell filthy jokes. But a glance at Mrs Sedgworth told her that the other lady was very interested in having some of the dainty cream-filled sugary pastries, and so Dottie immediately said she would have some. Gervase frowned slightly, and Dottie suspected she would hear about this once everyone had gone. She ate as quickly as she decently could in company, then rose from the table, saying, 'I think the ladies and I will take our coffee in the drawing room, and leave you gentlemen to talk.'

She smiled at Gervase as she said this, and received only a curt nod in response.

With an inward sigh she left the room, holding the door for the other ladies to precede her. As they reached the drawing room, Dottie was surprised to see Gervase's secretary there, waiting.

'Mrs Holcombe,' she said, hurrying forward, her hand outstretched. 'How lovely to see you. Though I'd expected you for dinner.'

Mrs Holcombe gave a wry smile. 'I'm sorry, perhaps I misled you. I was invited to coffee,' she said.

Dottie received the unspoken message. 'No, no, it's my mistake. Next time,' she said, forgetting that she did not plan to be here for 'next time'. 'It would be lovely if you could join us for dinner.'

If Mrs Holcombe seemed surprised, it was nothing to the look of disapproval on the face of Evangeline Parfitt. Dottie knew she had made an error of judgement. The ranks of society were far too rigidly observed here, she remembered, too late. These people were not the type to invite a 'mere' secretary to dinner, although if convenient, and if their numbers were low or odd, they might deign to invite her for coffee.

A maid came in with a tray of cups and saucers, and Michaels was right behind her with another, larger tray with the coffee, sugar, milk and cream, according to the taste of the guests. A third tray was borne in by another maid, and held plates of chocolates and other sweet treats: Dottie's favourites, miniature Florentines and tiny slices of Battenberg. Away from the frowning eyes of husbands and fiancés, the ladies helped themselves eagerly. Even Gervase's mother ate a Florentine, carefully removing one black silk evening glove to do so.

Dottie sat in the corner of a sofa, and Mrs Holcombe sat in the corner of an adjoining one. Mrs Sedgworth, her plate piled high, took the seat next to Dottie. Mrs Parfitt and Miss de Paul began to set up two tables for Bridge on the other side of the room.

As soon as the other two began to do this, Mrs Sedgworth said to Dottie in a low voice, 'I must speak with you privately. Can you come to me for morning coffee tomorrow? I'm sure Gervase would have no objections; he'll think we're getting to know one another for his sake.'

Dottie was surprised. She agreed immediately, but wondered if she had somehow misunderstood what Mrs Sedgworth was suggesting. She glanced at Mrs Holcombe, but she was stirring her coffee rather fiercely.

Mrs Sedgworth said, 'It's all right, we can talk in front of Mary. Dottie, dear, I know you don't know me at all, and this must seem very strange, but I need to talk to you about Gervase. You seem so—well, again I'm sorry my dear, it's really not a criticism—but you seem so very young. And well, innocent. I feel you ought to know certain things. Please, don't say anything about this to Gervase. I'm rather sticking my neck out in speaking to you like this.'

Dottie was almost at a loss for words. What else could she say but, 'Of course. I shan't say a thing.'

'Eleven o'clock, then? Tell Gervase I shall send Jimmy to pick you up, so there'll be no need to worry about how to get to me.'

'Thank you,' Dottie said, but got no further.

'I hope you're a good Bridge player, Dorothy,' Evangeline Parfitt called. Her tone was a little sarcastic, and prompted Dottie to say,

'Oh, I think I'll be all right.'

She didn't particularly enjoy Bridge, but she could play an average game. She thought it was an odd way to spend the evening of the first dinner party she'd attended—hosted—with Gervase. Conversation would surely have been a better way of getting to know Gervase's friends and parents? And besides, there were now nine of them.

'I don't play,' Mrs Sedgworth said. 'I expect you were just thinking that there are too many people? But I don't play, I'm afraid. Though I enjoy watching. And I've brought my knitting with me.' She indicated a flowered calico bag by her feet.

'That's why I'm here,' Mary Holcombe said. 'To make up the second four.'

Dottie nodded.

The door opened, and the men came in rather sooner than Dottie had expected them. Michaels brought in fresh coffee, and the port, sherry and brandy decanters were put to good use, and everyone took their seats at the tables.

*

Chapter Five

The evening seemed to last forever. By eleven o'clock, Dottie could barely keep her eyes open, but still the game trickled on between them.

She was not a brilliant player herself, but made a reasonable partner to the Major who was kind and forgiving of any mistakes she made, and generous with praise for her one or two bright moments. He smiled at her and called her M'dear, which reminded her of M'dear Monty, the family friend and solicitor Sir Montague Montague who had been such a wonderful help lately in Sussex, and of every other male friend of a certain age and type who had dined at her parents' home over the years.

Gervase was at the other table, to Dottie's great relief, and played an ambitious, aggressive game in partnership with his mother, his father and Miss de Paul being their opponents. Their two games were closely run, with Gervase and his mother winning by a narrow margin on each occasion.

Dottie was glad to be at a table where the game was not taken quite so seriously. Though Mrs Holcombe seemed to be a very good player, she was somewhat hampered by the

Honourable Marcus who had only the sketchiest understanding of the rules of play. Mrs Holcombe and the Major, if they had been partners, would have had no trouble at all beating the other two very quickly.

During any lull in the games, Dottie was at leisure to glance across at the other table to observe their game. It was a good thing that the players—all proficient apart from Venita—were engrossed. It made it less likely that either Miss de Paul or Gervase would notice that Marcus Armstrong was annoying Dottie by attempting to nudge her with his knee or his foot under the table.

She'd moved as far away from him as feasible whilst still able to reach the table. Now she was forced into making her irritation known by frowning at him and glancing down in such an obvious manner that none of the others could be in any doubt that he had touched her.

Armstrong apologised in a sulky voice for 'stepping on her toe', and withdrew his knee. Dottie began to relax again.

Venita de Paul, entrancingly blonde and blue-eyed, batted her eyelashes and asked Gervase for advice on at least two occasions. And he's not even her partner, Dottie thought.

Her gaze rested on them for a few seconds before her attention was demanded for her own game. A minute later, she glanced back in time to catch a smile exchanged between Miss de Paul and Gervase.

It was almost one o'clock when the guests finally departed. Dottie yearned to get to bed. Mrs Sedgworth reminded Dottie of their appointment the following day in front of everyone, and when Gervase looked surprised, the lady said simply:

'You won't mind if Dottie comes to have coffee with me in the morning, will you? I thought it would be nice for her to get to know at least two of the old codgers in the neighbourhood.'

Gervase's surprise began to closely resemble a frown. 'D'you know, I'm so sorry, Christobel, but I already have another engagement tomorrow.'

Mrs Sedgworth said with a laugh, 'Oh we shan't want any men around. Dottie and I want to talk about frocks and hairstyles. Jimmy will call for her at ten to eleven, and bring her back at half past twelve. Now then, we must go. Goodnight all!'

Mrs Holcombe had already slipped away unnoticed by anyone except Dottie who had thanked her for coming and helped her on with her coat, Mr Michaels being busy with Edwin and Evangeline Parfitt's outer wear. As the Parfitts were saying goodnight to Gervase, Mr Michaels was able to escort Mrs Sedgworth to the car, shielding her with a huge black umbrella.

Dottie said goodnight to the Sedgworths then returned to stand beside Gervase as he was still talking to his parents. Evangeline Parfitt shot Dottie a look, and to Dottie's astonishment, said to her son, 'Really, Gervase, the poor girl is dropping with exhaustion. Why on earth you had us all here the day she arrived, I don't know. Goodnight, Dottie. We shall see you tomorrow.' She kissed her cheek, before turning to snap at her husband, 'For God's sake, Edwin, get a move on. You can tell him all that tomorrow.'

The Chief Constable of Nottinghamshire halted mid-sentence, said a hurried goodnight, directing a kind of half-mast salute at Dottie then meekly followed his wife out into the night.

Finally the front door was closed. 'At last,' Gervase remarked, with a smile at Dottie. His meaning was unmistakable. Her heart sank.

The butler still hovered. 'Will there be anything else, sir?'

'No Michaels, that's it for tonight. You may go.'

'Very good, sir. Goodnight Miss Manderson. Goodnight Mr Parfitt.'

'Goodnight Mr Michaels,' Dottie replied. She began to head towards the stairs, hoping to get away with a brief comment or two and a quick kiss.

But he caught her hand in his.

'Dottie,' he said, and his tone warned her of the inevitable topic he was about to raise. Her heart sank even lower.

He brought up a hand to cup her cheek, and leaned close to give her a kiss more intimate than was welcome. Then she remembered she was supposed to be playing a part, in order to help William. She responded as best she could. It was so hard to pretend to feel passion for him when she hated the mere thought of his touch.

'I shall come to you in an hour or so,' he informed her.

That did it. She didn't trouble to hide her surprise. Or displeasure. 'Gervase, really, I don't think that's at all...'

'Oh come, come, Dottie.' His tone was impatient.

'No Gervase. I'm very tired, and even if I wasn't...'

He frowned down upon her.

But she wasn't willing to have a row with him right now. Instead she said with the maximum firmness, 'Goodnight, Gervase. I shall see you in the morning.'

She didn't wait for an answer, but turned, gathered her skirt up a little and went up the stairs. She expected at any moment to be grabbed by him, or for him to shout at her, or to demand that she stay and listen to what he had to say, but she had reached her room before she realised she was still alone, and nothing had happened.

Inside the dark room, she leaned against the door, aware that her heart was pounding.

The maid had been in to light the fire and turn back the bed. The firelight was comforting.

There was a key in the lock. It prodded her as she stood against the door. Had the key been there earlier? She couldn't remember, but on impulse she turned it now and on hearing the loud click in the quiet room, she felt safer, albeit foolish for what was doubtless an over-reaction.

She went to the window and stood looking out, leaning back against the frame. She could dimly make out a tracery of the treetops, grey against the not-quite-black sky, but other than that, there was nothing to see.

Her thoughts turned inwards, and for the first time, she

wondered if she had done the right thing in agreeing to help William by coming here this weekend.

Her feelings about Gervase had blossomed into full-blown dislike. Fear was also present. She wondered how far he would be prepared to go to get what he wanted. If she thought his attentiveness had lessened, how much more it would surely lessen towards any woman once he had attained his object and—for him at least—the chase was over. Not that she had any intention of changing her mind—nothing could be further from the truth, but it was an insight into his character that she hadn't been aware of before.

Where was William? If only he was somewhere nearby. She felt alone and vulnerable. She didn't feel safe under Gervase's roof.

Mr Michaels was here, she reminded herself, remembering with gratitude that he had already taken steps to help her, doing what he could to prevent Gervase from taking advantage. And there was the rest of the staff here, of course. She was tired, and it was making her imaginative and silly. Of course she was safe here. Gervase would never do what she feared.

He had changed of late, and noticeably. It was not just her imagination. He was all impatience and irritability with her, fault-finding and lacking the warm charm that had first made her forget what William meant to her.

Perhaps she should make an excuse and leave in the morning? The very idea of staying another two days made her feel ill. Just talking to Gervase was next to impossible, never mind flirting with him, or letting him put an arm about her or kiss her.

She could make an excuse, and get Mr Michaels to order her a taxi in the morning to take her to the railway station. Then when she got back home, she...

She heard footsteps in the hall. She tensed, remaining where she was, in the dark corner by the window, her eyes fixed on the door. She heard first one, then another door open and close. She heard muffled cursing, then the footsteps started again, coming closer all the time.

He was looking for her.

She felt like a small creature cornered, terrified. Her heart must surely give her away, it seemed to pound against her ribs. This was ridiculous, yet it was actually happening. She held her breath and waited.

The footsteps were right outside. There was a soft rattle and the tiniest squeak, and even in the dark she could see the handle turning first one way, then the other. She heard his not-quite-so-muffled curse when he discovered the door was locked. She didn't dare move.

There was a sharp rap on the door. Dottie leapt half out of her skin at the sudden noise.

'Dottie, dearest?' This was Gervase attempting to sound calm and loving. She heard the rough edge to his voice which gave him away. He was angry. She didn't move, daren't speak.

He knocked again, harder this time. 'Dottie? Are you asleep? Dottie, I'm sorry if I scared you. Let me in, dearest, I'd like to talk.'

He waited. Was that the sound of him breathing, or was it all in her imagination? She could picture him on the other side of the door, itching to kick it wide, but desperately trying to hold onto the threads of his temper.

He banged on the door again, but didn't speak.

She didn't move from where she was, and was almost too afraid to breathe in case he heard her, which was stupid, as he obviously knew she was there.

After another long moment he swore violently under his breath, the sound of it little more than a rasping hiss, but it prickled her as if he was right there with her. She heard a soft movement, and then he went off down the hall. In the next moment she heard the bang of his door.

Then she could breathe.

She rushed into the bathroom, and put on the light, clinging to the edge of the china basin until the nausea subsided. Her gratitude to Mr Michaels doubled. After a few minutes she washed hurriedly and put on her nightgown. She was shivering.

She was tempted to leave the light on all night for

comfort. But she put it out and got into bed, sitting there huddled under the covers and wondering if he would return and try again. She was so glad she had decided to lock the door as soon as she came in. It had been purely by chance that she had done so.

In the morning, she thought, he will be either sulky or angry. I will be the one at fault, the uncaring one, the cold, selfish one. Or else he will make me believe I am childish, with so much growing up still to do. He would be the victim, misunderstood, rejected. There was nothing she could do now, so there was no sense in worrying about it.

But she lay awake for hours, listening for the return of his footsteps, only falling asleep as the new day dawned.

As soon as Dottie awoke, she was aware of an oppression, like a heavy weight on her, but it took her a full minute to remember what it was.

Then.

Everything that had happened the night before returned in a series of mental images: Mrs Sedgworth inviting her to coffee and a talk about Gervase, something she felt Dottie should know, something Gervase must not hear. It could only be something terrible, Dottie thought, and based on what William had told her, this filled her with dread. 'I'm sticking my neck out rather,' Mrs Sedgworth had said.

But that wasn't all.

Gervase, trying her door, trying all the doors first of all before reaching hers, then trying hers, practically knocking the door down, and swearing angrily when she didn't open the door to him and he found the door locked. Gervase furious.

There was a knock at the door now, and Dottie jolted in shock. Then she heard the maid calling, 'Your tea, miss.'

Dottie jumped out of bed and ran to open the door, the key making a very audible grating sound in the lock. Dottie couldn't help herself, she had to glance along the hallway. If the maid found it odd, she of course said nothing, but just came in and set the tray down on the bedside table.

'Shall I open the curtains, miss?'

'Yes please.'

Her voice didn't sound too shaky, Dottie thought. Hopefully the maid would just think she was a little nervous, it being her first night in a strange house, and nothing more.

She really wanted to know if Gervase was up. How was he acting. Was he in a good mood, or banging about the house and snapping at everyone. But she didn't feel able to ask the maid anything of that sort.

The curtains were tied back neatly from the windows, revealing another dreary wet day that brought little light into the room.

Dottie sat on the side of the bed and poured a cup of tea.

'Shall I run you a bath, miss?'

'Oh yes, that would be lovely, thanks.'

She had easily two hours before Major Sedgworth would be arriving to convey her to his home. The more time she spent in her room and away from Gervase, the better. Besides, the hot water might help her to relax.

Eventually the maid departed. Dottie agonised over whether or not to lock the door again but decided against it. It would surely look very odd if she kept the door locked the whole time.

She locked the door of the bathroom, though.

The water was deliciously hot, and the maid had added Dottie's own bath salts under the running tap so that a soft fragrant foam covered the surface of the water. The air was steamy and leaning back with her eyes closed, she almost fell asleep. But as soon as her mind returned to the recent events, the tension came back and she was alert again.

Mrs Sedgworth had said something about it being safe to talk in front of Mrs Holcombe. Gervase's secretary was, it appeared, completely in Mrs Sedgworth's confidence. What did that imply? It puzzled Dottie enormously. But hopefully all would become clear over their coffee. She only hoped she would learn enough to be able to bring the weekend to an early end and go straight back to London with something useful for William's case.

It was so hard to remember the exact words and looks of the other ladies. Was she right in interpreting Mrs Sedgworth's invitation as a desire to caution Dottie against marrying Gervase? Or was she reading far too much into the whole situation, especially in the light of last night? It was all too intriguing. So long as she could both help William, and get back to London. Those were the only things that mattered now.

In the meantime, how was she supposed to manage another day in Gervase's company? As she rubbed herself dry and applied a beauty veil to her whole body, then reached for her wrap and tied it securely about her waist, she was thinking of a plausible excuse for why she hadn't opened her door to him last night.

She could say either, that she'd been in the bathroom and had not heard him knock—he wouldn't want to admit he had fairly pounded on the door in his temper, after all— or she could say she had been so exhausted by the train journey, the recent pressure of work, and then the dinner party—all that good food and wine—that she'd simply fallen asleep the second her head touched the pillow. Perhaps she should add the use of some sort of earplugs or something—say she always found it hard to sleep when not in her own bed. She felt fairly happy with both of these alternatives and was mulling over a kind of amalgamated version of the two as she opened the door to leave the bathroom.

She practically walked straight into Gervase.

Taken aback, she nevertheless managed to smile at him. 'Good morning! I know I'm a bit late coming down to breakfast, I shall only be another few minutes. Sorry, dear, I was *so* tired.'

He'd clearly been thinking and had decided to use what Dottie thought of as his 'petulant brat' approach. He actually had his bottom lip sticking out. Irritating in someone of eight years old, it was utterly ridiculous in a man of thirty-seven.

In a sulky tone, he said, 'I came to your room last night, but the door was locked. Didn't you hear me knock?'

She turned away to go over to the dressing table. Did this ploy actually work with other women, she wondered, not for the first time. Far from making her want to please him and give him anything he wanted, it made her itch to slap his stupid face.

He followed her across the room. She went to sit in front of the mirror and began to brush her hair. 'Oh is that what that was? I'm afraid I was in the bathroom. I thought I heard something but...' She shrugged and smiled at his bad-tempered face in the mirror. 'I thought it was just someone banging in a nail or something. Admittedly I thought it was an odd time of day to put up a picture. Oh Gervase, I feel so weary today. It was such a long day yesterday.'

She beamed at him again, looking perfectly relaxed now and the picture of health. Gervase frowned as usual.

'And you didn't realise it was me, knocking on the door?'

'Sorry dear.' She fished in her case for some coldcream. 'What was it you wanted?' She knew she was provoking him, but felt annoyed enough to fight back, in her own small way. She wondered just how honest he would be. Not very, as it turned out.

'Just to see if you had everything you wanted.'

It sounded incredibly weak as an excuse. She continued to smile lovingly at him as she dotted coldcream on her forehead, cheeks and chin.

'Oh, Gervase, dear! How kind of you. But you needn't have worried, Mr Michaels and the maid have been very helpful.' She smoothed in the coldcream then with a soft facecloth, began to wipe off the excess. Some light foundation. A dash of mascara, and a swipe of pale lipstick, a dusting of powder across her nose, and she was done.

She put on a necklace. Then added another. And another. A long strand of amber-coloured beads, a chain of plain silver links, another strand of beads, this time of freshwater pearls of a lovely uniform deep cream. She slipped on her pearl earrings, then a bracelet and observed herself in the mirror.

'I think that will do,' she said, turning this way and that to check her complexion. She got up. 'If you'll just give me a few minutes, I'll get dressed then come down to breakfast.'

He came forward and put an arm around her, pulling her close and immediately nuzzling her neck. He put a hand inside her wrap to caress her bare shoulder. She pushed him away with an attempt at playfulness.

'Goodness, your hands are freezing! Now then, off you go, I'll be down shortly.'

He was watching her, his expression guarded. 'I had intended you to have the room connecting with mine at the other end of the hall.' He still sounded like a sulking schoolboy.

She gave him another bright smile, this time one of commiseration. 'Such a shame. Mr Michaels told me it needed decorating or something. Oh well, perhaps another time.'

'The ceiling came down. It seems to have happened suspiciously quickly.'

'It's a good thing it didn't come down when someone was asleep in the bed. They might have been hurt, Mr Michaels said.'

Through gritted teeth he said, 'It's just Michaels. You don't need to call him Mr Michaels, he's not one of us.'

'Gervase! Everyone deserves to be treated with respect, whether they are a wealthy assistant chief constable, or whether they are in service in his household.'

'That's how the bloody communists talk. I won't have that kind of thing in my house.'

'Tsk tsk, Gervase, language!' She looked into his ill-tempered face, and with great concern said, 'You don't have high blood pressure, do you? I think you ought to see a doctor. You've gone awfully red in the face. Now, then, I really must get dressed.'

'You can get dressed in front of me. I am your fiancé, after all.'

She gave him a level look. 'Not yet you're not. And even

if you were, that's not the same as being married. Not in my book.'

He glared at her. There was a moment of indecision, then he shrugged, turned and left the room.

She sank down on the bed, trembling.

Breakfast was, hardly surprisingly, a frosty affair, with Gervase glowering and silent, at one end of an overly long table, and Dottie at the other.

It was such a relief to be going out shortly.

When they had finished their meal, he said, 'Come Dottie, let me show you the grounds.'

In Dottie's view, they were neither extensive enough nor impressive enough to warrant such a grand term, but instead were what she privately defined as a very pleasant, large garden, though she knew Gervase would be offended by such a prosaic name.

It was clear he had little interest in gardening, knew nothing whatsoever about plants, and cared even less. Perhaps, she thought, in taking her outside, he was trying to make amends for his earlier temper by being amenable. But soon she began to wonder if he only wanted to appear amenable in order to get information out of her by more subtle means.

'So kind of Mrs Sedgworth to invite you to visit her.'

'Yes.'

'Was that her own idea, or did you ask?' he asked, plucking a daffodil then sniffing it. Clearly the scent didn't please him, for he then threw the flower aside.

She was surprised by the question, and took a few moments to analyse the meaning behind it. How suspicious I've become, she thought.

'Goodness, no,' she said, 'I wouldn't dream of such a thing. She's practically a stranger to me. One has to wait to be invited by a brand new acquaintance, at least.'

'I suppose. Well, I'm sure you'll have a pleasant time.'

'Gervase? Would you prefer I didn't go?'

He seemed startled by that. 'Heavens, no. I'm not saying that at all.'

'I think it's very kind of your friends to welcome me into your social circle like this,' Dottie said. 'It's not easy to get to know a new set of people when they've known each other forever. Although I suppose that was the purpose of inviting everyone to dinner last night.'

'Oh quite. It will help you to be a more polished hostess in the future.' He glanced at her, saw her face, and demanded, 'Now what have I said?'

'Gervase,' Dottie kept the worst of her waspy irritated feelings out of her voice, making an effort to be calm. 'Surely it's natural that I am perhaps a little less polished than you might wish? But there's no need for you to make me feel so unsophisticated. I'm trying my hardest to get to know your friends and your social position here. But it's hardly going to happen overnight, and I need you to support me, not criticise.'

Mr Michaels was approaching across the lawn. 'Excuse me, sir, miss. Major Sedgworth is here.'

'Blast it,' said Dottie. Then shot a smile at Michaels. 'Thank you, I'm just coming.'

Michaels bowed and turned away.

Gervase said, with every appearance of truthfulness, 'I'm sorry, my dearest. I promise to try harder. I keep forgetting that this is all very new to you.' He kissed her cheek, then moved to hold her in his arms, one kiss leading to another. 'Dearest one,' he murmured against her cheek.

Dottie extricated herself with difficulty, and with a last smile at Gervase, hurried to meet the Major.

As Gervase waved them off, he said through the window to the Major, 'Give my regards to your dear wife, Sedgworth.'

The Major nodded and said he would.

Dottie said, 'See you later, Gervase. About half past twelve, I believe.' She shot a smile at the Major who nodded in confirmation.

'That's fine,' Gervase said, and as the car drove away, he added his parting shot. 'That will give you plenty of time to get ready for the photographer.'

He stepped away from the car, another self-satisfied smirk on his face at the sight of Dottie's look of surprise.

'What photographer is that?' Sedgworth asked.

'I have no idea,' she said. 'But I've a sneaking suspicion we are announcing our engagement to the press this afternoon.'

*

Chapter Six

Michaels went back to the kitchen as soon as the car had gone.

He was glad of a cup of tea and the chance to put his feet up. He sighed. A frown creased his brows. His heart was heavy.

'Why, Mr Michaels, you're very glum this morning,' the maid in the kitchen remarked.

He nodded. 'To tell you the truth, Lizzie, I'm a bit worried.'

'What are you worried about, Michaels?' That was Cook. Even though her legal name was Mrs Michaels, under this roof she was known by everyone simply as Cook. She darted a glance at him between opening the oven door and giving whatever was inside an experimental prod with a skewer. She examined the skewer with satisfaction, and wiped it on her apron. The oven door was slammed shut again. She looked at Mr Michaels for his reply.

He simply shrugged and sighed again.

'Lor, I reckon them'd had words, I do,' said Maureen as she came in. She poured herself a cup of tea then flopped down onto one of the wooden chairs at the long kitchen table.

'Why do you say that?' Cook asked.

'Locked her door, didn't she? I had to wait for her to get out of bed to let me in with her tea. She looked scared to death when she leaned out the door to see if he was about. Didn't none of you hear him? Last night, just after one o'clock it was. Opening and slamming all the bedroom doors till he found her, then banging on her door fit to wake the dead? And the language! Enough to make your hair curl.'

Cook and Michaels exchanged a look and a nod.

Michaels relaxed visibly. 'That explains a lot,' was all he said. But he was smiling as he drank his tea.

As they drove away, the Major embarked on a rambling story which had started out with how they had come to know Gervase but which had rapidly become a full and complete history of the Major's life with Mrs Sedgworth from the moment they first met.

Dottie listened with most of her attention though it wandered from time to time, but she thought it must be wonderful to have such a long, shared history.

The day was brightening up, and here inside the car it was comfortably warm. She began to relax. After all, an hour and a half away from Gervase was an unexpected bonus and the mere thought of it made her spirits rise. She sat back to enjoy the rest of the story and the passing scenery.

They were driving through the village. The sun had brought a gaggle of small children and their mothers to the village green. The post mistress was washing down the windowsill of the post office and pausing, cloth in hand, to chat to passers-by. The vicar was enjoying a conversation with two plump ladies who were laughing at something he'd said. And a young woman in a smart blue costume and a matching blue hat stood in the door of the village pub, looking up and down the street as if she was waiting for someone.

The woman was Moira Hansom.

Dottie shrank back in her seat, and wondered what—or who—had brought Moira all the way from London to a small village in Nottinghamshire when she had told her fiancé she was in Bournemouth visiting her family.

Was William staying at the same pub? He had told Dottie he would be coming to the area, but as yet there had been no contact from him. No note, no telephone call or message, no letter. Nothing. Was he here? Or off somewhere pursuing his enquiries, or even perhaps still in London? She wanted to know where he was. She just wanted to hear his voice. Without him she felt cut adrift.

'Here we are, told you it wasn't too far,' the Major announced as he turned the car into a quiet lane that contained four nearly identical neat little houses, and not much more.

'Lovely,' said Dottie, sincerely. It was a pretty location, just the sort of place where everyone wants to live, she thought. Quiet, attractive, close to the village yet away from the busy roads.

The Major came round to open the door for her, lending her a hand to get down, then conducting her along a path to a door at the side of the house.

'Christobel. We're here!'

There came a voice from upstairs.

'I'll be down in a moment. Take Miss Manderson into the morning room, Jimmy.'

Jimmy Sedgworth brought Dottie into the sunny morning room. It was at the back of the house. The large picture window looked onto a long garden that was clearly the Major's pride and joy. He began to point out a few choice shrubs.

Behind them the door opened, and Dottie turned, smiling, to greet her hostess.

Mrs Sedgworth had clearly been crying. That her husband had been unaware of the fact until now was clear from his startled look.

But all Mrs Sedgworth said was, 'So silly of me, Miss Manderson. I'm afraid I'm not feeling quite myself this morning. Do excuse my appearance. I think I must be coming down with something.'

Dottie politely replied with, 'What a shame. Perhaps you overdid things a bit last night. It was very late when we broke up, so no doubt you're over-tired.'

'That's probably it,' Mrs Sedgworth said, her smile completely lacking in joy. 'I'm so sorry to put you out. I was quite all right when Jimmy left, but then it just sort of came over me.'

Dottie suspected Mrs Sedgworth wanted her to leave. She hesitated, hoping things would become a little clearer. They did.

'Well, my dear, you'd better go and lie down. Perhaps Miss Manderson will be able to spare us some time on her next visit.' The Major was already on his way to the door, preparing to go out to the car.

Mrs Sedgworth came to give Dottie a quick hug. It took Dottie by surprise as they were not exactly old friends.

Dottie said again, 'What a shame, Mrs Sedgworth. I shall hope to see you next time. Do take care of yourself.'

'I shall, my dear, I shall. Thank you for being so understanding.'

That was definitely relief on Mrs Sedgworth's face, Dottie thought. She said yet again, 'Well, goodbye, I hope you feel better soon.'

It all felt rather unreal. Mrs Sedgworth assured her husband that she would be perfectly fine after lying down quietly for a while. It was clear Major Sedgworth was just as puzzled as Dottie, but he said nothing.

Returning to Gervase's just ten minutes after leaving it felt strange, and neither of them seemed able to think of anything to say.

But it looked as though the short drive back to Gervase's house would take longer than anticipated. The local bus, coming around the corner a little faster than advisable, had nudged one corner of a loaded wagon, tipping it and sending potatoes, turnips, cabbages and other grocery essentials tumbling all over the street.

The driver of the wagon had a few insights on good

driving to share with the bus driver, and got down from his wagon to share them very loudly, with much jabbing of a grimy forefinger in the bus driver's direction. The bus driver wanted to explain to the wagon driver the finer points of parking on a narrow village street. The two men, red-faced and angry, were very loud indeed.

The traffic—usually very light—was beginning to jam the narrow village street. Major Sedgworth sat with both elbows leaning on the steering wheel, and stared at the mess in front of them.

'It would have been quicker to walk,' he commented.

Dottie murmured in agreement. Then, inspiration struck as she turned to look behind them.

'There's only one car behind us,' she said, 'and he's not very close. You could easily turn around just here and go back home. I can get out here and walk the rest of the way. It's senseless to sit here—we could be ages.'

The Major blustered, embarrassed to be taken at his word. 'Now, my dear Miss Manderson, that really wasn't what I was getting at...'

'I know, I know. But your wife needs you, and it's a fine day. I can easily walk that short distance. So if you don't mind, I'll hop out now, and you can get back. Really, I insist. You could be stuck here for half an hour or more, otherwise.'

He gave her a grateful smile. Dottie stepped out, gave him a wave and set off along the road, carefully skirting several lumpy mangelwurzels that had rolled to lean gently against a garden wall. An elderly pedestrian cast a quick look about her then placed a cabbage and two carrots into her shopping basket and covered them with her scarf. When Dottie glanced over her shoulder, she saw the Major was already executing a turn in the road. He tooted the horn, waved to her then drove back the way they had just come.

It was rather a relief to be alone and able to puzzle over the odd events.

What had occurred between the Major leaving home at, what, about twenty to eleven? Then collecting Dottie and arriving back at the house a minute or two after eleven.

Dottie wondered if it was simply that the Major and his wife had argued. Perhaps they'd had words—couples did argue, didn't they—then Mrs Sedgworth had brooded over something one of them had said, and got upset, and was then embarrassed—you would be, after all—when Dottie arrived and saw she had clearly been weeping.

But Mrs Sedgworth hadn't seemed the type to get upset easily over that sort of thing. Not that you could always tell, Dottie acknowledged, and certainly no one ever really knows what goes on in someone else's marriage. But to all appearances, the Major seemed rather a pet, and Mrs Sedgworth seemed to be perfectly able to stick up for herself.

Perhaps she had received some bad news whilst the Major was out fetching Dottie?

Whatever it was, Dottie fervently hoped Mrs Sedgworth would feel better very soon and they would have the chance to talk as originally intended.

Dottie was nearing the public house, and as she drew level, she couldn't help glancing in at the doorway, just in case she should catch another glimpse of Moira Hansom. There was another enigma, she thought.

On an impulse, she went inside the pub. Once her eyes had adjusted to the characteristic gloom—not to mention her nose adjusting to the characteristic hoppy smell—she crossed the low-beamed room to the bar.

'Yes miss?'

The gentleman behind the bar was about her father's age or a little older. She beamed at him.

'I just wondered—do you have a lady named Moira Hansom staying in the pub? Only, I thought I saw her earlier when I went past. We were at school together.'

'Why, yes, miss, as a matter of fact, we have.'

As easy as that, she thought, slightly surprised. She nodded and thanked the man.

'Did you want to leave her a message, miss? She said she was going out for an hour, so I don't reckon as you should wait for her.'

'Oh it's all right, thank you. I'll pop back a bit later. Umm... Is there a gentleman staying here at all? A Mr Hardy? A tall, fair-haired young fellow, very good-looking?'

'Oh no, miss, Miss Hansom is our only guest at the moment.'

She thanked him again and came away, conscious of a bitter sense of disappointment, which, she realised, would have been considerably worse if he'd said, 'Oh yes, he has the room next to Miss Hansom's'.

William was not here, then. Yet Moira was. How very odd.

A constable had now arrived to sort out the traffic situation in the village where there was still a lot of shouting going on. Dottie set off again, and within a few minutes had arrived at the gateway to Gervase's drive.

She began to follow the meandering route through the outcrops of trees and shrubs, past the wide lawn, and up to the front of the house. She felt reluctant to go back so soon, but there was nowhere else for her to go. Anyway, Gervase would surely wonder where she had been, when he heard about Mrs Sedgworth.

Just before she reached the house, a hissing sound reached her ears. Looking about her, she saw a figure gesturing to her from the side door of the house. She turned and went across.

It was Mr Michaels. He looked rather pink in the face.

'I beg your pardon, miss. Er—I couldn't help but notice you're back a little earlier than expected.'

Dottie was puzzled. Michaels' manner was extremely furtive.

'Yes. Mrs Sedgworth was unwell. I had to come back.'

He nodded. And hesitated.

'What is it?' she asked. 'Is there something wrong?'

'Well, er—it's—er, it's a bit awkward, like.'

Dottie stared at him. She had no idea what he meant. 'What's happened?'

'Mr Parfitt has a visitor.'

She continued to stare at Michaels.

'You see,' he said, attempting to clarify, 'he wasn't expecting you back quite yet.'

'Oh? Well, he needn't worry, I shan't bother him if he's working.' Dottie looked at Michaels face. He was still very uncomfortable.

'It's not... that is to say...Well, miss, it's just that he expected to have the house to himself for a while.'

A horrid thought was beginning to form in Dottie's mind. She gave him a straight look. 'Is his visitor a woman, by any chance?'

Michaels shifted his feet. He looked sheepish, as if it was he himself who had been caught. 'Well, I must admit it is, miss.'

Dottie could feel herself blushing. But she was also angry. What on earth did Gervase think he was—er—doing? How dare he put her in this ridiculous position. It really was too bad of him.

But then came a wonderful sense of escape. How fortunate that she knew the sort of man he was, and that her heart was safe from the pain of his infidelity.

'Disgraceful,' she murmured. She looked at Michaels.

'I'm so sorry, miss. I'm afraid this is a bad shock for you.'

'Not so bad as all that,' Dottie said. 'And while we're at it, strictly between ourselves, thank you for er—noticing—the problem with the bedroom ceiling yesterday. That was most fortuitous.'

'Yes, indeed, miss. Saved you a lot of bother, I'm sure.'

She couldn't help laughing at that. She looked around, uncertain what to do next. She began to feel annoyed with Gervase for causing this embarrassment.

'Good Lord,' she said. 'This is ridiculous. What am I supposed to do until he is 'free' again? Do I just pretend not to know—or what?' She sighed. 'My mother was right about him.'

Michaels crooked his elbow for her to take his arm. She did so and he patted her hand. 'If you don't mind the liberty, miss, mothers do tend to be quite good at getting to the real man behind the smile. As to what you should do, you could go out again, miss? I'll drive you anywhere you fancy.'

She shook her head. 'Where would I go?'

'In that case, you come into my sitting room, Miss Dottie. We'll have a glass of elderflower wine and chat about inconsequentials.'

She agreed. Curiosity made her glance across the hall towards the stairs once inside the house.

The wine was potent. The butler's sitting room was a tiny wedge taken off a corner of the servants' hall, and inside there was only just enough room for a couple of armchairs either side of the small fireplace, and on the opposite wall, barely two feet from Dottie's arm, a little table with two chairs. A telephone was on the wall just above one side of the table. The window was one half of a big frosted window shared with the scullery. It was warm and stuffy in here. A radio chattered softly on a shelf, and the fire crackled cheerfully. Dottie could have fallen asleep with no difficulty at all.

She relaxed. She had no idea if the rest of the staff knew what was going on, or if they were unaware and wondering why Dottie should be sitting so informally in Mr Michaels room. Possibly this behaviour of Gervase's was completely routine. In any case, no one spoke to her, or even to each other very much. They all seemed very busy.

And then she remembered Gervase had made some kind of arrangement for the afternoon. The sinking feeling came over her once more.

'Mr Parfitt has something going on later, hasn't he? He only mentioned it to me just as I drove away with the Major. He said something about a photographer.'

Michaels nodded. 'Yes miss. They've come down from those swanky magazines, *The Country Lady* and *Society Style*. They are conducting interviews with you about how happy and in love you and Mr Parfitt are, and taking photographs of the two of you together, to announce your engagement to the world.' He gave her a wry smile.

Dottie ignored the nerves in the pit of her stomach, but admitted, with a wrinkle of the nose, 'I guessed it would be something like that. My word, how am I supposed to get through all that? Are they here for dinner, d'you know?'

'Oh no, miss, just the photographs and interview at three o'clock until around four.' He was watching her closely.

She knew there was no point in pretending. 'This is a disaster.'

He nodded. 'I can imagine. If I may say so, you seem to be coping rather well. I'd expect tears and hysterics at the very least, and for you to pack your things and leave by taxi within the hour. And quite within your rights if you did any or all of those.'

'That's not possible at the moment,' she said. She could tell from his expression that he dearly wanted to know more, but he couldn't ask, of course.

'Well, I shall have to just—I don't know—do my best, I suppose. What else can I do?' She was asking herself not Mr Michaels. 'Fortunately I've got a decent frock with me. Can I borrow a maid to help me with my hair and everything? I should have brought my own with me, I just didn't think I'd need anyone.'

'Of course, miss. Might I suggest a light lunch at half past twelve, then a short rest? I'll send Maureen up just after two o'clock to wake you and help you get ready. It won't hurt if you keep them all waiting. The bride's prerogative.'

'I'll never be a bride,' Dottie said. 'This whole affair is doomed. Perhaps I should just pack and leave now whilst I can. And have those hysterics you mentioned.'

She sipped her wine and thought about that. She had wanted to help William, but she had been here for almost a day and still had no idea how to gain the smallest iota of information of any kind. Plus, the temptation to leave a note telling Gervase exactly what she thought of him was almost too great. She could be home in time for dinner if she left soon.

The fire crackled. The sound broke in on her thoughts.

Without thinking of convention, she said, with the utmost candour, 'Has he been involved with this woman for long? Do you think he really loves her? If I wasn't here, would he marry her?'

Michaels shook his head. 'She was on the scene long before you, my dear, and I don't think anyone could call it love. No, he's had time to marry her if that was what he wanted.'

The wheels in her brain clicked and suddenly she saw what was going on. 'Is she blonde, by any chance?'

'Pretends to be.'

'And quite—er—quite voluptuous?'

'Let's just say, she tottered in on those high heels she always wears and as I helped her off with her coat, I thought them bosoms might topple her onto her face.'

Dottie laughed at that. Mr Michaels winked at her. 'He likes them like that.'

Dottie looked down ruefully at her own somewhat smaller bust. She sighed. 'I think I know the lady,' she told him. 'She's someone I've met in London recently, though she and Gervase pretended not to know one another. But on the way to the Sedgworths just now, I saw her in the doorway of the pub. Her name's Moira Hansom.'

'That's her. Handsome is as handsome does, my old mum used to say,' remarked Mr Michaels, refilling both their glasses.

'My sister said the same thing,' Dottie murmured. 'But Miss Hansom is engaged to someone I know. Or was. Poor William. This must mean their engagement is over. For the second time.'

'She had a ring on,' Michaels said. 'A solitaire diamond on her left hand.'

William's ring, Dottie thought. Moira hadn't even the decency to take it off and pretend to be a free woman.

'I don't know what to do,' she said. 'If I tell him, he'll hate me for it. Her fiancé, I mean. He's a—a friend. But if I don't...'

Michaels nodded but offered nothing.

She decided to take the plunge. 'Confidentially, you see,

I'm only seeing Gervase again because this friend, William—Miss Hansom's fiancé—asked me to try to find out some things for him. You see, I had already broken things off with Gervase. He let me down badly just when I needed him the most, and I began to see he didn't really care for me.'

If Michaels was surprised, he said nothing, just continued to nod and listen.

'My f-friend William—well, in fact he's the man I really love but I made the most stupid, idiotic mess of things... Then I met Gervase, and I made things ten times worse. By the time I'd come to my senses, William was engaged to that-that woman. Oh I've made a shocking mess of it all.' She shook her head as she thought about it. 'But—well, William is a policeman—and you absolutely have to promise me you won't breathe a word. But there's some kind of secret investigation going on into Gervase's affairs. He's been accused of some terrible things. William needs proof if he is to do anything about it. He needs evidence. Without it they won't get anywhere. He asked me to help, so I had to get back with Gervase to try to somehow help William to get this evidence. Only, now...' She gave a great outward breath and fell into silent contemplation of the fire again.

Half to herself, she said softly, 'I just don't know how to find out what William needs to know. And now this—with Moira. It's just one more thing I don't know how to deal with. I just—I just want to run away back to London. But what use is that to William?'

There was a long silence. It took Dottie a minute to realise that Michaels was wrestling with something in his mind. She looked at him.

Softly she said, 'Mr Michaels, do you know something?'

'I might,' he said. 'I'm just not sure...'

'If you know something, please tell me,' she said. 'Really Mr Michaels, I'm begging for your help.'

Michaels said, after a moment's thought, 'You went to see Major and Mrs Sedgworth, didn't you?'

'Yes. But Mrs Sedgworth wasn't well enough to receive

visitors, so I had to come back.'

'As soon as you left with the Major, Mr Parfitt made two phone calls. One was short, just for a minute at the most. That was to the pub in the village. I know because heard him give the number.'

'To Moira Hansom,' Dottie surmised. Gervase had no doubt rung her to let her know 'the coast was clear'. No wonder he'd made relatively little fuss about Dottie's arrangement to go out.

Michaels nodded. 'The other call was a little longer. But again, I was in the hall, and the study door was open, and I heard him say, 'Ah Christobel, my dear, just wanted to let you know they are on their way.'

Dottie stared at him. 'Do you mean he said something to her, something that upset her? Because—well—I know I said she wasn't feeling well, but the truth is she had been crying. It was clear she was terribly upset about something. She said she wasn't feeling well, but that was just an excuse. It didn't make any sense—her husband was every bit as surprised as I was. But I could hardly demand an explanation.'

'No indeed, miss. I was in an awkward position, as I wanted to get on with the silver in the dining room, which as you know, is quite close to the study, and Mr Gervase having a strong, carrying sort of voice...'

Dottie hid a smile.

'Naturally, I tried not to listen in on Mr Gervase's conversation. As soon as I could, I went over and closed the door, to give him a bit of privacy.'

'Of course,' Dottie said. Her thoughts were already leaping ahead. 'I don't suppose you accidentally caught a word or two?'

'As it happens,' he said with a smile, 'I did catch a bit. Mr Gervase was mid-sentence, but I heard him say, in what we staff are in the habit of calling his menacing tone...' He broke off to explain to Dottie. 'Now that sounds unforgivably rude, miss, I realise that. And I don't doubt we take liberties, but it's not that we think Mr Gervase is a menacing gentleman, only that he has a tone which, if you didn't know the gentleman, could be mistook for menacing. Miss.' He looked at her to see if she believed him. Clearly he wondered if it had been an admission too far.

She grinned and nodded. 'Of course, Mr Michaels, I know exactly what you mean. So what was this snatch of a sentence that you just caught as you closed the door?'

'He said, 'Just remember what I said last night. Can you really afford to do this?"'

'Hmm,' said Dottie. 'Any barrister would probably just say he'd been offering her some financial advice or something like that. But just suppose it was something to do with whatever she planned to say to me? Because she was planning to tell me something significant, I'm certain. She as good as said so last night. No doubt too, it was all there in his tone, no matter how innocuous he could claim his words were.' She sipped the last of her wine, set the glass aside, and said, 'If only I knew what it was she wanted to say. I wonder if she would tell me if I went there again and pleaded with her.'

'I might know something about that,' Michaels said.

Dottie stared at him.

'Well, there's been a rumour or two flying around these last few months. I know we shouldn't listen to rumours...'

'Yes,' Dottie said firmly. 'You should. They usually turn out to be true.'

He laughed. 'You could be right there, miss. Well we servants get to chat with other servants, and we hear things.'

'I prefer the word staff,' Dottie said. 'Servants sounds so—subordinate. It's not as though this is some feudal estate in the middle ages.'

He gave her a wry smile. 'Not that much different, miss, I can tell you. Not here. But there's been a rumour about Mrs Sedgworth having run down a man and killed him.'

Dottie looked horrified. 'Oh no! Really? How terrible!'

He admitted, 'Now I can't remember who told me or where, or even when. I certainly don't know if it's actually true. But last Spring, when the Major was away for a short while to do with his old job, it's said that Mrs Sedgworth was driving home late one night from a dinner engagement and hit someone walking along the road. Well it's said she rung up Mr Parfitt from her house all in a panic and told him what had happened, and she begged him to fix it for her. And according to the rumour, fix it he did.'

Dottie thought about that. 'It's a shame we don't know more about it.'

'If you like, miss, I can see if I can find out anything more, and let you know. All I know is, I didn't take the call from her. But that don't mean she didn't call.'

'Something she said last night, when I was concerned we might be overheard by Gervase's secretary. She said, more or less, that it was all right to talk in front of Mrs Holcombe, she said Mary could be trusted. Do you have any idea what she might have meant by that?'

'Not really, no,' he said, shaking his head. He got to his feet. 'Mrs Holcombe comes here from time to time. A nice, quiet lady. Now miss, if you'll excuse me, I've a few things I need to see to. You can stay here if you like, and I'll let you know when the other lady leaves.'

She nodded gratefully, and he left.

Dottie sat there thinking and staring into the fire.

Half an hour later, the door opened just a crack and Michaels peered through. In a low theatrical whisper he said, 'She's going to be leaving any minute now, Miss Manderson. Mr Parfitt is just taking her to the door now. If you hurry to the side door, you'll see her go by. Unless you don't want to see...'

'Oh yes I do!' She had to be sure it was Moira. Dottie leapt up and followed him to the side door. She dashed across the gravel to take up position behind some massive shrubs. She was just in time to hear the front door close and the sharp crunch of gravel beneath shoes. Then she saw blonde hair pushed up beneath a blue hat. A blue suit. She saw the full hips and bust as the woman rounded the curve in the drive. A self-satisfied smile was on the red painted mouth.

Moira Hansom was returning to the village.

Dottie returned to the butler's sitting room. After a few minutes Mr Michaels returned.

He came in eagerly. 'Well? Was it her?'

Dottie nodded. 'Most definitely.'

Michaels said, 'I think if I was him, I'd want to know. Your friend, I'm talking about. He won't blame you, at least not once he's thought it over.'

Dottie nodded again.

'Now then, miss, I suggest you give it another twenty minutes or so then you can 'arrive back'. But we'll have to be careful you don't bump into Mr Parfitt in the meantime. I wonder, do you think you could stand to stay put here?'

'Oh yes, I'm fine here, thank you.' Then she added. 'Am I in your way? I could go somewhere else.'

He wouldn't hear of it, of course. They worked out a few details, then he left to attend to the dining room. Lunch would be served in about half an hour.

When the time came, Dottie slipped out of the side door, round to the front, to make a show of arriving at the front door and loudly greeting Mr Michaels as if she hadn't just seen him one minute earlier.

Gervase emerged from his study looking suave and relaxed. He was clearly in a much better mood, so Dottie supposed she owed Moira some gratitude for that. He kissed Dottie on the cheek and asked, without a shred of guilt, if she'd enjoyed her visit to the Sedgworths.

'Dottie said, 'Ye-es. It was nice enough, I suppose, though Mrs Sedgworth had very little to say. She wasn't feeling well when I arrived, so the conversation was a little one-sided.'

'What a shame,' Gervase said.

Dottie thought he seemed quite pleased. Clearly whatever he'd said to Mrs Sedgworth, he was completely convinced it had done the trick.

Dottie couldn't resist adding, 'It was odd, because the

Major told me she was in fine form when he left to collect me.'

'Ah well, you ladies are all the same. Changeable, sensitive. It's your hormones among other things, though I doubt old Christobel has too much left in that department. You wait and see, she'll be fine next time.'

Dottie didn't trust herself to do anything other than smile. If she had the chance of seeing Mrs Sedgworth again, she'd tell her that she knew Gervase had telephoned her.

'Lunch is ready, dearest,' Gervase said and guided her to the dining room, seating her at the table with every appearance of genuine gallantry.

Michaels had been about to pour Dottie's wine for her, but she said no thank you, asking for a glass of water instead. Again unable to resist the temptation, Dottie asked Gervase, 'And what did you do while I was out? Anything interesting?'

He halted, his glass of wine halfway to his lips. He looked quite taken aback, as indeed did Mr Michaels.

Gervase appeared to be racking his brains for something to say. Dottie waited patiently, watching him with bright enquiring eyes and a devoted smile.

'Er, no, not terribly interesting. I just finished looking over a report ready for next week. It's meeting after meeting for me, all very dull.'

'Oh.' Dottie gave him a pitying look. 'Poor you, dear. It must be hard, having to bring your work home with you.'

'It is indeed. But I shall be able to take my mind off it by thinking of you, my sweet.'

Dottie cringed inwardly, though outwardly she continued to smile. She had to hold in a burst of laughter as she saw Michaels, passing behind Gervase with a dish of vegetables, roll his eyes in disgust.

'Now then, once lunch is over, I have a few letters to write, and then I will be greeting the photographers and the reporters. I know I've rather sprung this on you, Dottie dear, but I'm sure it will be absolutely fine. So here's your ring, if you'd just put that on.'

Caron Allan

He frowned at her as he slid a small ring box across the table towards her. 'You have brought a decent dress or two with you, haven't you? You'll need to change for them. If not I suppose my mother could...'

'There's no need, Gervase. I have managed to bring a *decent* dress with me, thank you, in spite of not knowing what you had planned.' She noted that he didn't seem at all chastened by her response. How quickly he has stopped pretending, she thought again. And this was a far cry from the romantic proposal of every young woman's dreams—a somewhat tired little box pushed across the table between mouthfuls of lunch.

She set aside her cutlery and picked up the box. She opened it, curious, even though not excited.

The dim stone was a huge diamond set on a thick gold band and surrounded by tiny emeralds, each one edged in a dark circle of accumulated dirt. It was an old setting, and had clearly been in the family for many years. It bore the grime of at least two centuries: it was filthy. Surely, he could have at least had it cleaned? Even if he couldn't be bothered to have the setting updated, surely he'd have realised this was not the engagement ring she would have cherished hopes of? The ring was absolutely hideous.

'Does it fit?' he asked.

He was watching her. She couldn't think of anything to say about the ring that wasn't a criticism. She was reluctant to put it on, but it couldn't be avoided. She shut her eyes momentarily and slipped it on, the heavy gold cold against her skin. The ring was too big by several sizes. It immediately swung down so that the stone was on the inside of her finger, the weight of the filthy stone pulling it around.

'Hmm,' said Gervase. He frowned again, as if Dottie was just being difficult. 'It's a bit big. I'll get that fixed at some point.'

'Thank you.' She didn't bother to inject any enthusiasm into those two words, but it didn't matter. He was no longer listening to her anyway.

'Apricot tart, sir?' Michaels asked. Gervase said yes to

that with a great deal more enthusiasm than he had shown towards his new fiancée.

*

Chapter Seven

Dottie came downstairs an hour later feeling extraordinarily on edge. She was wearing her new dark red wool dress with the flaring skirt and the shiny big black buttons down the front at a slant and on the shoulders. It was another of her own designs, and was selling like hot cakes, she reminded herself as an encouragement. She loved the dress, but she was afraid Gervase would hate it. She hoped that he would at least approve of it, because if he didn't, he would be put out, and she didn't feel up to handling yet another angry scene.

She was also worried about the interview, and the subsequent appearance of that interview in the two society magazines and possibly even in the newspapers. Only now had it occurred to her that the interviews would be seen by friends and family, and she'd had no chance to warn her parents or Flora, or anyone. She'd been hoping to keep the resumed relationship a secret, certain it would only be for a few more days, and known only to a few people. Now it looked as if it was going to become public knowledge almost immediately.

She halted on the bottom step. Some people had just

come in at the front door. Michaels was already showing them into the drawing room, and through the crack of the open door, Dottie could see Gervase waiting just beyond the threshold, ready to greet the journalists. As she moved from the bottom step to the hall floor, she heard him say, '...can't think where that girl has got to...' and he did indeed sound put out. Her heart sank.

Still, it couldn't be helped. She'd had no notice, after all, so he had only himself to blame. She called as she came towards the door, 'On my way, dear. Sorry about the slight delay. I lost an earring.'

'A lady's prerogative, surely,' a gentleman said gallantly, smiling and stepping towards her, his hand outstretched in greeting. 'Algernon James, from *Society Style*. Delighted to meet you, Miss Manderson. I've heard of you from my sister and her friends. I believe they are new clients of yours. Mrs Porter. Elspeth Porter.'

Dottie immediately relaxed. This was her element. She beamed at him, saying warmly, 'How lovely to meet you, Mr James. Thank you for coming. Of course I know Mrs Porter, she's a charming lady and so kind about everything we do at *Carmichaels*.'

Mr James introduced his photographer, Peter Phelan. Dottie greeted him with a smile and a handshake, and turned to the others.

Gervase frowned, she noted, but Gervase would no doubt frown at everything she ever did. He probably thought she was too informal, too friendly, and certainly he felt she lacked the required dignity. He probably thought she should be like his mother who was practically all dignity. Dottie reminded herself it no longer mattered what he thought.

Gervase was saying, 'And this delightful young lady is Miss Birnie, the journalist from *The Country Lady*. Really my dear, you don't look old enough to be a senior journalist.'

Dottie inwardly cringed at Gervase's fawning attempts at flirtation. From the slight tightening of her smile, Miss Birnie felt the same.

Then suddenly, unexpectedly, Dottie felt as though she'd walked into a wall. Gervase was saying, 'Miss Birnie is here with her photographer too—I'm afraid I didn't catch your name.'

'Carl Brown,' said William Hardy, and held out his hand to Dottie to shake. His lips were straight beneath an obviously fake moustache, but his eyes smiled at her from behind a pair glasses. But it was undeniably, unmistakeably him.

Dottie couldn't remember what she did next, but she found they were all sitting down, smiling politely at one another. Her heart was singing with happiness. Then in the next moment, she remembered Moira Hansom, staying in the village, and only this afternoon, a 'guest' of Gervase. Her heart sank again. And she marvelled that Gervase did not appear to recognise William behind his all-too-apparent disguise.

The interviews began.

Naturally Dottie wasn't required to say very much. The only question directed at her was from Miss Birnie, 'Have you chosen your wedding dress yet?'

Before Dottie could reply, Gervase directed a predatory smile at the reporter and said, 'Naturally, we will consult with one of London's top designers.'

'I expect Miss Manderson knows them all personally. Or will you be designing your own dress, Miss Manderson?'

'Carl Brown' stepped forward and snapped his camera at Dottie's hesitant look over her shoulder at Gervase.

Gervase snapped back at Miss Birnie, the flirtatious persona thrown aside, 'I hardly think that will be suitable. We shall need a thoroughly professional designer to design Miss Manderson's wedding gown. The girl will hardly get married in something she's knocked up at home like someone's kitchen maid.'

There was a brief electric thrill on the air as both the journalists caught Gervase's tone and scented a story. Dottie sighed inwardly. Gervase may think he knew what he was doing, but he lacked the subtlety to see himself as others saw him.

Miss Birnie said next, 'Do let us see your engagement ring, Miss Manderson. Carl, get a picture for our readers.'

Dottie held out her hand, with a heavy sense of knowing exactly what would happen.

As expected, the ring swung down with the weight of the revolting old stone. As 'Carl's' camera flashed, all he got was a photograph of the gold band. Looking down Dottie saw that the band was notably marked and a little worn in places. There was no disguising that it looked awful.

Miss Birnie's smile froze in place. Even the three men with her seemed to note that the ring was not the usual bright and sparkling affair. Dottie couldn't help it, she looked at 'Carl's' face. She could see he was angry. Very angry. She had expected him to be amused, even possibly disgusted. But angry? Was he angry with her?

He got up from his position on the floor in front of Dottie where he had knelt to take the close-up, muttered something about needing another flash bulb and left the room. Mr James' photographer, Peter Phelan, came closer to take his pictures. The ring kept slipping around.

In the end, ignoring Gervase's comment of, 'For God's sake, Dottie, control it, can't you,' Miss Birnie, seemingly desperate to get one half-decent photograph of the ring, placed a cushion beneath Dottie's hand, and that held the ring in place. Phelan took his photos. Then 'Carl' returned. As he took his pictures, he managed to give Dottie a reassuring smile from behind the camera. She beamed back at him openly.

The interviews continued with more questions of the usual type: how did you meet, how and where did Mr Parfitt propose, where did Mr Parfitt plan to honeymoon, how did Mr Parfitt see the role of the wife of the eminent local figure, the assistant chief constable. Gervase held forth pompously, and Dottie looked at her hands in embarrassment as she heard the drivel and even downright lies that came out of his mouth. He'd make an excellent politician, she thought. She hardly recognised the completely fictionalised story of their meeting and his romantic proposal. Dottie's part was to sit there and listen, and of course, smile.

Then it was time for a few final photographs. Miss Birnie arranged her subjects in front of the French windows, whilst Mr James preferred to have them stand in the hall, with Dottie on the first step, which made her slightly taller than Gervase, a fact that luckily went unnoticed by Gervase himself, as she instinctively knew he wouldn't like that. Mr James moved Dottie's hand so that it was resting on top of Gervase's, which was resting on the newel post. Normally a romantic image, Mr James was frustrated to see that the bride and groom appeared to loathe being so close to one another.

Tea was brought in, and the journalists had the opportunity to spend a little more time with the esteemed Mr Parfitt and his fiancée in a more relaxed manner. Another photo was taken of them together on the sofa, posing rigidly as a happy couple behind the cups and saucers. Then the cameras were all packed away, and tea became the main order of business. Cook had excelled herself with the delicious cakes and savoury offerings, and these were consumed rapidly and with great appreciation.

Gervase had clearly decided to be charming. Not to Dottie, of course, but he was witty and talkative with Miss Birnie, before turning his attention to Mr James. The two men talked of their interests and work. Soon they were deep into a discussion about the role of the police in the modern world, and Dottie leaned back against the sofa and went into a daydream, knowing she was no longer useful.

Until Miss Birnie said to her, 'I imagine you will find it something of a change of pace, when you move to here from London?' She said it quite casually, and Dottie could tell it wasn't part of the interview, nor was it a trap to try and get Dottie to say something indiscreet.

But before Dottie could reply, Gervase cut in with a terse, 'I thought the questions had finished? I don't remember this one being on the list?'

Dottie glanced at him in surprise, but the journalist just smiled sweetly and said, 'As one woman to another, I was just curious as to whether Miss Manderson felt the move would be as beneficial to her career as it is to her personal happiness.'

'Her *career*?' Gervase—no longer even pretending to be civil—addressed Miss Birnie with such venom that Peter Phelan, 'Carl Brown', and Algernon James paused their conversation to stare at him in astonishment.

Dottie felt sure that Gervase had forgotten that his guests were, first and foremost, reporters. She was practically holding her breath as she watched in dismay as Gervase said with a sneer, 'Let me tell you, young lady, my wife's *career* will consist of caring for and supporting me, caring for my home, and bearing my children. That is a woman's career.'

A stunned silence met his words. He couldn't have made a stupider statement, or phrased it more offensively, Dottie thought. She remembered, not for the first time, that he was inclined to lash out when offended, and throw caution to the wind. Not good attributes for someone in his position.

Miss Birnie, far from being upset, looked like the cat with the proverbial cream on its whiskers.

Hurriedly Dottie said, 'Naturally, it will require a lot of careful planning, but I am confident that the business in London won't suffer because I'm not able to be there every day. I have an excellent and experienced staff, and I will consult with them constantly about important decisions.'

As soon as she spoke, she could see from his expression that in his view, she was siding against him and matters had taken a turn for the worst. He was glaring at her wrathfully. Clearly there was about to be a Scene.

Mr James leapt to his feet, waving a hand at his photographer. 'Excellent, excellent, Mr Parfitt, Miss Manderson. Well, I think that's all we need for *Society Style's* readers. Thank you so much for giving up your valuable time. And of course, our sincerest good wishes for your future happiness.' His eyes were on Dottie as he said this, and she nodded and gave him a lovely smile.

Miss Birnie said the same, and shook hands with them

both. Dottie saw Miss Birnie's discreet attempt to wipe her hand on her skirt as she let go of Gervase's grip. Dottie hid a smile, but as she turned away, looked into 'Carl Brown's' face. He was angry again, and she wanted nothing more than to throw herself in his arms and ask him to take her away from here.

She followed them out into the hall, and as Mr Michaels helped Miss Birnie and Mr James on with their overcoats, Dottie managed to whisper to William, 'I need to speak to you. Are you staying locally?'

He shook his head but said nothing. Gervase loomed in the doorway, pale and furious. He looked right at William, and yet still did not seem to recognise the man he had met on at least four occasions. Gervase was no detective, Dottie thought.

Miss Birnie came to say goodbye for the second time, leaning forward to say to Dottie softly, 'I hope I haven't caused any difficulties for you.' She looked really concerned.

Dottie smiled at her. 'I'm sure everything will be fine,' she said.

'If there's any problem...'

'There won't be,' Dottie assured her again. In a louder voice she asked, 'When will the interview be published?'

'Oh, er, Tuesday in my paper, and I think it will be the following Monday for Algy's. That's right, isn't it, Algy? Monday?'

'Oh yes, that's right.' He gave them both another polite nod and left.

Gervase was standing close by, watching them now with a clear sense of dismissal. Michaels, Phelan and Brown/Hardy carried their equipment out to the cars, and Mr James followed on behind them. Miss Birnie, sending Dottie a last look of apology, said goodbye yet again and went outside, the door gently shutting behind her.

There was an immense cold silence in the hall.

'Gervase,' Dottie began.

He held up his hand to silence her. 'It's all right Dottie, I'm not angry with you. I know you were just saying what you thought they wanted to hear. I don't blame you in the least. Now look, I'm going upstairs for a bath. We're not due at my parents until half past six. Did I tell you?'

'No, but Mrs Holcombe did.' She smiled. An evening with someone else—even his parents—was infinitely preferable to an evening alone with him.

He gave her a cool nod then turned and went upstairs.

Dottie immediately went outside to see if there was any sign of William. But Michaels was returning, the guests had gone.

'Mr Gervase gone up for his bath?'

'Yes, Mr Michaels.'

'That lady reporter said it was a disaster. Was it?'

She gave him a slight smile. 'Near enough as makes no difference.'

'That photographer fellow that was with her gave me this note for you.' He held out a piece of folded paper.

Dottie said, 'Oh Mr Michaels, I could hug you!'

He grinned, bowed and went back to the kitchen.

The note was brief. 'Meet me outside under the larches at midnight, or later if he is still up. I'll wait. Burn this note. W.'

In many a romantic novel, Dottie thought, the heroine kept hold of the secret note she received, then the villain— Gervase fit that role so completely here—would discover it then rant and rave at the heroine, then usually lock her in a turret, or tie her up in a dungeon or to a railway track. Dottie was in no humour for that. She hurried to the drawing room, tore the note into four small pieces and fed each piece to the hungry flames, watching carefully as the paper browned, flickered and curled with the flame, then died away into grey sooty ash. She felt very proud of herself for being so sensible.

It was just after four o'clock. She had until midnight. Or whenever Gervase intended to take himself off to bed. Ugh, she thought, another thing she'd need to prepare herself for. She'd have to tackle that issue later, because she hadn't time for that now. She had a more pressing problem.

She went through to the kitchen. Cook and the maids, one daily, two living-in, were there turning out cupboards and scrubbing down shelves. They looked round as she came in.

Cook jumped up. 'Yes, miss? Can I help you?'

'I was looking for Mr Michaels.'

'He's outside having a smoke, miss.' Cook pointed to the back door. Dottie said thank you, remembering to call her Mrs Michaels—how often she forgot Michaels was married to Cook—and went outside to find him.

He was perched on a large upturned flowerpot in a sheltered corner of the garden. He had a lighted hurricane lamp beside him, though she would have found him easily enough—it was not quite dark, and he was silhouetted against the curtain of the lit room behind him. The tip of his cigarette glowed as he drew on it. Then he saw her.

'Miss Manderson!' He sounded a bit surprised.

She caught sight of the book he was reading, turning the book so that the lamplight fell on the page.

"A Duke for Isabella?"

'It's a very nice story,' he said, pretending to be affronted by her grin. 'And she's a very nice girl. No smut.'

She laughed. 'I'm glad to hear it.' She watched as he carefully placed a cigarette paper to mark his page then slipped the book into his pocket. Then she said, 'I'm sorry to bother you during your break, Mr Michaels. Thank you for giving me that note. The man who gave it to you is planning to meet me here tonight at around midnight, but...'

'I doubt you'll be back from the Edwin Parfitts by midnight,' he said. 'Their dinner parties tend to go on a bit.'

'Oh dear.'

'Here, miss, sit yourself down.' He leapt up from his flowerpot, and hurried off, reappearing almost immediately with another. He got it positioned to his satisfaction, and with a smile and a 'Thank you', Dottie sat.

He puffed on his cigarette.

Then Dottie said, 'So you think we'll probably still be at Gervase's parents at midnight?'

'I assume so, it's a ball, isn't it?'

Dottie shrugged. 'I have no idea. He only mentioned it a few minutes ago. Fortunately Mrs Holcombe tipped me off when she collected me from the station yesterday.' She shook her head. 'Was that only yesterday? But anyway, I hardly know them.'

'Best way, miss, in all honesty. He's all right if you don't mind them a bit pompous, but she is a cold piece, and known to not suffer fools.'

Dottie sighed. 'You're not making me feel any happier about this evening.'

'Did you bring a ballgown with you, miss? If not, I could ask around, we might be able to get you one...'

He was such a pet, she thought. 'Actually I've got one that I hope will do,' she said. 'It's really too bad of Gervase not to be clear about what he has planned or what he expects. Never mind, you don't need to hear all my woes. I have another problem apart from having to go to a ball and not being back until late. The gentleman who gave you that note asked me to meet him under the larches. I'm a town girl, Mr Michaels, I don't know a larch from a dandelion.'

Michaels laughed, and patted her knee, then remembering himself, said with genuine alarm, 'Oh miss, I do beg your pardon! I quite forgot myself!'

Dottie laughed. 'It's quite all right, Mr Michaels, just show me these dratted larches.'

'This way.'

He led her to the front of the house, to a sheltered little copse beside the end of the drive. The copse was the perfect spot for an assignation: the trees, the curve of the driveway, and the angle to the house all contrived to make the place almost hidden from the notice of any onlooker. There were perhaps a dozen of the trees, each with a broad growth of dense branches. The grass was tussocky and unmown beneath them. If Dottie had not been accompanied by a superior authority on the subject of trees, she would have dismissed them as 'some kind of pine'.

'The larches, miss.' He pointed. Dottie grinned at him in the near-darkness.

'Thank you. My friend says he will wait as long as it takes.'

Michaels nodded. 'None of my business, miss. You can be sure Mr Parfitt won't know a thing about it.'

'Thank you,' she said again.

'And are you sure about the dress?' he said, turning to head back to the house. Dottie fell in step beside him.

'Oh I'll be all right. I've got a good dress that I can dance in, and the shoes and everything. I haven't brought a really nice wrap with me, but I can take an ordinary coat and blame Gervase for not warning me.'

'If you're sure, miss.'

'I am, thank you, Mr Michaels. Goodbye for now.'

As she turned to go, there was a metallic clatter on the stones at her feet, and something bounced on the gravel. Dottie lunged forward and retrieved her engagement ring from the ground.

'That's the second time the blasted thing has fallen off.' She wiped it on her sleeve then replaced it on her finger.

'Just a little bigger, miss, and it would have made you a fine bracelet.'

Dottie laughed, and went inside, leaving him to finish his cigarette.

The evening was better than she had feared. To begin with, Evangeline—Gervase's scary mother—was too busy hobnobbing with her favourite guests to bother with her son's fiancée. At dinner, Dottie found herself seated between two courteous elderly gentlemen who were charmed and a little dazzled to have such a sweet young thing placed between them. The two men were old friends, and kept her entertained throughout the meal with tales of their misspent youth.

She could almost have forgotten that things were not as they appeared. But Edwin Parfitt proceeded to make a toast to the happy couple, who stood to receive everyone's good wishes, Gervase grabbing her hand in a grip that made her wince. Nevertheless, Dottie smiled her thanks around the room as the guests repeated the toast and raised their glasses.

The proud parents beamed at their son, and even smiled at Dottie with something approaching warmth. What would Mr and Mrs Parfitt say or do, Dottie wondered, if they knew there were people close at hand who were actively seeking to tumble Gervase Parfitt from his privileged pedestal. Whilst Edwin was merely dull, Dottie was certain Evangeline could be every bit as ruthless as her son appeared to be, and watched over him almost obsessively. Then Dottie remembered that Gervase was the only one of her three sons who was still alive, and felt sorry for her. To bury and mourn for not one but two sons must be a terrible experience. Perhaps she owed Evangeline a little more sympathy than she'd felt for her up to now.

After dinner there was a half-hour break for coffee, then the ball began. The musicians set themselves up in the ballroom, rather a grand name for the large, but not quite large enough, bare room at the back of the residence.

Dottie danced first with one of the elderly men who'd been beside her through dinner, then the other. Neither of them were very spry nor fully conversant with the latest dances, but they both managed a creditable waltz and seemed delighted to have done so. Dottie felt happy and relaxed.

Next, Edwin Parfitt offered her his arm, and saying with a smile, uncomfortably similar to his son's, 'Would you do me the honour, Dottie dear?'

She was surprised to hear him address her so warmly and with a smile. She accepted, and was pleased to find he was a good dancer. His conversation was general and undemanding, and she enjoyed her two dances with him.

Gervase danced with her for the next two dances. She was afraid he was still irritated with her, having seen so little of him since the afternoon. But although he spoke little, he appeared to be in a good mood.

She had already danced for two full hours when one of Gervase's friends, a young fellow who gave his name as Gordon Wisley asked her to dance. As they went round the floor for the first time, for the sake of something to say, she asked if he had known Gervase for a long time.

'Lord, no. I've only known him a year or two. My father is Chief Constable of Derbyshire, and Gervase and I met through some bash my father gave a while ago. It might even have been when Parfitt got the job.'

Dottie nodded, endeavouring to appear interested to just the right degree. Privately she was wondering if he might be a useful source of information to tap, but it seemed unlikely he'd say much with so many people about. The son of the chief constable might well hear things at home in confidence, but he'd hardly be aware of any wrongdoing on Gervase's part, especially if there was any possibility of it implicating his father.

Having just made up her mind about this, she was surprised when the young man told her: 'He promised to help me with my career, contacts and so forth, but we've rather drifted apart lately.'

Intrigued, she simply said, 'Oh?' and waited.

'To be honest, old Parfitt got me out of hot water a couple of times. I was very grateful but, well, he won't let me forget it. Things it wouldn't do for the old man to know, what?' He tapped his nose, suggesting this should be kept secret. He swayed precariously.

Dottie laughed gaily. 'Oh dear! People should have shorter memories in those cases.'

'Rather!' His addiction to these popular sayings made him appear even younger than he was. Dottie began to think he might be nearer her own age than Gervase's. He twirled her round in a not very successful flourish, narrowly avoiding Dottie's future mother-in-law, who glared at them.

'And are you following your father into the police force, Mr Wisley?'

He said rather breathlessly, as Evangeline moved away,

'Not bloody likely. Excuse my French. And do please call me Gordon, otherwise I shall feel like such an old buffer.'

She beamed at him. Gervase's mother was a safe distance away now, as was Gervase himself. She said, 'Gordon, I think most people understand that young men have their high spirits now and again, so I doubt it would be much of a shock for your father, even if he is the chief constable. After all, he was young once.'

'Well I'm supposed to be going in for law, and he is rather inclined to lecture me on propriety. Takes the moral high ground, don't you know, so best if he doesn't know. And old Parfitt loves a party.'

He was slurring his words slightly; she wondered just how much he'd drunk and she wondered how much she could get out of him before the end of their dance.

'Nothing so very terrible, I'm sure,' she said, rephrasing her earlier words. She beamed at him again.

'What would you say if I told you, gambling, raucous parties, lots of booze, a few other dodgy substances and of course, girls.'

Dottie was rather shocked. But she didn't let her smile falter, and said again, that it sounded all par for the course these days.

He looked briefly quite sober. 'One of the girls died. Fearful shame, that was. He should have kept an eye on her. She wasn't used to it. Parfitt hushed it all up. Wouldn't do for my father to know about tht.'

She made a sympathetic face, and just then the dance ended, and everyone turned to applaud the band. Her heart was pounding, but not from the dance.

The bandleader introduced each member of the band who then performed a short solo, then the bandleader announced a slow waltz and the vocal talents of Mr Hal Levy.

Dottie couldn't see Gervase immediately so she headed to the edge of the dancefloor, planning to sit out—she wasn't in the mood for slow-dancing. She accepted a glass of champagne from the tray of a passing maid, and moved back to lean against the wall and watch the dancers on the floor. She sipped her drink and let the music wash over her, replaying Gordon Wisley's words.

The song was a slower version of *The Very Thought Of You*. It was one of the songs that were playing when she danced with William for the first time at the ball at the Regency. It was one of her favourites, and the romantic words made her long to see him. She wondered if he was already there under the larches—now she knew what *they* were—and waiting patiently for her to arrive.

The song was cheered loudly as it ended, and calls were made for it to be repeated, so Mr Levy obligingly began the song again.

Dottie finished her champagne, set down the glass on a table and leaned back against the wall once more, half dreaming, thinking of William. The champagne had gone to her head very quickly. She was shielded partially by a jutting statue on a plinth from the far end of the dance floor. It was as if she wasn't really there, a very restful sensation. The music played, the song filled the air, the couples moved. But reminiscing was making her sad. So she stood up straight and forced herself to pay attention to the dancers, smiling at the one or two people she slightly knew.

And there on the other side of the room, visible once or twice through the dancing couples, was Gervase standing and talking to someone who was most definitely Moira Hansom. They were speaking earnestly and both glancing furtively about them. As the couples moved and parted again, Dottie caught a glimpse of Gervase looking around. She thought, he's looking for me. He's afraid I'll see him with her.

The next time the crowd parted, he was alone, and Dottie could have believed she had dreamt the whole thing, but for the blonde figure a few yards away, stepping out through the French doors into the garden.

Dottie was curious to see if he would follow her out there. He did.

The song came to an end for the second time, and she was glad of it. The sweet words tugged at her emotions, filling her with longing to be with the man she loved. And then another slow romantic melody filled the air.

It was another half an hour before Gervase appeared by her side. 'Ah, there you are. I've just been out for a smoke. Can I get you another drink?'

'No, thanks, I've just finished one.'

'Well, we'll have another dance if they play something a bit more fun. This crooning maudlin stuff is so dreary.'

The band struck up a faster beat, and Gervase took her onto the dancefloor again.

'Gervase, actually I'm all in. Do you think we could leave soon?'

Predictably, he frowned at her, but said, 'All right, if you want to. I'll go and say goodnight at the end of this number.'

In fact it was three more songs before they managed to get away. Dottie went with Gervase to say goodbye to his parents.

'Lovely evening, thank you both so very much,' she said and felt like a good little girl thanking the grown-ups for her party.

Evangeline inclined her head but said nothing. Edwin kissed her cheek and made a few pleasant remarks. They said goodnight and finally left.

In the car on the journey back, Gervase had talked non-stop about various friends he'd spoken to, many of whom Dottie had not met. Predictably, not once did he mention Moira Hansom.

As Michaels had said, it was well after midnight, nearly one o'clock in fact by the time they got back to Gervase's house. As they came along the sweep of the drive, the headlamps picking out each shrub in turn that was closest to the road, Dottie couldn't help glancing across at the little crowd of larches. But it was too dark to see if anyone was there.

As soon as they stepped into the house, Gervase said, 'Would you like nightcap, or are you going straight to bed?'

His tone was resigned, as if he already knew what she would say. She felt rather sorry for the man who seemed to have finally realised that the woman he was supposed to be marrying no longer wanted his company. She assumed a rueful expression.

'Sorry Gervase, I really am so tired.'

He nodded. 'And going back to London tomorrow.'

'Yes.'

He nodded again. After a moment, he said without looking at her, 'Well, goodnight, Dottie. Sleep well, my dear.'

'Thank you. You too.' She waited to see if he would try to kiss her. He didn't. He went along the hall to his study, so Dottie went upstairs, feeling horribly like the worst fiancée in the history of the world.

In her room she changed into warm dark clothes, then dithered, feeling uncertain what to do. She should be going out to meet William, but with Gervase still in his study... She had a vivid mental picture of him coming outside, catching her with William, suspecting the worst— which wouldn't be a million miles from the truth, she had to admit—and quite possibly things turning nasty. She knew it was unlikely they would end up duelling at dawn with antique pistols, and crossly dismissed the vivid picture supplied by her imagination. Nevertheless, she knew that tempers would flare on both sides, and William's chances at making a case against Gervase would be over.

She put out her light and went to stand by the window, looking out. Of course her room was at the back of the property, so she knew she would not be able to see William from there. But she could see a patch of grass and stone outside illuminated by the light from the study below, so she knew Gervase was still in there. She sat on the sill and wondered what to do.

The sky was clear and the stars seemed bright, close, like the spangles on an evening gown. She relaxed. There was no need to worry, William had said he would wait as long as necessary. He would know she had to wait until the time was right.

A shadow moved amongst the trees. She waited and saw it again, so it wasn't just her overactive imagination. A slender darker-than-dark something slipped between the trees, edging up to the terrace and halting there, partially protected by a tall bush that bore nondescript little white flowers with no fragrance.

Dottie's heart was in her mouth. What on earth did William think he was doing? She couldn't see so well from this window, so she moved across to the other window that stood partially open. She waited a moment then saw the shadow slip from behind the bush and move silently across the terrace and into the patch of light. Dottie heard the tap on the study door. The curtain was thrown back as the door was opened. And Dottie saw then the person was certainly fair, but definitely not a man.

Moira Hansom said as clearly as if Dottie stood beside her, 'You got rid of her, then?'

Gervase's response was muffled but his warm, light tone told Dottie he had laughed and said something to confirm that. The door was closed. The curtain was pulled back in place.

'Well.' Dottie stepped back from the window, not sure whether she felt betrayed or relieved.

Clearly Gervase was now going to be 'busy' for some time. In view of what had happened, there seemed no reason to delay going out to meet William.

She put on some sturdy outdoor shoes, and grabbed her coat. She slipped into the hall, closed the door of her room, locked it and pocketed the key. Quietly she hurried along the corridor to the back stairs. The night light burned there, and she was glad to be able to see her way. She ran lightly down and in less than a minute was outside in the chilly night air, crossing the grass and the gravel to the stand of larches.

She reached the meeting place. The shadows were deep under the trees, and even though she'd known he would be there waiting, she got a momentary fright when she bumped into the solid form of William Hardy.

To her surprise, he hugged her close. He smelled of shaving soap and coffee. She closed her eyes and stayed there for a moment with her head against his shoulder.

'How are you?' he asked against her ear.

Reluctantly she stepped back. 'I'm all right. Are you?' She could hardly see him, just the dark shape of him. Couldn't see his eyes or his mouth at all.

The shape appeared to nod. 'I'm fine,' he said. 'I saw you come back about fifteen minutes or so ago.'

'Yes, we had to go to a ball at his parents'. I'm lucky to get back so early. I pleaded tiredness.'

'It's all right. I saw you go, and so didn't really expect you back too early. That's why I brought the flask of coffee with me. Look, I hate to get to business so promptly, but have you managed to find out anything?'

She told him the snippets she had so far: that Mrs Sedgworth had been going to tell her something about Gervase, but in the end hadn't. She told him about arriving at the Sedgworths only to come straight back. That Mr Michaels had told her he had heard Gervase telephoning to Mrs Sedgworth. And the rumours that Mr Michaels had mentioned about the car accident. Finally she added what she'd learned from the young man at the Parfitts' ball. Told like this, it didn't amount to much, and it wasn't exactly proof, but William seemed pleased, saying it was a good start.

'Where are you staying?' she asked.

'I'm over at my uncle's in Matlock. It's convenient but a bit further out than I would have liked. But I couldn't really stay right here in the village.'

Dottie shivered. 'Golly no!' she said, though not for the reason he would think. She said, 'I'm going home tomorrow, or rather, later today. After I've said goodbye to Gervase, I think I'll get the cabbie to set me down at the Sedgworths, and I'll just pop in and see if I can get anything out of her. She might be feeling better, and ready to tell me what she'd hinted at on Friday night. Hopefully if she knows I'm going back to London that might make her talk.'

'Are you telling me he hasn't the decency to drive his fiancée to the station? You've got to take a cab?' She felt him shaking his head in disgust.

'I don't actually know how I'll get to the station. It's possible he might take me or get Michaels to take me.' Changing the subject she said, 'I couldn't believe it when you turned up this afternoon as a photographer!'

He laughed softly. 'Your face said it all. And I saw you glance at Parfitt a couple of times.'

'I don't know how he didn't recognise you!'

'He only notices women.'

Dottie couldn't argue with that.

'I'm glad you're going back to London. I hate the thought of you here with a man like him. Though I must admit, I'd thought you would be staying until Monday?'

'I told him I couldn't, that I had to get back on Sunday. Though in all honesty, I felt like going home the second I arrived. I can't pretend that I like him a moment longer.'

'I'm talking to a few people over the next couple of days, so hopefully I'll get something useful from them. I don't know how soon I'll be back in London. Take this paper, it's got my uncle's telephone number on it, just in case you need me. I ought to have given it to you before.'

She groped in the dark and found his hand with the paper. She put the paper in the pocket of her coat.

'I know I haven't found out much,' she said. 'It's been harder than I expected, just getting away from him. And I don't really know where to look or who to ask, let alone what to ask them. I can't exactly search the place with him there.'

'No, no, Dottie, darling, I don't want you to risk putting yourself in danger. Don't ask people questions. You've done enough already. I should never have asked you.'

If it hadn't been dark, he might have noticed her staring at him. As it was, he realised what he'd said. But there was no point trying to shrug the words off. He pulled her against him and kissed her softly. Her lips were cold.

'You're frozen. You'd better go in. Goodnight.'

She whispered it back to him, then turned and scurried

away around the side of the house, and up the back stairs, fumbled the key into the lock then once inside, locked the door again, at every moment expecting the light to snap on and to see Gervase standing there, his face red with fury. Not that he had any reason to talk, she reminded herself. She hurried to the window—but of course, it pointed the wrong way. She couldn't see William from here. She kicked off her shoes, pulled the counterpane from the bed, and drawing an armchair up to the other window, settled herself down to watch to see when Moira left—if she hadn't already, of course.

As she sat there, she wondered again if she ought to have told William about Moira. Would he be hurt? She had no idea how he really felt about Moira. He was engaged to her, yet he repeatedly, by his looks and his stolen kisses, he told Dottie his heart belonged to her.

She looked out into the night. There was still a light patch on the ground, so a light still burned in the study. That did not necessarily mean Gervase still had company, although it seemed likely. The luminous hands of Dottie's travel clock showed that it was not yet two o'clock. How late would Moira stay?

She was so glad she would be going home tomorrow. She would never come back to Gervase Parfitt's house. As soon as she reached London, she would telephone him and tell him it was all off again, and if he lost his temper, she would just put the phone down on him.

Finally, for once and for all, it would be over.

*

Chapter Eight

Dottie rose late the following morning, and, guilty when she saw the time, rushed to get ready to go downstairs.

Gervase was at the breakfast table already, but almost as bleary-eyed as Dottie. He glanced up and said good morning as she came in.

She repeated the greeting without even thinking about it, and said, 'Are we going to church this morning? If so I think I'm too late for breakfast.'

He gave a snort of laughter. 'I hadn't planned to go to church today. I don't as a rule, except on special occasions.'

She took a seat opposite him. He poured her a cup of tea. He passed the milk to her, offered her sugar which she declined, slightly irritated by the fact. After eight months of 'seeing' one another, how could he still have no idea how she took her tea? I bet he knows how Moira takes hers, she thought acidly. And she was still rather shocked by the fact that he didn't go to church regularly. They observed one another across the table.

'I thought you might like to go for a drive?'

'That would be lovely,' Dottie said sincerely.

'Where would you like to go? I don't mind where I take you, town, country, indoors, out. The weather should be half-decent today, according to the news on the radio.'

'Could we go to that place you took me last summer? Only not into the caves—that was rather a disaster. But the view...'

He nodded and smiled, remembering.

Dottie remembered too and felt sad. He had been so kind to her that day, and so romantic. She had really thought they were falling in love with one another that afternoon. He had seemed, if not perfect, then very close to it.

She never been into underground tunnels or caves before. She had not had the slightest inkling that she would be as terrified as she was. That had been a dreadful shock, and a humiliating one. She had never known terror like it. It had been completely irrational, but he had been so kind. She would always feel grateful to him for how he had reacted to her clinging fear. She couldn't help sighing now. It had all been a lie. What a waste of eight months.

She looked at him as he returned to his newspaper. In spite of everything William had told her about him, and even though Gervase's recent behaviour had been deplorable, she was convinced there was good in him somewhere. What made him choose to behave the way he did? Why had he chosen to manipulate and deceive? She reached for a slice of toast.

He glanced up to add, 'Perhaps a late lunch or afternoon tea in Matlock Bath again?'

'Lovely,' she said. She only hoped they wouldn't bump into William or his family, though they lived nearer to Matlock itself, so it wasn't very likely.

'Well I've finished here, but I could do with spending a few minutes looking through some papers in my study. Shall we aim to leave in about half an hour? Will that give you enough time?'

'Oh yes, that would be perfect.'

He left, and she settled back, immediately more relaxed now he had gone. It would all be fine. It would be an easy day, easy and pleasant. The majestic Heights of Abraham—avoiding the caves of course, what she privately thought of as the Dreadful Depths of Abraham—then the quiet charm of Matlock Bath. The drive would be pleasant. Then tea somewhere, and before she knew it, she would be on the train back to London. She hadn't found out anything, but it couldn't be helped, she would just have to leave the detecting to William Hardy.

The maid came to clear the table as Dottie wiped her hands on a napkin, and left to go upstairs. From her position halfway up the stairs, she could see that the study door was standing slightly open. Michaels was there talking to Gervase.

She thought little of it and went up to get ready. Twenty minutes later, when she went downstairs again, Gervase was coming out of his study in a rush.

'So sorry, dear. I forgot the time. Back in a minute.' He hurried past her and up the stairs. She thought his expression was a little odd.

Michaels was coming through from the kitchen and saw her. He halted. He looked around to make sure no one—Gervase for example—was there. Then, 'Have you heard the news, miss?'

'No?'

He drew a little closer. And in a low voice, said, 'Mr Parfitt didn't tell you what I told him just now? I'm afraid you will be shocked, miss. It's Mrs Sedgworth. She took some pills last night. The Major found her stone-cold dead this morning. In a terrible state, he is. Their maid telephoned just now to tell my wife.'

Dottie stared at him. Her hand was at her mouth. She couldn't believe what she was hearing. She shivered, and said, 'Mr Michaels...' but she couldn't think of anything to say, couldn't seem to think at all.

Michaels took her by the arm and guided her into the morning room and helped her into a chair. She was shaking her head in response to his question. 'No, Gervase didn't say... but I was upstairs... Oh that's awful. Poor Major Sedgworth. Poor Mrs Sedgworth.'

Gervase was coming down the stairs, she heard his steps. He was whistling a merry tune though he stopped as he came over to her. 'Sorry to keep you waiting,' he said with a smile as he came into the room. 'Are you ready?'

He's happy, she thought, astonished. He had looked rather odd when he went upstairs, and that's what it was. He's happy, really happy.

He beamed at her. Michaels and Dottie stared back at him.

Dottie shook her head, her hands outstretched. 'Oh Gervase, I can't. I've just heard about poor Mrs Sedgworth. It's so upsetting. She was so kind to me when she was here on Friday evening. And now...'

He attempted to assume a sorrowful expression but it didn't fool Dottie. 'Yes it's such a shame. But it's not as though you knew her.'

'I don't feel the same about going out now.' She drew a long breath in. 'Has the Major got someone with him? Do they have a family, I can't remember? I'd hate to think of him sitting at home all alone with this having just happened.'

Gervase shrugged and looked at Michaels who was poised to leave. Michaels said, 'The maid said she'd rung up a son. So I expect...'

'Yes, probably.' Dottie's mind filled in the blanks: now for the Sedgworth family, the process of mourning would begin. She sighed. 'It's so sad. My goodness, I can't believe it.'

Gervase was looking impatient. His expression made complete sense to her. He had been happy. The look on his face that had struck her as odd at the time: that was his look of triumph, the look he got when something was going his way. Whether it was a winning hand at Bridge, or the smiting of his enemies...

She wondered about that. Was it ridiculous to ponder whether Mrs Sedgworth's fatal dose of pills had been the poor woman's own idea, administered by her own hand?

'You needn't stay until four o'clock,' Gervase said suddenly. 'If you feel too upset to go out this morning, perhaps it would be best for you to get back to London a little earlier than planned. You might feel better in your own home, with your family.'

It seemed an oddly-timed suggestion. It took her completely by surprise. Dottie's first thought was that he wanted her out of the way. Her second was to wonder if Moira Hansom was still staying at the pub.

But if he was encouraging her to leave, she was tempted to do exactly that. She hesitated. He came over and crouched down beside her. He took her hand in his.

'Dottie dearest, of course I'd like you to stay, but—well, it'll be rather upsetting for you. I hadn't realised what an impression dear old Christobel had made on you. And you're so soft-hearted, you'll find it impossible to settle down for the rest of the day. Best if you go back home and you can talk things over with your parents.'

In theory what he said made sense. It was as if he knew exactly what to say to her. Yet the very fact that it was him saying it made her suspicious. However she had made up her mind. He was right. If they didn't go out, there was nothing else she wanted to do here. She certainly didn't want to spend all that time in his company. He was giving her the chance to get away, and she was going to grab it with both hands.

'If you're sure you don't mind,' she said. 'I think I will go home a bit earlier.'

Again that expression. He looked as though he had just won first prize. He wasn't capable of hiding his pleasure behind a more appropriate expression of sadness. She'd just given him exactly what he wanted and he was delighted. What on earth was he up to? Oh well, she wasn't going to waste any more time on him. She had the chance to go, with no tantrums or difficulties from him. And therefore go she would.

It took her only a few minutes to pack, and she was ready. Michaels brought her luggage down, with Lizzie carrying a couple of lighter things. Gervase was waiting for Dottie in the hall. She wasn't even surprised when he said, 'You don't mind if Michaels takes you to the station, do you? I might as well go back to my work in the study as you're not going to be here.'

Dottie wondered if the study held the same work that had occupied him last night. If only she had the sheer nerve to go and see for herself.

He put his arms around her and pressed his cheek against hers. 'Have a lovely journey home, dearest. It's been a wonderful weekend, and all because of you.'

Not a word of truth in that, she thought, but she smiled her dutiful smile. His lies had made her a liar too.

'I'll ring you tomorrow,' he promised and kissed her. 'And don't fret yourself about Christobel Sedgworth. Whatever was making her unhappy, it's all over now. She's at peace now, the poor dear.'

He beamed as he guided her to the front door. Michaels and Lizzie carried her things out. The car had already been brought round to the front of the house. Gervase saw her into the car, waved briefly from the front step, then as the car turned the sweep of the gravel drive, Dottie glanced back and the front door was closed. Gervase had gone inside already.

'Not exactly inconsolable,' Michaels commented.

'He's not, is he? I think we both know he has his consolation. Although I must admit I hadn't expected to leave quite so promptly.'

'Me either,' he agreed.

As they drove past the Sedgworths' a few minutes later, he said, 'There's the police.'

Dottie looked. And saw William Hardy on the lawn, talking with two men in suits and overcoats.

On an impulse, Dottie said, 'Could you stop the car? I must just have a word with them.'

If Michaels was surprised, he was nevertheless the consummate butler. He brought the car to a halt just a few yards beyond the Sedgworths' gate.

Dottie got out and went along the path to towards the house. The policemen turned. Hardy said something to them, then moved to meet her.

He kept his hands in his pockets, and his distance from

her, but his smile and his eyes were warm. Dottie found she was being escorted back to the waiting car.

Hardy said, 'You've heard, then?'

She nodded, turning round, anxious eyes towards the house. 'I know you won't be able to tell me anything. I just wondered if she'd—well—did she do it herself, do you think?'

He nodded. 'It seems that way. The husband said she'd been upset all day yesterday. He said he didn't know what it was. Said she didn't eat a thing all day, she was so upset.'

Dottie said in a low voice, 'Is it possible it had anything to do with Gervase's telephone call to her?'

'There's no actual proof at the moment. I'm certain the Major knows more than he's willing to say. However, there's no denying there's a possibility this has something to do with Parfitt. How did you find out?'

'The Sedgworths' maid rang to tell Gervase's cook.'

'And how did Parfitt take the news? Did he seem surprised? Upset?'

Dottie shook her head. 'Quite the opposite, he was happy, relieved even. Almost to the point of being excited. He was surprised I didn't feel like going out today as we'd planned. '

William frowned. 'I see. So where are you going now?'

'Back to London. Gervase felt I'd be better grieving in the privacy and comfort of my own home.'

William's laugh was bitter. 'After spending the best part of the day sitting alone on the train? What a gentleman.'

'I know.' Dottie bit her lip and looked at him. What she wanted was for him to put his arms around her to comfort her. That wasn't possible in such a public situation, and especially when he was working. So she said, 'I really feel he is involved in this. He seemed almost gloating. Oh, William, he's vile!'

Discreetly he held her hand and squeezed it. 'If he was responsible for this, I'll get him for it, have no fear about that. I shall talk to the telephone exchange as soon as I can. There's a good chance they will be able to confirm that call of Parfitt's to Mrs Sedgworth. He'd know she was all alone, with her husband on his way back after collecting you.'

'And,' Dottie said, 'He could be certain of speaking to her, not the Major, and in private. Even if the maid answered the phone, he could simply say that he called to let Mrs Sedgworth know we were on our way.'

'Exactly. It sounds to me as though he knew she planned to talk to you, or perhaps just feared she might, so he clearly knew exactly what she would say. For some reason, he had to prevent that. Possibly it was to do with this rumour of a road accident you told me about. He may have been threatening her or blackmailing her, and she couldn't bear the pressure any longer.'

'Poor Mrs Sedgworth. I wish—I so wish I'd had the chance to speak to her. Oh I do hope she told the Major what was wrong. The thought of a secret so terrible that it ate away at her like that. That she really felt the only way to be free of it was to take her own life!' Dottie shivered, and folded her arms across herself to try to keep out the cold. 'People who love one another should never have secrets.'

'As we've discovered,' he said, his voice barely above a whisper. She looked up at him and her eyes filled with tears. She couldn't speak.

'Need a handkerchief?'

She shook her head. 'I've got two of yours in my bag in the car.' She managed a little smile at that.

He patted her arm and said, 'Go home, Dottie. I'll keep in touch and let you know what's happening. Now, I must get back to work.'

'Are you here in an official capacity?'

'Let's call it semi-official.'

'Would it be better if I stayed? Though I can't possibly go back to Gervase's.'

'Isn't there a pub nearby?'

'Yes, but I can't possibly stay there either, because of M...' She caught herself just in time. 'Because Gervase might find out I was there. It's a bit too close.'

'Go home to London, Dottie. I'll probably be back

myself in a day or two. We can talk then.'

She nodded. 'All right. But can you please tell the Major how sorry I am.'

'Of course I will. Poor devil. He seems to hardly know what's hit him. Got a daughter coming over from Lenton, and a son coming from Manchester tomorrow. He'll need them.'

Dottie nodded. 'Well goodbye for now.' She held out a hand to him.

He shook it, his eyes mocking. 'How very formal. Do I have to go back to calling you Miss Manderson?'

'Well I'd like to kiss you goodbye, but with Nottinghamshire's finest watching, I can't very well do that.' She turned and went back to the car.

Michaels said, 'Are we going back to Mr Parfitt's, miss, or to the station as planned?'

'To the station please.'

'Very well, miss.' He released the brake. As the car pulled away, she saw him glance in the mirror. 'Find out anything?'

'Unfortunately not. It's very frustrating.'

'You'll only just make the train, miss.'

He was right. When she got to the station the train was already in the platform. Michaels and a porter bundled her into the nearest door and threw her luggage in after her as the guard blew his whistle and frantically waved his flag at them.

The train began to move. Dottie yelled out of the window to Michaels, 'Let me know what's happening!'

He yelled back with equal gusto, 'I will, miss, safe journey!'

She stowed her luggage in the overhead rack and pulled off her coat, hat and gloves. The heating was going full pelt and she knew she would roast if she didn't get rid of that outer layer.

She had the carriage to herself. She leaned back against the plush seat to mull over the events of the last two days.

It was heavenly to sleep in her own bed that night. Even

better not to have to lock her door against the arrival of any late night visitor.

She left that part out when she told her parents about the weekend, finishing with the death of poor Mrs Sedgworth. Although, she had to leave out William's presence, and that he was investigating Gervase, who may or may not have been responsible for Mrs Sedgworth's terrible actions. All in all, she felt as though she'd left out far more than she was able to tell them. Nor could she tell them anything about Moira and her involvement with Gervase.

'At least you don't need to see Gervase again. It sounds as though it truly is over between you, dear. I hope you're not upset about that?' her mother said.

This reminded Dottie of something else she urgently needed to tell her parents.

'Just to let you know, he ambushed me rather on Saturday. He'd arranged for people to come from a couple of magazines to do an interview and take pictures. It was about his engagement. Our, I should have said, *our* engagement. As I say, they asked a few questions and took photos.' She didn't mention who took them. 'Er—I'm afraid these will be published this week or next week.'

Her father shook his head, clearly unhappy. If only her mother had been equally restrained. But she wasn't. She spoke hotly and at length for several minutes, finally finishing with, 'And everyone we know will see it and think that it's true. Honestly, Dottie, what on earth were you thinking?'

Dottie thought it was progress that her mother called her Dottie not Dorothy. She sighed and apologised for the umpteenth time. She could already think of at least a dozen people she'd need to telephone to tell them it wasn't true. One of them was Gervase, of course. She wasn't looking forward to breaking up with him yet again.

'He gave me a family heirloom for an engagement ring,' she told them. She opened her bag to look for it but couldn't find it. She wasn't overly concerned. 'It must be in my main suitcase. Or in the dressing case. It's there somewhere, anyway.'

Half an hour later, having caught up with their news, she went to bed.

The following day was a hectic one. She rang several people, starting with her sister, to let them know the report of the engagement was a fake.

She had a busy day at the warehouse, only just getting home in time for dinner. It wasn't until a certain policeman turned up at the door later that night that she realised she was still engaged to Gervase—he was the only one she hadn't remembered to telephone. Neither had he bothered to phone to see if she got home safely, or to swear his undying love.

Her father shook William's hand, really pleased to see him. The two men disappeared into her father's study with a bottle of whisky for half an hour. Then William spent ten minutes listening to Dottie's mother, and finally he had time to say to Dottie:

'Would you like to go for a walk?'

She was surprised, but pleased. She ran upstairs to change her skirt and put on outdoor shoes, then tidied her hair and quickly patted on a little more powder, as excited as if it was a proper assignation.

Her parents seemed thrilled to see her going out with him. She hoped they weren't too pleased: she must remember to remind them he was technically engaged to someone else. All these strange engagements, she thought. How complicated life was.

It was chilly outside, but once out of sight of the house, he gave her his arm, which she practically hugged, and walking closer to him—or perhaps just because of the exercise—she felt warmer. At first they talked generally: when had he arrived back, had she had a good journey, had he had a good journey, how busy London seemed after the country. But by the time they reached Trafalgar Square and sat on the steps outside the National Gallery, he turned the topic to business.

'Whilst I have no doubt whatsoever that Parfitt was

involved somehow in Mrs Sedgworth's decision to make away with herself, there is nothing so far to prove that he did anything to make her feel that was her only choice. He admits to telephoning, but says—just as you suggested—that it was simply a courtesy call to let her know that her husband had collected you as arranged, and that you were on the way back to their home. When he was asked why the call lasted so long, he said that he told her about the reporters who were coming that afternoon, and also asked her to inform you, as he had forgotten to tell you about the arrangement.'

'How did he react to being asked to account for making the call?' she wanted to know. After all, Gervase always loved having all the power, and didn't like his judgement being questioned. Beside her, she felt William shrug his shoulders.

'I didn't speak to him about it. But the Sergeant who did was very tactful indeed. Said he'd simply wondered if Mrs Sedgworth had said anything to him about feeling upset or what she planned to do. Parfitt seized the opportunity to vent some righteous indignation on the Sergeant, pointing out at considerable volume that if the lady had said anything, *of course* he would have immediately rushed to help her.'

They were silent for a while, watching the world around them. It may have been a cold late-winter's evening but the streets were busy, and there were still large numbers of people going into the gallery and milling about. Strains of choral music came to Dottie on the night air, seeming almost magical.

'A concert or something going on at St Martins-in-the-Field,' William commented, nodding towards the church almost next door to the gallery. There was the excited chatter of tourists, the ever-present pigeons cooing and flapping their wings.

A couple approached them and in halting English asked William to take a photograph of them together on the steps of the Gallery. He obliged, the flash bulb of the camera just one abrupt flare amid a flurry of flashes. The couple were delighted and thanked him and went on their way. Dottie smiled. It was kind of him. He was an obliging fellow. She liked that about him. She smiled again to think of him as Carl Brown, society photographer, only two days earlier.

He came to sit next to her, and pulled his coat and his arm around her. She nestled into his warm body, and said, 'By the way, how on earth did you get them to take you on at that magazine?'

He laughed. 'Oh that was easy. Miss Birnie is the niece of my chief superintendent. He asked her for a favour. I spent the whole day before attending weddings and getting tips from the usual man. It's helped my photography skills no end.'

'So I saw!' she laughed, nodding towards the couple that had just left. Silence fell on them again. A warm, safe silence. She leaned into him, he held her tight and close.

After a moment, he said, 'Cold?' She nodded. He hauled her to her feet. 'Come on, let's go inside. They're open for a while yet.'

They walked, arm in arm, through the halls, stopping here and there to look at the art works. The place was not too crowded, and they were able to stop and look as much as they liked. And as they went round, William talked.

'The Major definitely knows more than he's letting on, but he's keeping quiet. And if it's what we think it could be, I'm not particularly surprised. The Sergeant you saw yesterday is looking into road accidents in the area for the last couple of years. The Major started out by saying he didn't particularly notice that his wife was upset before he came to collect you, but now he's changed it to saying she may have been, but he didn't notice because he was outside most of the morning. I find that a bit hard to believe, myself. Surely a chap would notice if his wife was upset to the point of tears. Even if they'd been married donkey's years, you'd still think he'd notice. I would.'

She looked at him. Things immediately seemed personal, awkward. 'Would you?'

He turned away. 'Of course.'

She said nothing. She followed him to where he stood in front of a massive canvas that took up the whole wall. She wanted to put her arms around him. She wanted him to kiss her, to take her home with him to his house, to take her inside, shut the door and shut out the world.

They moved to the next painting.

He sighed. Seeing no one else was in this small side gallery, she said, 'Is everything all right?'

He looked at her for a full minute. Several elderly ladies came in, chattering about the artist, consulting their guidebooks. William said in a low voice, 'No, it's not.'

He went out. He was making for the exit. She hurried to catch up with him. He gave her his arm with a mumbled apology, but it wasn't the same. The spell was broken. He took her home, and left her on the step with only a kiss on the cheek.

*

Chapter Nine

Two days later, on the Thursday morning, Dottie was once more travelling up to Nottinghamshire. She had been called to give evidence at the inquest into Mrs Sedgworth's death. The inquest was to be held that afternoon at two o'clock, and she planned to take a taxi directly from the railway station to the village hall.

She had hoped she wouldn't be called. It seemed a long way to go to spend five minutes standing before the coroner and telling the little she knew, but she'd been told she had to attend, and so she was stuck with it.

Then she'd had to think of a way to avoid staying at Gervase's house without making him angry. Because if there was one thing she just couldn't face, it was having to fob off his advances again. Or his sulks, which were almost worse.

She telephoned Gervase on Tuesday evening. It seemed prudent to let him know she was travelling up for the inquest and would be staying overnight. The possibility of bumping into him if he wasn't expecting her—it would be too awkward. To her surprise he had not been called as a witness, and had no plans to attend. It seemed he had no interest in the death of someone he had only a few days earlier claimed as a dear friend.

'In any case, I shall be at a conference in Bournemouth,' he told her. "Policing into the Future'. Load of nonsense. Modern claptrap.' Then he allowed his voice to become low and husky: his idea of how passion should sound. 'I shall miss you, dearest. I had almost thought of asking you to join me in Bournemouth, but then I realised your parents would never allow it. Thank the Lord we shall soon be married.'

Dottie ignored an urge to slam down the telephone. This was the most 'passion' she'd heard from him since Saturday. Or was it Sunday? She couldn't remember. She felt a little ill at the mere idea of him.

'Yes indeed,' she replied and wondered if he'd noticed the complete lack of passion on her side. She might have been agreeing that cabbage was superior to cauliflower.

'Any way, you've got to come up here for the inquest, so we would still be apart. But, my love, you are more than welcome to stay at my house whilst I'm away. I'm sure the servants will take very good care of their future mistress. I shan't be there, obviously, but after all, this will be your home too in the near future. So if you'd like to, feel free to stay.'

It would definitely not be her home, *ever*, she thought, but since he was offering... It would certainly suit her to stay at his house, especially without the major disadvantage of Gervase being there.

She said with genuine warmth, 'Oh Gervase, that's very generous of you, thank you! If you're sure you don't mind, that would be lovely, and so convenient.'

'Think nothing of it, dearest. The only problem is, you'd have to put up with a cold buffet for dinner on Thursday night, as it's everyone's evening out. Michaels will be there, in case you need anything, but other than that...'

'I'm sure it will be fine,' Dottie said hastily, worried he might change his mind, mainly because a plan was already forming in her mind. 'I shan't need anything, though in a big house on my own, it will be nice to know there is someone else there on hand, so to speak.'

'That's settled then. I shall let the servants know to expect you sometime in the afternoon. Are you coming by train?'

'Yes, it'll be another two weeks until my cousin has finished with my car.' She thanked him once more, then after a few minutes of dull conversation, they said goodbye.

In the little church hall in the village, Dottie was called to take the stand. She made her oath, one small shapely hand on the Bible, then was invited to sit.

The coroner said, 'Tell me, Miss Manderson, how you became acquainted with Mrs Sedgworth.'

Dottie explained about the dinner party at Gervase's house the previous weekend. She felt obliged to be creative when it came to relating how Mrs Sedgworth had come to invite her to the house for coffee.

She said, 'We'd only been chatting for a few minutes, but it was no secret among his friends that Mr Parfitt and I were about to announce our engagement. Mrs Sedgworth rather took me under her wing. I think she could see I was a little shy of some of Mr Parfitt's friends. She said something like, 'We must get to know each other better, as we shall practically be neighbours. Come tomorrow for coffee, we shan't need the men, we'll have a nice girly talk about wedding dresses and such.' We had talked a good deal about gardening, that sort of thing. I thought she seemed very kind, and rather the motherly sort.'

'I see. Thank you, Miss Manderson. Now tell me, what happened the following morning?'

'The major very kindly arrived to collect me as we'd arranged.'

'And was there anything unusual in his manner, so far as you could tell given your short acquaintance?'

'Oh no, he seemed perfectly relaxed and we chatted about this and that all the way there.'

'And when you reached the house, Miss Manderson, what happened then?'

Dottie hesitated briefly. She felt disloyal talking about the Sedgworths like this—but she had to say what she saw.

'Mrs Sedgworth came from upstairs. I saw immediately that she had been crying. She was embarrassed. I think she knew that I could tell.'

'Did Mrs Sedgworth say anything to explain her appearance?'

'She said she wasn't feeling well, and didn't feel up to having visitors. She apologised and asked me to come again next time I was staying in the area.' Which is now, she thought suddenly, and her lip gave a wobble as the sadness hit her again.

'And how did Major Sedgworth react?'

Dottie said, 'He seemed very surprised, but I don't think he felt he could ask her anything in front of me. He offered me coffee then took me back to Gervase's—I mean, Mr Parfitt's house.'

The coroner's clerk recorded Dottie's evidence, the coroner thanked Dottie and told her she could step down.

She went to sit in an empty seat beside the major, his red-eyed daughter and his son who wore a grim, determined expression. She gave them all an apologetic smile and nod.

The coroner deliberated for a few minutes, reading over his notes, then discussed something with the clerk and the police sergeant Dottie had seen with William outside the Sedgworths' house on Sunday. Then with a tap of the gavel to quieten the room, he said:

'I find that the deceased, Christobel Agnes Sedgworth took her own life whilst of unsound mind. Let the record show a verdict of suicide. This inquest is at an end. My thanks to everyone who assisted the court.'

Major Sedgworth hung his head, and his daughter broke into stifled sobs, pressing a black-edged handkerchief to her mouth and nose with a black-gloved hand. Her brother patted her knee and seemed close to tears himself.

The verdict was hardly a surprise, Dottie thought, but it must be awful for them. If only the coroner could have softened the verdict with a more generous ruling such as accidental death.

As she came away, she saw William at the back of the hall. She went over to join him, happy he was there. She cast a glance about her in case Moira should be with him. She wasn't.

'You were very clear and composed,' he said.

'I've done this before, as you no doubt remember. It helped, knowing what to expect.'

'Hmm,' he said. 'At least you didn't commit perjury this time.' Then he caught her guilty look and his own became one of astonishment. 'Now look here, Dottie, surely you didn't...'

'It's all right,' she told him. 'You don't need to brutalise me. I just left out what Mrs Sedgworth said about having something about Gervase to tell me. I wasn't sure whether you wanted me to mention it or not.'

He relaxed slightly. 'It's probably a good thing to leave that out for now.'

'Are you on duty, or...?'

'No, I'm a mere citizen this afternoon.'

'Staying at your uncle's again?' She was jostled by some people squeezing past. William drew her out of the way. It was frustrating; they couldn't talk properly here.

'Yes.'

'Of course. Very nice. But in your capacity at large in Nottinghamshire as a mere citizen, you didn't bring your fiancée with you?'

He frowned. He always did frown when she mentioned Moira, Dottie had noticed.

'No. She's still with her uncle and aunt. Back Saturday evening.'

'And where do these charming people live?' Dottie asked him in a light, teasing tone. It took all of her social skills to appear calm and happy. Because inwardly she was beginning to have a horrid suspicion. Not for the first time. She knew exactly what he was about to say.

He said it now. 'I'm sure I've mentioned it before.

Bournemouth.'

'The south coast. Lovely. Shame it's not a bit warmer.' Her mind was clamouring, but she couldn't possibly tell him, not here, not right now. Besides, what if it really was just a coincidence?

The other times hadn't been a coincidence, she remembered. Moira coming to Gervase's study late at night. And in the middle of the day. Cropping up at the ball at his parents' house. A long way to come from Bournemouth, Dottie thought, just for an hour of Gervase's company. She looked at William, thinking how can he not know this? An intelligent man, a detective. How could he not be aware of the deception going on right in front of him?

'What about you? Staying at Parfitt's place, I expect.'

'Oh yes,' she said, and here she was on dangerous ground. What if he asked where Gervase was? 'He's away at a police conference for a few days. But he very kindly said I could stay at his house.'

'Nice.'

'Very.'

Almost everyone had left apart from the Sedgworths. Dottie saw that the major was talking to the coroner and a clergyman. Dottie didn't know whether to suggest that they wait and have a word with him, or whether it would be better to simply leave.

'Good afternoon, Miss Manderson.'

Dottie turned to see Gervase's secretary, Mrs Holcombe, standing there.

'Mrs Holcombe. I didn't realise you were here. How are you?'

'Very well, thank you. And yourself?'

Dottie said she was well, thank you. They exchanged a few words about the sad occasion. Then, seeing Mrs Holcombe looking at William with undisguised interest, Dottie said, 'I'm sorry, I don't think you two have met. This is my friend, William Hardy. Mr Hardy is visiting his family in the area and heard I was here. I know Mr Hardy from London. It is Mr Hardy who is related to Mr Allsopp whom I believe you said you know?'

'Only very slightly. How do you do, Mr Hardy.' Mrs Holcombe smiled at him, and William treated her to his most charming smile in return, and shook her hand.

'Mrs Holcombe is Gervase's secretary, Mr Hardy,' Dottie said, hoping her formal manner would be noted by him.

'And you knew the Sedgworths, I understand?' he immediately said. 'You were a friend of Mrs Sedgworth?'

Mrs Holcombe agreed that she and Mrs Sedgworth had been good friends. She was clearly upset.

'Mrs Holcombe, will you join us for tea at the village pub? I'd really like to talk to you.'

'The pub?' Mrs Holcombe seemed rather scandalised by the idea. But she said, 'I'm sorry, I'm afraid I don't go into public houses, Miss Manderson. Er—well, I'm a Methodist, you see. So I'm afraid I couldn't, even though it would only be for tea. But why not come to my house? It's not far. A few minutes' walk. I'd be delighted...'

Her invitation seemed to be extended solely to Dottie. William hastily excused himself, saying he had to go and have a word with someone. Dottie said goodbye to him reluctantly and very formally. Then she and Mrs Holcombe set off along the road.

'A Very Attractive Man,' Mrs Holcombe commented with a smile. 'Is he married?'

'Engaged,' Dottie said.

Mrs Holcombe nodded. 'And what does he do for a living?'

Dottie hesitated. She wasn't sure if he would want her to say. Not that he was exactly working undercover. But would Mrs Holcombe clam up completely, if she found out William was a policeman?

So she said as lightly as she could. 'Oh, he's in the same line as Gervase.'

Mrs Holcombe stopped in her tracks. 'Oh?' She glanced back along the road to where the Very Attractive Man was talking to the other policemen. 'He's in the police?'

'In London. The Metropolitan Police. Not as high up as

Gervase. He's an inspector.'

'But he's not here to work? I mean...?'

'Just having some time off to spend with his family.' Dottie had to risk a lie here. Judging by the dismay on Mrs Holcombe's face, Dottie instinctively felt that Mrs Holcombe might retreat if she thought William was actually on an investigation. Dottie was not prepared to lose her chance of finding out what Mrs Sedgworth had been going to tell her.

Mrs Holcombe said nothing more. They walked on. A minute later, she stepped through a gateway, saying, 'Here we are.'

Here was a small thatched cottage with a front garden that in summer would be full of bright flowers. Already early shoots were poking shyly above the soil, sheltered from the worst of the winter winds by the sturdy wooden fence. One or two daffodils were ready to unfurl from their papery casing.

Once inside, Mrs Holcombe invited Dottie to make herself comfortable in the parlour. Taking Dottie's coat and hat away to hang up, Mrs Holcombe then went into the kitchen to put on the kettle to make the tea.

The parlour was neat, bright and airy, and ran the full length of the house from front to back, with a window at either end. Dottie found the room charming, and comfortable in spite of being sparsely furnished. The clear lines and lack of fuss or clutter was restful, especially after the emotionally demanding nature of the inquest.

Dottie drifted into a kind of daydream as she sat looking into space. She only roused herself when Mrs Holcombe came in with the tea-tray.

'I almost fell asleep. It's so peaceful here, a real haven.'

Mrs Holcombe seemed quite touched by that. 'Thank you. I love it here. I've lived here all my life, actually. My mother came here as a bride in 1892, and she lived here until her death in 1932, so a good long while.'

'You must miss her.'

'Yes.'

'And your father, does he still...?' Dottie tried to phrase

the question delicately, suspecting she already knew the answer would not be a happy one.

'Oh no, he died last year. It's just me now.'

'And Mr Holcombe,' Dottie suggested.

Mrs Holcombe halted abruptly in the act of pouring their tea, her expression was one of dismay. A dull brick-coloured blush spread from her neck to her forehead and ears. 'Oh—er...' She seemed unable to explain.

Dottie felt for her. She said hastily, 'I'm so sorry, where are my manners. I didn't mean to pry. Do forget I asked. My mother's always telling me I talk too much.'

Mrs Holcombe concentrated on the tea. For the next few minutes they were occupied with adding milk and stirring. These ordinary tasks gave Mrs Holcombe time to compose herself.

Then Dottie said, 'I thought the inquest went well. Though it's a shame that the coroner couldn't, for the major's sake, have ruled death by misadventure, or accidental death. But I suppose he couldn't exactly rewrite the rules. But poor Major Sedgworth, he looked a shadow of himself.'

Mrs Holcombe nodded. 'Did he tell you how she was the rest of the day you were supposed to have coffee with her?'

Dottie said, 'No, he didn't.' She waited, but her hostess contributed nothing further, so she said, 'I do wish I knew why Mrs Sedgworth invited me to coffee with her that morning. I felt sure she wanted to tell me something. Perhaps you have some ideas about that?'

It wasn't subtle, she knew, but she felt she had to push a little.

Mrs Holcombe, avoiding Dottie's eye, said, 'I? Oh no sorry. I can't help you at all. Surely she was just being friendly, as you said at the inquest. Welcoming you to the area. It's the sort of thing she would have done.'

'I got the impression you and she were close friends.'

But Mrs Holcombe denied it just as Dottie had somehow known she would. 'Oh no,' she said again. 'We'd met once or twice recently at various social events that Mr Parfitt had been kind enough to invite me along to. I just thought she seemed a pleasant woman.'

'And you don't know anything about her?' Dottie asked. She knew as soon as she'd said it that she'd been too blunt. She had to feel her way so carefully with Mrs Holcombe. The slightest wrong word or phrase seemed to make her close up completely. How could she get her to talk? She was certain Mrs Holcombe knew more than she was telling.

'Do excuse me, I must just put the kettle back on to boil, in case we need a top-up.'

Dottie felt frustrated. She wanted to be friends with Mrs Holcombe, she felt they *could* become friends, and yet, Mrs Holcombe wouldn't trust her. Could it be that she was afraid of something? Or *someone*, perhaps?

Dottie sat back, cradling her teacup, and waited.

When after several minutes, Mrs Holcombe hadn't come back, Dottie got up to go and look out of the window. She saw a small but impressively neat kitchen garden behind the house. She stood watching a blackbird pecking between the few last cabbages and leeks.

Finally Mrs Holcombe returned. Dottie turned and said, 'Your kitchen garden is beautifully kept, Mrs Holcombe.'

As she turned back from the window, her eyes alighted on a framed photograph of a man, a woman and two girls, one quite small, perhaps three or four, the other appeared to be in her late teens. The older child was quite obviously Mrs Holcombe.

Mrs Holcombe made a laughing comment about the garden, but her wary eyes were watching Dottie. She held herself rigidly, as if afraid of what Dottie might say about the photos. Dottie said nothing immediately, but returned to her seat and picked up her cup and saucer. Over the rim of her cup, she remarked blandly, 'Photographs are such a comforting reminder, aren't they?'

Then she began to tell Mrs Holcombe about Flora's children and the efforts the family had gone to, trying to get some good photos of them sitting side by side.

Another cup of tea and twenty minutes more of unrevealing conversation, and Dottie felt able to rise, thank Mrs Holcombe for her kindness and say goodbye. The whole visit had just been a waste of time.

At the door, Mrs Holcombe said, 'I hope we will see each other again soon, Miss Manderson. I expect you'll visit the area frequently up to your marriage?'

'Oh very likely.' Dottie smiled. 'And are you quite sure you don't have any suggestions as to what Mrs Sedgworth wanted to say to me?'

Mrs Holcombe, neatly turning the tables on her, said, 'Can you remember what you and she had been talking about when she invited you to go for coffee?'

'No, I was hoping you could remember.'

'I'm sorry, no,' Mrs Holcombe said. 'Well perhaps it will come back to you later. Do let me know if it does. I shall be racking my brains about it.'

As Dottie came away, she couldn't help wondering why she felt as though she had been the one being interrogated.

'I've made up a fire in the drawing room, miss, and also in Mr Parfitt's study. I wasn't sure which room you might prefer to sit in. The drawing room is grand and more up-to-date, but the study is rather cosier if one is sitting alone. And there are plenty of books to choose from, though perhaps not all to your taste, miss.'

Dottie looked at Michaels, wondering if there was any hidden meaning to his words. His expression was mild, giving no indication of any kind.

'I imagine Gervase's taste in books is quite unlike mine.'

'True, miss. Although there are books of what you might term a general sort. It's turned much colder this evening, miss, so to my way of thinking, with Mr Parfitt away, I thought you might like to be snug and cosy in the smaller room.'

She thanked him, adding, 'It's not often I get the chance to sit in his study, as he is usually in there—er—working. So it will make a nice change from the drawing room. It was very good of Mr Parfitt to invite me to stay here even though he knew he would be away.'

'At a conference, I believe, miss?'

'Yes. In Bournemouth.'

'Very nice, miss. Very bracing, the sea air is, and good for the constitution. Even in the middle of winter.' He moved towards the door as if about to leave, then turned back to add, 'Oh by the way, miss, your dinner, or supper, as Cook calls it when it's laid out as a buffet, that will be in the dining room on the sideboard as usual for you to serve yourself when you're ready. I'll bring it through directly. There's some soup, and some little pies and roast potatoes. It's not a cold buffet. Not at this time of year, miss.' He shuddered at the thought.

'Thank you, Mr Michaels, that sounds lovely.'

'I'd say the study would be the best place to start.'

'Start?' She gave him a puzzled look.

'Yes miss. Then later you may prefer to switch to the drawing room for a change. So as not to spend the whole evening in one room. It can be dull, if you're on your own.'

Again, she could find nothing in his words that anyone might use against him, and yet...

'Thank you, Mr Michaels,' she said again.

'It's no trouble at all, miss, my pleasure entirely.' He gave her a slight bow and a definite smile, and left.

It felt quite daring, going into Gervase's study when he wasn't there. But Michaels was right. It was very snug in here, perhaps because of the darker, more masculine colour scheme, or the bright fire, or the heavy curtains pulled across the windows to shut out the miserable weather.

She perched on the edge of one of the sofas, slipped off her shoes, and stretched toes and fingers towards the fire, enjoying the warmth after the biting wind and rain.

She could hear the sound of the butler going back and forth, carrying dishes into the dining room for her meal. Down in the kitchen and scullery, the cook and other maids would be cooking, clearing away, and cleaning all the pots and pans and china. It seemed so much trouble for the whole staff to go to, providing food for just one person. At home, none of the Mandersons' staff had the same evening off except on very special occasions, and in any case, she was hardly ever there alone.

Dottie looked about her. It was more like a small sitting room than an office.

There was a desk, of course, and the usual pair of leather armchairs beside one of the bookcases, with a small table set between them for drinks or books. There was another larger table too, in case books needed to be lifted down in quantity, though she guessed that only the staff ever looked closely at the books, no doubt as they cleaned. She couldn't remember ever seeing Gervase read a book.

The area in front of the fire held a deep plush rug, two long sofas and a coffee table. It was very similar to the drawing room layout. These sofas were a match for those in there. The room was smaller, the furniture placed closer together, but other than that, there was little difference.

A small side table held a radio. Dottie went over to it now and turned it on. After a minute or so, it was warmed up and the sound filtered through. It was some kind of political discussion about 'the European Question'. Men with upper-class accents argued with one another politely and with no real passion. Dottie wrinkled her nose and changed the station, turning the dial carefully. Soon she was rewarded by the sound of the announcer saying, 'And now, live from the Belle Vue ballroom in London, we bring you an evening of dance music.'

'Ooh good!' she said, and stayed with that station. She stood in front of the fire for a while swaying gently in time to the music.

She shook her head in wonder as she thought how impossible this would be if Gervase was here. To think she had ever thought herself in love with him. That too seemed impossible now. It had become so hard to conceal her feelings. She was sure he was having the same difficulty. He said the right things—most of the time—almost as if he had made notes on the right thing to say at the right moment, but his expressions told their own story. Now that he had Moira in his life, Dottie was very much surplus to requirements.

In any case, Gervase didn't seem to be one for cosy evenings at home. He seemed to have some engagement or other almost every night. She couldn't picture him sitting with her in the evenings, alone and relaxed, perhaps chatting or reading. Or just the two of them dancing to some love song on the radio.

William, on the other hand...

She indulged herself in her favourite daydream where she pictured herself doing something—sewing, or designing a new evening gown or something like that—sitting at the table in William's kitchen, and he would be there too, sitting at that same table, going through some work papers, reading witness statements or making notes, or even just reading for pleasure. In the background the radio would be playing softly. They would glance at one another from time to time and smile. Or one of them would make them both a cup of tea. They'd talk. It would be lovely.

You couldn't do that with Gervase. With Gervase you had to lock your door at night. Of course if it was William... She sighed wistfully. She'd never lock William out of her room. In fact, she'd insist on them having the same room. It was quite common now, even among her own class where the family home had plenty of rooms to choose from, for married couples to share a bedroom. To be with William every night, to wake at night and hear him breathing—probably snoring loudly, she admitted—beside her. To wake to find him there. To be held in his arms and kissed. To...

There was a sharp tap on the door that jolted her out of her daydream. The door opened. Dottie stopped moving to the music and stood there, embarrassed, like a schoolgirl caught mooning over a film actor's picture.

'Everything's ready in the dining room, miss, whenever you are.'

'Oh thank you. I'm sorry to give everyone so much extra work when Mr Parfitt is away and you probably reckoned to have an easy day.'

'Miss Manderson, it's our pleasure.' He grinned at her—
a very human grin that made him seem a lot younger. 'I'm
glad you've got the radio on, miss. I wasn't sure if you
would notice it, tucked away there in the corner. A bit of
music always brightens you up, I always say. Just ring if
there's anything you need, miss. The girls are off, but I'll
still be here.'

She thanked him and he departed.

She moved about the room, trying and failing to
imagine Gervase doing any work here. She could imagine
him laughing and talking with his male friends. Drinking
and smoking, most definitely. Or 'carrying on' with some
woman. Moira. Or someone else. There would always be
someone else's fiancée to conduct a liaison with, yes, she
could easily imagine him doing that. Even after they were
married, should such a thing ever come to pass, he would
be one of those men who always had some other woman
on the side. No doubt at every social function there would
be some lovely thing there, and you'd ask yourself, is it
her?

But working in here? No. She had great difficulty
picturing him working. By an association of ideas, she
went to sit in the large leather chair behind the desk. Very
comfortable, was her first thought. It was one of those
seats that tilted forward slightly, to give the sitter a more
comfortable position when working at the desk.

She leaned her elbows on the desk and propped her
chin as she looked about her.

Everything was just so. The blotting paper in the blotter
was fresh and clean. The pens and ink were neatly placed
in one corner and perfectly free of dust. Beside them was a
little stand with rubber stamps and an ink pad; the pad
was clean—there were none of those oozy inky marks
around the edge of the pad that come from not placing the
stamp in the centre properly. The stamps themselves were
still of the same clean red rubber with which they had left
the factory. In the other corner of the desk was a low
shaded lamp. That was all.

Dottie thought about her desk at the warehouse. Its

cluttered surface had very little room for such things as stands bearing rubber stamps. There were odd buttons, scraps of paper, bits of ribbon and lace, scissors, needles, dress-making pins and safety-pins. There were bolts of fabric and designs heaped up on orders, invoices, notes to herself, notes from other people. Tape measures. Buckles. Dress-maker's chalk. More buttons. And, as like as not, a cup half-full of cold tea. When she sat at her desk, she was surrounded by the tools of her trade.

She looked about her. Just where were the tools of Gervase's trade? At the police headquarters in Ripley? In his office there? She wondered. Perhaps she'd ask Mrs Holcombe the next time she saw her. Dottie was willing to bet Mrs Holcombe's desk resembled hers at the warehouse, and that Gervase's desk in his office was just the same as his desk here. She suspected Gervase was not one of life's workers. He enjoyed an easy time of it, and felt entitled to do so by virtue of his background and now of course, his much-vaunted status.

Still vaguely pondering that thought she pulled out the top drawer at her right hand. This was fairly full, but still not truly cluttered. No papers of any sort. Just the sort of old stuff everyone shoves into a drawer: drawing pins, glue, a couple of those rubber finger things for counting bank notes very quickly or going through a pile of papers. More rubber stamps—what on earth did he need all those for? Pencils. Broken pens and spare pen nibs. A pen knife, three not-quite-empty ink bottles in black and blue-black. An eraser. A bulldog clip for holding papers together. Sixpence in pennies and ha'pennies. A piece of dusty sealing wax. But no seal, she noted—that was the only rubber stamp he didn't seem to have. Rubber bands. A lot of old rubbish really, it could probably all be thrown away and never once missed, she thought.

Beyond the room, outside in the drizzle, Gervase Parfitt was looking in through the tiny gap in the curtains and watching her movements.

He had approached cautiously, seeing the light on in his

study. Clearly he'd have to wait until the person was gone. If it was that fool Michaels he'd better not be snooping.

Gervase watched her dancing about to the music on the radio—he couldn't hear the music but had seen her turn the radio on. He thought, not for the first time, that she was graceful and appealing, and felt furious that she had refused and evaded him. It was a good thing Moira wasn't so unkind. Not that he expected to marry Moira: his parents had never approved of her, but he had to admit, she was easy to get along with, and they understood one another.

He pulled his collar up around his neck to keep the worst of the weather out, then watched as Dottie took a seat at the desk. He saw her opening a drawer. He was practically holding his breath, afraid of fogging up the glass and missing something.

Unaware she was being watched, Dottie pulled out the top left-hand drawer.

This was more interesting. There was a small pile of papers, and underneath those, a couple of little account books, of the sort that her mother and cook used to keep track of expenses and bills paid. A quick glance showed her a few figures in columns with the odd name here and there on each page. Christobel Sedgworth, Katie Cutler, Gordon Wisley, Fred McRae, and Moira Hansom were just a few of the ones she noticed. The names intrigued Dottie, but she couldn't work out what the figures meant. She assumed the figures were money, some in red, some in black, but what did it mean? She shoved them back into the drawer. She would mention the books to William.

But there was rubbish too—an old cigarette end with red lipstick smeared on it. She wrinkled her nose in disgust and put it in the wastepaper bin. Two old cinema ticket stubs. A photograph of an elderly woman, by her clothes and the setting, clearly not a relative, as she had to be working class, perhaps a nanny or former member of staff, someone like that. Although on the back of the photo it said, 'Mum, May 1928'. It was most definitely not

Gervase's mother—and like all men of his background, he only ever called his mother, 'Mother', never the cosy, working-class 'Mum'. The photo intrigued Dottie enormously. She spent several minutes looking at it. The woman looked friendly and reassuringly normal. Her smile was small and a little stiff—no surprise if she'd had to hold that pose for the time it took to expose the film back in 1928. Was it reading too much into it to say the woman also looked a little nervous? Dottie had seen that wary half-frozen expression before on the faces of older ladies in photographs. They weren't as used to being photographed as younger people were.

'Who are you?' Dottie asked the woman. Perhaps she was the mother of a previous member of Gervase's staff, and they had left it behind when they moved on to another job. Perhaps he'd kept it in case they asked for it? If someone had lost a treasured photo of their mother, they'd be terribly upset. Not that it was like Gervase to concern himself with the feelings of others, especially not those whom he considered his social inferiors.

Dottie put these things back and continued her nosing about.

There were two more drawers on each side. The second one down on the right contained a folder of what could only be described as highly pornographic pictures. Dottie closed the folder hurriedly as soon as she realised what she was looking at, and put it back in the drawer, her cheeks hot.

The bottom drawer on the right was locked.

On the left-hand side, the middle drawer contained a metal cashbox and a small bunch of keys. With a guilty sense that she was taking too much advantage of the situation, and the abhorrence of prying that was due to her upbringing, she nevertheless grabbed the keys and tried each one in the lock of the bottom right-hand drawer. None of them fitted. So she turned back to the metal cashbox, lifting it out onto the desktop. She reached for the bunch of keys again. This time she found a key that looked about right, and tried it in the lock. It turned perfectly easily, the lid coming up quietly and smoothly to reveal a hearty little stash of money.

Dottie stared. It appeared to be mainly £5 and £1 banknotes but with a few £10 notes too. She didn't waste time counting the money but from the size of the heap, bound by rubber bands, she guessed there was likely to be several hundred pounds: a fortune! And in the bottom of the box, lying loose, there were a couple of dozen crowns and half-sovereigns.

Even though she was alone, she could feel her cheeks flaming with embarrassment at her snooping. She'd got rather carried away and now felt guilty and uncomfortable. With a sense of urgency, she quickly locked the box again and replaced both it and the keys. She closed all the drawers and decided it was well past time to go and get some food.

Gervase was livid. How dared she pry and spy like that? Poking about amongst the personal things in the desk. Searching the contents like a cheap little sneak? Moira had been right about her. As he peered through the gap in the curtains, looking in from outside like some dirty little thief, he thought about how he'd like to go in there and wring her neck. His fists clenched now just at the thought of it.

It was almost worth it. No one would know he'd been there. With the staff out of the way, no one would find out until the morning, or at least not for a few hours. It would only be what she deserved, the two-faced scheming little bitch, and put an end to this thorn in his side once and for all.

She'd come pretty close to finding him out, had actually had her hand on some very damning stuff, but the idiot didn't know what she was looking at. Luckily for him. He'd need to deal with this before things got out of control, he was too much at risk.

He'd almost laughed when she'd found the pictures. How very like her, little miss prim, to blush like a child and push them away. Too moralistic, too idealistic by half.

Not that she'd recognise any of the people in the photos, but even so. Oh she just wasn't worth the effort. To think she'd turned on him in this way, taking advantage of his absence to spy, pry and rummage through his things. He'd make sure she regretted that.

Dottie crossed the hall to the dining room, seeing and hearing nothing unusual as she went, yet still trying to shake off the eerie sensation of not being alone in the house, even though she knew it was only dear Mr Michaels somewhere in the back of the house, no doubt in the kitchen or his minuscule but cosy sitting room.

The soup was still hot. Carrot and herb, she thought. The scent of it made her stomach growl. She ladled some into a bowl, and added some bread and butter, a small hot meat pie of some sort, then on second thoughts, added another. She cut herself a slice of apple pie, slathered on cream, put everything onto a tray along with a glass of water and a glass of white wine. It was quite heavy as she carried the tray back to the study, and sat cross-legged in the corner of a sofa beside the fire. The radio was still playing dance songs, and all in all, she felt very cosy and comfortable.

Half an hour later, the plates were empty, as were the glasses. The dance programme had ended and now the news came on. Dottie listened to the start of yet more depressing reports of unrest in mainland Europe, an anxious knot in the pit of her stomach. Gervase, William and her father agreed only on one topic: sooner or later, there was going to be another war. Her mother said, 'Nonsense,' with a toss of the head and a tone of voice which firmly closed the subject every time.

Yet Dottie knew it was not that her mother was living in a world of make-believe, nor that she really thought it *was* nonsense. It was more that, having lived through the terror of the first war, the 'war to end all wars', she felt an absolute horror at contemplating the possibility of a second. Her mother had often said, the waiting was the worst.

Dottie and Flora had talked about it when alone. The notion that their men—that thousands, if not millions, of women's men—might have to serve, might be lost forever, was too awful to bear. All those sons and husbands, lovers and fathers. She didn't want to hear this when she was all alone. She changed the station hurriedly and found some classical music. Surely even a bit of opera had to be better than the news?

But it was coming towards the end of *Pagliacci*, and as the clown's fateful words rose on the evening air, Dottie shivered and felt the goosebumps crawl down her arms. The very air seemed chilled, and before it could take a hold of her mood, she turned off the radio with a rapid hand.

The silence was deafening by contrast. She hadn't been quick enough to turn it off, and she felt sombre now, creepy and fidgety and full of fears that made her start at shadows. She sat wondering if she should just give up and go to bed.

She carried her tray back to the dining room. As she crossed the hall, Michaels was coming towards her. He hurried to relieve her of the tray.

'I wondered if you'd like coffee, miss? Or anything else? A port, perhaps, or sherry?'

'I'm quite all right, thank you. I will probably go up to bed shortly.'

'Very good, miss. In that case, if you don't need me again tonight, as soon as I've cleared the sideboard, I shall turn in too. An early night is always very welcome, especially in the wintertime. I have locked the front door.' He hesitated as he turned away towards the dining room door. 'Er—you may hear cook and the girls coming in at the back door at about eleven o'clock. I hope they won't disturb you. They're usually very quiet. But if you do hear anything, that's all it will be. Nothing at all to worry about.'

They said goodnight.

Dottie went back to the study. She returned to her spot in the corner of the sofa and sat thinking. The brief exchange with another human being had cheered her mood. She felt like continuing her investigation.

She remembered she had not checked the bottom left drawer of the desk. She did so now. She got a shock as she looked down to see what the drawer contained. There was only one thing: a revolver. She looked at it for a few seconds, but didn't touch it. She closed the drawer.

She felt frustrated by her lack of success, though if pressed, she couldn't have said what she had hoped to find.

In any case... and why hadn't this occurred to her sooner? ...surely Gervase wasn't foolish enough to keep anything incriminating right here in his own study?

She went to the bookshelves and poked about there, checking for dummy books or concealed handles to secret rooms. But rather disappointingly, they appeared to be just bookshelves, and the books were just books.

Dottie sank back onto the sofa, and gazed into space. She huffed out a long breath of air, and as always, her rebellious fringe blew up into the air then she felt it gently float back into place, framing her forehead and temples.

It was so galling. She had endured a difficult weekend the previous weekend, all in the name of helping the man she loved, and what had she to show for it? N...

Nothing?

No. Frowning she went back to the desk. She pulled all the drawers out again and looked at the things she had looked at before. The cinema ticket stubs. She looked at them now with fresh interest.

Why keep them? Gervase was not a particularly sentimental man. He didn't go in for sighing looks—except in respect of what Dottie termed 'bedroom matters', when he thought he was being seductive and loving, rather than merely irritating. He didn't go in for tokens of love. He composed no painfully embarrassing sonnets. He sang her no love songs of his own devising. He hadn't sent her flowers since those first few weeks of their relationship. He didn't keep the first whatever: first rose, first letter, first theatre programme, or whatever to commemorate their time together. He was not a keepsake type of chap. So?

These were just the usual ticket stubs made of thick pink paper. They were printed with the usual serial number, in this case two consecutive numbers, 7724 and 7725. The paper was not fresh. It appeared a little faded and old, not exactly decades old, but neither were they three weeks' fresh. The name of the cinema was printed on the reverse: The Rialto, Nottingham.

She put the stubs back where they'd come from, then picked up the photograph of the old lady again. This also had something else printed on the back: Jinkson's of Nottingham.

She thought she heard a slight sound. It made her jump up guiltily, but she couldn't tell what she had heard. As before, she became aware of the liberty she was taking. In a hurry, fingers trembling, she replaced the photo where she had found it, quickly and quietly closed the drawer then came back to sit on the sofa in front of the fire.

That money bothered her too. She wondered if she was simply making mountains out of molehills. The money could simply be the wages for the staff for the next few months. That seemed probable and innocuous. That had to be it, of course. She had been so silly, thinking it was a sign of something sinister. She felt the lightness of relief.

It was just a practical, prosaic means of dealing with an ordinary household responsibility. She smiled at her own foolishness. William was to blame, she thought, making her see threat and danger everywhere, turning ordinary things into a mystery.

She sighed. She was bored, she was tired. It was time to go to bed, although barely a quarter past nine. At least if the staff did make any noise coming back from their evening out, in one and three-quarter hours' time, she was unlikely to hear it: with any luck she'd be sound asleep.

As cook and the two live-in maids came up the drive from the village street at around ten minutes to eleven o'clock, they were startled out of their discussion of who was the most swoon-worthy out of a choice of Gary Cooper, Clark

Gable, Jack Buchanon, or Ronald Colman, by a sudden movement across the far end of the drive ahead of them, close to the corner of the house. A tall figure—a man—ran across the gravel and into the bushes on the other side.

Maureen, young and easily frightened, let out a kind of strangled squeak in shock, whereas Cook shouted 'Oi!' in a very robust manner. The figure halted momentarily then fled, easily outstripping them both and disappearing into the shadows.

Cautious with suspicion, the three women let themselves in at the back door, and once the kitchen light was on, Cook hurried to lock the door behind them.

'In case he comes back again!' she said, arming herself with a rolling pin. 'He'll have me to deal with!'

The young maid squeaked again and looked at Cook with admiration. Cook had one, and only one solution to all of life's difficulties: put the kettle on, not an easy task with a rolling pin in one hand.

Trying to follow Cook's calm example, Lizzie gathered up the few empty dishes onto the tray. She said, 'I'll just quickly wash these few pots, so they're not left until morning,' and she carried them through to the scullery.

Cook said, 'My Michaels hasn't brought back the Thermos. The soup was in that. I'll go and fetch it, it'll need a wash too. You know how hard it is to clean if the soup gets all stuck round inside.'

'If there's any soup left, I wouldn't mind it for a spot of supper before I go up,' called the Lizzie over her shoulder.

Only a matter of seconds later, the maids heard Cook's running feet coming back. Looking round to see what the matter was, she saw Cook's eyes were wide with shock.

'We've been broke into!'

'What? Never!' Maureen was on her feet and rushing to Cook's side.

'I swear. The dining room window's been smashed in. There's glass all over. Come and see!'

They went hurrying back together.

They stood in the doorway and stared at the gaping hole in the window. A breeze billowed the curtains and brought in the cold night air. The slivers of glass on the carpet twinkled gently in the light from the chandelier overhead.

'The young lady!' Maureen said. 'What if she's hurt!'

As one they left the dining room and ran up the front stairs, too alarmed to go through to use the back stairs. They rapped on Dottie's door.

'Come in,' she called out, sleepy and struggling to sit up, blinking in the light spilling in from the hall.

'Oh miss! Are you all right?'

Puzzled, Dottie said, 'Yes, I'm quite all right, thank you. Why? What's happened?'

'Oh miss,' said Cook again. 'We've been broke into!'

*

Chapter Ten

'The police is on their way,' Cook told Dottie as she came downstairs two minutes later, still knotting the belt of her wrap.

From the back hall, Michaels came in—a striped dressing gown over striped pyjamas worn with work boots—and asked what was going on.

They told their story of the man they had seen as they came along the drive. Michaels ran back to the kitchen to return with a poker in one hand and a cleaver in the other.

'Stay here, ladies,' he said. 'There could be someone still in the house.'

Dottie said, 'I really don't think...' at the same time as Mrs Michaels said, 'They must of gone by now, Bob.'

'All the same,' he said grimly. Slowly and carefully he began to go from room to room. The four women clustered together at the foot of the stairs, watching him anxiously, but with a touch of excitement.

He eased open the dining room door as silently as he could, then used his elbow to snap on the light and braced himself in the doorway.

There was no one there. He went across to examine the

window, clearly the entry point, taking care not to touch anything. Apart from the broken window, and the scatter of glass, nothing was out of place. He risked putting down the poker for a few seconds to open the drawers of the dresser. They could plainly see all the silver was safely in place.

'Nothing missing from here,' he called. 'Keep out of here, though, in case the police need to see it. I'll clear up that glass later.'

The ladies had no intention of going into the room in any case, but Dottie thought it was sweet of him to be so considerate.

He withdrew, and made his way to the drawing room.

His wife said: 'Bob, me duck, I don't think you should. Wait till the police get here.' Her hand was clutching her throat, her initial courage gone. Lizzie gripped Cook's arm, and Dottie's too. Maureen, standing behind all three of them, had eyes like saucers in the dim light, her face pale and tense. Dottie gave her a smile.

'How we'll all enjoy talking about this once the danger's over,' she said.

Maureen managed a little smile in return.

Michaels threw open the drawing room door and with a loud, 'Aha!' turned to face into the room, weapons raised, his elbow again doing the job of turning on the light.

There was no one there. The room looked just as it always looked. Not so much as a cushion was out of place. The little knot of ladies behind Michaels heaved a sigh of relief, though Michaels himself looked a little disappointed.

'The study, then,' he said. 'Just to make sure.'

He performed the same moves, but this time as he snapped on the light and stood ready to confront a villain, Dottie could see that beyond him the room was in disarray. This, then, was where the burglar had gone to work. The drawers of the desk had been pulled out and the contents scattered. All of them. Even the locked drawer had been yanked out with something like a crowbar, Dottie surmised, judging by the splintered wood of both desk and drawer. About a third of the books were off the shelves and littering the floor, some torn, some just lying in heaps. There were papers everywhere.

At that moment someone pounded on the front door and shouted. Inside the house, they all jumped, startled, then Cook said, 'That'll be the police.'

Michaels ran to let them in.

Cook sent Lizzie and Maureen back to the kitchen to get some coffee and sandwiches ready. It would doubtless be some time before anyone got to bed. 'And everyone knows the police drink their own weight in tea and coffee,' she grumbled to Dottie who nodded. In her experience, yes, they certainly did.

Michaels lay aside his weapons and began to gather up the scattered papers. Dottie put a hand on his arm.

'I'm sorry, Mr Michaels, but you can't do that. The police will want everything left just as it was.'

'But these are Mr Parfitt's *private* papers, miss. I'm sure he wouldn't want...'

Dottie shook her head. 'Leave it. They will want to speak to you. And they will want to see this room.'

She turned to see two uniformed men and a man in a suit coming through the hall in their direction. The suited man introduced himself as Sergeant Fulford of the Nottinghamshire police. Dottie had seen him before with William, both outside the Sedgworth's house and at the inquest. If he recognised her, he said nothing.

To Michaels he said quite sternly, 'Leave that at once. You're not to touch anything until my men and I have examined this room thoroughly.'

Michaels dropped the papers he was holding, and assumed a meek acquiescence. 'Of course, sir. Sorry sir.'

Fulford despatched the two uniformed men to look around the house, in case an intruder was hiding there.

As succinctly as possible Michaels, Cook and the two maids told the policeman what had happened. The maids seemed upset by the presence of the police. Dottie noticed they looked at Mr Michaels a good deal as if asking for his confirmation of events. Not that he would know, because like me, he was in bed, Dottie thought.

Sergeant Fulford viewed the broken window in the dining room, then returned to the study. Dottie and the staff were asked to leave. Dottie went to the drawing room, and the staff returned to the kitchen. Presently Maureen came along with sandwiches and coffee for Dottie. Dottie wasn't hungry but the coffee was hot and comforting.

After another five minutes or so, Dottie heard the tramp of feet as the uniformed men went upstairs. When they eventually came down again, Fulford sent them off to look around outside.

The sergeant came to the drawing room, mainly for the coffee and sandwiches, she suspected, then asked Dottie a few desultory questions: where was the home-owner, what was her relationship to the home-owner, did he know she was there, when was he returning, what had she been doing when the break-in occurred, and so forth.

He didn't seem especially interested in the investigation. Dottie considered that he was put out at having been called from his bed late at night, the status of the owner of the house notwithstanding. He disposed of three sandwiches and two cups of coffee, snapped his notebook shut and prepared to leave with a casual, 'If you have any more upsets, please call the local station.'

Gervase will be livid, she thought. She could almost hear him saying in his clipped sarcastic voice, 'Do you know who I am?'

'I'll send someone out in the morning to check for fingerprints,' Fulford said from the door. 'Probably a waste of time, though. We never catch 'em. But anyway, no one is to go into the study, nor can you use the dining room until we say so. Thank you for your cooperation. Goodnight.'

And he left. Michaels persuaded the women to go to bed, promising to keep an eye on things until it seemed the uniformed men had finished outside. He locked the door of the dining room. A fierce draught was blowing under the door, and he lay an old thick curtain across the bottom of the door to keep the worst at bay.

'I'll get someone out first thing to fix that window, miss, we can't have that wind blowing through the place.'

Dottie nodded then said goodnight and went up to her room. A glance out of the window showed the two policemen still going back and forth with their electric torches shining. Not that they will find anything or anyone now. He'll be long gone, she thought.

She got into bed, and was asleep almost immediately.

It seemed as if Lizzie woke her just minutes after she fell asleep, but the alarm clock showed that it was almost nine-thirty.

'There's a policeman downstairs miss. He's not that fellow who was here last night. This one's some good-looking chap from London.'

Dottie leapt out of bed and began rummaging through her suitcase, selecting and discarding clothes.

'Shall I bring you up a cup of tea, miss?'

'Oh no, it's all right. I'll be down in about ten minutes. Will you tell Inspector Hardy that? And give him some tea, too please.'

'Of course, miss.' Lizzie bobbed and left.

In a rush, Dottie washed, dressed and added some discreet make-up—she was sure that blemish on her chin wasn't there yesterday—and more or less tamed her hair, all within the promised ten minutes.

He was waiting in the drawing room, perched on the edge of one of the Chippendale-style chairs, a delicate china cup and saucer balanced on his knee. He looked very uncomfortable.

Dottie stood in the doorway, trying to resist the urge to run and fling her arms about his neck. Instead, she clasped her hands in front of her, and asked him if he'd like to come through to the morning room, where she was going to have breakfast.

He followed her through, pulled out a chair and sat down, placing the cup and saucer on the table with an alarming rattle. He pulled a face. 'Sorry. Don't think I broke anything.'

She shook her head, grinning. 'Men!' she said. She removed the delicate china and gave him a clean, more robust cup and saucer of tea, remembering how he took it. 'Better?'

'Much. Thanks.' He reached for a slice of toast, buttered it and ate half before he put any marmalade on it. He laughed at her raised eyebrow.

'Didn't have time to eat anything this morning. I've been at the police station since seven.'

'In that case...' She heaped bacon and eggs onto a plate and passed it to him. 'They've made far too much just for me.'

'Nice place you've got here.' He looked around with a grin, which came to rest on her.

'It's a lot nicer without Gervase, I must say.'

She looked at him. He certainly looked ridiculously gorgeous this morning. She felt hot and flustered, and here he was calmly eating breakfast in the camp of his enemy. How dare he be so at ease, grinning at her like that when she hadn't had so much as a cup of tea. She poured herself one now.

'I understand you had some excitement here last night?'

'Well, I don't know about excitement. I slept right through most of it.'

'I'm rather glad you did,' he said. 'But I've read through the statements taken by Sergeant Fulford. The cook and both maids were returning from their evening out and actually saw the man outside, apparently, as he was making his getaway.'

'Yes. He got in through the dining room window, but only seems to have ransacked Gervase's study. The drawers were pulled out of the desk, a locked one was smashed open, the drawers' contents seem to have been thrown all over the place, and books pulled out of the bookcases.'

'Anything missing?'

'I don't know. We were told to get out as soon as the police arrived, and before that, I wouldn't let anyone touch anything. They did start to pick up papers, but I told them not to, that the scene shouldn't be touched until the police had seen it. So I don't think too much damage was done.'

William nodded. 'It could have been worse. Thanks for keeping everyone back as best you could. Staff will do it, I'm afraid, it's their training. I'll take a look in a bit, and ask Mr Michaels and you to go with me to see if you can work out if anything has been taken.'

'Are you taking over? It doesn't seem important enough to warrant Scotland Yard getting involved. Although it is odd that there should be a break-in just now. But surely no one knows you are investigating Gervase, do they?' Apart from Michaels, she thought, suddenly feeling guilty. She ought not to have said anything to him.

Before he could respond, Michaels himself came in, bringing more hot water for the teapot. Dottie noticed he didn't turn a hair at seeing a strange man sitting at his employer's table, eating bacon and eggs. Clearly everyone 'below stairs' knew William was here.

She introduced William, saying, 'This is the man I met under the larches the other evening. Inspector William Hardy of Scotland Yard.'

'Ah, our photographer from *The Country Lady*. Carl Brown, wasn't it, sir?'

'Er, yes, that's right,' William admitted. He exchanged a look with Dottie.

'I must admit, I'm surprised that our little break-in is being investigated by the big-wigs from Scotland Yard. Sir,' he added as an afterthought.

'Miss Manderson and I are friends,' William explained. 'And as I'm staying in the area with family, and I'm also slightly acquainted with Mr Parfitt, it seemed appropriate to offer my help. The local people will be sending out their chap to look for fingerprints and such at some point this morning.'

Michaels nodded.

'The Inspector would like you and I to go to the study with him in a minute, to try and see what if anything is missing.'

'Of course, miss.' Michaels was already by the door.

'Perhaps you'll ring when you're ready for me.'

William did not seem in any hurry. He was spreading butter onto more toast.

'He's obviously a lot more observant than Gervase, if he recognises you from other day,' Dottie said.

'Hmm. Impressive observational skills. He could be a detective.'

'William?'

'Hmm?' He looked up from his food.

'Perhaps it's time I admitted something to you.'

He stared at her now. 'You're not the thief, are you? I'm fairly sure the cook and maids were correct when they said it was a man they saw going away from the house, not a beautiful young woman in a smart frock.'

Her worried look softened into a smile. 'Beautiful?'

He grinned at her, 'You know you are. Carry on. Tell me your confession. I can't guarantee to get you off. Though I must admit I can't picture you somehow scrambling through a broken window.'

'No. I didn't. But I wanted to tell you that I spent a couple of hours in the study last night. I had my dinner in there, it was warmer in there, and as I was on my own...'

'...It just made sense to use the study rather than sit like Miss Haversham at one end of a long dining table all alone?'

She laughed. 'Exactly. But, well, I had a bit of a nose about... looking for something to help you.'

'And what did you find?' He got up to fetch some more bacon, and poured himself another cup of tea, and one for her too.

'Not much really. The drawer that was locked was obviously out. There was a bunch of keys but none of them fitted it. Another drawer held a cashbox. I got that open all right. It contained a pile of bank notes. At least a few hundred pounds.'

'Staff wages, do you think, or?'

'I assume so.'

'Anything else?'

'A gun.'

That surprised him. 'Loaded?'

She shrugged. 'I didn't check. There was also an old photo. And a couple of old cinema ticket stubs. William, that's your third piece of toast!'

'I'm hungry. What was the photo of?'

'Who, you mean. An elderly lady. I'd say working class from her apron and the fact that she was standing in front of a small terraced house. On the back it said 'Mum, May 1928."

She finished her coffee and pushed cup and plate away. She waited a few more minutes for the human dustbin to dispose of his breakfast. She watched him wipe his mouth on a napkin, push his chair back and rise.

'Shall we?' he said.

As William looked around the study, Dottie rang for Michaels. He had clearly been waiting for the call, as he arrived almost straight away.

William said, 'Now, can I just ask you both to look but disturb things as little as possible. I really only want to know if anything is missing, or not as it should be.'

Michaels immediately pointed out the cashbox, lying open and upside down on the carpet. 'That's new.'

Very carefully, picking his way through the litter of other items, William took out his handkerchief then used it to pick up the cashbox. The box was completely empty, as they'd guessed, and no money lay on the floor.

'Do you know how much was in here, Mr Michaels? Or what it was used for?'

'No sir, I'm afraid not.'

'Staff wages perhaps?'

Again, Michaels shook his head. 'No sir. The staff wages are always kept in my office. Mr Parfitt used to draw the money from his bank each month and give it to me to hold until paid out.'

'I see,' William said. 'Have you checked the money is still there, after last night's events?' William asked.

Michaels looked dismayed. 'Er, no sir, I haven't. I think I'd better go and do that now.' He turned to go, saying over his shoulder in a panicked voice, 'Excuse me, sir.'

He returned in less than a minute, looking relieved. 'No, it's all right. It's all still there.' He let out a long breath. 'Phew.'

Dottie patted his arm. 'That's something at least.'

William said, with a frown, 'So what was the money for? Why keep such a large sum in the house?'

Michaels shook his head. 'I'm afraid I just don't know sir. I've never seen this box before.'

William went to the kitchen to talk to the rest of the staff. Cook said he could talk to them each in turn in Mr Michaels' sitting room. That suited him perfectly, as his experience had shown him that if questioned together, junior staff would usually defer to any opinion expressed by the most senior member of staff. He stood a better chance with them one at a time.

Out of respect for her position, he turned on his most winning smile and said to the cook, 'If you can spare me a few minutes, I'd like to ask you a couple of questions.'

She pulled off her apron, tidied her hair and issued directives to the maids. Then she bustled into the butler's sitting room with him, letting him sit facing the door at the table, with his notebook and pencil ready.

'This is cosy,' he said looking about him. 'Very nice. Do you sit in here at all?'

'Sometimes. I put the radio on. I like to hear some of the old tunes, you know. Reminds me of the dances we went to when we was kids.'

'Very nice,' he repeated. 'Now, Mr Michaels told me that the staff wages are kept in here until paid out.' She was already nodding, so clearly she knew that. 'And where are the wages kept?'

She pointed to a little cupboard that was essentially a board put across the corner to form the door of a triangular cupboard. The board stood about three feet tall, and above it was a shelf with a couple of photographs in frames standing on it. There was a small hole in the door, so the cupboard was opened by a key. William felt it didn't seem particularly secure, but no doubt the money was in a locked box inside.

He nodded. 'Convenient. Is it kept in a locked box?'

She shook her head. 'Oh no, it's just on the shelf in there.'

'Is that secure?'

She hesitated. 'Well, it's not *not* secure. You'd have to know where it was and get hold of the key.'

'True.' He glanced down at his notes. 'How many staff do you have here?'

'Well there's me and Michaels, and the two live-in maids, and a daily three times a week. Then if there's a special do on, Michaels will be told to get some extra help in. Or sometimes, if it's involving Mr Parfitt's parents, they lend us their people.'

'I see.' He wrote this down. Not that he needed to, but he thought she would feel he was taking her very seriously. 'And on the night of the robbery, you and the two live-in maids were both out for the evening?'

'Yes, sir. Because Mr Parfitt was away, we wouldn't be needed, so he'd said we could all go out together, which was very good of him. It's not often we all go out together.'

'And you went to the pictures?'

'Yes sir. That new film, *Five Days in Paris*. Very romantic it was, a bit too romantic, if you take my meaning. I didn't know where to look half of the time. But the girls enjoyed it. He is very good-looking, that Malcolm Matthews.'

William grinned. 'Ah yes, I've heard that film has caused some comment over it's—er—*romantic* content.'

'Yes indeed.' She grinned back at him, perfectly relaxed now.

'Now let me see.' He glanced down at his notes again. Not that there was anything there, it just made it clear they were now back to business. 'What are the names of the maids?'

'There's Lizzie. Lizzie Corby. She's been with us for two-and-a-bit years, came just before Christmas.'

'That would be Christmas 1932?'

'Yes. Then there's Maureen. Maureen Stagg. She's only been here about seven months or so. She's only just sixteen. Lizzie, she's eighteen.'

'I see. Thank you, Mrs Michaels. And they both live in, you said.'

'Yes they do.'

'You're happy with their work?'

'Oh yes, they're both good girls. Or they'd be out on their ear.'

'Has that ever happened?'

'Oh yes, sir, we had one girl last year, Clara she called herself, though she was just plain Clare Smith on her birth certificate. She only lasted three weeks. I wouldn't have her in the place, too flighty, and that flirty with Mr Parfitt... it was a disgrace. She'll get herself into trouble one day, I should think. That's all that was on her mind.'

'Oh dear, not at all suitable.'

'Definitely not, and I wasn't about to put up with it.'

'Quite right too. Is it possible that whilst she was here, she knew where the money was kept?'

'No. We don't ever discuss it with the maids. Michaels brings the money into the kitchen in the little envelopes and the girls think it's been given to him that way by Mr Parfitt. Besides, that's not the money what was taken, is it?'

'No,' he admitted. 'I'm just trying to see the case from every angle. Now coming back to last night. Everything was just as usual when you and the maids left?'

'Yes.'

'And did you see Mr Michaels? He stayed here, didn't he?'

'He did, yes. It's his evening out on Tuesday as a rule, unless Mr Parfitt needs him to stay in for some reason. He was sitting in here, with his cigarettes and a glass of stout. He had the radio on, some comedy play, and he was listening to that. Mind you, he had the door open so if Miss Manderson had rung, he would have heard it, he wasn't ignoring his duties.' She seemed worried about getting that across.

'Yes of course. Miss Manderson said he had told her about the arrangements for her evening meal, and that later, he brought the dishes through to the dining room.'

She looked tense. He wondered if she thought he was trying to put together a case against Michaels. He said, 'It might be the case that the burglar had been watching the house for some time, saw you three ladies leave the house, and knew that with only one or two people left in the house, he had a good chance of getting in, getting what he wanted and getting out again without too much bother.'

It was the right thing to say. Her fears were immediately reassured, and she relaxed.

'Well sir, I don't know why he didn't take some of them valuables from Mr Parfitt's room. He's got gold cufflinks and the like, and there's some old paintings upstairs, and things from his grandmother, jewellery and ornaments and such. I should think they'd fetch a pretty penny.'

'I believe the burglar was disturbed. Perhaps he thought all the staff were gone for the evening. Or perhaps he was just after one or two specific items. We don't know at the moment. Now, if you could just take me through what happened as you came back onto the property after your evening out.'

She told him how they had been walking along the drive, talking about the film and their favourite actors, when they had noticed a figure emerge from behind the shrubs on the corner of the house, as if from the back door. He had run across the gravel of the drive and disappeared the other side through the trees.

'Could you see what he looked like?'

She folded her arms and shook her head. 'No, not at all. It was too dark and he was too far away. And fast. He ran that fast, like one of them sprinters at the Olympics. We barely had a chance to notice him and him was gone.'

'But it was a man?'

'I just assumed. It wouldn't be likely to be a woman, would it?'

'Probably not. How tall would you say he was?'

'Quite tall. Not as tall as yourself, sir, but taller than my husband.'

'Thank you.' He wrote that down. 'And did he have on a hat, or was he bareheaded?'

He watched her debate the point with herself. In the end she said she couldn't remember.

He smiled and thanked her. 'I think I'd better speak to the maids too, just to cross every T and dot every I.'

She got up, her relief evident. 'I'll send in Lizzie, sir.'

'Thanks. I promise I won't keep them long.'

'That's quite all right, sir.'

When Lizzie came in, it was with a cup of tea and a large slice of date and walnut cake. She hovered nervously.

He beamed at her. 'That is very welcome, thank you,' nodding at the tea and cake even though he'd eaten a huge breakfast less than an hour earlier.

She blushed and smiled. 'I thought it might be.'

'Please sit down, just a couple of questions, nothing to be worried about.'

But she was nervous. Talking to the police made everyone nervous, he knew, even if they hadn't done anything wrong. She perched on the edge of the chair as if ready to rise as soon as someone came in and caught her. She gripped her hands together in her lap.

'So,' he said, looking at his notes. 'You're Lizzie Corby and you've been here a little over two years.'

She nodded.

'Like it here?'

'It's all right. Hard work.'

'I bet it is. All those stairs, all those fireplaces to clean and lay. Not to mention all the dusting and the sweeping, and the kitchen duties on top of all that.'

'At least I've got Maureen to help me. She's a good laugh too, we're good friends.'

'That's nice. It must be lonely here otherwise. Maureen's better than Clara?'

'Oh her!' She tossed her head. 'She was an awful fool, that one. I expect she got herself in the family way, the way she was carrying on.'

Just what the cook had said, Hardy thought. Had the

girl really been like that, or was Lizzie just repeating the general talk from the kitchen? He said, 'Did she keep in touch after she left?'

'Not her, no. But she and I wasn't especially friends.'

'I see.' He took a moment to have a bite of the cake, wiping his fingers on his trousers as she hadn't brought him a fork to use. 'That's delicious,' he said.

She blushed again. 'Thank you, sir.'

'You made this?'

She nodded, justifiably proud. 'I hope one day I'll have my own little cake shop. That's my dream. Don't tell anyone, they'd just laugh.'

'I don't see why they should. If this is anything to go by, you'd be the perfect person to run a cake shop. I hope it works out for you.'

She was still blushing, shyly pleased.

'Now coming back to last night. Everything seemed quite as usual as you all came in the gate? And then what happened?'

'We was just talking and laughing about the film, you know. And walking up the drive to go round to the back door.'

'You didn't use the side door?'

'Oh no, sir. The staff doesn't use the side door. That's only for Mr Parfitt and his guests and such.'

'What about deliveries?'

'Everything comes to the back door, sir, the bread, the fish and meat, the grocer, the postman, everyone.'

'I see.' He let her see that he was writing it down. 'And so no one uses the side door, in the normal way of things?'

She shook her head, and gave him another smile.

'Before you went out, did you go round the house checking everything was secure?'

'Before we went out? Me?' She was puzzled enough that he thought he had his answer.

'Or anyone else?'

'Not in the middle of the day, sir. It was only just four o'clock when we went out. And the house wasn't empty.'

'Of course. But who usually locks up, and when?'

'Mr Michaels locks up, always. And he does it when he's going to bed, in the summer. In the winter, he does it when it gets dark.'

'So at this of year it would be at what time?'

'About fiveish. It's usually dark about then.'

He nodded.

'Right. So when you came back last night, what was the first thing you noticed?'

'Noticed, sir? Or saw? The first thing I saw was the man run out from behind the rosemary and rose bushes by the corner where you go round to the back door.'

'Was he this side of the bushes, or behind?'

'He was definitely behind them.'

'So he came from the back of the house?'

'Yes.'

'And then what happened?'

'I just saw him come out, he looked towards us, and we stopped dead in our tracks, sir, then he fair legged it across the grass, then the drive, then into the trees.'

'Fair legged it? So he was running quickly?'

'Yes sir.'

'If you'd tried, could you have caught him?'

'Ooh sir, I wouldn't run after a burglar, sir, he might attack me.'

'True. And very sensible. All right. Let's suppose you knew who it was, and that he wouldn't harm you, just for fun, say, could you have caught him?'

She laughed. 'Oh easy. He ran, but not like his life depended on it. Not in my heels, mind, but in my work boots.'

'Did he run to the trees and stop, or did he keep going?'

She shook her head 'No idea, sorry.'

'It's all right. You're being very helpful, Miss Corby.'

She smiled and blushed again. He was willing to bet no one had ever called her Miss Corby before. She was just Lizzie to one and all. He drank some tea, and ate some more of her delicious cake.

'Can you describe the man? Was he tall, short, medium?'

'Quite tall.'

'Thin, fat?'

'Just medium.'

'What was he wearing?'

'A dark overcoat, short, you could see it dark against the gravel, it only came to his bum, sir.' She blushed at saying the word bum—bottom or behind—to a policeman, especially a good-looking one like this one.

'Oh? So like a car coat?'

'Yes sir, exactly like that. Mr Michaels's got one for when he goes out in the car.'

'Anything else?'

'Boots, I think. They made a lot of noise as he ran. I didn't have time to notice much else.'

'Did he have on a hat?'

'No.'

He was surprised at her definite tone. 'Sure?'

'Quite sure, thank you,' she told him crossly, then immediately apologised, remembering who she was speaking to.

He laughed. 'Don't worry. I just wanted to be sure. Mrs Michaels said she couldn't remember.'

'Oh well, that's not much of a surprise.'

'What do you mean?'

She looked away, fidgeted with her apron. She didn't want to tell him what she meant, clearly. He waited. She glanced back at him, then leaned forward.

'Look, I want to help, I do. But if anyone finds out, they'll have my guts for garters. But I don't want to get in any trouble.'

'Tell me, Miss Corby. I promise no one will hear a word of it from me.'

'Well, I know she's not as young as she was, but I reckon she saw him all right and knew him. I recognised him myself, so I don't know how she could say she didn't know him.'

'Who was it?' William felt the familiar soft thrill of excitement he always had when he got a firm piece of evidence in a case.

'It was Mr Parfitt.'

William sat back and stared at her.

She immediately became defensive. 'I'm not accusing him just for the fun of it. It was him, I swear it. But please, please don't say that I told you. I'll lose my job and everything. He can be nasty if you cross him.' This was hissed across the table at him, and she looked over her shoulder anxiously.

'Lizzie, it's all right. I was just surprised, that's all.'

'You thought I was going to say Mr Michaels? Well he might of known about it, I s'pose. But it was Mr Parfitt what ran across the drive. But he might not of had nothing to do with the burglary. Or he might of been after the burglar, if he saw him running away. Anyway, even if she saw him, Mrs Michaels wouldn't say anything in case she got into trouble.'

'You let me worry about that.'

He let her go, not wanting to detain her too long. Maureen came in, but he got very little out of her. He wondered if she'd been told to keep quiet; she seemed too scared to speak. She didn't really have time to see the figure, it was too dark, he ran too quick, he was tallish, but then again, she didn't really see. Hardy wasn't getting anywhere with her, so he thanked her and said she could go.

He went to find Dottie. She was in morning room flicking through the pages of an old magazine, bored.

'I'm off now,' he said.

'Did you find out anything?'

He just grinned at her and tapped his nose.

She laughed. 'Sorry, I forgot who I was talking to for a moment.' She got up and hurried over, walking with him into the hall. She helped him on with his coat, and gave him his hat.

William said, 'When are you going back to London?'

He was standing in the doorway looking out at the front drive, seemingly very interested in his car, a huge beast in dark crimson, sporting four doors and a sliding roof that would be very nice and easy to open even if you were

187

driving, unlike the folding roof on Dottie's own car, which seemed to always jam in the rain when she needed to close it quickly.

'Tomorrow,' she said.

'I see.'

Quite what he saw, she couldn't have said. She wanted to tell him that Moira and Gervase were having an affair, but she wasn't sure how hurt he would be by Moira's betrayal, especially considering this was their second engagement. They had been engaged several years earlier, but Moira had broken it off when his family had lost all their money. Dottie felt Moira didn't deserve a second chance, but that wasn't her decision to make, of course. Still, she wasn't quite sure about his feelings, and so for now she said nothing.

William said, 'And when does Parfitt return home?'

'Monday morning.'

He shot her a surprised look. 'You're not waiting to see him when he gets back?'

She smiled. 'See, clever clogs, that's how you became an inspector.'

He laughed. She loved to hear him laugh. It always seemed to come from nowhere and surprise her, a hearty, robust sound.

'I need to talk to you,' she said, coming to a decision. 'I think it could be important.'

'Is it about the robbery?'

'Part of it is. And something else I've found out.'

He considered for a moment. Then, 'Would you have dinner with me tonight?'

'Yes, of course, if you like.'

'Seven o'clock? I'll call for you.'

She nodded. He walked over to his car, and drove off without a backward glance.

Dottie went in and shut the door.

She found Michaels in the dining room, watching as the glazier, from the outside, carefully lifted out the old pane, a spotty youth there to help him. Inside, Maureen was sweeping up the tiny fragments and shards as best she could.

'One of them new-fangled vacuum cleaning machines would work a treat on this, Mr Michaels,' she grumbled.

'Well, we haven't got one of them, so you'll just have to get on with it, missy. But take care you don't cut yourself. Like needles, some of them tiny bits are.' He turned to Dottie. 'Did you want me, miss?'

'Only to let you know I shall be out for dinner.'

'Very good, miss.'

'And I wanted to ask you something.'

He smiled. 'Of course, miss, anything.'

Turning away slightly, and lowering her voice, she said, 'Did you see if Mr Parfitt's gun was amongst the mess in the study?'

Michaels looked startled. 'His gun? Miss?'

'There was a gun in one of the desk drawers. I've just realised I didn't notice it. I was wondering if it had been taken by the burglar.'

'I didn't notice one, miss. I didn't even know Mr Parfitt had a gun.'

Dottie nodded. 'He'd never mentioned it to me. Also, there was a photograph. A picture of an elderly lady. On the back, it said 'Mum, May 1928'. And there were two cinema ticket stubs, pink paper. I want to see if they are still there.'

'Let's see.' Michaels went off. Dottie trailed after him as far as the study doorway.

'Mr Michaels, do you think we should contact Mr Parfitt and tell him about the break-in?'

'We could do, miss. Though he'll be home on Monday, so I had thought of just leaving it until he gets back. After all, everything should be as good as new. More or less. I didn't want to spoil his weekend.'

'Hmm.' Dottie was torn, not sure which was the best course of action. She decided to leave it to Michaels. He knocked on the open study door. The uniformed policeman came over and said, 'I'm afraid we're not quite finished in here, sir. About another fifteen minutes, give or take.'

Beyond him, they could see the fingerprint man busy with his brush, gently blotting what looked like grey dust onto the edge of the desktop. The faces of the drawers were all lined up on the floor. They thanked the policeman and Dottie went back to the morning room.

She was restless for action. But she sat in a chair by a window, and looked out at the garden.

'Coffee, miss?'

'Yes please.' What else was there to do, she thought.

What was going on? She had so many ideas, different and conflicting. If only things were simple. If only she could line everyone up and demand answers from them one by one. Truthful answers. Why was life so complicated? She felt worn out with trying to work out what was happening. And bored to tears at the same time.

Michaels came back with a tray bearing coffee and a couple of small cakes. 'I know it's not been long since breakfast, miss, but these are that small and light, you'll hardly notice them going down.'

'They look delicious. Mrs Michaels is far too good to be a domestic cook, Mr Michaels. She ought to be a pastry-chef at some top London restaurant. Or have her own establishment.'

He beamed at her. 'I'll tell her you said so.'

She remained in the chair for the next fifteen minutes. And then a little more. It was closer to twenty-five minutes later that Michaels came to tell her the glazier and the police had finished their work and departed. They had the house to themselves once more.

The drawers of the desk were now stacked in a wobbly heap on top of the desk. Grey dust seemed to cover everything. Of course, it was just the detective's job to test everything for prints. It was the maid's job to remove evidence of the testing.

'I'll get Maureen to come in and clean up in a minute. I thought you and I might check the state of things first.'

'Good idea,' Dottie said.

The two large drawers from either side were smashed. Three of the smaller drawers were more or less intact, and the fourth had no handle, and one of its sides was reduced practically to splinters. As she moved some of the bits of wood, she saw the photo lying there. She felt unaccountably relieved to see it there. On impulse she showed it to Michaels.

'Any idea who this is?'

He shook his head. 'No, Miss, I don't know the lady.'

He seemed sincere, and completely incurious. She put the photo in her pocket and went back to what she was doing.

The space under the desk was completely empty. If Dottie had harboured hopes of hidden panels, or secret documents taped to the underside of the desk, or any other espionage-inspired things, she was disappointed. She placed the three unbroken drawers back in position. Michaels began to pick up the scattered items, whilst Dottie tidied the loose papers. She had no real idea where anything went so just placed the stacked papers in the three usable drawers. Gervase would have to sort it all out when he got back.

Michaels placed the books back on the shelves, more or less in the right order. Soon the carpet was clear of belongings and ready to be cleaned to get rid of splinters and dust.

There was no sign of the gun.

Dottie found the ticket stubs under a toppled chair lying on its side, and quickly pocketed them. She had no idea if they were important. It seemed unlikely. But at least she could show them to William, along with the photo.

The empty cashbox was put into the gap where the bottom right-hand drawer would have been, sitting on the wooden floorboards beneath the desk.

Soon they had finished. Michaels went to find Maureen. Dottie looked around. She had a niggling feeling she'd forgotten something. She felt certain something else was missing, but what was it? It was some time before she realised it was the folder of pornographic pictures and the two small account books.

*

Chapter Eleven

Dottie had more or less forgotten that it was not for the pleasure of her company alone that William had invited her to dinner. She spent a good amount of time bathing, doing her hair, and fussing over her make-up to get it just right. Then there was the agony of indecision over her clothes. Finally she settled on what she thought of as a good 'all-purpose' dress: long enough and dark enough to be quite formal, but in a lightweight, flowing fine wool, because it was, after all, still winter. The soft flounce of the skirt was handy for any unexpected dancing—she *never* missed an opportunity to dance—yet suitable for weddings, funerals, afternoon tea and even business appointments, not that she had many of those.

It also had the advantage of having been worn before in his presence. She was conscious of not wearing new clothes every time she saw him. She was worried he would think her frivolous and expensive.

She added a couple of long necklaces, the usual one of amber beads here and there on a long silver chain, and another of green glass beads that resembled chrysoprase. She put on earrings that matched the green glass; they provided the perfect finishing touch. Or not quite. As she was about to leave her room, she darted back to the dressing table to dig out Gervase's hideous engagement ring. She put it on. It immediately swung round on her finger. With a huff of impatience, she pulled it off again and threw it back onto the dressing table. Twenty seconds later, and she grabbed it again. She ought to wear it as she was going out in public. She only hoped it didn't fall off her finger and go down a drain or something.

She did a final twirl in front of the dressing mirror and was satisfied. The pimple on her chin had taken the hint and disappeared, and her unruly hair was as tame as she could get it.

At five to seven she went downstairs, glancing automatically towards the front door. She smiled, a flutter of joy lighting up inside her, to see the lamplight shining on William as he came up to the door. She ran to open it before he rang.

He was wearing a dark grey suit. It was a smart one, newish, and most definitely not one of the several cheaper sort he usually wore for work. Nor was his tie was a work tie, it was of the kind she might have chosen for him herself. His hair gleamed in the lamplight, damp and slightly curling at the nape, and he was freshly shaved. Was it just her imagination, or had he too forgotten that this was supposed to be a business dinner?

Michaels came through, but on seeing that Dottie was there and the guest had been brought in, he wished them a pleasant evening and returned to the kitchen.

'Ready?' William asked her.

She nodded, and out they went. He held the door of the car open for her, then ran round to get in. The headlamps picked up the first drops of rain as they drove out through the gates and onto the village street.

'Where are we going?'

'A hotel near my uncle and aunt's.'

For a mad second or two, Dottie's imagination furnished a shadowy liaison in one of the hotel's rooms, but William continued, 'The restaurant is quite good, and more importantly it's not usually too crowded. I've asked for a quiet table. I'm rather worried about being overheard as we discuss a certain well-known local person.'

'Of course,' said Dottie, crossly dismissing her imagination as a fool. This is strictly police business, she reminded herself. 'Good idea.'

He glanced at her. 'You look lovely this evening.'

'Thank you, William, and so do you.' It was only the truth, she thought, but he laughed it off as if she'd told a joke. He did not readily accept compliments.

Not sure what else to say, she fell back on a well-used topic. 'How's Eleanor getting on? Is she going to stay up here permanently, or does she plan to return to London?'

'No, she'll be here permanently now. Oh she'll visit from time to time, I don't doubt, but she's engaged now, you know.'

'No, I didn't! How lovely!'

'They got engaged practically the second she was eighteen. He's a decent young fellow, only just twenty-one himself. But he's a hard worker, full of ideas about how to run a business, it seems, and as my aunt says, what else can we do but support them?'

'You don't think they're right for each other?' Dottie asked. She turned to watch his face. He wrinkled his nose slightly, half shook his head.

'Oh, it's not that. They're just so *young*.' He halted the car at a crossroads and gave all his attention to the road. As they pulled away again, he added, 'He's the first fellow who's taken her about. And...'

'You feel responsible for her? You're worried about her?'

'Exactly.' He shot her another quick look, and a rueful grin. 'Probably it's usually the girl's father who feels like this.'

Dottie laughed. 'You're not that much older!'

'Almost eleven years. Feels like twenty sometimes.'

'So when is the happy day?'

'It's set for the 1st of June. They're having an engagement party the Saturday before Easter. I think it's the about the 19th or 20th of April. Remind me later, I've got an invitation for you in my pocket. She asked me to give it to you. It's only for you, I'm afraid, I hope that's all right. Though I believe she plans to invite Flora, George and your parents to the wedding itself.' He was looking in the rear-view mirror to check the road behind. 'Obviously I had to tell her that it was all off between you and Parfitt. That's all right isn't it?'

'Of course it is. This vile great rock on my hand is going back to him the second your investigation is over. I'm only wearing it in case someone sees me, though goodness knows who that might be.'

She held her hand out. The ring slipped round as always so that the dirty diamond bumped the dashboard.

'Wretched thing,' she grumbled. 'I'm more likely to lose it long before I give it back to him. It's miles too big.'

He smiled. 'It's hideous.'

'It's very old. A family heirloom he reveres, which is apparently sufficient excuse to avoid buying me something pretty as an emblem of his so-called love.'

'Dottie, it's not a real diamond, it's glass. The ring isn't old, it's merely dirty.'

She looked at the ring in renewed disgust.

William said, 'Jo Birnie said to me, 'They don't exactly present the picture of a couple madly in love, do they? If I was her, I wouldn't take him for £10,000.' Why didn't he at least get it cleaned and fitted for you?'

She shrugged. 'No idea. He didn't propose to me, just sprang all this on me out of the blue. Sort of shoved it across the table at me.'

'Hmm. I thought he was completely smitten?'

'Clearly not. He just thinks I'm suitable.'

'Eminently teachable,' William murmured.

'What?'

He shook his head. 'Sorry, sorry, I shouldn't have said that. I was just remembering something he said to me the first time I met him. It was at your parents' anniversary party back in November.'

'He said that?' Her lip curled slightly in distaste.

'I'm sorry, I shouldn't have said anything. He was

bragging. He wanted me to envy him. Which, of course, I did, I do. Perhaps he was a bit drunk?'

She stared at him. 'Tell me exactly what the said.'

He was turning the car through a narrow gateway. 'Oh Dottie, I can't. It was foul.'

'He *is* foul. No manners, once he's got past the initial stage of making an effort. No real feelings for me. He expects everyone—including me—to faun all over him because of his great status. Which he clearly attained by illegal and immoral dealings. He's a charlatan, a fraud, a good old-fashioned conman.'

All he said was, 'We're here.' He turned off the engine. He opened his door, got out, and like the gentleman he was, came to open her door and help her out. 'Mind the puddle!'

His hand was warm, his clasp firm. Without letting go, he pulled her hand through his arm, and led her up the steps to the hotel's entrance.

Coach lamps gleamed from either side of the double glass doors. A uniformed doorman leapt forward to open one of the doors for them, smiling and nodding in welcome.

'Good evening, madam, good evening sir.' He took their coats and hats.

William and Dottie went through to the dining room. She approved of the plush carpets, the richly coloured draperies, the chandeliers and mirrors. It was all lovely. There was a pleasant hum of conversation. It was rather like a good restaurant in London, but without the noise and bustle. Or the crowds. There were pots of tall plants and plenty of lattice work to provide privacy at the tables, and in the corner a young lady in a smart black dress played a charming melody on a baby grand piano.

The head waiter approached, and William gave his name. They were taken to an intimate table for two. The crystal gleamed, candle flames bobbed and danced, and when he pulled out her chair for her and Dottie took her seat, she couldn't help but forget this was supposed to be a business meeting, and she was filled with happiness.

William took the seat opposite her. His smile was a little tentative, she thought. Was he nervous? She smiled back.

'It's lovely here,' she said. 'You were right about this place.'

'Wine?'

'Yes, please.'

William barely turned his head, and the waiter was there with a wine list and a recommendation.

William said to Dottie, 'What do you think? Does that sound all right to you?'

Usually her escorts didn't bother to ask her opinion. Luckily she had had this wine before.

She nodded, 'Yes, that's a very nice one.'

He nodded to the waiter, who departed.

'Shall we eat first then talk over coffee?'

She nodded again. She looked at him. Her eyes were soft and lovely. His heart did that same odd little flip it always did when he looked at her.

It felt as bold as a public announcement when he reached across the table and put his hand out. He held his breath. She put her hand in his. To mask a sudden rush of emotion, he touched the engagement ring with his thumb, and said:

'You're right, it's a hideous lump of a thing.'

She looked at him. Then she pulled the ring off her finger and put it into her evening bag, snapping the clasp shut on an unhappy episode in her life.

'I'm not going on with that anymore,' she said. 'I can't do it. It's not fair to Gervase, and—well—I just can't pretend any longer.'

'Indeed. I know exactly what you mean.'

The courses came and went. Dottie hardly noticed what she was eating, all her awareness was focussed on the man sitting opposite her.

They talked of their families. Of Flora and George's children, William said, 'I haven't been to see them for almost a fortnight. I'm sure they'll have grown by the next time I visit.'

They talked of their work. Dottie told him how things were at the warehouse, and he watched her, animated, excited, as she talked. How quickly she had become a confident woman, capable of running her own business, competently managing the day-to-day requirements of that business. He felt proud of what she was achieving, and could see she was proud of herself in her gentle, rather apologetic manner.

'I've learned so much in the last eight months or so,' she said. 'People have been so kind.'

But, he thought, people were kind to her because she took an interest in everything and everyone, because she respected them and was honest and sincere. And besides all that, the real love she had for what she was doing shone through, as did her intelligence and her natural flair for style. Just thinking of Parfitt's sneering dismissal of her career and interests made his blood boil.

They talked of his work too. She already knew that he had been seconded to the Metropolitan Police headquarters at New Scotland Yard for the duration of this investigation into the conduct of Gervase Parfitt.

'It's not likely to lead to promotion, more's the pity,' he said. 'But it could—I hope—be a very useful addition to my record. Though I have to say, it's been far more difficult than I'd anticipated, looking into the behaviour of a colleague. At every moment I'm aware that there but for the grace of God, I could have done some of the same things he has done. We all have the opportunity to further our careers by taking the easy way out when faced with a difficult investigation, or placed in a position of trust.' He shook his head, and concentrated on pushing a small piece of potato around his plate. Without looking up, he said, 'I feel rather like a traitor, snooping and prying into another fellow's conduct.' He shot her a glance. 'I know you think I'm delighting in the prospect of ruining his career, that I'm looking forward to his disgrace as a kind of petty revenge for his feelings for you. But truly, I'm not. I've got quite a sense of dread over it all finally coming out, and I feel like a rotten cheat about it.'

'But you're not a rotten cheat, William, or a traitor.' She just stopped short of calling him 'darling'. She placed her hand on his arm. 'I know you're not enjoying this. That's why you're the perfect man for the job. You understand all too well the pitfalls of your profession. You know all about human weakness, and the importance of integrity. You *are* the right one to do this.'

He began to speak, but the waiter came to ask them if they wanted coffee.

William looked at Dottie again. 'Would you like some?'

She nodded.

William said yes, they'd have coffee. The waiter quickly cleared the table and left.

William leaned forward and took her hand once more. 'Dottie, I'm afraid some rather awful things are going to come out of this whole affair. I'm worried you will be hurt by it.'

'Don't be, William. I went into this with my eyes open—or, at least, more or less open. You've warned me, several times. You've told me the kind of things you're investigating him for. In any case, I've seen for myself what he's like—I know what kind of man he is.'

William nodded. Then said, 'In that case... There's something you ought to know. Dottie, I'm afraid Parfitt's not at a conference this weekend.'

The waiter arrived with a tray. He set down a gleaming chrome coffee pot in the centre of the table, added a sugar basin, a jug of cream, two cups and two saucers, two shiny teaspoons, and a plate of chocolates.

With the waiter gone again, Dottie looked at William, and said, 'I know he's not. But, well, there's something else. I've been wondering how to tell you. Or whether I had the right to say anything.' She was watching his face. Her heart was pounding. She said it in rather a rush. 'Gervase is having an affair with Moira.'

His expression didn't change. That surprised her.

She said, 'You knew?'

'Suspected. A pretty strong hunch. He went back to her place that night. Remember how he so gallantly offered to give her a lift back after the Valentine's Ball? And somehow he knew her flat was near his hotel. How did he even know she had a flat, let alone where it was? Ever since then, she has been quite elusive. Always dashing off to see relatives and sick friends. People she's never so much as mentioned before.'

'She was here last weekend. She stayed at the pub in the village. I saw her there. Then she came to the house. Mr Michaels showed her in, and then when she left, I watched her walking away from the house. And—I'm so sorry—I saw her arrive late one night. He let her into the study from the garden. That was the night I met you under the larches.'

Was his heart broken by the revelation? She watched him anxiously. He sighed. He looked at her. His mouth twitched at the corner in a lop-sided smile.

'We can't half pick 'em!'

She laughed. 'We're idiots.'

'I'm not devastated, Dottie. I only ever wanted you.'

'Oh.' Her eyes prickled suddenly.

He took her hand again and squeezed it tight. 'I should have come after you when you got off the train at York last summer. I was too scared to be late back to work, too scared I'd lose my job, because how could I support a family, with no job? But I should have... I wanted to...'

'It doesn't matter. I was an idiot. You're my man, William Hardy. Let's stop this foolishness now.'

He nodded. 'I shall speak to Moira as soon as I get back to London. She might make a scene, but I doubt it. She already knows how I feel about you.'

He bent his head to kiss the back of her hand, and an older woman at an adjacent table said, 'Oh how sweet!'

Dottie laughed and beamed at her, dashing away a sentimental tear. The man at the other table raised his glass to Dottie and William in a toast to their happiness.

The air was now clear. Finally. They both knew where they stood. Dottie poured their coffee.

'Now then, Inspector. Back to work. I'll tell you the pathetically small amount I've found out, though it's mostly guesswork.'

She told him about the two small account books she'd seen, and how she had later realised they were missing. She reminded him again of the missing gun and the money. She took the photo out of her purse and handed it to him.

'Mr Michaels didn't recognise her, and I got the impression he hadn't seen the photo before. There is a studio name on the back, by the way.'

He turned it over and read out the name. 'Jinkson's of Nottingham. I don't recognise the name. But it could be useful.' He got out his notebook and wrote that down. 'I'll get someone onto that.'

'So I was wondering if it's the property of a former member of staff, perhaps? It mightn't mean anything.'

He handed it back to her. 'It's not so very old. Presumably the person who is the child of this woman is not very old either. Your age, or mine, probably.'

'True.' She put the photo away again. Then she showed him the ticket stubs she'd found under the sofa.

He turned them over in his hand, with a frown of concentration. 'Why keep these? Why were they there? Sentiment? Love?'

Dottie shook her head. 'Gervase isn't given to sentiment. There's one thing Gervase loves above all things: power. I'm certain he wouldn't keep any of these things without a reason. He's not the sort of man to go in for keepsakes.' A sudden memory came to her. 'I've just thought. I found a cigarette butt in one of the drawers too. I threw it in the wastepaper basket—I just thought it was rubbish. But now...'

'You think it's another item from his odd collection?'

'It had red lipstick on it.'

'Moira's red? Or?'

Was he worried? She looked at him but couldn't decipher his expression. She shrugged. 'Possibly. I'd have to see the two shades side by side to be really certain, but it could have been Moira's shade. Even if it was, that lipstick isn't exclusive to her, the cigarette could have been smoked by any number of women. It needn't mean anything at all. And presumably a barrister would say as much in court.'

'I'll ask Michaels to look for it. The maid has probably already emptied the bin. It's very likely been thrown into the furnace by now. Was there anything else?'

She thought for a minute. She blushed a little at the memory.

'What?' he said.

Looking down at her coffee cup, she said, 'There was a folder of pornographic pictures. I-I didn't look at them closely, obviously. As soon as I realised what they were, I shoved them back in the drawer.'

He grinned. 'And were these missing, or still there?'

'They're gone too.'

'Were they pictures of women?'

She stared at him. 'What? Yes, of course they were!'

'You can get pornographic pictures of men too, you know. If you know the right people.'

'Well, I don't, thank you very much. Yes, these were definitely women.'

'I think I need to come back and have another look around, and talk to the staff again. Particularly Michaels. He might know about the pictures. Have one of these, they're very moreish,' he suggested, pushing the plate of chocolates towards her.

She took one and bit into it, savouring the sweet taste which contrasted perfectly with the bitterness of the coffee. She was still thinking about the contents of Gervase's desk.

'We still don't know what was in the locked drawer, but whatever it was, it's long gone. The drawer had been smashed open, as you saw. And I didn't notice anything new lying about, so perhaps we'll never know about that. Then there was the gun, of course. I'm fairly sure now there was no ammunition. I can picture the drawer in my mind. I think there was only the gun.'

He nodded. 'I wasn't happy to hear his gun is missing. But it's not especially surprising that he had one. A lot of these fellows brought back guns from the war. As trophies, or, just out of habit, they'd been carrying them for several years, it was second nature. There are unlicensed guns all over the country, unfortunately. The armed forces got back most of the weapons they issued, but of course, if a man was killed or injured, his weapon would be quite likely to be picked up by someone else. It was quite common for a demobbed soldier to hand back the weapon he was issued with, yet hold onto one or two unofficial ones. And as I said, they could have been taken as trophies too.'

'Taken from dead enemy soldiers?'

'Exactly. Or illegally obtained abroad and smuggled in.'

'Do you think this was a purely chance break-in, just a robbery? I mean, the money in the cashbox was taken. Perhaps the man just went from room to room until he found the study and knew he could fairly count on finding something valuable in the desk.'

'Did you lock the cashbox after you opened it to look inside?'

'Oh yes. But the key was on the bunch in the same drawer, so there would have been no need to search for it.'

'Hmm.' He poured more coffee. He offered her a top-up, too, but she shook her head.

'No thank you, I shan't be able to sleep if I have any more. The last thing I want is another restless night tossing and turning.'

His pupils immediately became huge. He grinned at her.

She raised her eyebrows at him. 'William! Behave yourself.'

He was still grinning as he stirred a little splash of cream into his coffee. 'Sorry. Just pictured you unable to sleep, tossing and turning... Just out of curiosity, what might you be wearing whilst doing all this tossing and turning on your bed? That little lace and satin number I noticed in your room last year?'

She pretended to be scandalised. 'Well really! And my mother thinks you're such a nice man.'

'I am. Usually.' He stared into her eyes.

Feeling rather hot and bothered, she forced herself to break the look and turn away.

He finished his coffee, and said, 'Back to our discussion. The robbery was not a genuine one. It was an inside job.'

She was already shaking her head before he finished speaking, though admittedly with little conviction. William continued: 'One of the maids, Lizzie Corby, told me that as the three staff came along the gravel drive they all saw a man running away from the back of the house and into the shadows. The other two agreed with this, but they didn't say much more than that. However Miss Corby said she recognised the man as Parfitt. She said the man was about the same height and build, and wore no hat, so she presumably saw that he had light-coloured hair—I can check that—and he wore a short dark coat such as Michaels wears for driving. She was utterly convinced. It was as plain as day to her that it was Parfitt she saw running away. She thinks the others recognised him too, but kept quiet out of fear of losing their jobs.'

Initially Dottie had been shocked by this, but the more she thought about it, the more it began to seem possible. 'We know he's not really at a conference in Bournemouth, so he could easily be staying in the area.' She thought back to the uncomfortable, prickled feeling she had in the study that evening. Had he been watching her? Perhaps even made some sound she subconsciously noticed? Parfitt as the burglar was a possibility she had not even considered until now. 'But what would he have to gain by robbing himself?'

He sighed. 'Well, obviously there's still a lot we don't know.'

'Remember the visit I paid to Mrs Holcombe's after the inquest?'

'The one I was so rudely excluded from, you mean?' He said it with his usual grin that made her want to kiss him.

'That's the one. I was hoping to get something out of her. Mrs Sedgworth's deepest darkest secrets, for one. At Gervase's, Mrs Sedgworth said that I could speak freely in front of Mrs Holcombe. I told you I thought they were friends. But Mrs Holcombe didn't tell me anything. It was as if *she* was trying to get information out of *me*. She seemed to think that I knew something that would be useful to her.'

William made another brief note, saying, 'Interesting, though I don't see how that helps us at the moment. Now then, I have another favour to ask of you.'

'What was the first favour you asked?'

'To come up here and wear that horrid ring.'

'Ah yes. You owe me more than dinner for that.'

He grinned. 'True.' He dropped his voice. 'I'm happy to pay up. What do you want?'

To his disappointment, she simply told him to behave himself again.

He rolled his eyes and said, 'Very well. I should have said, I have yet another favour to ask you, as I grovel unworthily at your dainty feet.'

She smiled. 'They are dainty, aren't they?' she said complacently, with a glance down at her ankle. 'Very well, you may ask.'

He flipped back a few pages in his notebook. 'Ah yes, here we are.' He nodded, and glanced at her, and leaning forward, in a very low voice, he said, 'Look, this is highly confidential, as you know, but I'm telling you this for background. I got this from Sergeant Fulford. A certain Mrs Enid Parkes went to see Parfitt at the Derbyshire police headquarters in Ripley last month. However, as she quickly discovered, it's not possible to just go in and see someone of his great eminence without an appointment. She made rather a fuss at the front desk and was asked to leave. Started shouting and trying to hit the young constable with her walking-stick. As they shoved her out of the building, not very gently I imagine, she said she was going to the newspaper to tell them what Parfitt had done. And she said something along the lines of, 'And believe me, I could tell them plenty about that high and mighty so-and-so—I won't trouble you with her actual word—I could tell them that he went back on his word, and after my son did what he did, I got nothing."

Dottie stared. 'What does that mean?'

'That's what I want you to find out. The incident was recorded in the station's daybook, so it was easy enough to get her address. She had a son. He was arrested and subsequently convicted of two counts of murder and he was hanged last December. He was her only son, so he had to be the one she was talking about. If I give you the address, could you visit her and try to persuade her to tell you all about it? I've already called on her myself to speak to her but she wouldn't let me in. Said she wouldn't have anything to do with a copper.'

'Of course I will.' She took the notebook from him and copied down the address in her diary. 'It's a shame I don't have my own car back. It'll be tricky getting to this place and back again. I'd probably be best to get a taxi.'

'Lord, yes, take a taxi,' William said. 'The police can pay you back your expenses.'

'All right. Thank you.'

They finished their coffee. William paid the bill. Dottie was sad that the evening was coming to an end. He would take her back to Gervase's and that would be that. At least they'd dined out together, and it had *almost* been an assignation. They'd managed to cram in a bit of flirting, at least.

They walked out to the car. They were arm in arm again, and it felt so perfect.

They drove back to Gervase's house in near silence. He halted the car at the front door, and once more, got out to open the car door for her, offering her his hand. As she stepped out, he wrapped an arm around her and tilted his head to kiss her, the first touch of his mouth a soft enquiry, but immediately becoming demanding, passionate. She leaned against him, heart pounding.

'I wish you didn't have to go,' she murmured.

'So do I, but it really wouldn't do.' He was regretful, but almost laughing.

'Then you'd better go. I'll see you in London in a day or two, with my taxi fares neatly entered into an invoice for you.' She grinned at him in the light of the headlamps.

All he said was, 'You're gorgeous. Goodnight, darling.'
One last, quick kiss, and he was gone.

The next morning, Dottie said goodbye to Mr Michaels
and took a taxi to the railway station, where she deposited
her suitcase, hat box and dressing case in the left luggage
office. Then she took another taxi to the address William
had given her for Mrs Parkes.

The taxi came to a stop outside a dilapidated terraced
house in a deprived area of similarly all-but-falling-down
properties. If the driver of the taxi had misgivings about
setting Dottie down in such a neighbourhood, Dottie
found it was all just as she'd expected. After all, the
woman was elderly and without an income, or as good as.
Where else could she afford to live?

She debated whether to go up the steps to the front
door, or down the steps to the basement. A basement
room or rooms would be cheaper, therefore she opted to
go down the area steps, and knocked on the door. As she
waited for someone to answer, she scratched a thin tabby
cat behind the ears. It purred frantically.

'She'll have no end of that,' said a voice.

Dottie turned to see the original of the photograph she'd
taken from Gervase's study. She had it in her handbag
now. *Mum. May 1928.* Oh certainly the woman was older,
her hair almost silver now, rather than the darker grey it
appeared in the photo. Her face was lined and her figure
spare. But it was her.

'Mrs Parkes?' Dottie began, but the woman held up a
hand.

'I don't want no do-gooders from the church round her,
telling me where I'm going wrong.'

Dottie smiled. 'I'm not from the church. I'm here to ask
a favour, certainly, but I think you'll be surprised what it's
about.' There was some shouting behind her which made
her jump. She'd like to get inside if possible.

'Hmph. There's not much surprises me these days, me
duck,' the old woman said, but she took a careful step or
two back into the house, using a walking stick to support

her right side. She left the door open.

Dottie took that as an invitation to enter.

She went into a warm dimly-lit kitchen, hung about with men's shirts and undershirts in various degrees of dampness.

'I takes in washing,' Mrs Parkes said by way of an explanation. She seated herself on a hard, upright chair beside a small table, hooking the handle of the walking stick over the back of the chair. She indicated to Dottie that she could take the other. Dottie did so.

'That's hard work,' Dottie said.

'I've got to eat. No one else is going to look after me. Now, what do you want?' She was staring at Dottie, but her expression was defiant rather than hostile.

Dottie said, 'I'm sorry that you lost your son.'

That surprised Mrs Parkes, and she suddenly looked upset. Dottie felt horrid. She leaned forward to put a hand on the woman's arm.

'I'm so sorry, Mrs Parkes. I didn't mean to ambush you like that. Of course, it's still very raw.'

Mrs Parkes's mouth was a straight, firm line. She stared at Dottie again and said nothing. Outside there was more shouting and a dog barked.

Dottie tried again, 'I'm sorry to bring up such an unhappy subject...' but before she could continue, Mrs Parkes was on her feet, feeling behind her for her stick.

'I knew you was here about him! Who sent you? The social? The police?'

'The police,' said Dottie. She prayed Mrs Parkes would let her get a bit more in before throwing her out. 'My friend is a police inspector. He tried to see you, but you wouldn't speak to him, so he asked me to come.'

'And why would I speak to you, Miss Posh Girl?'

'Because I found this photograph of you in my fiancé's desk, and I want to know why he had it.' Dottie lay the photograph on the kitchen table. Mrs Parkes made no attempt to touch it or even look at it properly.

'And who might your fiancé be, when he's at home?'

'Gervase Parfitt,' Dottie said.

The old lady was surprised. More than surprised. Her face turned a worrying greyish shade.

Dottie said, 'Are you all right? Shall I put the kettle on? You've had a shock, a cup of tea might help.'

'I'm all right,' Mrs Parkes said, giving herself a bit of a shake.

She'll tell me to leave now, Dottie thought. Well, I tried my best.

Mrs Parkes reached for her stick, then went across to the stove and lit the gas. She set the kettle on it, and got two chipped cups out of the press. She scattered a very small quantity of tea into a pot, and came to sit down again.

'How'd you come to be engaged to him? He must be old enough to be your father.'

'Not quite,' Dottie said. 'He's seventeen years older than me. I know it's a lot. But I just met him last year and fell for his charm. The only trouble is, once you get to know him, you realise he's not quite so charming as he seems.'

She met Mrs Parkes' appraising look. The old lady gave a cackling laugh, completely lacking in humour.

'I reckon you've hit the nail on the head there, girlie.'

'Well, things are not working out between us. I'm planning on breaking the engagement.'

'He's the type as would sue you for breach of promise.'

'He can try,' Dottie said. 'But after what I've found out, I don't think he'll dare.'

'So you've come here fishing.' It wasn't a question. Dottie nodded, thinking Mrs Parkes seemed like a woman who preferred the truth.

'I know he's done some terrible things,' Dottie said. 'Though I only know a little about it. My friend is from Scotland Yard, and he is trying to get proof of what Mr Parfitt has done. We believe you might be able to help us. Would you be willing to tell me how you know Mr Parfitt?'

'Will I have to go to court and swear on the Bible?'

'I don't know,' Dottie said. 'I'm afraid that's not up to me.'

The kettle boiled just then, the shrill whistle piercing

the air. It was a relief when Mrs Parkes hastened to remove the whistle and make the tea. As she was doing this, she seemed to be thinking.

When she returned to her seat at the table, she said, 'Well I've kept quiet like Parfitt told me, but what good has it done me? None at all, that's what. And I suppose, if I send you away, there'll just be some other fool banging on my door, asking me the same questions.'

Dottie grinned at her. 'Probably.' She waited. She sensed that Mrs Parkes wanted to talk. She was rewarded, because finally:

'My son George, he was a bad lot, as they say, always in trouble from a boy. But he was good to me, he loved me and took care of me, and I loved him too. He was my only one. I know most likely everyone says this, but it's true. He lost his job—not through his own fault, they just got rid of the men, couldn't afford to pay them no more. Then he got in with a bad crowd. At first it was just small things, but bit by bit the small things turned into big things. Bad things. But he wanted into this gang, and they made him prove himself by doing something big. So he robbed a pub—the Purple Emperor, it was, out at Blackhall. The landlord put up a fight, and got punched, and then as George was getting away, in a panic he coshed some chap, one of the customers from the pub, and the man died.'

The noise from the street had receded. Dottie shivered in spite of the damp heat in the kitchen. It was as if she were there outside the pub watching as a desperate young man tried to make his escape. Goosebumps stood out all down her arms. These weren't just names on a page. These were real people, with real struggles, and somehow Gervase had made their struggles worse. She hardly dared to move in case Mrs Parkes changed her mind and told her to get out.

On a long shuddering breath, Mrs Parkes said, 'Well he felt bad for what had happened, and he turned himself in. Said he'd beg the court for mercy. I begged him not to, I couldn't bear the thought of him spending his whole life in prison, even though he'd killed a man. It's not as though he planned to kill someone. I said to him, 'What did you think would happen, that the landlord would just hand over the money?' He said to me, 'I didn't think, Mum, that's just it, I was that desperate. I told him I had a knife. I hadn't, but he didn't know that. Anyway, he gave me the money. But fists flew, and I had to make a run for it. Then a couple of customers chased me outside, and I grabbed the first thing that came to hand.' That's how he told it, and I believed him. He grabbed a bit of a fence post that had broke off near the door. He just picked it up and when some fellow came at him, George whacked him with it. Spur of the moment.

'Your Parfitt chap, he was the chief superintendent then. His men was looking into the case. He said that if George made a full confession, the judge would go easy on him, because he hadn't gone there with a weapon. He told George he could be out of prison in as little as ten years. I thought, given what we'd expected, that ten years wasn't too bad. I thought I could live with that. With any luck, I'd still be around to see him when he got out.' Mrs Parkes paused to take a sip of tea. 'But of course, it never happened.'

She got up and went over to the sink, though Dottie couldn't see that she did anything. Perhaps she just needed to move about, no doubt she got stiff from sitting too long. She came back and sat again, putting the stick to one side and taking her teacup in both hands.

Dottie felt as if she had turned to stone. Through stiff lips, she forced herself to say, though she already knew, 'What h-happened?'

'Sentenced him to hang,' Mrs Parkes said. 'My boy—my baby. After he'd give himself up. After all he'd told them about the gang, and about the robbery, how he'd just lashed out, not really meaning to hurt anyone. Someone came forward and said he'd picked up the bit of fence post on the way in, but that weren't true. He appealed, but it got turned down flat. There was nothing we could do. I just wanted to die myself. If I could of taken his place...'

Dottie was fighting back the tears. To indulge her own

emotions would be an insult to Mrs Parkes's grief, so she sipped the tea. It was too hot, but it braced her, weak though it was. Mrs Parkes continued:

'I wrote to that Parfitt fellow, asked him if he could help us. I reminded him he'd promised to get George a lighter sentence. He said he couldn't do anything. That we had to 'allow justice to take its course."

There was silence in the kitchen. Outside the dog barked again, and Dottie felt as if she had come back to firm ground. A glance at Mrs Parkes showed the woman was still wrestling with her emotions, and Dottie waited to see if there was anything else.

There was. And this was the key now, Dottie instinctively knew. This was something she could take to William.

'The last time I got a letter from my George, he told me Parfitt had come to see him. He'd told George there was nothing he could do to save him, but that if he'd plead guilty to another killing they couldn't get anyone for, Parfitt would see to it that I got enough money to live comfortable for the rest of my life. He told George he'd be bringing an end to the torment of this dead girl's mother, who thought she had killed herself. And that she'd get her insurance pay-out if the death was ruled a murder. Of course, if I'd been there, I'd have told George not to do it, that it didn't sound right, but he'd already done it. He signed Parfitt's paper, and Parfitt took it away with him.'

Dottie stared. 'He signed a paper?'

'Yes. George said he wrote it all out. Parfitt told him what to put, and then my boy signed it as a true statement. And Parfitt signed him a bit of paper to say I would receive the sum of five thousand pounds. Then he took the statement away with him to give to the judge.

'Well, I daresay, to them five thousand pounds is neither here nor there, but it's more money than I can even imagine. At first I said I wouldn't take it, but then, when it was clear nothing could be done, I thought I might as well. It was too late to change what George had done. I'd never see my boy again, nothing could save him, but he'd tried to do this one last thing for me, to make up for all the bad. So then I made up my mind to buy this little sweet shop and tobacconist with a flat over.'

'Then why didn't you?' Dottie asked.

'Because I never got the money.'

'Oh!' Dottie sat back, thinking about that.

'When I got my boy's things back from the prison in Birmingham, after—you know—there was no piece of paper signed by your intended. And no one ever came near me or spoke to me. Then after a few weeks, I began to feel very angry. They'd taken my son. He'd done his best to make amends. So where was my money? It was the least they could do. By rights, he should have had ten years in prison and come out. But no, that weren't enough for them. So where was my money?

'Well I wrote him, first off. I thought perhaps there was just some sort of a delay. Or I told myself he might of lost my address. You know how it is—you try to explain it to yourself, but in the end, you just can't. Anyway, there wasn't no answer to my letters, so I went there to see him, only of course no one would let me in. I went to the desk and raised merry hell but they just threw me out, threatened to arrest me for being drunk and disorderly. I've never been drunk in my life! I went back again another time. That got me a thirty shilling fine for disturbing the peace. So here I am, sixty-nine and taking in washing for next to nothing.'

She looked at Dottie. 'And what will you and your friend do about it? Nowt, I expect. I mean, them coppers all cover up for each other, don't they? And Parfitt's your intended, so you won't want him shamed or disgraced, will you? Stands to reason. Mud sticks, and you won't want it sticking to you, Miss Posh Girl. I suppose after all it was really him what sent you here to see what I'd say?'

Dottie shook her head. 'No, truly, he doesn't know I'm here. He'd be furious if he found out.'

'Hit you, does he? He looks the type.'

'He hasn't yet. But there have been times I thought he might,' Dottie admitted.

Mrs Parkes shook her head. 'You can't help me, duck. You'd best get off home to your mother. And find yourself a nice man. That Parfitt sort will leave you crying.'

Dottie stood up. 'I'll tell Inspector Hardy what you told me. He might ask you to make a statement. He'll need that if he's to prove a case against Mr Parfitt.'

Mrs Parkes gave a cynical laugh. 'They always want you to write it down on their bit o' paper, don't they? Makes it seem real. But then the paper goes missing, and it's just your word against theirs, and no one will believe someone like me.'

'I do, Mrs Parkes, and so will Inspector Hardy. He's not like Mr Parfitt. This one is a good man.'

The old woman just shook her head. 'Oh send him round. I'll sign his bit o' paper. I don't care anymore.' She picked up the photograph now and stared, not at the picture, but at her son's handwriting on the back.

Mrs Parkes directed Dottie to the bus-stop, and eventually she got back to the railway station. The bus journey had given her plenty of time to think. Now her mind was made up. She retrieved her luggage, went outside and hailed another taxi to take her back to Gervase's house. Her work here was still not finished.

*

Chapter Twelve

It was immediately clear that yet again her unexpected arrival back at the house caused Michaels some embarrassment, but she detected, too, a certain amount of triumph in his expression as Dottie marched past him to the morning room.

She opened the door, and entered to find Gervase—returned a day early from his 'conference'—apparently wrestling on the sofa with a female who, on realising they were no longer alone, hastily pushed Gervase aside and straightened her clothing. It was, of course, Moira Hansom.

Dottie—neither angry nor shocked nor hurt—merely rolled her eyes and said, 'Good God! Not again! You two don't waste much time, do you?'

She fished in her bag for the hideous engagement ring and set it on the coffee table.

'It's time we ended this charade, Gervase. I'll leave it to you to notify everyone.'

'I know about you and William! I know you want him for yourself!' Moira snapped, her eyes flashing angrily as she fumbled to button her blouse.

'Of course.' Dottie shrugged. She didn't stay to argue. In the hall, she asked Michaels to call another taxi.

'I'm not sure where to go,' she said. 'I need to stay in the area for various reasons.'

'I can recommend a nice hotel, miss, not too expensive, but very clean and the food is good.'

She smiled at him. 'Thank you, that sounds perfect.'

'Miss Dottie, if I may say, don't upset yourself over him. He's not worth it.'

'Don't worry about me, Mr Michaels. I'm not heartbroken. Thank you for your help and your kindness. And please give my thanks to Lizzie and Maureen, and my best wishes to your wife.'

'Thank you, miss. And—may I trouble you for your home address, just in case it's needed.'

'Of course.' She quickly jotted it down on a page of her diary, tore it out and gave it to him. He only just had time to pocket it, before Gervase's shout from the doorway made them both jump.

'What the hell, Dottie?'

She sighed. Of course. Gervase must have his scene. She turned to face the man, his shirt still open, undershirt hanging out, tie dangling loose from his collar, and his face flushed deep red. In the harsh light of the late winter sun, he looked more like fifty than his true thirty-seven years of age. His lifestyle was taking its toll, she realised. The flushed face no doubt indicated high blood pressure, his waistline was expanding, his temper was irritable. No longer the attractive, energetic man she had thought him only eight months ago.

'What is it?' She could hardly keep the revulsion from her voice.

'Now look,' he began. He halted. Dottie thought, I could almost write this script for him. Cue the change of tactic.

He tried the puppy-dog eyes and whiny voice she had always despised. 'Dottie darling, please! It was a momentary error of judgement. She means nothing...'

'You're a liar. And you mean nothing to me, Gervase. I'm leaving. It's over. Don't ever contact me again. I loathe you, by the way, and this expression you're adopting now, that you think makes you look so appealing. Honestly, if you don't stop it, I shall take off my shoe and throw it at you. It's ridiculous in a man of your age.'

He went into the cold rage stage. His temper had never been fully directed at her before, though she'd seen it a couple of times. She was already taking a step back when he lashed out. Even so, his hand caught her a heavy slap across the face and almost knocked her down.

She staggered back with a gasp, groping for the little side-table to steady herself. She was dumb with shock. It took several breaths to pull herself together and stand upright.

His look was one of satisfaction. His eyes held no contrition, no realisation that he had gone too far. She knew that for him, his actions were not only right but entirely justified. He would always view any woman as beneath him. He would require total unquestioning obedience and respect. Well not from me, she told herself.

Mr Michaels, horrified, ran to assist her. Dottie straightened her shoulders and put her chin up. She looked Gervase right in the eye and said, 'If you ever lay a hand on me again, I shall have you charged with assault. And I shall make sure that everyone knows what a truly despicable man you are.'

She half-expected him to turn on her again, but as he made a slight movement, Michaels stood in front of her.

'Now, now, sir, the young lady is just leaving. No need to lose your temper.'

Dottie hurried to the front door, not looking back, except to briefly glance at the morning room door where Moira stood leaning against the jamb, shock overcoming her anger.

Dottie went outside. She drew in several deep breaths. The shock was hitting her now. She began to be afraid he would follow her outside. She trembled, sudden sobbing breaths choked her. She heard a step, and whirled round. But it was Moira coming out.

'It's all right,' Moira said. 'He's gone to his study. Here's your hat box and dressing case. Michaels will no doubt bring out your suitcase.'

Of course, Dottie realised, my luggage.

Moira hesitated, then said, 'He seems so nice at first. Gervase. So—you know—full of sex appeal, so good-looking. But he does lash out. You have to learn how to handle him.'

'I have no intention of doing that, thank you,' Dottie snapped.

Moira's crimson-polished fingertips went to her mouth. 'My God, your face! It's bright red. And you're bleeding!'

Dottie put her hand up to her cheek. Sure enough, it came away with a thick streak of red. 'That signet ring he wears,' she said. 'It must have caught me.' Her hand was shaking, like her voice.

'Are you all right?' Moira asked.

Dottie nodded.

Moira said, 'Look, I know we don't like one another. But I never meant for this to happen. I didn't mean for you to get hurt.'

The taxi was already coming through the gates at the end of the drive; it was the same one that had set her down just a few minutes earlier. Michaels brought Dottie's suitcase out of the house.

Dottie said, 'How could you do this to William?'

Moira gave a bitter laugh, shaking her head as she did so. 'He won't care. He was never mine, he's still yours. Give him this and tell him I'm sorry.' She pulled off her ring and gave it to Dottie.

'Really? You'd rather have Gervase?'

'We go back a long way. He's done too much for me to leave him now, and vice versa. I'll make him marry me this time.'

'But you can see what he's like!'

'I told you, I already know what he's like. But he'll give me the life I want. William won't ever get to the top, he's too nice to get on in this world. And I'm not the sort of girl to put up with being just—ordinary.' Moira turned and went inside.

Dottie put Moira's ring into her bag and took out one of William's handkerchiefs. She used that to wipe her face, looking into the little mirror of her compact to assess the damage. Her hand was still shaking, she could see it reflected in the mirror. She felt like sobbing.

'Nonsense,' she told herself fiercely. That bucked her up a bit.

Michaels put Dottie's luggage into the taxi and told the driver the name of the hotel she was going to.

As the taxi drove away, Dottie waved to Mr Michaels, who was looking worried.

The driver, watching her in the rear-view mirror, said, 'You all right, duck?'

'Yes thank you. Better now.' She gave him a wobbly smile, then winced as she became aware of the pain in the whole of the left side of her face. At least it was finally over.

The hotel was small, but pleasant. The manager looked askance at the young woman standing in front of him, much calmer now, but still sporting the signs of a physical dispute of some kind.

Why, Dottie wondered, should she be the one to feel guilty for the marks on her face? Did battered wives feel this way? Did they apologise for sins they had not committed? Bruises and cuts they had not inflicted?

She smiled at the manager, put her shoulders back and her chin up. In her most imperial voice, she said, 'A room with a private bathroom, please, and I'd like lunch sent up right away.'

That told him.

'Yes miss, of course. It'll be room seventeen. If you'll just sign here.'

Within half an hour of arriving at the hotel, Dottie was wondering why she had done something so rash. If only she'd gone back to London as planned.

But the truth was, she had been so moved by Mrs Parkes' story, and so angry at what had happened, she couldn't simply 'abandon' the old lady and return to

London as if she hadn't sat there and listened to her talk about her grief. Coming face to face with a victim of Gervase's relentless climb to the top of the social ladder had made her all the more determined to help William.

But she also couldn't deny that if she'd just gone back to London after leaving Mrs Parkes, she would never have had that dreadful scene with Gervase. To hit her like that... Dottie still couldn't believe it, even though she could see the damage in the mirror with her own eyes. She looked as though she'd been struck across the face by a whip. She replayed the scene again and again in her mind, and it still didn't seem real.

Lunch was brought up to her, and having eaten it—Mr Michaels was right, it was very good—she felt better. She took the coffee and sat on the bed to consider her options.

She would have to ring her parents to let them know she had decided to stay on. Now that she had the rough outline of his hand and a huge weal across her cheek from Gervase's signet ring, she couldn't possibly go home. She'd have to stay here until it was better, or her father, outraged, would be calling Gervase out. Or if not her father, her mother would be quite as likely to challenge Gervase to prove himself a man. Her parents would say that hitting a woman was as low as a man could stoop. She sighed.

It astonished her that she still felt somehow it had been all her own fault. She almost felt as if she owed him an apology, yet she knew that was nonsense. She could only hope that a little more make-up than usual would conceal the worst.

She had planned to meet William tomorrow or the next day in London, to let him know what Mrs Parkes had told her. Now what was she supposed to do? He was in all probability still staying with his uncle and aunt, but she felt shy of telephoning him there.

There was a tap on her door, and a maid put her head in and said, 'I've come for your tray, miss, if you've finished with it?'

'I have, thank you.'

She nodded and came into the room, 'I hope everything was satisfactory?'

'It was delicious.'

'Also, miss, there is a gentleman in reception asking to see you.'

Dottie was surprised. What was Mr Michaels doing here? It had to be him, because no one else knew where she was. Had he come to make sure she was all right? He was such a dear.

She followed the maid along the hall and then as the maid went through the baize door to go down the back stairs to the kitchen, Dottie continued down the main staircase.

Her approach was almost silent. The thick carpet muffled the sound of her steps, and the stairs were completely free of creaks—not a common occurrence in Dottie's experience.

There was a man standing in reception, waiting. He stood with his back to her as he read something on the noticeboard, and hadn't yet noticed her. Her heart pounded. She should have made up her face to cover the mark, she didn't want him to see it, but it was too late to do anything. She was only able to see his back, but of course she would know William anywhere.

The manager was watching her, presumably in case this was the man she had already had an altercation with. But Dottie sent him a smile and a nod to say everything was all right. He relaxed noticeably. Another kind man, she thought. Thank goodness not all men were like Gervase.

Then, 'I assume Mr Michaels told you where I was.' She held her breath, waiting for his reaction.

He turned. His concerned look gave way to a furious one in an instant.

'My God!' he exclaimed. 'Michaels told me what happened, but this is absolutely bloody...'

She put a hand up to stop him. 'William, please. Please don't, I can't take it. No scenes just at the moment.'

He shook his head. His right hand came out to try to sweep her into his arms, but she held him off. 'Don't,' she said. 'I'll cry. I'm trying not to...' Her voice wobbled to prove it. 'Let's just sit and have a sensible conversation.'

The manager called over, 'There's a sitting room for guests through the archway there, Miss Manderson.'

It was a relief to be sitting down with William in the cool quiet room.

She said, 'Look, I know you want me to tell you all about it, but I just can't at the moment. I'm too shaky and upset. And please don't blow up and lose your temper, or shout at me, because I can't cope with that either. I just want you to be nice and calm, and to talk to me about boring things, or nice things like flowers or kittens.'

'I'll get him for this,' William said savagely, but keeping his voice low. 'If it's the last...'

'Stop it, William. Be sensible. You've got more against him that the fact that he slapped me. In the grand scheme of things, really this is nothing, we both know that. Let's just forget about it.'

He didn't reply to that, and she had a suspicion she hadn't changed his mind. Instead he said, 'Have you eaten?'

'Yes, thanks. I've just had a very nice lunch, and I wolfed down all three courses in about ten minutes' flat.'

He smiled a little at that. But beneath the smile his temper was seething. He would have to speak to Parfitt about this. This kind of thing could not simply be accepted without rebuke.

She managed a shadow of her usual smile. 'So you see, I've still got a good appetite, and this little cut will heal in no time.' She dismissed it with a wave of the hand.

It didn't look such a little cut from where William was sitting. But he made an effort to do as she asked and calm himself. Therefore he asked about her visit to Mrs Parkes.

She told him all about the visit, finishing with, 'And she will tell you anything you want to know, and she understands you want to use it in court and all that sort of thing.'

William could hardly believe she'd been so successful. But then, people warmed to Dottie, and would usually tell her anything. He took her hand. 'Thank you for doing that. I knew if anyone could get the old girl to talk, it would be you.' He wanted to kiss her. She pulled her hand away, still needing some space.

'I felt very sorry for her,' she said. 'Obviously her son was a bit of a bad lot—yes, yes, I know that's putting it mildly—and she said as much herself. But she loved him, he was her only child, and in his own way he tried to take care of her. After talking to her, I just felt I couldn't go back to my nice little life in London without trying to help her. I just want to help... I know it seems mad.'

'Michaels said...' He saw her expression and held up a hand to calm her. 'I know, I know. But I have to ask you. Michaels said Moira was there. With Parfitt. Is that true?'

'Yes.'

'I see.' He didn't seem to know what else to say.

'William, she knows exactly what he's like, yet she still...'

'Loves him?'

Dottie shook her head. 'It's not love, though she said she would make him marry her. She likes the lifestyle he can offer, and his status. When he—did what he did—she came out to see if I was all right. William, you need to warn her about the investigation. Otherwise she could be caught up in it.'

He nodded. 'She knows. I found her looking through my papers once when I came back from having a bath. I should have put them away, but I wasn't expecting her to arrive when she did.'

Dottie said, 'She gave me your ring to give back to you. She said...' Too late she realised she couldn't tell him what Moira had said about him. He was waiting for her to finish what she'd been about to say. So she added, rather lamely, 'She said she'd be grateful if I could give it back to you and tell you she was sorry. Er—it's in my bag upstairs, I'll go and get it.'

He put a hand out. 'Don't bother, later will do. So are you going back to London in the morning?'

'No, I'm staying here.'

'Really?'

'I can't go home looking like this. Can you imagine what my parents would say? You can give me something to do to help you. Or are you going back to London?'

'No, I'm staying on, especially now this has happened. Would you like to come to dinner? I'd like you to meet my uncle and aunt. And Eleanor has been pestering me to bring you over.'

She was already shaking her head. 'Not today, I'm sorry. And thank you, it's very kind, but not today. I don't really want to meet them whilst this is still so raw.' She touched her forefinger to her cheek.

He nodded, pushing down disappointment mingled with rage at Parfitt. 'Of course.'

They looked at each other.

'Give me something to do,' she said. 'I need to be busy, and I need to help you, and to help Mrs Parkes. I just want it all over and done with.'

'Perhaps you could talk to the major? If he'll talk to anyone, I think it will be you. And the secretary must know something. How could she not? If you try her again, she might be more forthcoming. Especially when she sees...'

Dottie sighed. 'When she sees what Gervase has done to me? I imagine it will come in useful from that point of view. And with the major too, he's such a sweet old softie. All right, I'll tackle both of them, the major this evening, and Mrs Holcombe tomorrow.'

'She'll be at work tomorrow. It's Monday, don't forget.'

'Oh yes, blast it.' She thought for a second or two. 'I could meet her for lunch. She must get a lunch break, surely?' Then she groaned. 'Oh blast again. I keep forgetting I haven't any transport. Well, I'll have to see about another taxi.'

'I'll drive you.'

'Don't be silly, darling, you've got more important things to do, I'm sure.'

He was looking at her intently. Then she realised that she'd called him darling again.

But all he said was, 'I'm not going to argue about it. I'll

take you to Mrs Holcombe's. I'll stay in the car whilst you talk to her.'

It wasn't quite what she had wanted, but he was not in the mood for a discussion. At least she could keep an eye on him this way. She didn't want him going to Gervase's house and punching him. It was Gervase who was supposed to be going to prison, not William.

She nodded. 'All right. When do you want to go?'

He said, 'After dinner? Or before?'

'Let's go now,' she decided. 'Then we can go to Major Sedgworth's afterwards. There, all done in one afternoon.' She deliberately kept her voice bright, not wanting him to know all she wanted was to huddle up in bed and feel sorry for herself.

But she knew he wasn't deceived. He gave her a searching look. 'Sure? We don't have to see either of them today. Or I could go to see them alone. Or...'

She got to her feet. 'No, we'll do it now. I need to change and freshen my make-up. Ten minutes. Is that all right?'

'Of course.' He reached for a newspaper, and settled back in his armchair. 'Take your time, Dottie, love.'

*

Chapter Thirteen

Mrs Holcombe opened the door and didn't trouble to disguise her surprise at seeing Dottie there. She invited her in, nonetheless, staring openly at the injury to Dottie's cheek. She raised her eyebrows, but said nothing.

As soon as they were sitting down, Dottie said, 'Let's put our cards on the table, Mrs Holcombe. What do you know about Gervase Parfitt?'

If Mrs Holcombe found this forthright approach shocking, it was nothing to Dottie's tension as she held her breath, waiting to see whether or not she would be shown the door. She was aghast at her own brazenness.

But Mrs Holcombe didn't tell her to leave, though she looked wary. After a moment she said, 'Why? What have you heard?'

Dottie didn't reply, she just waited to see what her silence would do. After a moment, Mrs Holcombe asked, 'Why should I tell you anything?'

'Because you know what Mrs Sedgworth wanted to tell me.'

'She would never have told you anything,' Mrs Holcombe said impatiently. 'All she wanted was to find out what Parfitt had told you about her.'

Puzzled, Dottie said, 'Why should Gervase tell me anything about Mrs Sedgworth?'

'Well, he obviously knew something that she didn't want to become common knowledge. She thought he might confide in you, tattle to you about his friends. I'm not quite sure why, but she believed Gervase and you had been having cosy little chats about all the scandals he has helped to hush up.'

'We haven't,' Dottie said.

'Of course not. I told her he wouldn't, he had too much to lose. But she was worried and not thinking straight.'

'But why now? I've been seeing Gervase since last summer.'

Mrs Holcombe's shoulder jerked in a kind of shrug. 'Because of the engagement. Everything was about to change, and you would be living here, in a small village where reputation is everything, and not in London where there are millions of people, and no one knows anyone. You would be here, talking to people who knew her, people she might meet every day. Once this terrible secret of hers was out, she felt her life wouldn't be worth living. She would be despised and ridiculed. Everyone would *know*.'

Dottie was horrified. 'But, Mrs Holcombe... I would never do such a thing...'

'Christobel didn't know that. She was past reasoning. She was desperate. She had to be sure. Hence the invitation.'

'But what on earth could be so very terrible? What was her awful secret?' Dottie asked, although she already knew the answer to that.

Mrs Holcombe drew back, and clasping her hands, contrived to look saintly. 'I know nothing about it.'

From that, she would not budge. She got up and led the way to the door, saying over her shoulder. 'I'm afraid I have an early start in the morning, and so much still to do this afternoon before I go to Evening Service. Good afternoon, Miss Manderson, and thank you for coming. It was so kind of you to call again.'

Dottie had no choice but to go. She came out of the house and walked along the road to where William's car was parked.

He was reading, but looked up to watch her coming towards him. As always when he saw her, his spirits lifted. She was lovely. But now, her face wore a troubled look in addition to the long angry-looking scratch.

She told him the little she had learned.

'Well,' he said with a sigh, 'Let's hope Major Sedgworth is a bit more helpful.'

He let them in, smiling to see them. They hung up their coats and went into the little sitting room. The maid had just brought in tea.

'Shall I be mother?' Dottie asked, and with a nod and a grave smile from the major, began to pour out the tea, and pass the men their cups and plates. She knew she was giving the perfect performance of a little girl at a grown-up tea-party, but it didn't matter a jot. The major was relaxing, and that was what counted.

'Been in the wars?' he asked Dottie, nodding at her.

She could feel herself blushing. How had she forgotten about her face? She stammered something about it being nothing to worry about, but William interrupted her, giving the major an angry, man-to-man look.

'Parfitt did that to her this morning. Slapped her across the face. His signet ring caught her and scratched her cheek. I think it's fair to say the engagement is off. And I for one am glad it is.'

The major was shocked. In fact, Dottie thought he looked really upset.

'Not quite the ticket, Parfitt. He couldn't do anything that would surprise me. Or sink him lower in my estimation. Rotten through and through. A thorough-going B-word, if ever there was one. Have a cake, m'dear.'

Dottie smiled at him. And although she didn't really want it, she accepted the cake he offered.

William said, 'Major, I'd like to ask you something rather difficult.'

Major Sedgworth looked as if he'd been expecting it all along. He straightened his shoulders, set his jaw and looked more like a military man than Dottie had ever seen him.

'Copper, aren't you?'

'Yes. I'm an inspector from Scotland Yard.'

The major nodded. It was just as he had expected, it seemed. 'Thought as much. And—er—you're in love with this young lady here?'

Without a moment's hesitation or even a glance at Dottie, William said simply, 'Yes.'

It was all very unromantic and matter-of-fact, Dottie thought. But there, he'd said it, and in front of someone else. She couldn't help smiling.

'Ask away, dear boy. Been expecting it. But to warn you, I don't know much. She kept me out of it. More's the pity. I'd have called him out. Perhaps that's what she was afraid of, I don't know.'

'Major,' Dottie said in a lowered voice, 'What about your family? Your son and daughter?'

'Out at the moment. Gone to see someone or other. Old schoolfriend of my daughter, I think. Back in time for dinner, they said. I think they just needed to get out of the house for a while.' He shot her a look. 'But thank you for thinking of them, m'dear.'

She smiled at him.

The major turned to William, who got out his notebook and pencil.

'Your wife indicated to Miss Manderson that there were things—one assumes discreditable things—that she ought to know about Gervase Parfitt.'

'Hmph.' The major dropped his chin on his chest and appeared deep in thought. He said nothing further.

Dottie said, 'Major, I'm sure you were very fond of your wife, and the last thing anyone wants is to tarnish her memory in any way. But you and I both know that she invited me here that morning to tell me something. Something specific, not just as a general kindness to a newcomer. You were as surprised as I when we arrived here and she claimed to be unwell. She had been crying. She couldn't have been upset before you left, or you wouldn't have come, you'd have simply telephoned to tell me she wasn't very well, and then arranged a different day. What upset her so badly? Surely she told you?'

Major Sedgworth turned troubled blue eyes upon her. 'Thought the world of my wife. Met her when I was nineteen. She was only sixteen. I had to wait two years before her father let me court her. I wasn't even supposed to hold her hand, let alone kiss her.'

Dottie had heard all this is the car the other day, but she listened anyway, touched by the old-fashioned romance of it.

'Though we managed to sneak a couple of kisses over the years.' He laughed heartily at that. William and Dottie smiled politely.

The major continued: 'He was a tyrant, her father, and with six daughters to marry off, he knew how to keep a close eye on 'em. But it was worth it. I loved her with my whole being. Don't know what I'm going to do...' His voice gave out on the last two words.

Dottie's eyes filled with tears. She squeezed his hand.

After a few moments, he said. 'As I said, Christobel was brought up very strictly. As was I. My father was a bishop and took his duty to his flock very seriously. But once we were married—I suppose it goes with the army lifestyle— so many soirees, dinners, receptions, celebrations, dances, you name it, not to mention difficult times to endure. I— I'm afraid we both became rather too fond of a tipple. In fact I'd go so far as to say it was quite difficult to get through the day without a glass of something towards the evening. I drank far more than was good for me. And m'wife hardly less.'

He broke off to offer them more tea. They both declined, but he rang anyway. Once the maid had appeared, he said, 'Drop more tea, m'dear.' She bobbed and left again.

Major Sedgworth said, 'Where was I? Oh yes. Well, I don't know the details. Honestly. If I did, I'd tell you.'

To Dottie he looked as though he had aged ten years in the last week, he looked worn out. She could easily imagine him sitting here for hours every day reminiscing and upsetting himself. What a good thing it was he had his family with him. Though she could understand why they might need to get out of the house for a while.

'Last year, in March of 1934, I was away from home for just over a month. I had been asked to do some lectures for a new intake of recruits at my old base down in the south-west. To be honest it was rather fun, and I wasn't at all sorry to go—it was mostly pontificating, reminiscing and such, which all we old blokes love, of course, along with a reunion with some fellows I'd knocked about with over the years. An excuse for a good old-fashioned booze-up.

'When I got back, I saw immediately that something was up. Something had happened, but Christobel didn't want to tell me about it, she just waved it aside, said it wasn't anything serious. I suppose eventually I realised that he had something over her, that Parfitt fellow. But it was easier to ignore it, just forget about it, anything to avoid a row.

'You see, we never really took to him. Parfitt, I mean. One hears rumours in a village, of course, and we didn't think he was our kind of chap. Yet suddenly, my wife's inviting him to this and that, and we're traipsing back and forth to his place. Hobnobbing. Even though I see that Christobel really hates it, nevertheless, it's all, 'We must go,' she says. And 'He's our neighbour,' she says, 'we must be friendly.' 'Think of the talk if we snubbed him,' she says. Shouldn't have thought anyone would notice or even care if we did, but she was so set on it, I was happy to tag along. Anything for a quiet life. Quiet life, happy wife, don't they say, eh?'

'Then a few months ago, I'm thinking over a few things, and the lousy weather is getting me down. I suggest to my wife we might invest the money her parents left her in a holiday home down on the coast. We could let it out, I suggest, and take breaks ourselves when we fancy it. It's one of those things people are doing now. And it seemed like a good idea. My money's all tied up in investments, but not hers. She'd only had it a year or so, we hadn't really decided how to make the best use of it.

'I had quite a bee in my bonnet about it. It seemed such a good opportunity. I'd heard from a very reliable friend about four little villas all owned by the same family, all coming up for sale. Not a five-minute walk from the beach, sea view, nice little village, everything. The perfect spot for a relaxing holiday or a long weekend. It seemed ideal. So I put it to Chris, as I say, and what does she tell me?'

Dottie thought she knew the answer to that, and judging by William's grave expression, he did too.

'All gone,' the major said. 'She broke down in tears and told me. It was all gone. She'd given it to someone, she wouldn't say who, to keep them quiet about something that had happened whilst I was away. Wouldn't say what. So finally I put two and two together, and I don't think I was far out. She'd obviously pranged the car and had to have it repaired. No real problem there, these things happen.

'But it didn't explain the money. Car repairs wouldn't have taken her whole inheritance. Obviously she'd been paying hush-money to someone. And as far as I was concerned, that could only mean one thing. She'd probably had too much to drink at one of these get-togethers, and knocked some poor blighter down. You don't pay hush-money for anything minor. But every time I asked her, she just burst out crying and I couldn't get anything out of her. All she would ever say was, that it was over, and it was too late to fix it. So I let it go. Fool that I am. But... well, if it wasn't Parfitt she was paying, I'll give you £50.'

The door opened a crack and the maid peeped in cautiously. The major waved her in. 'Yes, yes, it's all right. Just set it down and go, m'dear.'

She scuttled in with a tray bearing another teapot, and a collection of clean crockery. She took away the used things and left once more.

'So you don't have any definite knowledge?' William

asked.

The major shook his head. 'As Miss Manderson said, on that morning when I left to come and collect her, Chris was as right as rain. Then—well—you saw what sort of state she was in when we got back.'

'Mr Parfitt was seen making a telephone call as soon as you and Miss Manderson left,' William told him.

'To this house?'

William nodded.

'Just as I thought,' said the major.

He poured himself a cup of tea, again offering them both another cup. Once more they declined. He stirred in milk and sugar, then said to William, 'Would it be possible to find out if anyone died on the road in this area in March of last year? That's when I was away. That's when it had to have happened. A bit late in the day, I realise that, but I—I just need to know.'

'I've had a man looking into it,' William said. 'But he hasn't been able to find anything so far.'

'Do you think Mrs Holcombe knows anything? I rather got the impression that your wife had confided in her,' Dottie said.

The major shrugged. 'Sorry, m'dear. I don't really know. They got along all right, but weren't exactly the closest of friends. I suppose we do—did, I mean—see Mary quite a bit at various things, with her being Parfitt's secretary.'

'Is that all she was?' Dottie couldn't help asking.

The two men stared at her, and she blushed. 'Sorry, but I just thought... I mean, knowing what sort of man Gervase is, I just thought...'

'He likes 'em young and pretty,' Major Sedgworth said gently. 'Luckily for her, old Holcombe's a bit long in the tooth for Parfitt. From the rumours I've heard, it's common knowledge that he always has some pretty little thing on his arm.' He broke off, embarrassed, and apologising profusely, adding, 'Oh my dear Miss Manderson. Put my foot in it again. So sorry, m'dear.'

Dottie waved it aside. 'Don't worry, Major. You're quite right. It's all true.'

'It was rumoured that if some well-to-do fellow was entertaining friends or business associates, say for a weekend house party or something, then Parfitt was the chap you went to, to fix up the entertainment. Ladies, you know,' he said in clarification, and going a bit pink in the face. 'Not that I was ever counted amongst his closest friends, luckily, so I don't have any personal experience of this, but that is what I've heard, or surmised from comments over brandy and cigars after dinner, that sort of thing. All far too sordid for my taste. Then of course, the rumours about something happening and being hushed up. Which struck a chord with me anyway, because of Chris. There was drug-taking too, from what one of the fellows said.'

Dottie nodded. 'I've heard similar rumours.'

'Do you have any details?' William asked the major. 'Can you remember who told you this, or who was there when it was discussed?'

'I've a feeling I was having drinks after a game of golf with a few fellows, and I remember at the time thinking, that's something that's been suggested before, and if it's true, he's even more vile than I thought. There were five or six of us. Me and Parfitt, of course, and—oh let me see...'

'Was his father there? Edwin Parfitt?' Dottie wanted to help him remember.

Major Sedgworth shook his head. 'No, Parfitt is quite careful what he lets slip in front of his father—*he's* the chief constable of Nottinghamshire, don't forget, so he needs to keep out of anything disreputable. One of the other fellows said something along the lines of wasn't it time they had another of their special weekends. There was a bit more, but I'm afraid I can't really recall... Parfitt shot me a look as though he didn't like them mentioning it in front of me, not sure how I would take it. Oh what was the chap's name?'

Again Dottie tried to prompt the old boy. 'Was it that Armstrong fellow who was there last week?'

The major snapped his fingers. 'Spot on! Well done, m'dear, yes, it was him.' He turned to William. 'The

Honourable—or in this case—the *dis*honourable Marcus Armstrong. A young brat, moneyed class, never done a day's work, you know the type. Yes it was he who mentioned it first, and gave a kind of sneaky laugh, like bathwater going down the drain. Hate the young so-and-so.'

'And the other two? Or three?' William was writing it down in his notebook.

The major was frowning into space, racking his brains for the answer. 'I've got no recollection of one of them. And the other, well I'm not sure, but I've a feeling it was young—oh what's his name? I can't think of his name at the moment, but he's the son of Parfitt's boss, the Derbyshire chief con.'

William raised his eyebrows. That meant he was *very* interested, Dottie knew. She smiled slightly as she looked at him, feeling suddenly very proud of him.

She said, 'I've met him, William. It's Gordon Wisley. I told you what he said to me at the engagement ball at Edwin and Evangeline Parfitt's place. Gordon seemed quite sweet, and desperately worried his father would find out what he'd been getting up to.'

William nodded, making another note.

The major said, 'That's the fellow. Young Gordon's all right. A bit lacking in the brain department but he's a fairly decent young fellow.'

'I met Gordon at the Parfitts' ball last week, we danced and chatted. He mentioned that Gervase had helped him out of a scrape. As I say, it was clearly sufficiently scandalous that he was worried his father might find out.'

'I'm beginning to think that's what all this is about,' William said. 'That Parfitt helps his friends out.'

'For a price,' said the major. 'Quite a high price, at that. Old Parfitt must be worth quite a few bob these days. By the way, I still have the bill from the garage too, somewhere. Found it yesterday going through some things. Chris always used to complain I never threw anything away. She was right too, but it should be here somewhere. Is that likely to be useful to you, Inspector?'

'My goodness, yes, definitely!'

William and Dottie exchanged an excited look as the major went over to his bureau in the corner of the room, pulled down the flap and began to sift through the heaps of papers. It was several minutes before he said:

'Ah yes, here we are.'

He held the page out to William, who took it and read it then passed it to Dottie.

A relatively small sum of money had been paid to a garage and the invoice was dated 2nd April 1934. The description of the work was vague, but mentioned denting and scraping to the front bumper and a smashed headlamp.

'I suppose if you hit someone when you're driving a car, you'd be likely to cause damage to your front bumper, headlamp and possibly to your windscreen,' Dottie suggested.

William and the major both nodded.

'And the car was not in need of repairs before you went away?' William asked. The major shook his head.

'It was in good order. Recently serviced, so I know all was well.'

William held up the invoice. 'May I use this?'

The major nodded.

'Would you be prepared to make a statement or give evidence if called before an enquiry panel?'

'An enquiry panel?' The major was rather taken aback. But then he shrugged. 'Oh all right. If it helps put that b...' He shot Dottie an apologetic look. 'B-bounder away,' he hastily amended.

'We can only do our best, Major.' William pulled out an official pad from his briefcase, and for the next half hour, he and Major Sedgworth worked on the statement.

They drove away, but William stopped the car a few minutes later at the side of a quiet country lane.

'Why have we stopped?' Dottie asked.

He turned in his seat. 'I just wanted to make sure you're all right.' Very tenderly he stroked her cheek, feeling the ridge of the cut. 'Are you? All right?'

'Not really,' she said.

He put his arm around her shoulders and pulled her against him. They sat in silence for a several minutes. She began to relax against him. She closed her eyes. Her cheek was aching...

Suddenly a thought came to her and she shot bolt upright, almost hitting his chin with the top of her head. 'My parents! Oh William, I completely forgot to let Mother and Father know I won't be home tonight. They'll be worried sick!'

He started the car. 'Right. I'll take you back to the hotel, you can telephone from there. Then we'll go out for dinner. If you can bear a little more of my company, that is.'

In her head, she said, *always*. With a nod and a slight smile, she said, 'Marvellous idea. I'm ravenous.'

As before, the meal was almost at an end before they began to discuss what they knew.

'Mrs Parkes' son was persuaded to confess to a crime he hadn't committed,' Dottie said. 'Why? Who really killed that woman? Was it Mrs Sedgworth? Because looks as though that's exactly what happened, don't you think?' She looked at him earnestly.

'I do. Between Michaels' rumours of Parfitt helping her deal with a traffic accident, Parfitt calling Mrs Sedgworth and saying something to upset her the day you went to visit her—possibly to prevent her confiding in you—along with what the young fellow told you at the ball, and what the Major has now told us about damage to his car...

'Yes it seems all too probable that she knocked someone down and killed them, or seriously injured them, and phoned Parfitt to ask him for his help. If she'd been drinking, and the police had got involved—other than Parfitt, I mean—then things could have looked very grim for her. Not to mention the scandal if it ever got out.'

'Then there are the parties...' Dottie didn't really want to think about what might have happened at those. She said only, 'Gordon Wisley told me someone died. A girl. Somehow he was involved, and Gervase helped him out of a hole, so that his father wouldn't find out.'

'Serious damage to his own reputation or criminal activity on the part of his son would undermine the chief constable's authority, and how the police board view his integrity.'

'Would he lose his position as chief constable?'

He nodded. 'It's likely. In his position, he's supposed to be squeaky clean and above reproach.'

'Like Caesar's wife,' Dottie murmured.

William stared at her. 'What do you mean?'

'Well, in Shakespeare's play, Caesars's wife had to appear to be above reproach, so that she wouldn't suffer the consequences of...'

'Yes, yes, but...' He thought for a moment. 'Are you saying that Parfitt is acting on secret instructions from the chief constable?'

She was surprised. 'Do *you* think he might be? The chief constable couldn't get involved in anything crooked. Too much of a risk to his career. He might promise to protect Gervase in return for a little private help.'

He nodded. 'Interesting. I hadn't thought about it from that angle. I'd rather assumed that Parfitt has ambitions for the chief constable's office, and is using everything he can to get there. But, you're right, it could be a kind of 'you scratch my back, I'll recommend you for my job when I retire' situation.' He made a note in his trusty notebook.

'Though I don't see Gervase being patient enough to wait until someone retires. How old is the chief constable?'

He grinned. 'I shall endeavour to find out.'

She smiled slightly and finished her wine. 'So what's our plan of action?'

'I shall talk to Gordon Wisley. Then I'll go to see Mrs Parkes—thank you so much for that, it could be a really vital piece of the puzzle. Next I'll try to confirm from Gordon Wisley whether or not someone died at a party he either hosted or was a guest at, and how Parfitt was involved. Then I'll match that up with police records, and also search police records again for a road accident involving a female victim around the time of Major Sedgworth's absence, in or around the area of Blackhall, where young Parkes robbed the pub.' He sighed.

'It sounds like an awful lot to do,' Dottie said.

'It is, darling, but we've got to know.' Without thinking he took her hand and kissed the back of it. She took his hand and kept hold of it. They gazed at each other for a full minute, before he said: 'Look, Dottie, you're all in, time to get you back to your hotel.'

He noticed she was pale now, as she always was when tired or frightened. Or hurt. Or anxious. The mark from Parfitt's hand had faded slightly during the course of the afternoon, but the cut from the ring stood out across her cheek, a four inch scratch that was a deep red line, and on either side of it, a half-an-inch deep blueish-grey border bruised the skin. The sight of it rekindled his rage at Parfitt. How dared he lay his hand on her! According to Michaels, it had been forceful enough to almost knock her to the floor.

'William! You look absolutely furious with me.'

'Not you, Dottie. I was thinking about what he did to you.'

She looked in her bag for her mirror. A glance showed her she looked rather a mess. A blob of make-up was never going to disguise that. As she replaced the mirror, she saw the ring. She put it into his hand.

'Sorry William. I told you Moira asked me to give you this. You'd better have it back. Perhaps you can sell it or something.'

He said nothing, just looked at it then dropped it in his pocket. She knew he wasn't likely to be emotionally wounded by the failure of the engagement, but perhaps his pride... Flora and her mother always told her how fragile a thing a man's pride was.

She said, 'They've clearly been seeing one another for a while.'

He nodded. 'I don't care about that. It's over between

us, so it's nothing to me what she does. So long as he

doesn't hurt her too.'

'She saw what happened. She knows what he's like. They already have an intimate relationship, so it's probably for the best that they do get married.'

'Did he ever try it on with you?' He surprised her by asking.

'Oh he tried, of course. In fact...' She broke off, remembering her arrival the first time. 'Michaels knew what he intended. Michaels sabotaged the room I was supposed to be using, so that I had to be put in a different one. Gervase was so angry, though I'm sure he had no idea that the damage in the room was deliberate. Good thing, too, or Mr Michaels would be out of a job.' She told William all about it, and watched his anger resurface as he heard how she had shivered in her room as Parfitt shouted and pounded on her door in the middle of the night.

When he could trust himself to speak, William said, 'Obviously Michaels knew Parfitt was in the habit of seducing—or even attacking—women that stay with him.'

'It was a good thing Mr Michaels decided I was a nice girl who wouldn't do that sort of thing.'

'Let's go,' he said abruptly. He paid the bill and they went out to the car. It was frosty, and the cold air nipped at her throat and her eyes.

William said, 'I wonder if he's hosted any of those 'parties' at his house. I think I shall speak to Michaels again, see if I can get him to tell me anything. I'm certain he knows what's been going on. If anyone does, it would be the butler.'

'Mrs Holcombe, too,' Dottie pointed out. 'She *still* hasn't told me the truth, I just know it. Again, like a butler, a secretary is in a privileged position, often knowing a lot of private information.'

At the hotel door, she said, 'You don't need to see me inside.'

He was disappointed. He had hoped for an opportunity to kiss her. So he made do with a rather too brotherly kiss on her unhurt cheek, and said goodnight.

He watched her go into the lobby and then he went back to the car.

*

Chapter Fourteen

The next morning, William left her outside the Lion and Lamb hotel next to the market square in the centre of the town of Ripley.

'I'll meet you at about four o'clock,' he said. 'But if I'm delayed, I'll ring up and get them to let you know.' He made a note of the telephone number in his notebook.

She nodded. 'I'll be fine. Don't worry about me.'

'What are your plans?' He was looking at her suspiciously, a slight frown creasing the bit in between his brows. She felt as though the look went right through her. Golly, Dottie thought, I'm so glad I'm not an actual suspect. She guessed he would be scary in an interview.

'I'm going to lure Mrs Holcombe away from her desk and hope that, on neutral ground, she'll be a bit more forthcoming.'

He looked unconvinced. 'Well be careful, I don't want you running into Parfitt. Right then, see you later. Be good.'

Not for the first time, purely instinctively he bent to kiss her. She kissed him in return, and the kiss became longer and more passionate than either of them intended. It was quite difficult to stop.

He gave her a look that made her feel quite shivery. He raised his eyebrows and said, 'Well. Er—it might be half past three.'

She laughed and went into the hotel.

At the desk, she said, 'I'd like to reserve a table for two for afternoon tea, please.'

'Certainly madam. For what time?'

'Four o'clock.' She gave her name and the clerk confirmed he'd reserved a table for her.

'And can I also book lunch for two?'

'Yes of course.'

'The only thing is, I don't know what time. I need to speak to someone first, to find out when she can be here.'

'Let me know any time before eleven o'clock, madam, and I'm sure we will be able to suit you. Will there be anything else?'

'May I use the phone?'

'Of course. There's a booth just round the corner and to the right.'

'Is there a book?'

'Yes madam.'

She thanked him and went to make her call.

She found the phone book, and flicking back and forth, found what she was looking for: a telephone number for general enquiries at the police headquarters on the outskirts of town.

She got through quite quickly, and asked to speak to the assistant chief constable's secretary. When asked her business, she said—wondering as she did so if it was a criminal offence to lie to the police—that she was calling about the assistant chief constable's new dress uniform. She was put through immediately.

She had then to explain her deception to Mrs Holcombe, and pray she wouldn't hang up the phone or report her. She didn't. Dottie said,

'I'm in Ripley. Do come to lunch with me at the Lion and Lamb. Surely you get a lunch hour?'

There was a pause, then Mrs Holcombe said, 'All right. Thank you. I can be there at half past twelve, if that's suitable?'

'That's perfect,' Dottie said. 'I'll see you then. Oh—er— please don't mention this to Mr Parfitt. I don't want him to know I'm here.'

'I won't,' Mrs Holcombe assured her.

With almost three hours to while away before lunch, Dottie looked through the telephone book to find out if there was a Rialto cinema or theatre in Nottingham. There was. She went to the see the hotel clerk and asked for directions to a taxi firm. The man kindly offered to call the taxi for her.

'Where shall I say you wish to go, miss?'

'The Rialto, Nottingham.'

'Of course, miss.'

Ten minutes later she was on her way to Nottingham and praying the taxi could make it there and back in time for lunch. It wasn't a long way as the crow flies, but the roads were mainly rural, winding through small towns and villages, and as Dottie knew, that meant dawdling behind tractors, livestock, local buses, and clusters of chatting neighbours.

But they made it there in good time. Dottie negotiated with the driver to wait outside with his meter off, in exchange for a decent tip.

The Rialto was a little busier than she'd expected. It was Monday, so there was no matinee performance, but there was a rehearsal going on for a play starting at the weekend. People were coming and going, shouting and carrying things, and there was no one on duty behind the counter.

She looked about her as she waited. The place wasn't large, but it had a cheery air to it. The décor was in good condition, wood gleamed with polish, as did the chrome. The Rialto doubled as a variety theatre and a cinema, boasting two auditoriums, one on either side of the front lobby, and business was clearly good at the Rialto.

Eventually a young woman noticed Dottie and came over.

'Costumes?'

If only, Dottie thought, she'd love to do something like that, but she shook her head. 'No, sorry. I'm here with an enquiry about some old tickets.'

The woman looked puzzled but directed Dottie to the counter, going around to the opposite side to assist her. Dottie opened her bag, opened her purse and drew out the ticket stubs. She handed them to the woman.

'I know it seems like a stupid question, but can you tell me anything about these?'

The woman's eyes were round with excitement. Her glossy black hair swung forward like a heavy silk curtain as she leaned close, making Dottie think of Cleopatra. 'Are you one of them detectives?'

After only a slight hesitation Dottie said, 'As a matter of fact, I am.'

'Are you working on a case right now?'

Dottie nodded.

The woman looked at the scraps of pink paper. 'I suppose someone had these as an alibi?'

Dottie grinned. 'That's what we think.'

'Ooh!'

'Is there any way of finding out anything about them?'

'I can't tell you very much. Like, I can't tell you who bought 'em, or where they sat, or anything like that.'

'Do you know when they were sold?'

'I should be able to give you a rough idea. I'll be as quick as I can.'

Dottie nodded as the woman hurried off.

She was gone several minutes, but came back looking quite pleased. She held a red-covered book in her hand. 'Well,' she said.

Dottie was already smiling. This was going to be good.

'We get our ticket rolls delivered every fourth Wednesday. We get seventy-five rolls of 250 tickets. And the manager records them in the book, and I counter-sign. We have to do it for the owner, it's part of the accountancy procedure.'

'I was hoping you'd say that,' Dottie said.

'Looks like it might finally come in useful after all, then. I've gone back through some old account books. I found the ones you want in last year's book. These tickets, being numbers 7724 and 7725, would have been almost at the end of a roll. We have to take the numbers off at the start and end of each shift, and if we change rolls mid-shift. This is the shift book, where we record the ticket numbers. If you look here, you can see that your numbers were sold on Monday 2nd April last year. It shows here they had to change the roll that evening at half past nine. These would have been sold before half past nine but after the shift started, which was five o'clock. In fact quite a bit after, as the starting number taken at the beginning of the shift was 7596.'

Dottie made a note of all this information. 'If I ask a friend of mine to come and speak to you, would that be all right? He's a policeman. He might need to use this as evidence if the case goes to court.'

The woman was pink and excited. Her eyes shone. 'Oh yes please! Will I have to give evidence in court?'

'I'm afraid I don't know.'

'Oh, I do hope so. How exciting. Wait till I tell my sister, she'll be so envious.'

'Is there any way of knowing what film was on? Or if they saw a show?'

'These pink ones are tickets for the cinema. The theatre ones are a kind of bluey grey. Now, let me see...' She hurried off and returned a couple of minutes later, this time with a book with a black cover. 'Right then, this is the film book. We check the reels in and out in this, so we know we've sent back everything they supplied to us. Or else we're fined for the loss, you see, so we have to be very particular.'

'Of course.'

The woman ran her finger down a long list of dates, titles and numbers. 'Here we are, on the Wednesday night before the tickets were sold, we received *Keep It Quiet*.

Ooh that's the one with that good-looking Cyril Raymond, isn't it? I like him. And Jane Carr. I love thrillers, and that one kept me on the edge of my seat, wondering if they would be able to help him in time. I remember coming to see that with my sister.'

'I remember it too, I went with *my* sister.' With a smile, Dottie wrote down the name of the film and the date. She was excited to have found out so much. She thanked the woman profusely, and asked her name.

'Let me write it down for you,' she said. 'It's Indian. Most people can't spell it.'

'Miss Gitanjali Kaur?' Dottie said when she read what the woman had written. Dottie thanked her and said goodbye. She was relieved to find the taxi still where she'd left it.

She was back in Ripley with forty minutes to spare. She congratulated herself on a job well done. And hoped William would think the same.

When Mrs Holcombe arrived, she made no secret of her curiosity. As soon as she arrived, and gave Dottie a quick hug, Dottie knew something had changed.

They sat. Their table was perfectly situated: the dining room faced away from the now bustling marketplace. Here it was quiet, with a view of a tiny postage-stamp sized lawn bearing the summer's white-painted tables, and surrounded by a high wall. In the middle of this pleasant scene, a robin hopped about, once or twice pausing in its pursuit of bugs to cock a bright black eye at the two ladies. Only a few other people were lunching at the hotel, and none of them sat close by.

Dottie smiled and nodded at the waiter, who hurried over to take their orders. Drinks arrived: a glass of wine for Dottie and a glass of lemon squash for Mrs Holcombe. Dottie took the bull by the horns, so to speak, and immediately said, 'Obviously after what happened yesterday morning, my engagement to Mr Parfitt is over. In fact, that was one of the things that triggered the scene. I had given his ring back. I left the house in the morning, went to see someone, then purely on impulse, I came back to the house instead of going back to London. Gervase was already there at the house with his mistress, back a day early from the conference he had pretended to attend in Bournemouth.'

Mrs Holcombe nodded. 'Yes, I must admit, I thought it was odd I hadn't been asked to make any travel arrangements for him. Usually if he is away for professional reasons, I have to make his reservations, arrange his cars, that sort of thing. So I'm afraid I *was* suspicious.'

She glanced at the cut across Dottie's cheek, then hurriedly looked away. Dottie had almost forgotten about it, but now she felt as though it covered her whole face. The make-up and powder she had so carefully applied that morning were clearly not doing a very good job of concealment. Dottie's hand went to the cut instinctively.

Mrs Holcombe said, 'My dear Miss Manderson, I'm terribly sorry, I should have said something sooner. This is all my fault. I've hardly slept through thinking about it. If only I'd been frank with you from the start. I know you've been trying to get me to tell you what I know. But I was afraid. Mrs Sedgworth tried to persuade me... But...'

'You talked to Mrs Sedgworth about—what? About me? Or about Gervase?'

'Both as a matter of fact. When I met you at the station, I was a little shocked by how young you were. Forgive me, I'm not trying to insult you.'

'Everyone says that, although I shall be twenty-one in a few weeks,' Dottie said, annoyed with herself as she knew she was blushing, and thus further proving just how very young she was. 'That was why Mr Michaels pulled down the ceiling in the bedroom I was supposed to occupy. He thought it was dangerously close to Gervase's own room.' She paused then added, 'I'm very grateful to Mr Michaels for doing that. After what happened later... I think I was lucky to escape with just a slap across the face.'

Mrs Holcombe looked horrified. 'Well, I just thought you looked very young, and you seemed very decent. I called Mrs Sedgworth as soon as I left you and told her. I said I didn't think she needed to worry about what you might know or say. I-I told her I liked you, that you were *nice*. She was upset to hear that. She said she thought you couldn't know what he was.'

'And what is he?'

'Do you need to ask? A brute. A vile manipulator of everyone he meets. A beast who preys on the vulnerable and weak. A user of people. He has no morals, no decency. He thinks everyone else is only on this earth to serve the needs of Gervase Parfitt.'

'Is that all?' Dottie asked.

They broke off as the waitress came over with their watercress soup and a basket of tiny warm loaves. It smelled heavenly, and even in the middle of a conversation like this, Dottie's mouth watered. The warm bread crumbled crisply between her fingers as she broke it to dip it into her soup. The soup soaked the bread which dripped onto her chin as she put it into her mouth. The soup was perfect.

Mrs Holcombe was watching her. Dottie wiped her chin and her fingers, and hastily apologised. 'Do excuse me, I always seem to revert to childhood when I'm hungry, and completely forget my manners.'

Mrs Holcombe laughed. 'Don't worry about that. It is good soup. I've never been here before, it's really very charming.'

Dottie picked up her spoon, dipped it and took the soup in a manner her mother would have approved. She said, 'Now what were we saying?'

'It was you who spoke last. You asked me if that was all. Isn't it enough?'

'No, it's not enough to get him sent to prison,' Dottie said. She was taking a huge risk here. If Mrs Holcombe decided to remain loyal and tell Gervase of their conversation, William's investigation might be seriously damaged.

Mrs Holcombe paused with her spoon halfway to her mouth. She set it down again, gave herself two or three seconds to think about those words of Dottie's. She said, her voice carefully null, 'Prison?'

'Yes.'

'Are you serious?'

'Yes.' Dottie stared at Mrs Holcombe. She had grown so pale, Dottie was afraid she might faint.

But Mrs Holcombe said, 'Is there an enquiry, or something?'

'If I tell you, you have to keep it secret. You can't tell him. It's absolutely vital he knows nothing about it.'

'I give you my word.'

'Very well. Scotland Yard are looking into Gervase's affairs. You met the man after the inquest into Mrs Sedgworth's death. He's been sent up here to find out things. I'm helping him to gather evidence.'

Dottie could hardly believe her eyes. All reservation was gone. Tears were now running down Mrs Holcombe's face. She began to search in her bag for a handkerchief. She put it to her face, turning away so that no one else could see. After a moment she blotted her eyes and blew her rather pink nose.

'Are you all right? You can tell me anything.'

'Oh I'm so sorry to be silly and embarrass you in public. How kind you are.'

'Not at all. And I'm not embarrassed.' Dottie leaned forward and spoke in a quiet voice. 'Take your time.'

It was another minute before Mrs Holcombe was composed. Dottie continued with her soup, waiting until Mrs Holcombe was ready to speak.

'I can't tell you how long I've hoped... After my father... yes, you're right. I do know something. I'll tell you, but I'm afraid it may take some time.'

This was just what Dottie had been hoping for—not that she'd expected the efficient secretary to become emotional. But Gervase had left a lot of victims in his wake, so it was no surprise that they would have unhappy tales to tell.

Mrs Holcombe said, 'My father was an inspector in the police. About ten or twelve years ago, he became something of a mentor to a young graduate from the police college. It was Mr Parfitt, of course. He came to the local force as a sergeant straight from the college, and had to learn the ropes, before he could progress up the ranks. This is quite usual, I believe.

'According to my father, Parfitt was personable, intelligent, well-connected, his father was a well-known high-ranking officer in the neighbouring force. Gervase Parfitt showed promise, and my father was glad to take him under his wing.

'But that didn't last very long. He quickly discovered that Parfitt had a knack for turning things to his own advantage. Things would happen, or cases would just not match up with expectations, or work out a little too neatly. I'm explaining this very badly. But my father knew something was up, his experience told him that Parfitt was crooked. He went to his superiors, but his concerns were dismissed. Then rumours began to circulate that my father was jealous of Parfitt's success, his youth and popularity, and that Parfitt's natural ability as a police officer would see him outrank my father in no time.

'And it did seem as though that could be true. My father admitted he felt too tired to compete with the youngsters. They learned things at college that it had taken him his whole career to discover. But it was Parfitt's attitude more than anything. He didn't have the right moral tone, my father called it. But that didn't hold him back. Within two years he was a junior inspector, another two, a senior inspector, then he became a chief inspector, followed by a promotion to superintendent, then chief super, until last year he was appointed Assistant Chief Constable, and I myself have heard him say, he plans to be Chief Constable within another year.

'He has powerful friends. When anything troubling or suspicious happened, he'd always miraculously be somewhere else with a dozen witnesses. Witnesses withdrew their statements, or else they appeared as if by magic just when they were needed. Anyone who raised objections or criticised Parfitt seemed to disappear—oh, not always literally, I don't mean. But my father was one of them. He was summarily dismissed after being accused of taking bribes. He denied it. He always taught me that there is one thing we have that we can never replace, and that is our integrity. My father would have sooner died than do something to compromise his integrity. But evidence was put forward, conveniently manufactured, and no matter what my father said, no one supported him, and no one believed him. After almost thirty years on the police force, he was fired.

'Well he managed to get a job as a night-watchman. It was the only work he could find. He wasn't old enough to retire, so he had to work, of course. A night-watchman. After thirty years on the police force! Two years ago, he got pneumonia and died. It was outdoor work, you see. The place where he worked—they only had a little hut where the men could sit, have a cup of tea, that sort of thing. One of the fellows had brought in an oil-stove to heat the place, but the owners removed it, saying it was a fire hazard. So the hut was very cold. And damp. And, well, Father became ill.

Mrs Holcombe's voice wobbled to a halt. She reached for the handkerchief again. Dottie put her hand on the woman's arm.

'I'm so sorry, Mrs Holcombe.'

'Mary, please.'

'Dottie,' said Dottie.

The waitress came to clear their soup plates, gave them a concerned look then hurried away with the dishes.

Dottie said, 'So did you become Gervase's secretary to try to get back at him in some way?'

'Not at all. It was purely by accident, although Ripley's not a very big place. But no, I had to earn my living. My husband had passed away the year before my father. His name was David. He was a prison chaplain. He had a weak heart and nothing could be done. But we had fourteen happy years together, so that's something, I suppose.'

'No children?'

Mary shook her head. 'Sadly not.'

253

The waitress returned with their main course. The roast chicken was golden brown and looked juicy. Wisps of scented steam curled upwards to Dottie's nostrils. The vegetables were a little overdone to Dottie's taste, but Mary attacked them with relish. Dottie wondered how well Mary lived, alone and on a secretary's income. It seemed that this was a rare treat for her. If I lived alone and worked all day, Dottie thought, I shouldn't feel like cooking a proper meal most of the time. I'd probably exist on boiled eggs and toast.

As if continuing that thought, Mary said, 'As I say, I had to earn a living. My father left me the house, and a small amount of money that enabled me to do a secretarial course.' She paused and looked at Dottie with an apologetic expression. 'I—I'm afraid I allowed them to think I'd been a secretary for a lot longer than I actually have. It was too good an opportunity to miss, and after all, how often does a good job come up for a woman of my age? I'm forty-two, in case you're wondering. Fortunately, I am quite good at organising and keeping track of things, and that seemed to impress them. My typing is rather slow, but it's accurate, so again, they seemed satisfied with my ability.' She looked down at her food. 'I'm so thankful for my job. And everyone has been so kind to me. The chief constable—I'm not certain, but, well, I think perhaps he wasn't quite so convinced by my claims, but he had the final say in whether or not I was hired, and he has always gone out of his way to be kind.' Again she darted Dottie that confiding, uncertain look. 'He is a widower, and so perhaps he is a little lonely. I know he has a son. Perhaps he sees me as a kind of daughter.'

Dottie suppressed a smile. 'How old is he?'

'Oh he will be fifty in August. He plans to have a big party with his family. His brother is travelling up from Cornwall with his family to stay for the weekend. Sigmund—I mean—Mr Wisley is very excited about it'

'That sounds lovely. I hope he invites you.'

Mary hid a smile but admitted, 'He has asked me to attend. In a purely supporting role, of course.'

'Of course.' Dottie grinned at her over her glass of wine.

Mary smiled now, and blushed adorably. For the first time, Dottie saw the sweet person beneath the secretarial efficiency, the woman who had obviously captured the heart of the lonely chief constable. Dottie felt a pang of happiness for them. She would keep in touch with Mary and see how this gentle romance unfolded.

But for now, romance was set aside.

Mary said, 'I knew the Sedgworths through my father. When he was a police inspector, he used to play golf with Major Sedgworth. And so I got to know Mrs Sedgworth quite well, better than I implied, certainly.' She gave Dottie another apologetic look at which Dottie dismissed with a smile and a shake of the head. 'Something happened when Jimmy—Major Sedgworth—was away two or three years ago. She didn't tell me directly, but I got the impression it was serious, something rather terrible. It transpired that Mr Parfitt was blackmailing her over it. Oh it didn't come out right away, all in one go. But gradually I pieced it together. That something had happened and she had lost her nerve for driving.

'Once when I was driving the two of us home late at night, she became very agitated as we passed a certain spot on Gibbet Hill. And she urged me to slow right down, to make doubly sure no one was coming from a side-road. She said, 'Oh sometimes men come out quite quickly on a bicycle, and if they haven't lit their lamp, you might not see them.' Her hand was shaking as she said that to me, and by the time we reached her house, she was in a terrible state, almost in tears. Then too, she was short of money. Far shorter of money than she should have been. But her husband didn't seem to realise, or at least, not at first. And of course, it was clear that even though neither she nor her husband liked Mr Parfitt all that much, they socialised with him and his friends very frequently. So you see it all began to come together in my mind like a jigsaw puzzle.'

Dottie nodded. 'Yes, I can imagine. I think I would have thought the same. And so how did you come to take the role of Gervase's secretary?'

'Purely by accident, as I said. I was just asked to help out temporarily. I could hardly believe my luck. His previous secretary left rather abruptly—in the family way, and not married. They couldn't keep someone on in that situation, the poor girl. But sadly I haven't learned very much. I had hoped to overhear something, or to spot something lying about on his desk, but apart from a letter from the previous secretary naming him as the father of her child, and demanding money to support the baby, I have found nothing.'

Dottie blushed to the roots of her hair. Mary put out a hand.

'I'm so sorry. I completely forgot...'

'No, it's all right. And I know exactly the kind of man he is. I'm beginning to think he has illegitimate children all over the country. I definitely know of one other, a very sweet little boy, actually. Simon, he's called.' Dottie felt a momentary sadness, but Simon was now living with grandparents who loved him, so hopefully he was beyond Gervase's influence, which was a very good thing.

'No doubt there are more of his children out there. Mr Parfitt is well-known as a womaniser. He's incredibly vain, pompous, and goodness knows what else. But he is not sloppy about business matters. I've found out virtually nothing that could help me prove he set my father up to take the blame for what he himself had done. He is all too good at covering his tracks. I'm afraid I've rather given up hope of clearing my father's name.'

They ate in silence for several minutes, until at last, Dottie pushed her plate away. Mary placed her knife and fork neatly together and did the same.

'That was delicious, Miss—Dottie, thank you.'

'I hope you have time for a dessert and some coffee?'

Mary nodded, her smile broad, her sorrow set aside once more. 'Oh definitely!'

'A girl after my own heart,' Dottie said. The waitress cleared the table, and returned to the kitchen with their order.

They fell into a companionable silence. When the desserts and coffee came, they ate, and drank and said little that wasn't related to the food.

As they were finishing, and it was clear Mary would have to leave soon, she said to Dottie, 'Do you know what it was that he had over Mrs Sedgworth? Was it this car accident I was just suggesting?'

Dottie said, 'We still don't have much actual evidence. But from what you and a couple of others have said, it very much looks as though she ran someone down in the car, and well, it seems likely that they died. We think she turned to Gervase in a panic because Major Sedgworth was away.'

'If he hadn't been away, I doubt she would have been driving,' Mary said. 'Her night vision isn't very good, so Jimmy tended to do all the driving. Are you certain Parfitt has been blackmailing her?'

'As far as we can tell. We're still trying to find enough proof.'

'From what one reads, there are people who just enjoy having something over others, it gives them a sense of power. They do it for the thrill of the other person's misery, not for any financial reward.'

'It's horrible,' said Dottie with a shake of the head. 'But very like Gervase.'

'I'm so glad you're no longer involved with him, my dear. You really are far too good to throw yourself away on such a man. But—did it break your heart, when he...?' Mary nodded towards Dottie's face.

'No. It just meant that in less than a minute I went from mere dislike to utter hatred.'

'I believe he's already back with his old flame. My neighbour saw them together at a restaurant she and her husband go to.'

Dottie stared at her. 'What?' Then realising how that sounded, she apologised but Mary waved it aside, saying:

'He's with that woman he was with for years. Moira Hansom.'

'You know her?' Dottie could hardly believe it.

'*You* know her?' Mary repeated.

'Well yes. I met her in London a couple of weeks ago. She was introduced to me by *her* fiancé, who is that same policeman who is here from Scotland Yard, William Hardy. Although she broke it off with him yesterday.'

'That can't be right.' Mary looked puzzled. 'It was easily a year ago. I heard the fellow had died. If he hadn't, I'd wondered if she would have gone through with it, they seemed so ill-suited.'

Dottie stared again. 'I wonder... I don't know if we're talking about the same man? William only introduced me to Moira, oh, two weeks or so ago, as his fiancée.'

'No,' Mary said definitely. 'Moira Hansom's fiancé died last Spring. But so far as I can make out—and this is only based on gossip, although as you probably know, gossip is usually correct—she was still secretly seeing Parfitt, even when she was engaged. On several occasions she's been unofficially included as his 'wife' when I've made bookings for him to travel out of the area. She is the original gold-digger, although perhaps that's why they get on so well.'

'This fiancé of hers,' Dottie said, 'Do you remember his name at all?'

'Er—let me see, the first name was Phillip. Er—Phillip—Selly, that was it. Phillip Selly. The poor man, it was awful. He was attacked outside a public house. It was in all the papers. But the police got the fellow who did it. He was hanged.'

'So I understand.' Dottie clasped her hands together in her lap, wishing she could put on her gloves. She was suddenly so cold. Her head felt a bit swimmy, and she knew that if she stood up now, she'd stumble, perhaps even fall over.

*

Chapter Fifteen

As William headed the car out of the tradesmen's gate at the rear of Parfitt's property, he was feeling very satisfied with how his case was progressing. He had Michaels's statement neatly written up and signed by Mr Michaels, declaring what he had seen and heard of Parfitt's call to the Sedgworth's house after the major had collected Dottie, and also the little he knew of Parfitt's connections and entertainment of certain well-known public figures. The document was now in the manila file with all the other evidence he had so far gathered. It wasn't a lot, but together with other evidence, it was suggestive, and therefore hopefully useful.

William was very happy indeed. At last it seemed that his chance of bringing Parfitt to book for his crimes was a good one. The list was an increasingly long list of very serious offences, and could well grow longer. With the right evidence and a few more statements, Parfitt's reign was going to come to an end.

William turned left onto the main road that led into the village, and as he pulled away, he had suddenly to halt the car as a pedestrian stepped off the curb and into his path.

He stared. The woman stared back. With an inward groan, he dropped his window down and said, calmly. 'Good morning, Moira.'

She was still staring. She came a little closer. 'What are you doing here? Were you looking for me?' She was frowning at him. Clearly, he was the last person she expected—or wanted—to see.

'More importantly,' he said, 'what are *you* doing here? It's a bit of a way from Bournemouth.'

She glanced from right to left and back again. Giving herself time to think, he thought grimly. He said nothing, waiting to see what she came up with. Her composure began to return. She attempted a light laugh.

'Look, I'm sorry if you're angry with me for giving back your ring. But Darling, deep down you know we were never suited. It just wouldn't have worked.'

'Staying with your lover, Gervase Parfitt? Thanks for the ring, by the way. Dottie gave it back to me.'

She stopped pretending. With a sneer she said, 'Oh I'll just bet she did. Couldn't wait to throw herself in your arms and sob on your shoulder about the big nasty man.'

He remained calm. She was just trying to defend her own actions. He didn't care about that anymore, although he was curious.

'Why did you come back to me?'

It took her by surprise. 'What? What do you mean?'

'Five, no six, years ago, you were engaged to me, then broke it off when my family lost everything. Then I heard you had taken up with some other chap. You were engaged to him, weren't you? But you didn't marry him. What happened there?'

'He died.' She looked away as she said it. He wondered about that. A psychologist might say she was being evasive.

'I'm sorry to hear that.'

Her answer was a shrug of the shoulders. Then, 'So I've answered your questions, now you can answer mine. Why are *you* here, Bill? Are you spying on me? Or is this your idea of petty revenge?'

He laughed, let off the brake and drove away. A glance in the rear-view mirror showed that she was furious with him for doing so. He was pretty sure she'd tell Parfitt. Hopefully they wouldn't work out what was going on. But if they did, well it was just too bad. Parfitt would know soon enough, in any case.

He was still thinking about Moira when he reached Mrs Parkes's. There was room to pull the car into a space a few yards along the road. He sent what he hoped was a forbidding frown in the direction of some youths hanging about looking for some trouble to get into. He knocked on the door.

She opened it almost immediately. She had clearly been expecting him. She ushered him through the damp kitchen to the parlour before he'd even finished introducing himself.

He took a seat on the rather springy sofa. Judging by how incredibly clean everything was, the room was never used, but a lot of care was taken. It smelled of furniture polish and dry rot. Leaning heavily on her walking-stick, she crossed the room to sit on an upright chair opposite him.

He asked her if she was still willing to give a statement. She nodded, fully understanding, and very keen to help.

'That sweet little girl told me you'd be along. Do you know her? Such a sweet little thing. Pretty little voice, and a lovely kind way with her.'

He smiled to hear Dottie spoken of in that way. Having heard Moira's views, it was good to hear someone lauding Dottie. Dottie was a tall woman, yet everyone thought of her as little. He said, yes, he knew the lady.

'Though not as well as you'd like, I'd bet. I bet she has posh young men queuing round the corner to take her dancing every night.'

'It's not exactly a queue,' he said with a grin. 'But I'm definitely at the front of it. She dances very well.'

She cackled in delight. 'Does she indeed? Well I never! 'She dances very well', he says. So you are human after all, you coppers!'

'Some of us are.'

'Derbyshire man, are you? For all you've got that public school voice, there's a bit of it there still.'

'I am,' he said. 'And proud of it. I was born just outside Matlock.'

'Oh very nice. I went up them hills once when I was a girl. It fair did me in, I can tell you. I never went back.'

'The Heights of Abraham? Yes, the road is extremely steep. Excellent for coming down on a toboggan when it's covered in snow.'

'It's like a cliff, sonny, like a cliff.' She folded her hands together. The time had come to get down to business.

'Shall we begin, Mrs Parkes?'

'Yes, me duck. Let's get it all down on paper, official-like.'

It took over an hour, but at the end of that time he had a full statement written out and she had signed her name to it after reading it through twice.

She made him a cup of tea. Hardy sat with her for another half hour, letting her tell him about her life, her son. He felt the same as Dottie: this woman deserved an answer. She was shrewd, proud and hard-working. And she was lonely, he could see that. Her only relative had been taken from her, and when hard times hit her in the future, there would be no one to help her. Yet she didn't waste time wallowing in self-pity. She did laundry for the well-to-do, and plenty of it, if her chapped and work-roughened hands were any sign. She had few possessions and she was proud of her parlour, and justifiably. She had worked hard her whole life to create this place where any visitor could sit in comfort. And when the time came, these precious few possessions would be sold to pay for her funeral. He wanted to help her if he could.

At last, and with genuine reluctance, Hardy said he would have to be going. She went to get his hat and coat. She pressed his hand.

'Thank you, Mr Hardy, for what you're trying to do. And tell the young lady, I'm so pleased to have that photograph she gave me. Oh not because I'm vain. It's not what's in the picture. It's what it meant to my boy. That he kept hold of it. That's why it matters.'

He nodded. 'I'll tell her.'

'Perhaps you could give her this. It's just something I thought she might like to see.'

Mrs Parkes handed him a dirty old envelope. It was sealed. He nodded.

'I'll make sure she gets it.'

'When she's done with these, I'd be glad to have them back. And make sure you marry her,' Mrs Parkes said with a croaky laugh.

William smiled. 'I'll do my level best.'

'Good boy. Well, off you go then, I've got things to do.'

But she stood at the door and watched whilst he drove away.

After Mary Holcombe had gone back to work, Dottie came out of the hotel and looked about her.

The February day was cold, but the sun poked through the clouds as often as it could manage, and the slight breeze made everything seem fresh and alive. It was a day to be out of doors.

She wandered through the little market, resisting the urge to buy anything—although the hams looked succulent and the cheeses tasty, the winter vegetables: plump cabbages, carrots, parsnips and late potatoes, looked as if they had been pulled from the earth only a moment ago.

Then as she looked across the square, a new idea came to her, and she quickened her step.

She opened the street door of the newspaper office and stepped inside, automatically patting her wind-ruffled hair back into place and wondering if her face was as red as it felt.

'Good afternoon, miss, how can I be of assistance?'

Dottie smiled at the elderly gentleman behind the counter.

'I was wondering if you could help me with something that happened in the area a little while ago.'

'If I can, miss.'

'Do you keep old issues here?'

'Every single issue, miss. Going right back to 1825.' His voice rang with pride.

Dottie beamed back. 'That's wonderful. Please can I look through them?'

'I'm afraid not, miss. But if you tell me which ones you want, I can bring them over to the reading desk.' He nodded towards a high long table placed against the wall. Several tall, well-padded stools had been added for the comfort of the readers.

Her forehead furrowed. 'Oh dear. I'm not sure which ones I need. I've heard about some events, but I'm not exactly sure when they took place.'

'If you can give me a few details, or a name, I can look through our index, then we might be able to find out which issue you need.'

'Lovely,' she said and beamed at him again. He blushed and grinned back at her, taking off his glasses to polish them on his waistcoat in preparation for his task. It wasn't very often a pretty woman came into his office. It relieved an otherwise dreary day.

An hour later, though, and Dottie was no longer feeling that everything was 'lovely'. She was feeling puzzled and frustrated.

She was now sitting in the little back room that served as a staff kitchen and sitting room. She was having a cup of tea with the elderly gentleman who had been attempting to help her to find what she wanted.

Mr Treadwell made them both a cup of tea that was almost orange in colour, and in flavour, violently tea-like with an undertone of rust. Dottie took two sips, repressed a shudder, and set her cup on one side.

'It must have been the break-in a couple of weeks ago,' Mr Treadwell was saying. 'At the time, we thought nothing had been taken. It was dismissed as youngsters out mischief-making. The police said they'd probably expected to find money on the premises.'

'It seems odd that they only took a few select papers. And knew where to find everything,' Dottie said, not quite bold enough to suggest it was likely to have been an employee.

But he understood her meaning. He looked at her over the top of his glasses. The look was intelligent. He nodded. 'An inside job, you mean. I did wonder about that...'

Dottie looked forlornly at the little pencilled list they had created. The first item was: 'Local man George Parkes charged with murder following public house robbery.' Next to that she had added a large X to indicate that the newspaper containing that report was missing.

The next item on the list was: 'Girl's hit and run death— Parkes admits he did it.' She had placed an X beside that, another missing newspaper.

The newspaper that dealt with George Parkes's execution was also gone. In fact every issue that carried some part of the story was missing, along with two other, earlier papers that mentioned some of Parkes' younger exploits. They now knew there were at least eight issues gone without a trace.

On a whim, Dottie asked about the obituaries. Mr Treadwell made a note to look for the announcement of the death of a night-watchman who was a former police inspector. Then, feeling as though she were doing something rather terrible, she asked him to find the death announcement of Major Garfield Hardy, William's father.

As soon as Mr Treadwell left to carry out his search, Dottie tipped away the orange tea, washed and dried up the cup and saucer, then replaced them on the communal shelf with the rest of the staff's china. She wondered what the time was. It felt as though she had been there forever, and she had an afternoon tea appointment with William she would not miss for anything.

Another idea came to her, and when Mr Treadwell returned a moment later with three newspapers, she added another query to his list. He beamed his cherubic smile, and assured her it was no trouble, it was much nicer to be busy than have nothing to do all afternoon.

They sat whilst he drank his tea and Dottie looked at the papers. She politely declined the offer of another cup. Mr

Treadwell, firmly of the belief that tea should be drunk every hour on the hour, made himself another.

The first obituary she read was the announcement of the death of former police inspector, Harry Evans about two years earlier. The obituary was extremely short and impersonal: *'Evans. Harry Evans, formerly of the Derbyshire Constabulary, aged 67, passed away at Dale View Nursing Home following a short illness, grateful thanks to staff, no flowers. St Jude's Methodist Church, Long Eaton, 3pm 16th March, all friends welcome.'*

There was nothing much to be gleaned from that. But at least she had the information.

She turned to the obituaries in the next paper, dated 1928, and what she found there made her heart bump with guilt. She read:

'Hardy. Maj^r Garfield Henry Hardy, formerly of the Derbyshire Light Infantry and the 2nd Battalion of the King's Own Regiment, aged 53, at his home, Great Meads, near Matlock, following a short illness. Major Hardy is survived by his wife Isabel Hardy nee Allsopp, and their four children. A private funeral will take place in the chapel on the Great Meads estate, Dalemead, Matlock.'

It didn't go far in satisfying her curiosity about William's early—and far more privileged—life. As Mr Treadwell returned with another paper for her, she asked, 'What's this extra one?'

'Oh, it's the same family, so I thought you might be interested. On page four there's a short article.'

'Thank you.' She carefully turned over the large sheets to find page four. A scan of the page revealed nothing at first, until:

'Great family seat sold: after four hundred years, Great Meads is broken up to settle debts.'

'My goodness,' she whispered. Four hundred years! It hit her in the chest like a physical blow. She knew exactly what this was. She felt so awful for reading about the tragedy of someone she cared about, but sheer curiosity made her keep reading. She told herself she needed to understand more about William's background.

'Mr William Hardy, 22, was on hand yesterday to oversee the sale of his family's former home and lands, the Great Meads estate, to satisfy his late father's creditors and to pay extensive outstanding death duties. Mr Hardy was lately at Oxford where he failed to complete his studies in Law, and according to a close personal friend, is now about to enter Hendon Police Training College.'

There was a good deal more about how the family were now living in London in what that same 'close family friend' had salaciously described as 'greatly reduced circumstances'. The piece ended with: *'Mr Hardy declined to comment other than to state he would do everything in his power to settle what was owed and he offered grateful thanks to his family's staff and tenants for their years of loyal support and service.'*

How sad it was, Dottie couldn't help but feel, to read of the decline of a once-great family. She was deeply moved by the mental image of the proud, determined young William, pledging to repay everything his father had owed. The loss of his own career prospects had led to the forging of a new career, one far less well paid, far more difficult and dangerous, and definitely less prestigious but clearly something he had a gift for. She admired him immensely for all of it.

But she was angry with the newspaper for its gleeful report, for intruding on the family in their time of grief and humiliation, and for putting it in the newspaper for thousands of people to enjoy over their morning tea.

She only realised Mr Treadwell had been absent again because he returned now, with one final newspaper. He handed it to her and she opened it, even though she had yet to look at the fourth one on the table in front of her.

'What am I looking for in this one, Mr Treadwell?'

'It's that engagement you asked for.'

'Ah.' She nodded. 'Thank you.' He sat down opposite her to drink his tea.

'Oh, Mr Treadwell, do you have the time, please?'

'Certainly, dear lady.' He pulled out a well-polished gold watch on a chain. I bet that was his father's, if not his grandfather's, she thought. He said, 'It's exactly nine minutes to four.'

Her eyes rounded in dismay. She had to be quick. Very quick.

She turned the pages until she came to the announcements. It felt as though it took most of the nine remaining minutes to find what she was looking for.

Rev Jonathan Ernest Selly, of the Garside Street Wesleyan Chapel, Ripley, and his wife Cora are delighted to announce the engagement of their eldest son, Phillip Ernest Selly to Miss Moira Hansom of Lowdale, Derbyshire. The wedding will take place on Saturday 9th June at the Garside Street Wesleyan chapel, at 2pm. All well-wishers invited. A buffet will be provided afterwards at the home of the Reverend and Mrs Selly.'

The newspaper was a February 1934 edition. Slightly over a year old. Dottie read it again with rapt attention. Then she scribbled a note of the details in her diary. I could do with one of those daybooks like William's, she thought. There was one more paper, but she had so little time.

'What...?' she began, but before she had a chance to finish, Mr Treadwell said:

'Four minutes to four.'

'Thank goodness.' There was just time.

The final newspaper was dated the same year as that of the report about the sale of the Hardy estate, 1929. She found the announcement and it said:

Mr William Hardy, formerly of Great Meads near Matlock, regrets to announce that his planned marriage to Miss Moira Hansom, only daughter of General and Mrs Hansom formerly of Lowdale, but now of Chesterfield, will not take place on Saturday 17th August as previously announced. Neither Miss Hansom nor General Hansom were available to comment. Miss Hansom's mother is the former socialite, Arabella Armstrong of Chesterfield, Derbyshire, daughter of Sir

Henry Armstrong.

To Dottie's dismay, the announcement then went on to outline once more William's family's debt-ridden misery from the earlier report. But there was no new information, and she really had to leave. She closed the newspapers and gave them back, holding her hand out to Mr Treadwell.

'Thank you so much for all your help. And of course, for the—er—tea. You've been an absolute angel. If you think of anything else, I'm staying at the hotel in Edgewick, the Harlequin. It's Miss Manderson. Thank you again. I'm afraid I must dash.'

She kissed him on the cheek and hurried out, leaving him pink and sentimental as he went to return the papers to their folders.

Dottie was glad to get back to the hotel. Now that it was almost the end of the day—it would be dark in less than an hour—the temperature was dropping and it was too cold to linger outside.

As she came into the hotel's entrance, a man got to his feet. With a rush of happiness she saw it was William. She practically ran to him.

He kissed her cheek. He might be any man meeting an acquaintance. How she wished he would pull her into his arms and really kiss her.

He gave her a severe look. 'You're a minute late.'

She laughed. 'A whole minute! My goodness, Inspector, you'll have to arrest me for loitering.'

'Don't tempt me,' he growled, but then he smiled.

They made their way to the dining room, Dottie giving her name. The waiter greeted her like an old friend, remembering her from lunchtime. He took them to the far end of the room, away from the pretty view through the window, which Dottie was sorry about, but at least it was quiet here, as the hotel was busier now.

William pulled out her seat for her before taking his own, and the waiter withdrew to give them a few minutes to talk.

'Had a good day?' William asked.

'Yes. Very good actually, although...' Her face clouded as she recalled some of the things she had read.

'What is it? Did something happen?'

'In a manner of speaking. But forget about that for now. What about you? Did you see Mr Michaels and Mrs Parkes?'

'I certainly did. Two statements, both neatly written up, signed, and ready for use.'

'Oh well done!'

The waiter came over with their afternoon tea on a huge tray: a two-tiered cake stand and separate large plate of sandwiches. He hurried away then returned with a large fat pot of tea, the milk and sugar, some small savoury pastries in a hot dish, and pots of jam, cream and butter. The waitress arrived almost immediately with their china and cutlery, then finally they were alone.

'I'm famished,' William said, looking at it all.

The human dustbin, again, she thought with a smile, remembering the gigantic breakfast he'd consumed the other morning.

'Well, don't just sit there, man, eat!' Dottie took a plate and helped herself to a miniature chocolate éclair.

'That's not fair,' he said in mock protest. 'You can't start on the cakes until you've eaten your sandwiches.'

'We're not six years old anymore, William. We can do as we please.' To prove her point she crammed the entire thing into her mouth in one go. With difficulty but an air of triumph, she chewed it.

He laughed and shook his head. Without even thinking, he said, 'I do so love you, Dottie Manderson.'

She almost choked on her food. She went rather pink in the face but managed to swallow the éclair without any unfortunate occurrences.

'Sorry,' he said. 'Forgot myself for a moment.'

'Again.'

'Yes, true. Again. Sorry.'

She couldn't decide what was worse, him joking about loving her, or apologising afterwards. She sipped some tea.

He reached for a sandwich, bit into it, set it down on his

plate, and still chewing, said, 'I nearly forgot. Mrs Parkes gave me this to give to you. A kind of thank you for the photo you gave her. I assume the photo she mentioned was the one you found in Parfitt's desk that was, in fact, evidence.' He raised his eyebrows in a question, but his smile said he wasn't taking it too seriously. He lay the envelope on the snowy tablecloth beside her plate.

She reached for it, saying, 'Forgetting rather a lot, lately, aren't you? How old are you? It might be senility. Oh. My. Goodness.'

Her smile vanished as she opened the envelope and began to draw out the contents: a little pile of folded newspaper clippings. Everything around her seemed to fall silent. She knew, before she read any of them, exactly what these were. She put her hand up to her mouth as she said another, almost silent, 'Oh'. Her hand trembled too. Tears threatened. And William made her love him just a little bit more by immediately setting down his cup, and taking her hand in both of his, his eyes troubled.

'Dottie, what is it? What's wrong?'

Her laugh was unsteady. She quickly scanned the first cutting she had unfolded until she found the name she was looking for. These were cuttings of the very articles she'd been searching for at the newspaper office. Or rather, Mr Treadwell had done the searching. And here they were. This was Mrs Parkes' own record of her son's final days.

She handed it to William. 'Read that. The date that she has written at the top must be the date the paper was printed.'

He read it slowly and carefully aloud: "*Condemned man makes shocking confession.* Police sources disclosed today that George Parkes, condemned to death for the foul murder of Phillip Selly, a public house customer brutally done to death in April of this year, has most shockingly confessed to another murder, saying that he wanted to die with a clear conscience. Police say that Parkes, 22, who will hang next week at Winson Green prison in Birmingham, confessed everything to the prison chaplain and said, according to our informant, 'I have something to tell you. My guilty conscience will not give me a moment's rest until I tell all.' Parkes then went on to admit to stealing a car and knocking a young woman down and killing her, as he escaped the scene of the public house robbery on the evening of 2nd April. A detailed statement is due tomorrow from Ripley police headquarters.' The date on this one is 19th December 1934.'

He read it again. He didn't see what Dottie saw. She took her diary out of her handbag and opened it to the page where she'd made her note just a short while earlier. She read it out in a low voice.

'I made a copy of an engagement announcement from the local newspaper from 7th February 1934. It says: *Rev Jonathan Ernest Selly, of the Garside Street Wesleyan Chapel, Ripley, and his wife Cora are delighted to announce the engagement of their eldest son, Phillip Ernest Selly to Miss Moira Hansom of Lowdale, Derbyshire. The wedding will take place on Saturday 9th June at the Garside Street Wesleyan chapel, at 2pm. All well-wishers invited. A buffet will be provided afterwards at the home of the Rev and Mrs Selly.*'

'Moira?' he said. He seemed unable to follow Dottie's line of thought. She nodded.

'*My* Moira?' he asked again, and his use of the possessive pronoun hurt her.

'Yes. Moira.' She couldn't help sounding waspish.

'So she was engaged to this fellow who was the man killed by George Parkes?'

'Yes.' Dottie stared at him, waiting for the penny to drop.

He looked puzzled, mulling it over for a while. Then to her annoyance, he said, 'Well, she told me this morning that her previous fiancé had died, though she didn't say how. This must be him, although I don't see how this gets us any further forward.'

She was annoyed by his lack of excitement, but mainly because now the thrill of discovery was over, she couldn't see what help this information was, either. She knew something was there, but like looking at a blurry photo, couldn't quite work out what she was looking at.

She looked at the next cutting, and the next, then saw that she needed to put them into chronological order. For the next few minutes she read the cuttings and sorted them. She and William pored over the cuttings to read the story in the right sequence.

'This is the first one,' she said. 'The paper's dated 11th April. '*Man Held In Connection With Public House Robbery And Murderous Attack.* George Parkes, 22, from Daleside Lane, Longford, has been charged with causing the death of Mr Phillip Selly as he sat outside the Purple Emperor with friends on the evening of 2nd April. Parkes went into the public house with the intention of robbing the place, but when making his getaway, he attacked Mr Selly, beating him about the head with a cudgel improvised from a broken fence nearby. Mr Selly, 27, of Ripley, died before help could reach him. Parkes was apprehended later the same evening by officers under the command of Chief Superintendent Gervase Parfitt, who said, 'Parkes represents the very worst type of criminal from whom it is the duty of the police to protect society: opportunistic, brutal, and utterly ruthless. He is the type of man who will cut down anyone who stands between himself and his objective.'

'Then there's this one from 3rd October,' she went on. "*Parkes Found Guilty – condemned to hang.* Yesterday, it took the jury just forty-five minutes to find George Parkes guilty of the wilful and callous murder of Phillip Selly on the evening of 2nd April. Sir Justice Markham pronounced the sentence of death, stating that the crime was the vile and sadistic act of a criminal who had repeatedly found himself on the wrong side of the law, and whose reign of misery and bloodshed had now been brought to an end.'

'Hardly a reign,' William objected. 'He killed one man then confessed, falsely we believe, to another killing. He wasn't exactly Jack the Ripper.'

'No, he wasn't, was he? Then comes the one we've already read, and now there's this one, much shorter, from the paper that came out on the 31st December, 1934.

"*Double murderer dead.* George Parkes, 22, was hanged at eight o'clock this morning at Winson Green prison, Birmingham, following his conviction of the murder of Phillip Selly. Parkes, who confessed to a second killing just one week ago...' then it goes on to recap what we already know. Poor Mrs Parkes, reading all this in the papers about her own son.' Her euphoria fizzled out completely, and her happy mood plummeted into gloom. She put the cuttings back into the envelope to look at later. She took a drink of her tea.

'What did you do today?' William asked.

She brightened a little. 'I had lunch with Mrs Holcombe. Oh, it turns out that her father was a police inspector, a Harry Evans. He was Gervase's first mentor, but Mary is convinced that Gervase discredited him and got him sacked from his job. He ended up working as a night-watchman, got pneumonia and died. She admitted she's been trying to find a way to make Gervase pay for that.'

'And after lunch?'

'I went to the newspaper office across the square. It turns out they had a break-in a few weeks ago. At the time, they thought nothing had been taken. Now however, the delightful Mr Treadwell and I have discovered that what was taken were several old issues of the newspapers in the archives. Actually it turned out that all of the papers I wanted to see were the ones that had been stolen. They included reports of George Parkes's arrest, his trial, and his death. These cuttings from Mrs Parkes are the same editions as the missing ones, I'm certain. Oh, and there was no report of any road accident about the time that Major Sedgworth was abroad.'

Finally he looked interested. He munched two more sandwiches and a chicken savoury as he thought about what she'd said.

But Dottie was feeling despondent. She didn't know if she was tired or just fed-up.

'I really thought we'd cracked the case,' she said. 'But now I feel as though we still know nothing.'

It was dark as they drove back to the little country hotel where Dottie was staying. She stared out into the night, and tried to still her growing sense of anxiety. When they reached the hotel, William went in with her.

At the desk he told the clerk, 'Miss Manderson will be dining out this evening.'

'I will?' She looked at him.

'You will. My aunt and uncle have invited you to dinner.'

'Do they know they've invited me?'

'Not yet.' He grinned at her. 'But don't worry. It will be perfectly all right. My aunt has been nagging me to introduce you.' He picked up the newspaper and prepared to sit in the waiting area. 'I don't mind waiting whilst you do whatever it is women have to do when they suddenly discover they are dining out.'

'Good, because I'm going to be ages, and you deserve it.'

She had a very quick bath. It was unusual for a little out of the way place like this, she thought, that they had such nice bathrooms and so much hot water. And thank goodness they had, because she had been desperate to wallow in some really hot, sweetly-scented, bubbly water.

She made up her face, taking extra care to cover up the scratch across her cheek that was still so sore. She brushed her hair vigorously then secured it back from her face leaving little curls hanging down about her cheeks to soften the severity of the style. She chose her jewellery: the earrings her parents had given her for her last birthday, and a couple of long silver chains.

She pulled out one of the dresses she had with her—it wasn't too badly crumpled, and hopefully no one would notice the mark on the left sleeve.

A final check in the mirror. Yes, she would do, she thought. In any case, it was the best she could manage at such short notice.

Feeling excited, but rather scared, she ran down the stairs to meet William. He got up, and coming towards her, gave her the look that told her the effort was appreciated, but said simply, 'Forty-three minutes. I'm impressed.'

And he led her to the door.

It was pouring hard now, the fickle British climate having, as usual, given almost every kind of weather in the space of one day. But the roads were quiet, and William was an excellent—and careful—driver.

Dottie's apprehension was growing. She knew how much his aunt and uncle meant to him, especially since his mother's death last year. It helped a little that she was already slightly acquainted with William's younger sister Eleanor.

Abruptly breaking the silence he said, 'I've got an appointment with the chief constable and his enquiry panel tomorrow afternoon at four o'clock. I shall have to lay out all my findings then, and they will decide whether there are sufficient grounds to charge Parfitt with something—perverting the course of justice, or bribery and corruption, or... Well, there are a number of options. But it means I've got to have all my ducks in a row by then. I called through to the office while I was waiting for you, to see if they had anything for me, and that was when I discovered that the enquiry had been moved forward by more than a week. I'm not sure why—but someone as eminent as the chief constable doesn't have to explain himself to a mere inspector. So yes, it's now tomorrow. I must admit to being fairly daunted by it.'

Dottie was alarmed. 'But we hardly know anything! I mean, I thought we still had time to investigate. Isn't there going to be a trial or something—a court case?'

'No, there has to be an enquiry first, to see if there's a case for Parfitt to answer. He'll only be arrested and stand trial if I can prove my case.'

'Oh dear,' Dottie said. 'I wonder how soon it will be before Gervase finds out what's going on?'

William concentrated on negotiating three consecutive sharp bends on the narrow road, then swerved and slammed on his brakes to avoid hitting a deer. He cursed under his breath. The animal froze for a moment then disappeared into the night.

'All right?' He looked across at her. She had one hand on the dashboard to brace herself.

'Yes, I'm fine.'

He drove on. 'Er—about Parfitt—well, obviously he'll know by now, because he's going to be there with his barrister.'

'What!'

'Didn't you realise?'

'No, of course not. How could I?'

'Ah. Well, he will have the opportunity to answer the accusations. And as I said, he will have a barrister present to advise him. They're probably working on their strategy right now.'

'Does he already know what he's being accused of?'

'Some of it.'

'So it's a bit like a trial.'

'They call it an enquiry panel. But essentially, yes, it's a small, private trial that takes place before the real thing. There will be myself, Parfitt, his barrister if he brings one, and he'd be a fool not to, the chief constable, a court stenographer and three area judges or magistrates. And perhaps one or two others.'

'Doesn't sound very private to me.'

He laughed at that.

She sat well back in her seat, her mind busily attempting to frighten her out of her wits by conjuring up scary legal scenes in a courtroom setting.

'You seem very calm,' she remarked, casting a glance at his profile.

'Not at all. I'm in a total panic. I'm convinced I haven't done anywhere near enough. But in many ways, it's out of my hands now.'

'Do you call witnesses, like in a normal trial?'

'Yes.' After a moment he said, 'By the way, I forgot to mention. After I saw Michaels this morning to get his statement, I met Moira coming out of the entrance to Parfitt's drive. I rather assume she'd spent the night, seeing that it was still rather early.'

'Oh dear,' Dottie said. 'What happened?'

'We had a little chat, that's all. She sends her regards.'

Dottie snorted. 'I bet!'

'And here we are,' he said, halting the car outside a plain, square, red-brick house on a quiet street.

'Oh dear,' Dottie said again, taking a deep breath. Her thoughts in utter turmoil, she grabbed her bag and turned to take William's hand as he came to help her out of the car.

*

Chapter Sixteen

There seemed to be a great many people. Dottie had only expected to meet an older couple, his aunt and uncle, and his younger sister Eleanor, who was a year or two younger than Dottie's own age, and whom she'd met two or three times before. But there were several other people crowding into the hallway to greet her. They were quite without any stiff formality here: William had simply thrown open the unlocked front door and walked straight into the house, calling out loudly, 'I'm back. I've got Dottie with me', in an easy way that made her smile.

As soon as everyone began to come out to meet Dottie, William said, 'I'm just going up for a quick bath, won't be long.' To her astonishment, he bounded up the stairs and disappeared from view, leaving her to face them all. The wretch, she thought in dismay, he did that on purpose.

Eleanor took Dottie completely by surprise by practically running at her and enveloping her in a tight hug. They were acquainted, but they'd never been as friendly as this before. Dottie was embarrassed but pleased. Eleanor released her, exclaiming, 'My goodness, it's about time!' Her arm through Dottie's, she turned to make introductions.

A gentleman of about the same age as Dottie's father came forward. He wore an old suit, rather baggy and battered-looking. He had a huge mop of grizzled grey hair and deep blue eyes disconcertingly similar to William's. He held out a hand to her. 'I'm Joseph Allsopp. Welcome, young lady. We've wanted to meet you for some time, as you've probably gathered.'

Dottie blushed and smiled, still feeling shy. She put her hand out to shake his, but he surprised her by bending to kiss the back of it in an old-fashioned, rather courtly manner she thought very sweet.

'Allow me to present my dear wife, Cassie.'

Dottie shook Mrs Allsopp's hand a little awkwardly and smiled at the lady. Mrs Allsopp smiled broadly back, a quietly pretty middle-aged woman. Her country tweeds were well cut but by no means new, but they added to Dottie's sense of a comfortable family home.

Dottie found her voice at last. 'It's such a pleasure to meet you all. I'm sorry to arrive unannounced.'

Another woman came forward. For a moment, as she stood partially in shadow, Dottie almost took her for William's deceased mother. It was a brief shock. Then as she stepped forward, Dottie could see her hair was fair not grey, and that she was young.

Holding her hand out, Dottie said, 'I think you must be William's sister Celia? We've never met but I've heard a lot about you.'

Celia grinned at her and kissed her on the cheek. 'I bet it's nothing to how much we've heard about you! And not above time, I can tell you. We've wanted to meet you since Bill first mentioned you, and mentioned you, and mentioned you, in connection with that poor fellow you found in the street, what, two years ago, eighteen months, something like that?'

'Almost eighteen months ago,' Dottie agreed.

'Not the most subtle of men, my brother.' Suddenly, Celia turned back to yell up the stairs, 'Hey! Go and have your bath, you wicked wretch, throwing the poor girl to the wolves then watching to see how she makes out!'

There was an answering laugh from the upstairs hall, and Dottie heard him moving away along the corridor. He had been spying on them the whole time.

'This is my husband, Roddy. Roderick Pickford,' Celia said. Dottie smiled at the tall thin red-haired young man in a dog-collar who grinned at her, and managed to quickly say, 'How do you do?' just as Mrs Allsopp said:

'Do let the poor girl come in and sit down.' She led the way into a spacious sitting room. To one side there was a large playpen set up, but its intended occupant was currently sitting on the floor with two young men beside a small train set. One of the boys was clearly William's younger brother Edward, he was so like William, she could hardly believe it. He got up and came forward with his hand held out.

'I'm Ted,' he said. 'Very pleased to meet you, Miss Manderson.'

She knew he was only sixteen, yet he was almost as tall as his brother, if not quite as broad-shouldered. His face bore a litter of freckles across the nose that made him look mischievous, as did the grin and the twinkling blue eyes.

She grinned up at him. 'Do please call me Dottie.'

The other young man picked up the toddler, who immediately put out his arms out for his mother. Celia settled him on her hip, kissed the little chap's curly pale red locks, and said, 'This is Roddy, our son. He's eighteen months old now, and rather into everything.'

Dottie laughed. 'I bet you need eyes in the back of your head.'

'Oh, I do!' Celia laughed. Everyone smiled fondly, and the ice was well and truly broken.

'He's adorable,' Dottie said. 'My sister has twins, but they are not quite eight months old, so they stay more or less where you put them most of the time.'

'For now!' It was clear from everyone's nods and smiles that they knew all the background of the 'twins', and Dottie was pleased about that. One less thing to try to keep secret or to have to explain.

The other young man was chivvied forward by Eleanor. She said, 'This is my fiancé, Andrew Gresley.'

Dottie shook hands with a reserved-looking young man of about her own age and her own height, who said quietly, 'Very pleased to meet you.' It lacked sincerity, but perhaps he was just shy, Dottie thought.

She smiled back and said simply, 'Thank you, it's very nice to meet you too.' To Eleanor she said, 'Congratulations on your engagement. William mentioned it might be given out soon, but I didn't realise that had already happened.'

'Well, it hasn't officially. Not until Andy's parents have made the announcement. But as far as we're concerned, it's on. Look, I've got my ring!'

She held out a hand for Dottie to admire the dainty sapphire and diamond arrangement on a gold band.

'It's lovely,' Dottie said, thinking it was a shame she couldn't tell them about the travesty Gervase had given her for their so-called engagement. This thought reminded her of William's meeting the next day with the chief constable, and she felt a sudden dropping lurch in her stomach at the thought. She thrust it away, not wanting it to ruin the evening.

They sat on the sofas and there was conversation about this and that. Later, Dottie couldn't really have said what they talked about. Ted and Roderick sprawled on the floor playing trains to amuse the little one. Dottie felt relaxed, as if she'd been coming here all her life. No one stared at the mark across her face, everyone was natural and friendly and kind.

After about half an hour, William returned, in casual trousers now, and an old jumper with a darned elbow. She'd rarely seen him in anything other than his usual work attire, and he looked almost boyish and relaxed. His hair was still damp from the bath, curling very slightly behind his ears and at the nape of his neck. She had to look away, afraid his family would see her devouring him with her eyes, but she longed to look at him. He joined his younger brother on the floor, sitting cross-legged to set a toppled wagon straight on the circle of track. The toddler came over to hug his neck. She didn't know why, but she was surprised to see the tender way William gathered the little one onto his lap, dropping a kiss on the child's hair, and leaning forward to grab a small toy horse to give to Roddy, who exclaimed excitedly.

Again she felt she had to look away, and was disconcerted to find Celia smiling at her, obviously aware that Dottie was touched to see the caring, paternal side of William's character for the first time.

It was a relief when a moment later, Cassie Allsopp said from the doorway:

'Dinner's ready everyone. Do come through, Dottie, dear. I've put you between Bill and Ellie.'

When dinner was over, they returned to the sitting room. After half an hour or so, Mr and Mrs Allsopp went out. They apologised to Dottie for leaving.

'We always pop along the road to spend a little time with my parents,' Cassie Allsopp explained. 'They're getting on a bit now, and don't get out much. We take them a few things from our kitchen, and sit and have a chat with them. Joe plays cribbage or dominos with my father. We shall be back at about ten o'clock or so. Will you still be here then?'

Dottie turned to William to find out, but he was already shaking his head.

'Probably not. I shall need to take Dottie back to her hotel.'

'It's a shame you didn't bring your things, dear,' Cassie said. 'You could have stayed with us. Well, another time then. I'd love to see you again soon, dear. It was lovely to finally meet you.'

Both she and her husband kissed Dottie's cheek and said goodbye. That left the younger set to amuse themselves. Ted suggested playing cards, but the others shouted him down, preferring Celia's suggestion of charades.

'There's no time,' William said. 'Dottie's got to leave in

about an hour.'

'Oh rubbish, Bill. We've got tons of time. I'll go first.' Celia stood up to mime for them, beginning with a play.

Dottie was wondering why he felt they had to leave so early to take her back. She could only suppose that it was because he wanted to get an early night before his important day tomorrow.

The game of charades was loud and boisterous. She quickly discovered that although the family were quite competitive, they had little regard for the rules of the game—which surprised her again, given that rules were William's profession—it was clearly far more important to make everyone laugh as much as possible. Dottie laughed a lot.

They said goodbye as one or two snow flurries began to drift down. Almost spring, and yet winter had returned for one last chance to reign. William took one look and grabbed her arm to hurry her out and into the car. She half-ran with a laughing backward glance at his family who waved from the door then went back inside.

William ran round to his side to get in, started the car and let off the hand brake within a few seconds, then asked her to look in the back of the car for a rug or something to put over her knees.

She found it and swathed herself with it. 'I like your family,' she commented.

That was the last thing either of them said for the next forty minutes. The snow increased, and the road was rapidly becoming a slide.

Outside the air swirled with snowflakes gleaming silver against the night. Grass verges and roads glittered with icy crystals in the light from the headlamps. Inside the car, with the rug pulled up to her waist and down over her feet, and with her coat collar turned up, her hat on, and her gloves too, Dottie felt deliciously warm and very soon began to nod in her seat.

It had been such a hectic day. She hadn't realised just how tired she was. She leaned comfortably against William's left shoulder and dozed.

She became aware of him saying her name gently once or twice and she pulled herself upright, full awake and disappointed to find they were outside her hotel.

'Oh. Are we there?'

'We are.'

'Oh.' She didn't want to leave him, didn't want to say goodnight.

He said, 'Look, Dottie. I know it's not exactly late, but if you're not too tired, can we have a quick word about tomorrow?'

'Of course.' She pulled the rug up to her chin and grinned at him, stifling a yawn. He put his arm around her shoulders and pulled her close.

'That young fellow, the son of the chief constable?'

'Gordon Wisley? I met him last week at Gervase's parents' ball.'

'Yes. Look, I want to go and see him, to try to get him to make a statement about what he knows. Will you go with me? I know it's last minute, but with the panel being brought forward, I'm completely out of time. Things I thought I could do tomorrow or the day after, I just don't know how much I'll get done.'

'Yes, if you like. We're not friends or anything, I've only met him that once. He's a bit of an ass, but a likeable one.'

She felt him nod and half-turn to her as he said, 'I'm hoping he'll be more forthcoming if you're there. I'm asking rather a lot of him, expecting him to talk to me. But I had expected a further week to prepare my evidence, and...'

'Won't he be incriminating himself? Not to mention his concern that his father might find out what he'd been getting up to.'

'I know. That's why I'm worried he'll refuse. I mean, I can arrange for him to be free from prosecution if he's done something fairly minor, in exchange for his witness statement. Unless he's done something serious, obviously, in which case I shall be required to bring him to justice.' He sighed. With his free hand, he rubbed his face. Dottie had only seen him do that once when he was desperately worried about a case.

She kissed his cheek. 'Pick me up at half past nine. We'll go and see him. I'll phone up and ask Mr Michaels for the address. Obviously I don't want to risk Gervase answering, not that it's very likely, so I'll wait until he's left for the office tomorrow morning.'

'Parfitt won't be in the office tomorrow. He'll be at home consulting with his barrister before the panel. He's under orders to stay out of the office tomorrow, and until such time as the panel concludes.'

Dottie hadn't expected that. Now that she thought about it, it seemed obvious, but it just hadn't occurred to her before.

'We'll think of something,' William said.

'Do you think Moira might know anything?' Dottie's suggestion was tentative. She didn't particularly want to bring up Moira right now, but they needed all the help they could get. She felt him shrug.

'No idea. Perhaps. She'll be staying at Parfitt's house, of course.'

Dottie squeezed his hand. 'It'll be all right, William.'

'Hmm. Probably. But I can't say I'm happy with what I have so far. This is the biggest case I've had to deal with, and I've still got next to nothing.'

'Rubbish,' she said immediately. 'What about those dinner party robberies last year? *That* was a big case. And involving several other police forces. And men with guns. This is just different, so you're feeling out of your depth. You're good at what you do. You'll succeed in showing that Gervase has committed some terrible crimes. You'll do it,' she added. And kissed his cheek again.

He turned his head, and his lips met hers, passion flaring from nowhere to transport them both away from the cold and the uncertainty. It was several minutes before he drew away with great reluctance, and said crossly:

'This isn't really the time or the place, is it?'

She laughed and said, 'No, darling, it's not, is it?'

Momentarily, she wondered if she dared invite him upstairs to her room, but decided on the one hand, the hotel clerk would doubtless stare embarrassingly at them as they went past, and on the other, Inspector Hardy needed a good night's sleep.

'Goodnight,' she said, and stroked his face with her fingertips. She kissed him once more and got out of the car.

He got out and walked her to the hotel door, hand in hand, in silence. Then he kissed her gently and let her go inside. He drove home carefully through the snow, praying it would come down deep and heavy during the small hours, and that the panel would be cancelled.

Dottie slept like the proverbial log, and felt as if she'd only just laid her head on the pillow when her alarm clock woke her. Half an hour later she was downstairs eating toast and drinking two cups of strong tea, and trying to ignore the nerves churning away inside her at the prospect of the coming panel.

Not that she would be allowed into the chamber where the chief constable would be holding his private hearing into Gervase's conduct. She would have to wait— somewhere—perhaps the same hotel where she'd gone yesterday. That would be handy if William had time to take her there. The waiting would be awful, she thought. Not knowing what was happening, whether things were going well. This was how it would be as a policeman's wife.

'How will William feel this morning if I'm like this?' she wondered.

Would this ruin his career if it didn't go well? Even if it didn't prevent him getting promotion, surely it would seriously dent his confidence? She pushed away her plate, unable to finish her toast.

As she went across the hall, with a sense of déjà vu, she glanced across to the seating area and noticed a man waiting there. She hurried to speak to him.

'Mr Michaels! I wasn't expecting to see you this morning.'

From his expression and his stance, it was clear he was upset.

'Has something happened?' she asked.

'I'm afraid it has, miss. Mr Parfitt has given me my cards.'

That was a shock. 'He's sacked you? But...'

'He's got wind of a few things. He knows I spoke to Inspector Hardy, and so he says I've abused my position of trust.'

'Well he'd know all about abusing a position of trust,' Dottie said. 'But I wonder how on earth he found out. From Moira probably. And Mrs Michaels, I assume she was sacked too?'

He nodded. 'Oh yes miss. She's gone to her mother's. We'll need to stay with her for a while until we can get another position.'

He was looking quite distressed. 'Miss Manderson, I know it's a cheek to ask, but with getting sacked, I don't see Mr Parfitt giving me, or either of us, a decent reference. And no one in their right mind would take us on without one. I just wondered if you would vouch for me if I need you to?'

'Of course,' she said. 'Just let your new employer know how to contact me in London. Do you still have my address?'

He nodded, relieved. 'I do, miss. I took the liberty of noting it down in case I missed you here. We've a small amount of savings, but not enough to keep us for the rest of our lives.' He was mangling his hat with his hands, wringing and twisting the fabric in his anxiety. Dottie gently took the hat from him and coaxed it back into shape.

She patted his arm. 'Try not to worry. Hopefully everything will come out all right in the end. Do you have enough to be going on with?'

He seemed taken aback by her offer of money. His pride asserted itself. Firmly but politely he told her, 'Oh yes, miss. We have enough for now, thank you.'

'Have you been called to give evidence today?'

'I'm to make myself available. They said I might not be called.'

Dottie nodded. 'I'll probably see you there. I'm not giving evidence but I'm going into Ripley with the inspector. I'm sorry, Mr Michaels, I must go and pack. Once the panel have made their decision today, I shall be going back to London.' A sudden thought occurred to her. She said, 'By the way, do you happen to know Gordon Wisley's address, or his telephone number? The Inspector needs it.'

'I know the address, miss. I need to check the telephone number.' He reached into his pocket and pulled out a small book. He riffled through a few pages. 'Ah here it is, miss.'

Dottie copied the details down in her ever-useful diary. 'Took the whole address book with you?' she asked him with a grin.

He nodded, embarrassed at being caught out. 'Yes, miss, I'm afraid I did.'

'Good thing too.'

She shook his hand and after reminding him to contact her in London if he needed anything, she said good morning. She ran up to her room, deep in thought.

At twenty-five past nine, Dottie hauled her baggage down to the reception area, her room now neat and completely empty. The hotel clerk—horrified to see her being so independent—slammed up the flap of his desk and rushed to help her to carry the bags to the front door where she waited for William.

William's car was just pulling into the area in front of the hotel. He got out and came to meet her.

To her surprise, he looked fresh and well-rested, every trace of nerves was hidden. He kissed her on the lips almost in defiance, and they smiled at one another.

As they drove along through the village towards the larger town of Ripley, Dottie told him about Michaels.

William said, 'I've had a call this morning telling me to expect a fight. I assume Moira has told him things. Not that it's likely to be a lot.'

'Who called you?'

'Parfitt's barrister. Rather unorthodox. I'm intrigued as to how many strings had to be pulled for them to get hold of the telephone number for my uncle's house.'

'Perhaps that came from Moira?'

He shook his head. 'I've never given her that number. But she knows the address of course, so perhaps Parfitt simply spent ten minutes with directory enquiries.'

Dottie laughed. 'Yes I can just see him doing that, I don't think. But he may have got her to do it. Did you tell her anything about the enquiries you've been making? Could she tell him anything damaging to your case?'

'All she could know is whatever she managed to read that time when I was out of the room at home.' He beckoned to the driver of a farm cart to go out across in front of them. The man waved a hand in acknowledgement. 'I've never discussed my work with her. She wouldn't have been interested, in any case.'

Dottie felt a warm glow inside. He had discussed various cases he was working on with her. That made her feel special. Until she remembered that half of the time, it was because he was telling her off for interfering in police business.

Gordon Wisley was still in bed when they arrived. That came as no surprise to Dottie, she knew plenty of young men like that. It was still quite early for a man of his type used to rising at lunchtime, drifting about his flat before going out to his club or to dine with friends. A well-to-do young man with no need to worry about making ends meet or working hard to earn a living. In any case, he had told her about his inclination for parties and socialising.

In spite of them disturbing him, he received them cordially, though clearly puzzled by their visit. He cast several questioning looks in William's direction. Tying the belt on his dressing gown, he invited them to come into the sitting room and to take a seat.

The room was rather cluttered. There was enough dust on the surfaces that Dottie could tell he had no maid to come in and clean for him on a regular basis. They managed to remove some of the heaps of papers and general tat to make enough room to sit down on a threadbare sofa whose springs had seen better days. Perhaps he wasn't so well-to-do after all.

'Look here, what's all this about?' Wisley asked, looking from one to the other. He reclined in his chair opposite them with every appearance of ease, but Dottie didn't miss the tension in the way he held his shoulders, nor the way his left hand trembled and refused to be still as he drummed on the arm of the chair.

'It's about those things you told me at the Parfitts' the other night.'

As soon as she said that, he thumped his forehead. 'I knew it! I knew I should have kept my big mouth shut. Wine and pretty girls. Always loosen the tongue, what? And make a man throw caution to the wind.' He looked at William again. 'I suppose you're from the police?'

William nodded. 'I am indeed. I'd be very grateful if you could elaborate a little more on the things you told Miss Manderson.' William hesitated before adding, almost as a challenge, 'Or was that pure pretence, just to show off? Wine and a pretty girl, as you say.'

Gordon was staring at his fingernails. Suddenly they seemed very important to him. He said, in a low voice, 'What if my father gets to hear about any of this? I mean, it's one thing to act like a complete fool with your friends. But I wouldn't for the world deliberately do anything that would hurt my father—or his career. It might not be very fashionable to say it, but I admire my father, and love him very much. Since my mother died five years ago, we're all each other has.'

William was about to speak, but Dottie said, 'Gordon, I know this is putting you in a difficult position. And I know Gervase is a friend of yours, but surely you can see he's not supposed to do the things he does? It's illegal. And he's using what he knows about people to bribe and threaten them. You've got to think about doing what's right. If you keep this up, you could still end up in terrible trouble. Best to make a clean breast of it, bring it all out into the open, and admit what you've done. Your father will be proud of that, won't he? That he's brought you up to do the right thing. Eventually.'

She could see he was leaning towards agreement.

William said, 'I'm sorry to put you on the spot. But this is vital information in a case I'm bringing before your father this afternoon. If you don't help me, Gervase Parfitt may very well stay in his position and continue to abuse it so that he can keep on hurting people.'

Gordon was paler now. 'This afternoon? So soon?'

Dottie nodded.

Gordon closed his eyes as if he couldn't face any of it anymore. 'Will he go away? Parfitt? To prison, I mean. Will Parfitt go to prison?'

William nodded. 'That's what I'm aiming for. Some of the things he's done—they're—well, they're extremely serious.'

Gordon was silent. He leaned forward in his chair, his shoulders hunched, his face buried in his hands.

'I know Parfitt is a friend of yours,' William began, but Gordon shot up onto his feet, one hand out to silence him.

'My *friend*? Not any more, but I won't say a word against him.'

Dottie said, 'What about that dreadful hole he got you out of? Can you tell us what that was all about?'

'Never. I can't possibly...' He fell silent.

'Please, Gordon, it's so important.'

He wouldn't look at them. He was chewing his lip, trying to decide what to do or say.

'Get it off your chest,' Dottie said. 'It's obviously troubling you.'

He shook his head. 'I tell you I can't.' He began pacing the floor, agitated. 'I just—I just can't. He has people...'

'Gordon,' Dottie pleaded.

'No, I... Oh it was too terrible.' He was struggling to remain calm, fighting to get the breath to speak normally. He sat down again, took a few deep breaths, then, his voice shaking with emotion, said, 'If you had been there... Her face. I will n-never forget her face. As long as I live, I will never...' He began to weep.

William and Dottie looked at one another. After a moment, Dottie took one of William's handkerchiefs out of her bag and lay it on the young man's knee. He took it and placed it over his face. It was several more minutes before the emotion subsided.

He composed himself enough to say, 'I could never stand up in a court and tell my father this. He'd be so ashamed. And he'd be ruined. I can't.'

Dottie said, 'Think about it.'

But he said, quite roughly, 'I tell you, I can't. I won't! You'll have to find someone else. Please. I'd be glad if you would leave now. I'm sorry, but I can't help you.' He was on his feet and heading for the door to show them out.

Dottie would have continued to plead with him, but William got to his feet. Before they left, William took a card from his wallet.

'That's my card. I'm appearing before a closed hearing in your father's chambers at four o'clock this afternoon. Please think carefully about what you know. I can't ask anyone else, there simply isn't time. You're the only one who can help. If you change your mind, please let your father's secretary know, she will contact me.'

Gordon made no move to take the card from him. William placed it on the arm of a nearby chair, then he and Dottie left.

Dottie felt sombre and discouraged as they walked down the stairs to the street door.

'It was all for nothing,' she said. 'What are we going to do now?'

He said nothing, but pulled her arm through his and turned towards the car.

'What now?' she repeated.

'I really have no idea.'

They sat in the car in silence.

After a few minutes, he said, 'I shall just have to hope that I have enough evidence.'

'Well,' Dottie said, starting to count them off on her fingers: 'There's Mrs Parkes, and Mr Michaels. And the major. Even Mrs Holcombe might be willing to tell what she knows about her father, and even that she suspects Gervase of taking advantage of her sister. And the very helpful woman I spoke to at the Rialto in Nottingham. She said she'd be happy to give evidence.'

'But what could she testify to? I don't even know what those ticket stubs have to do with anything. Or even *if* they have anything to do with anything.'

Dottie bit her lip. She'd been about to say, and the newspaper cuttings, but he was right. The vital link between all the disparate parts of their evidence was missing. As things were, it simply wasn't enough, and Gervase and his barrister would no doubt make mincemeat of the case.

He glanced at her and saw her despondent expression. 'Sorry, Dottie. You've been a huge help, honestly. But I just don't have enough.' He was silent for a moment, then added, 'I have a statement from another ex-policeman, stating that he saw Parfitt making payments to known criminals, so that's another piece of evidence. It might just have to do.'

Dottie's spirits rose slightly. She said, 'Surely that's enough just on its own? All you've got to do is prove Gervase has abused his position. You're not trying his case in court today. What about the identity parade racket Gervase was running? You worked out how he was using that, so you can present that to the chief constable. Is it worth taking another run out to Gervase's house? Moira is probably still there. I bet she knows what he gets up to. She might be willing to talk.'

He shook his head. 'The identity parade thing is too tenuous. And Moira won't talk to me, I'm sure of it. She plans to marry Parfitt, so she'll hardly help me to get him arrested.'

Dottie sighed and leaned back in her seat. She twiddled a strand of hair around her forefinger and gazed into space, racking her brains for something either helpful or encouraging to say to him. Nothing sprang to mind.

William leaned back too. A glance at his watch showed

him he had five and a half hours before he would be meeting the chief constable for the panel. It wasn't enough time. But the chief constable could give him another month and it still wouldn't be enough. He closed his eyes and tried to think, but all he could think was, he wanted to drive off right now with Dottie and start a new life together somewhere far away on the three pounds and ten shillings he knew he had right now in his wallet. By four o'clock they could be in Gretna Green, and married over an anvil, or they could drive south and get a boat from Dover or somewhere. They could be in France by dinnertime. Or... just... anywhere. Anywhere but here.

He turned his head to look at her, smiling to see the frown of concentration, the furrowed brow as she tried to think of something useful. She was wonderful, he thought. A gorgeous, sexy, funny, intelligent woman who had done so much to try to help him. The bruise around the cut across her cheek was beginning to lessen, but was still red, still all too clearly visible. He felt so angry whenever he thought of Parfitt hitting her. He shook his head as that anger rekindled now. He had to get Parfitt where he belonged: behind bars.

She took his hand. 'What else have we got? Can you get him for making payments to criminals? Or can you prove he helped Mrs Sedgworth to cover up the accident then bribed her over it?'

He sat up and stared at her. Then he took her face between his hands and kissed her firmly on the mouth.

'You are a genius, Dottie!'

He started up the car.

Thirty-seven minutes later, he halted the car at a garage. 'Come on,' he urged, leaping out, and he was halfway to the door of the ramshackle workshop at the side before Dottie was out of the car.

A man came out, wiping oily fingers on an even oilier rag. 'Help you, sir?'

William got his warrant card out. 'It's about a car you had in here three years ago. Would you have been here then?'

The mechanic nodded. 'It's my place. Been here nigh on ten years.'

William fished in his pocket for the invoice the major had given him. 'What can you tell me about this?'

As soon as they had finished at the garage, Dottie said, 'How far is it to that pub where George Parkes carried out the robbery?'

It turned out not to be very far at all.

As pubs went, it was not especially picturesque. It was a plain building set back off the road, and several minutes' walk from the village of Blackhall.

Looking about him, William said, 'My first impression is that this is the perfect place for a crime—no one in the village itself would know anything about it unless they were actually at the pub.'

'No witnesses to the getaway?'

'Exactly. But look,' he pointed out, 'no seats outside, even though the reports said that the dead man had been sitting drinking with his friends outside the pub.'

Dottie nodded. 'With the road sweeping round right in front, and that fence along the edge of the field, there's nowhere to put any chairs even if you wanted to. And there's nowhere for a car or any vehicle to pull in. It's a very inconvenient location.'

'Hmm.' William was thinking. 'I wonder if business is good.'

'Are we going in?'

He nodded, and linking his arm through hers, they made their way to the door. It was locked. William banged on the door. Above their heads, a window opened.

'Clear off,' the man yelled. 'The pub's shut. There's another one in Blackdale, the Lamb, two miles along the road.'

'I'm Detective Inspector Hardy of Scotland Yard. I'd like to speak with you on a police matter. Please come down and let us in.'

The man banged the window shut. It was easily five minutes before he opened the door. He looked belligerent, his feet planted wide, his arms folded across his chest, a scowl on his face.

'What d'you want?'

'Are you still in business?' Dottie immediately butted in.

'Who are you, his secretary?'

'Just answer the question,' William snapped.

'No, of course I'm not in business. Take a look about you. Business folded last year.'

'So the money Gervase Parfitt gave you wasn't much help, then?' Dottie felt William glare at her, but she kept her eyes fixed on the angry publican.

The man shrugged. 'It helped, of course. But it weren't enough. He only gave me half what he promised.'

William said, 'Shall we sit down. Best if you tell us the whole thing from the beginning.'

When they came out of the pub, they went straight into the village to speak to a man named Thomas Perkins as directed by the publican. Knocking on the door of a small thatched cottage in the centre of the village, Dottie was filled with excited anticipation. Would Thomas Perkins be there? Because if he was...

The door was opened by a tall thin man with a long cow-lick of fair hair that flopped over his forehead.

'Thomas Perkins?' William demanded.

The man was immediately on the defensive. 'Who wants to know?'

With an impatient sigh, William held up his warrant card. 'Just tell me if you are or aren't.'

The man crunched up his eyes to read the warrant card, his lips moving as he did so. After a long minute, he said, 'Fine. I am.'

'May we come in, Mr Perkins? I need to talk to you.'

When they left, it was close on half past two. Time was running out. Dottie had a frightening sense of the sand running through the hourglass far too quickly. But William was pleased with this latest small success.

'It all helps,' he said.

'Now where?'

'I don't know.' He looked at her. 'It's a bit early for lunch.'

'Definitely.' A thought came to her. 'How is Mrs Parkes getting to the hearing?'

'Oh she's not coming. She didn't want to go to court unless she was summoned. I tried, but she said no. I'm going to try to make do with just her statement.'

Dottie found that surprising. 'Will that be enough?'

He didn't look too happy about it. 'It will have to be. I didn't feel I could badger her. She's getting on a bit, after all. Her statement is quite clear and compelling, so I'm hopeful. But if this case goes to trial, she'll have to appear then.'

She nodded. She bit her lip, pondering. 'I suppose we could offer her a lift?'

He looked doubtful.

'Can we at least go and see her?' Dottie asked. 'Unless you've thought of something urgent to do?'

'No, nothing. If you want to do that, I don't see why not. If she comes to the Police Headquarters, they might be more inclined to call on her, and certainly her testimony will be even stronger if delivered in person.'

'She's a nice old thing, and very hard up, so if we can save her trouble and expense of getting there, it'll be worth it.'

'All right then.'

When they arrived and knocked on Mrs Parkes's door. However, she only opened it a crack, not wanting them to come inside. She looked rather sheepish. Dottie's heart sank. This looked like bad news.

'Oh it's you. I told them to let you know. You've had a wasted journey coming here.' She was about to close the door, but Dottie said:

'What do you mean, Mrs Parkes? Who did you tell? And what did you tell them?'

'I've changed my mind. I'm not doing it. I told them yesterday, you're to tear up that statement, you're not to use it. I've changed my mind. I'm not giving evidence.'

Dottie and William exchanged dismayed looks.

'But Mrs Parkes!' Dottie began, but the old lady was adamant.

'I don't want to talk about it. My mind is made up. That's an end to it.'

And with that she slammed the door and they heard her sliding the bolt across to make sure.

'Dottie,' William said. She turned to look at him. His tone was so urgent, her heart was pounding even though she had no idea what he was about to say.

'Dottie, I want you to go home. Now. I'll drive you to the station. We've got your luggage in the back, so there's no need for any delay. I want you out of here and back in London. You'll be safe there, at home with your family. I've got a feeling I'm not going to be able to pull this off, and I need to know you're safe. Just in case he decides to come after you out of pure spite. Because after today, he will know everything, and he will be furious. We both know he's the type to get his revenge if he can.'

'William, in forty minutes you are going before a panel to put forward your case against Gervase. There's no time for this. Set me down in Ripley as arranged, and go and do your best. That's all you can do, William dear.'

'But...' he began. She shushed him with a finger on his lips.

'No, William, I'm not leaving you now.'

*

Chapter Seventeen

William felt sick with nerves as he took his seat in the meeting room in the chief constable's chambers. Doubt filled his mind, and he asked himself for the umpteenth time who he thought he was, coming here like this today.

On the opposite side of the vast conference table was Gervase Parfitt in an elegant suit that clearly cost more than anything William owned. Both on Parfitt's left and his right sat a suited barrister, stern, polished, and professional right down to the gold cufflinks that closed the pristine white cuffs of their bespoke shirts. One of them frowned slightly as he regarded William over half-moon spectacles. William glanced down and only now noticed a greasy smudge on his tie, and a button of his shirt gaping open.

He was on his own save for the stack of papers he'd spent most of the night preparing once he'd got in from taking Dottie back to her hotel. A two-hour nap followed by a quick bath to wake himself up a bit, and he'd been back on the road to meet Dottie at their agreed time. The room was warm, heated by radiators that noisily expelled a great deal of heat. William felt drowsy and muzzyheaded. His confidence was in his boots.

On top of his stack of papers lay a list of the order in which he planned to present his evidence and the corresponding number of each item in the stack. If nothing else, he'd be sure of a good job as a secretary when all this was over. Not for the first time he wondered whether he should just give up the police force and take the job his uncle had been offering him for the last five years. But he'd never seen himself running a cotton mill.

A trickle of sweat ran down the middle of his back. His collar felt too tight and irritated the back of his neck. He knew no one could see it, but he had a hole in his sock; one of his toes was poking through uncomfortably. The smudge on his tie seemed at least twice as big as when he'd first noticed it and he became convinced it was all anyone else could see. He had no business here with these elegant people who looked more like city businessmen than police officers.

He sighed inwardly. Was this all just about his own ruffled pride? Was he pursuing a purely personal vendetta against the man he hated so much? He glanced again at Parfitt, sitting there laughing and chatting comfortably with his little cohort. Parfitt stretched back in his seat, revealing a silk waistcoat, the chain of a gold pocket-watch neatly draping from pocket to buttonhole, complementing the gleaming buttons of the waistcoat.

Parfitt sent him a jeering look, almost a smirk, and made some remark to the men beside him. They all laughed, looking across at Hardy.

All at once William thought, let them laugh. I'm here for a reason: to prove that Gervase Parfitt has continually abused his position and perverted the course of justice—and more besides.

The door opened. The stenographer came in and took up her position, and right behind her, came the chief constable, his secretary, and the three magistrates. They all took their seats.

The room felt crowded, and William's brief flare of confidence began to fizzle away once more. This is ridiculous, he scolded himself. I've been to court and successfully proved a number of cases; this is no different.

The chief constable cleared his throat and began by welcoming everyone to the meeting. The magistrates' clerk, the stenographer, the chief constable's secretary and one of Parfitt's barristers all immediately began to record the proceedings.

The chief constable went on to say, 'The purpose of this informal hearing is to establish whether there is any case to answer in the matter of the assistant chief constable's conduct. Our task is to find out if there are any grounds to suspect or accuse Gervase Parfitt of corruption, abuse of position, or perverting the course of justice, or indeed any other charge. Evidence will be heard before myself and the three magistrates into whose purview this enquiry falls.

'This is not a court hearing. But if the magistrates here present find justification for doing so, they may order that Mr Parfitt be removed from office, placed under arrest and formally charged, pending prosecution and the full penalty of the law.

'There is no one acting for the Crown in this matter because as I said, this is an informal hearing, but Inspector William Hardy of the Metropolitan Police has been empowered by the internal affairs department and the Home Office to conduct an investigation into Mr Parfitt's professional and personal conduct. Inspector Hardy will call witnesses to support his evidence. Mr Parfitt and his legal representatives will have the right of rebuttal and of cross-examining witnesses, just as in a courtroom hearing.

'As this hearing could materially affect Mr Parfitt's position, he has been permitted, even I may say, advised, to seek legal representation. I will now ask everyone to identify themselves for the record. We shall begin with myself and go around the table in a clockwise manner.'

As they each in turn gave their name and profession, William looked towards the window. Ten past four, and already it was growing dark outside. He thought of Dottie. All he wanted now was for this whole episode to be over, and to be with her. He felt that he'd been wanting that one thing his whole life.

He would be the first to present his case. But as he got to his feet, straightened his tie and prepared to speak, one of Parfitt's barristers, the one with the half-moon glasses, said:

'Mr Wisley, we would like to make a request, if we may.'

The chief constable looked surprised but a quick glance at the magistrates showed that they had no objections.

'Very well. What is it, Mr Turner?'

'Inspector Hardy intends to call a Mr Robert Michaels to give evidence before the hearing. We very humbly request that this witness be disallowed.'

William was aghast. The chief constable and the magistrates hardly less so.

'What is the reason for this?' one of the magistrates asked.

'The gentleman was for a number of years a trusted servant in Mr Parfitt's household, but had recently been indiscreet about household details and Mr Parfitt had therefore cause to dismiss Michaels from his service. Mr Michaels was heard by two witnesses to state he would extract his revenge. I therefore request that his testimony be withdrawn, since he clearly has an axe to grind, and is only here out of spite.'

William lay down his pen. This was a wretched beginning, and entirely his own fault. He should have known, even expected this. They would get what they wanted. He had been a fool to even try to make use of Michaels.

The chief constable had the briefest of consultations with the three magistrates. From their grave looks and nods, their decision was apparent before it was given.

'Inspector, Mr Michaels will not appear before us today, and his statement will be disregarded. Clearly he is not a useful witness in this case. I hope any other evidence you have will be of greater reliability, Inspector. You may proceed.'

There was nothing else for it. William simply nodded

and said, 'Yes sir. Thank you.'

Gervase Parfitt was looking troubled and reflective over templed fingertips. He'd clearly been practising the expression. As he glanced across at William Hardy, however, his eyes gleamed with triumph. There was the suggestion of a sneer about his nose and mouth.

William attempted to rewrite his notes in his mind. He cleared his throat and began to outline his case.

'Mr Parfitt, from the earliest days of his police career, has sought to use his position to benefit himself and his friends, manipulating evidence and abusing his position as an upholder of the law.'

He was speaking off-the-cuff, unable to recall his prepared opening remarks. As he tried to pull his case together, his mind was sarcastically repeating to him, "He used his position to abuse his position.' Does that actually mean anything?' He felt flustered and hot. Clearly it was a good thing he'd been forced to give up his pursuit of a career in law. He'd have been useless as a prosecutor.

Behind his hand, Parfitt smirked, confident, untroubled.

'I would like to bring my first particular case before this hearing, and show how Gervase Parfitt took charge of a situation to bring about a satisfactory outcome for himself and his friends.'

The magistrates were looking somewhat doubtful, and the chief constable was already looking glassy-eyed. Defeat felt imminent.

If anything, things got worse. Hardy, certain that Major Sedgworth would strike the perfect note with the magistrates, brought him in as his first witness.

'Major Sedgworth, you told me that your wife was extremely upset by a call she had from Mr Parfitt on the morning before her death, is that not so?'

'Yes indeed, beside herself,' the major confirmed, his Adam's apple bobbing several times as he swallowed nervously.

'And she told you that Mr Parfitt had demanded a large sum of money from her or he would reveal an uncomfortable secret to which he was privy?'

'That's correct.' Major Sedgworth sent an apologetic smile towards Gervase Parfitt that induced a sense of exasperation in William.

'As a result of this unhappiness, your wife then took her own life?'

There was a slight pause. Then the major nodded. 'Yes, she did.'

One of the barristers said, 'Major, were you at home when your wife received this telephone call?'

The major turned slightly to face Parfitt and his cronies. 'Er, no, sir. I had left the house, to drive to Mr Parfitt's house, to collect his guest, Miss Manderson. She was to take coffee with my wife that morning.'

'So how do you know that Mr Parfitt actually did telephone to Mrs Sedgworth?'

'My wife told me so.' The major's tone was surprised.

'And your wife would always tell you the absolute truth, no doubt?' The barrister's words were accompanied by a wide smile and a flash of large, yellowish rabbit-like teeth.

'Of course.' The major sounded a little defensive now, William thought, and more than a little put out. William himself had a horrid sense of knowing exactly where this was about to lead.

'And yet she didn't tell you what this mysterious secret was, or how she came to have shared it only with Mr Parfitt to the exclusion of everyone else, including yourself?' The barrister allowed his tone to sound politely disbelieving.

'Er—well, no, not as such.' Major Sedgworth shifted in his seat and tugged on his shirt collar.

'And in fact,' the barrister continued, 'even now, you have only the haziest of ideas of what that secret was?'

'I believe it was to do with a car accident,' the major said.

'Indeed? And did Mrs Sedgworth tell you what had happened?'

'Er—no.'

'So how do you know there was an accident at all?'

'I found a bill from the garage for some repairs.'

'I see. But your wife kept this from you?'

'Didn't want to worry me with it, that's all.'

The major sounded rather sulky now, William thought. It was like watching a car crash happening very slowly in front of his eyes. He could see what was going to happen, but could do nothing to stop it. Perhaps when they had the tea-break in an hour—if the whole thing hadn't already been called off by then—it might be best to go to see the chief constable, and simply throw in the towel.

'Have you formed any opinion as to the details of this accident or how, if at all, Mr Parfitt was involved?'

'Suppose she asked him for help, that's all. I was away at the time.'

'Yes, Major. You were away at the time.' The barrister clearly thought he was in a law court, from the way he nodded and gravely emphasised the major's words, looking at each magistrate in turn as he said it. 'Would it surprise you to learn that Mrs Sedgworth had hit a deer on the way home from Mr and Mrs Edwin Parfitt's home, where she had dined that evening? Or that your wife—an emotional lady, as we've already heard—was greatly upset by the event and needed the reassurance of a trusted family friend, a man who could tell her the right thing to do. And so she had telephoned Mr Parfitt to ask him to help her. He arranged for the collection and repair of the car, and himself drove out to pick her up and take her home. Would it also surprise you to learn that the phone call on the morning of Miss Manderson's visit, was simply a two minute courtesy call to let your wife know that you and Miss Manderson were on your way back to your home, and that she could expect you to arrive shortly.'

'Ah. Well, I s-suppose I didn't realise. And she had never mentioned the accident to me. I thought she'd hit a person, k-killed a person. She didn't say a thing about it.'

'Just so, just so. *You* thought, *you* jumped to conclusions. In the light of your recent sad bereavement, I think we can all agree, you were not likely to be thinking as clearly as you otherwise would. I'm afraid, Major, you have been the victim of an ambitious young police officer's bid to make a name for himself, without considering the feelings of those upon whom he trampled.'

'Oh I don't think Inspector Hardy...' the major responded immediately.

'Then the alternative is, that your wife didn't tell you what had happened because like many wives of military men, she was afraid of upsetting you, and thought it better you didn't know.'

The major blustered a little. 'Quite possibly,' he agreed with reluctance.

William had a falling sensation in the pit of his stomach. It seemed that Parfitt's men were prepared to go even further than he'd thought.

'Are you a violent man, Major? Was your wife afraid of you?' the barrister demanded.

'What? Now look here! That's damned insolence!' The major was on his feet, faced already flushing deep red with anger.

'Calm down, Major Sedgworth,' the chief constable said. He directed a frown at the barrister. 'Be careful, Mr Turner.'

'I apologise, Mr Wisley. I forgot myself for a moment. This is rather like being in court. However, I believe I've shown that there may have been things that Mrs Sedgworth kept back from her husband, and her unfortunate suicide was not due to any fear of bully-boy tactics on the part of the assistant chief constable, who remained a caring and considerate friend of the family.'

There was silence.

The chief constable then said, 'Major Sedgworth, thank you, you may leave.'

The major scuttled from the room with an apologetic look at Hardy.

As the major went out, someone else came in. A young man approached the chief constable and bent to speak to him in a whisper.

William assumed this was yet more bad news. The hearing began to feel doomed. He had known he had barely enough evidence to support his case, but within mere minutes, the rug was already halfway out from under him.

The chief constable nodded and the young man departed. Everyone waited to hear what new revelation would be announced.

The chief constable said, 'Inspector Hardy?'

'Yes sir.' William jumped up.

'I understand that your witness Mrs Parkes has withdrawn her statement and will not be appearing before us today?'

He was almost relieved. At least that wasn't something new. He acknowledged that what the chief constable said was correct.

The chief constable said, 'I understand that Mrs Parkes claims her statement was obtained by threat. She says none of it was true, and was a complete fabrication created by yourself. I may say Inspector that I do not approve of police officers threatening elderly women. Be careful you do not end up in a discreditable position. As they say, rather a case of the kettle and the pot, it seems...'

'Sir, I assure you, I would never threaten anyone, especially not an elderly woman,' William stated.

'Are you saying the witness is a liar, Inspector Hardy?' Parfitt asked, his tone lazy and amused. 'If that's the case, I rather wonder you wanted to call her at all. But perhaps all your witnesses are liars?'

There was an electric pause as Parfitt belatedly, and his barristers, realised this was a taunt too far.

The chief constable immediately turned to them and said, 'Be careful Mr Parfitt, you're the one whose conduct is under scrutiny today.' He turned back to William. 'Inspector, I shall allow you a thirty-minute break to tape together the tatters of your case.'

'Thank you, sir.'

The chief constable and the magistrates left the room. William went out right behind them.

He went down the back stairs and out into the yard behind the building. The air was frosty, the sun was almost gone beneath the horizon—only a thin orange band separated the navy-blue sky from the black earth beneath.

He leaned against the wall of the building, and closed his eyes. It was all in pieces. It was all too clear from Parfitt's attitude that he thought he would be walking away from this afternoon's affairs with his honour intact. By tomorrow he would be back to feasting on the misery of others. And Hardy would find himself facing his superiors to explain how he had failed so horribly to do his job. He sighed, and went back inside.

*

Chapter Eighteen

The chief constable had set a small office at William's disposal. Almost as soon as he entered, dumping his papers on the desk beside a window, he peeled off his jacket and the lamentable tie. A knock came at the door and a young man looked in at him.

'Excuse me sir, sorry for the intrusion. I've been asked to bring you this. And before you return to the meeting room, can you pop along to Miss Vardry's office, please. The chief's secretary.'

'This' proved to be a large tin mug of hot tea. The young man left it on it on the desk and retreated. William had no idea who the young man was, or who had asked him to bring the tea, but he was very, very grateful for it. William sat on the chair, got out his pen and pulled the papers towards him.

Michaels disallowed. Major Sedgworth's evidence largely refuted, Mrs Parkes withdrawing her testimony. What should he do now? Where should he concentrate his efforts in the—he looked at his watch—seventeen minutes remaining before the meeting resumed?

He drank the tea down before it even had a chance to

cool, spent a few minutes staring out of the window, and a
further few minutes scribbling furiously. With just five
minutes to spare, he gathered up his things and went out
into the corridor.

A sign on a door told him he had found the secretary's
office. He tapped on it, unsure of the usual protocol, but
went in without waiting for a response. He saw the same
matronly woman he had seen at the hearing making notes
for the chief constable.

'Ah, Inspector!' she said. 'I came to look for you a while
go.'

'Sorry,' William said. 'I went outside for some fresh air.'

She gave him a kind smile. 'All a bit much, wasn't it?'

He nodded. 'You could say that. What did you need me
for?'

'Well first of all, there's this.' And she handed him a
clean tie. He beamed at her, pulled off his old one and
replaced it hurriedly with a smart, clean tie. She smiled
back. 'That's better, dear. Now then, come with me.'

He followed her along the corridor to another room.
She opened the door and nodded inside. 'In there. I do
hope you know what you're doing. And there's only two
minutes before we resume, Inspector.'

Inside the waiting room, the major was puffing
furiously on his pipe, filling the air with clouds of smoke
that curled and gathered just below the ceiling like a cloud.

In the corner sat a young man, one knee bobbing
continually. Gordon Wisley. William went over.

'All right?'

The young chap began shaking his head. 'I thought I
could, but now I don't know. I don't know, I just don't
know. This is going to kill the old man. I don't think I can
go through with it.'

William's heart sank. 'Please. I really need your help
with this. It's all going to pot.'

The major said, 'Didn't exactly cover myself in glory,
I'm afraid.'

'Never mind, Major, you tried, that's the main thing. Mr
Wisley, if you don't help me, Parfitt will walk free, and

keep doing all the things he's been doing.'

Gordon Wisley still looked unsure and sweating.

William said, 'Look, I'm sorry, I've got to get back. Please don't back out now. I'll ask them to call you right away, then it will be all over and done with.'

He hurried back to the meeting room, just slipping into his seat as the chief constable arrived back with the magistrates.

As William was the one bringing the accusations against Gervase Parfitt, there was no need for Mr Parfitt's legal advisors to offer any kind of defence for him. At the moment they were amusedly content to allow William to throw his paper darts at Parfitt. William would have welcomed gaining more time due to the chief constable listening to a lengthy defence case, but it was not to be.

Across the table, the two barristers and their client barely bothered to contain their easy confidence, let alone their disdain for the policeman facing them.

William was invited to continue to outline his case, and trying to ignore the old music hall song of *A Policeman's Lot Is Not A Happy One*, that was for some strange reason going round and round in his head, he said, 'Gentlemen, I respectfully ask if I might move to a different case. I had planned to present this later, but I would like to—er—'

His brain failed him, apart from a residual murmur of '....*is not a happy one...*', and he couldn't remember what he had been about to say.

Gervase Parfitt didn't quite manage to conceal his snort of derision.

William was furious with himself. I'm unprofessional, I'm acting like a brand new trainee just off the beat, awed by the higher-ups, he thought. He looked down at his notes and took a calming breath. As he looked down, a glimpse of the borrowed—and clean—tie encouraged him.

The chief constable said, 'I take it you wish to make a fresh start with your evidence, and in doing so, you wish to change the order of the two cases you planned to bring before us today, yes? You will now bring the second case first and the first case after it?'

The chief constable was unsmiling, but, William thought, there was a glint of kindliness in the man's eyes. William was grateful. So grateful.

'Er, yes, that's correct. Sir,' he added as a hasty afterthought.

'Very well, Hardy. Get on with it, man.'

William suppressed a smile. He said, 'I'd like to set before you a new case. And if I may, I'll give a little background to this.'

A glance showed the magistrates looking stern but not impatient. They were attending to his words carefully.

William said, 'Mr Parfitt has committed a number of grave misdeeds during his years in the police force. He has taken bribes. He has paid out bribes. He has enabled and protected perpetrators of illegal activities to continue in those activities without being troubled by legal difficulties. He has been present at, taken part in, hosted and facilitated weekend house-parties where businessmen met together to arrange contracts for unlawful enterprises. In addition, on these occasions, Gervase Parfitt has procured drugs, and even women for the sexual gratification of the men attending these parties.'

'Preposterous,' Parfitt remarked. He stubbed out a cigarette with vigour, then with a perfectly steady hand, poured himself a glass of water from the decanter. 'An utterly disgraceful assertion.'

No one seemed inclined to dispute what Parfitt had said. The barristers were steely-eyed, the magistrates were as stern as ever, and the chief constable's expression was inscrutable. William wondered if he really was as ignorant of his son's affairs as previously supposed. Even the stenographer and secretaries were staring at William now in disbelief.

William continued, 'Therefore I would draw your attention to the statements I have filed, and...'

'These are suggestive, but largely circumstantial,' one of the magistrates commented. 'We'll need to see rather more proof than this, Inspector.'

'Absolutely.' William sent a worried look in the direction of the chief constable. 'I'd like to call Mr Gordon Wisley to offer an eye-witness account of some of the events I've just described.'

The chief constable said immediately, 'Mr Gordon *Wisley*? Did I hear you correctly, Inspector? You are calling my son to give evidence before us today?'

'I'm very sorry, sir. But yes, I am.' William's heart was pounding. At a nod from the astounded chief constable, the clerk went out. If young Wisley had decided he couldn't go through with it after all, William would not just look like a prize fool, he would be saying goodbye to both his case and his career. He held his breath.

The chief constable and William both stared at the door with trepidation.

The door opened. The clerk came in, and all they could see was an empty corridor. For a second or two, William thought he had lost everything. But then, in came Gordon Wisley, white-faced and visibly shaking, to stand in front of them and give his name and address to the stenographer.

Trying to keep his voice steady, William said, 'Thank you for coming here today, Mr Wisley. I know it was not an easy decision for you to make. Will you please explain how you know Mr Parfitt.'

Gordon said in a quiet but firm voice. 'Certainly. Gervase Parfitt has been to our family home on many occasions over the last two or three years, both socially and in a professional capacity.'

He halted, and looked around him. He glanced at his father then away again almost immediately.

The meeting room seemed very quiet now. Outside, seemingly miles away, there was a honking of car horns and a shout. William noticed that Parfitt was now watchful, tense, one hand clenched almost into a fist. Parfitt saw William looking at him and made a show of relaxing. He lay his hand open on his knee. His barristers were conversing earnestly behind him.

'Thank you,' William said. 'And would you say that you

and Mr Parfitt became friends?'

'Oh yes,' Gordon Wisley said with no hesitation. 'He took an interest in me. I suppose he thought he could help out a young fellow. I was just down from Cambridge, and wondering what to do with myself. My father wanted me to study law, but I have more of a head for figures. I thought I might try stocks and shares. I think Parfitt just wanted to lend me a hand.'

One of the barristers nodded to his colleague, who then stood up and said, 'Objection. The witness cannot possibly know Mr Parfitt's unexpressed thoughts about him.'

The chief constable frowned, and before any of the magistrates could speak, he snapped irritably, 'For the second time, man, this is a not a courtroom. Sit down and allow the witness to continue.' He nodded to William.

William said to Gordon Wisley, 'I see. And you thought Mr Parfitt could help you with that?'

'Yes. He told me he had good connections and offered to introduce me to a few fellows. He invited me to a couple of golf weekends, put me up for membership at his club. Said it would be useful to get me in with the right people. He said he could help me to meet friends of his who would guide me into the trade.'

'That sounds very useful. I imagine too, that you were flattered?'

'Well yes I was. I'm just a kid, after all, no experience in that sort of thing, and Parfitt's a man of the world, known in business circles, and with a lot of—er—well, clout.'

William tried not to smile at that. 'You mean, his position as the assistant chief constable allows him to meet a lot of people, some of whom have influence?'

Too late, one of the barristers attempted to object again, but Wisley was already speaking.

'Exactly. He is a fellow who knows people from all sorts of backgrounds.' He was starting to relax now, and eager to help. Though the main obstacle was still to come.

'But things didn't go quite as you expected?' William asked.

Wisley looked at his father again. The chief constable

was staring steadily at the notepad in front of him.

'No. I'm an idiot, I suppose. I know this was entirely my own fault. I—I'd been brought up better than this. And, well, I know I've let my father down.'

'What happened?' William asked gently.

'There were card games. I'm terrible at cards. But I never liked to say no. And Parfitt is a difficult fellow to say no to, in any case. I—I lost rather a lot of money.' Wisley's voice trailed away and he looked down at the floor. 'A lot of money.'

'How much?' William asked. He wasn't sure it was strictly necessary to know that for his case, but for Wisley himself, William thought it would be as well to get it out there in the open.

'A little over seven thousand pounds.'

There was a stunned silence in the room. William almost couldn't believe he'd heard the young man correctly. After a couple of heartbeats, he said, 'I'm sorry, did you say seven *thousand* pounds?'

Wisley nodded, miserable. The chief constable had a hand up to shield his eyes and appeared to be carefully considering his notes. Wisley's eyes darted towards his father, then Parfitt, then William then back to the floor.

'Yes. Mr Parfitt said I shouldn't worry too much. He said he would pay it for me and I could pay him back. He promised not to tell my father.'

'How did you plan to repay the money?' William asked.

Wisley shrugged. 'Oh you know. Marry a rich girl. Try to win a bit back on the horses. Sell my car. Try to get some kind of job. Nothing has worked so far, apart from selling my car. I now owe him six thousand and seven hundred.'

'Did Mr Parfitt seem concerned that you owed him so much money?'

'Objection,' said one of the barristers again, unable to help himself. He was quelled by a look from all three magistrates at once.

'Continue, Mr Wisley,' said William.

'Well you see, Old Parfitt...' he halted, bit his lip and tried again. 'Mr Parfitt told me he didn't mind if it took me a while to repay the money. He told me it was better that I owed it to him and not to the other fellows. He said they weren't the type you wanted to owe money to. He said he wouldn't charge so much interest, so he was helping me out that way too. He told me my father would never hear of it.'

'I see.'

'Well then a little while later, he said to me, 'Look do me a favour, will you?' and of course I said I would. I felt jolly grateful to him. He said he'd write off some of the debt if I helped him out. He was entertaining some friends for a weekend party. He said it was a business meeting really, and that he hoped to make a couple of good deals out of it that would earn him a decent return on his investment. Then he said, 'Tell you what, help me out with this, and I'll write the whole debt off, that shows much this means to me."

'Sounds simple enough,' William suggested. 'What easier way for you to repay your debt to your friend? You must have been delighted?'

Gordon nodded. 'I was. In fact, I couldn't believe it. It seemed almost too good to be true.'

At this, the chief constable closed his eyes, shaking his head in dismay. William felt deeply sorry for the man.

Wisley continued, 'The only thing was, he wanted to invite everyone to my family's hunting lodge up in the Dales. Fresh air and open country, Parfitt said. Focuses the mind, and just the kind of getaway that city businessmen need. Good for the soul, he said.'

'I presume your father knew nothing about this?'

Wisley pounced on that, saying with huge emphasis, 'Good Lord, no! My father had no idea at all about any of this. He would never... I didn't tell anyone.'

'And so, you and Mr Parfitt were joined at the hunting lodge when and by whom?'

'It was Easter last year, from Friday 30th March, to Tuesday 3rd April. I was at a loose end anyway, as my father was staying with his brother down in Cornwall. Regarding the chaps who came along, I've made out a list.

There were a couple of judges, and the rest were mostly businessmen. Oh and an MP.' He handed a piece of paper to the clerk, who carried it to the chief constable, who glanced at it, looked distinctly uneasy, then handed it across to the magistrates.

William said, 'I see. And as it was a hunting lodge, I presume there was some shooting?'

'Yes. Only rabbits and whatnot. Crows, you know. And clay pigeon shooting. Just larking about really.'

'And no doubt there were some slap-up meals, and plenty to drink?' William suggested.

For a second, Gordon Wisley smiled. He said, without thinking, 'Oh yes, we had enough to put a Roman orgy to shame.' As soon as he spoke, he realised what he had said. He dropped his eyes to the floor, blushing.

Gervase Parfitt was looking uncomfortable at last, though he remained silent. The chief constable was looking at his son, but his expression gave nothing away.

Wisley glanced across at his father. He said, 'Oh Father, I'm so sorry, I never meant for you to know any of this.'

The chief constable shook his head slightly and said to the stenographer. 'Strike that last bit from the record.'

She nodded and quickly did so.

The chief constable added, without looking at his son, 'I'd like to remind the witness to address all his remarks to the meeting.'

Gordon Wisley hung his head.

William said, 'A Roman orgy? Surely not as bad as all that?'

The air in the room seemed taut, alive, as if everyone was straining to hear every word.

'Yes, that's more or less what it was.'

'Now look here!' Parfitt was on his feet. The man on his left put a hand on his arm, and Parfitt resumed his seat. The barrister said:

'This whole afternoon is a cynical and perverted attempt to cast Mr Parfitt in the worst possible light. Surely we are all men of the world and can accept that occasionally things get out of hand at a party. Mr Parfitt cannot be held accountable for his friends' conduct, nor indeed their bad habits. Mr Wisley's gambling debts are not Mr Parfitt's responsibility, even if, as a friend of the family he attempted to offer help.'

William said, 'To begin with, these occurrences were not 'occasional'. And it's important to remember that we are not talking about one or two personal indiscretions of a private nature. We are taking about an assistant chief constable procuring—yes, I said procuring—drugs and young girls—*very* young girls, I might add, to provide so-called entertainment for his business acquaintances.'

Everyone looked at the chief constable. Pale, stern, he nodded. 'Proceed, Inspector.'

William said to Wisley, 'Tell us what happened on one particular night last Easter, Mr Wisley.'

Gordon Wisley took a deep breath. 'It was the Monday. Er, the 2nd of April. We'd been together all weekend, and to be honest, we were getting a bit sick of each other. Just after nine o'clock, Mr Parfitt left the house. He told us to amuse ourselves for a while. The other men laughed, and one of them said something like, 'Oh we always do, old chap, you know that.' Anyway, we played cards for a while. Parfitt was gone for an hour and ten minutes. I checked my watch. To be honest, it was all getting a bit much, and I wanted to leave them to it. Some of the men were very drunk and were inclined to rub one another up the wrong way. We'd got past the having fun part of being drunk, and things were getting a bit dicey, everyone irritable and starting to fall out with one another. That was another reason I wanted to get out. One of the other fellows—about my age, actually—had passed out. He'd taken some pills or another. Someone gave him them, and the young chap gave him a tenner for them.'

'Did you witness this exchange, Mr Wisley?' asked Mr Turner from the seat to Parfitt's right.

'What? Oh no. They were in another room. But the fellow came back to get the money from his wallet. He'd left his jacket on the back of a chair next to mine.'

'Then surely we have no actual proof that this was for

drugs of some kind? This young man was quite likely to be simply repaying a small debt. In any case, Mr Parfitt was not present at the time.'

'Well, I, er...' Gordon Wisley floundered and looked at William.

William, with a sinking sense of deja vu, just said, 'Do go on, Mr Wisley.'

'Well I was thinking of turning them in, wondering what to say or do. I mean, I was sure it wouldn't do old Parfitt's rep, er, I mean, his reputation much good if it got out things like that were going on. To be honest, I thought it was a good thing he wasn't there. Or my father. After all it was his property.'

William smothered a groan. Gordon Wisley was making a great case for Parfitt's side so far. He wondered whether he should cut the young man off before he did more damage.

Gordon Wisley continued in his rather rambling manner. 'Well, I was actually halfway upstairs, to go to my room, when Parfitt came in the front door. He had a bunch of girls with him, I think there were five. They looked— well, I took them for streetwalkers. They weren't dressed like proper ladies. He waved at me and said something like, 'C'mon, Wisley, the party's going to start now. You can't slope off to bed yet. Not alone anyway.' So I went downstairs again.' He paused, and drew in a shuddering breath.

This was it, Hardy thought, and it was either going to turn the tide or break his case into pieces.

For the second time Mr Wisley turned to his father and said very softly, 'I'm so very sorry.' Then addressing himself to the magistrates, he said, 'Well, some of the girls, they seemed to know what was expected. They went over to some of the men and sat on their laps and started to— you know—get to know them better. Two of the girls just stood in the doorway. Mr Parfitt gave them both a drink and said, 'Get that into you, it might warm you up a bit.' They looked terrified. And young—they looked so, so young. Parfitt put his arm around one of them and took her over to one of the other men. He said, 'Here's nice uncle for you, Jeanie. Make him happy and he might buy you a nice p-present."

'Then what happened?' William asked. He found it hard to raise his voice. Under his jacket, he felt cold to the bone.

Mr Wisley dropped his head in shame. 'They took the girls upstairs. I—I didn't go with them. I poured myself a drink. I was trying to decide what to do. It was cowardly, I know. I was scared to stand up to the men, and I didn't want them to laugh at me. But it felt so very wrong. And because it was my family's property, I felt I had to stay, to sort of keep an eye on the place. I didn't know what to do.'

A barrister said, 'Mr Wisley, it's quite clear that the young gentleman couldn't possibly know what happened if he wasn't in the same room as the events he's asking us to merely imagine. In any case, as already stated, it is not Mr Parfitt's responsibility to control his friends or tell them how to behave.'

'Pray continue, Inspector,' the chief constable said as if the learned counsel had not spoken.

William nodded. 'Mr Wisley, where was Mr Parfitt at that time?'

Gordon said, 'He went upstairs with the others.'

'But I doubt he went with one of the girls? Surely he simply went upstairs for a bath or an early night?' William suggested.

'No.' Gordon said. 'He went with one of the other men and one of the young girls. He said, 'We can share her, Alex.' Then he looked at the girl and said with a laugh, 'You'd like that, wouldn't you?' He slapped her on the bottom as he said it.'

William glanced towards Parfitt who was white-faced but composed.

'Utterly outrageous,' one of the barristers exclaimed. 'I cannot believe this tripe for a moment. This wretched young fool has been paid to stand here and lie to us.'

The chief constable peered over his spectacles at the barrister, and in withering tones said, 'May I remind you, *sir*, that the wretched young fool is my son. And whilst he is indisputably both a wretch *and* a fool, he is not, I can assure you, a liar.'

The barrister appeared to have turned to stone. He managed to croak an apology. Parfitt glared at him.

William nodded to Gordon Wisley who said, 'As I said, I didn't know what to do. I went up to my room. Fortunately no one was in there. I planned to put on a gramophone record as I didn't want to hear any—er—anything. But it was only a moment later that I heard the sound.'

'What sound?' William asked.

'The sound of a girl sobbing loudly. I felt I couldn't ignore that. I went along the corridor. There was one of the girls standing at the top of the stairs. One of the men, Alex Keene, the Member of Parliament for East Hurling, was trying to pull her back into a bedroom. He had his hand on her arm, and he was saying, 'Shut up, you idiot'. She was sobbing and saying they should send for a doctor or call an ambulance.

'I asked what was going on. Keene told me to mind my own business, only not in exactly those words. The girl said, 'It's my friend Jeanie. She won't wake up.''

'And then what happened?' William asked.

'She was yelling at Parfitt about some pills he'd given them. He hit her so that she fell to the floor, and he shouted at her to be quiet. Then he pushed me out and shut the door. He turned the key in the lock. I heard him going out later, at about a quarter to three. I heard the front door open and shut, and the sound of a car driving away. Then about an hour later, I heard him come back again. I went out onto the landing to see him. He was alone. He told me to go back to bed and stop fussing. When I asked him about it the next morning, he said he'd taken care of the problem, and that I should keep my mouth shut. When the girls left after breakfast, she wasn't with them, and her friend was still crying.'

"The problem?" William asked. 'That's what he called her?'

'Yes.'

'Anything else to add to that, Mr Wisley?'

'Just that, on several occasions since then, Parfitt has asked me for money, stating that if I didn't give it to him, he would tell the newspapers what I had done in my father's hunting lodge.'

'But it wasn't you who did it, so why did it matter what he said?'

'Parfitt said the papers wouldn't care if it was true, it would still be a big enough scandal that my father would be disgraced. So I paid him. As it was, three weeks ago, Parfitt persuaded me to break into the newspaper office and take a few back copies out of their files, he said it was in case any journalists managed to work out what had happened. He told me which ones to take. I-I know I shouldn't have done it, but again, I believed that he would try to implicate my father.'

Parfitt was on his feet now. 'I'm sorry, sir, I do realise that the witness is closely related to you. But he is young, and impressionable, and has clearly been coached by this police officer. I can honestly say, with my hand on the Bible if need be, that I have performed none of the disgraceful actions attributed to me. These are entirely false, and the fabrication of this ambitious inspector from London who has his own axe to grind. I'd like to point out that Inspector Hardy has a personal grudge against me and is pursuing a vendetta against me in order to discredit me and gain some kind of gratification from doing so.'

The chief constable looked startled. 'Parfitt, explain.'

Parfitt inclined his head in what William thought of as a toadying fashion. Parfitt said, 'I have been seeing the inspector's fiancée, er, romantically.'

There was a collective gasp of surprise. Parfitt attempted to look both ruggedly handsome yet boyishly self-deprecating.

'I'm deeply ashamed of how it happened. It wasn't exactly my finest hour, but I was introduced to Inspector Hardy and his fiancée at a ball a few weeks ago, and—well, I'm sorry to say that I allowed my heart to rule my head. I couldn't help myself. I admit I was weak. But true love only comes into one's life once, and it seemed foolish to neglect the chance. I was transfixed by the lady, and after two or three conversations with her, I realised that she was desperately unhappy, that she was engaged to a bullying brute of a man who cared not a penny for her, only for her money. Having fallen on hard times and lost his family fortune due to stock market prospecting, he was determined to restore himself by marrying a wealthy woman. I felt I had to save her. And for this he has hunted me down and trumped up all these lies against me, for the satisfaction of seeing me suffer.'

The magistrates were looking at Hardy now as though he had walked dog mess into the room on his shoe. He said nothing, but remained in his seat, outwardly calm, inwardly seething. Gordon Wisley was looking at his father as if waiting to be told what to do.

*

Chapter Nineteen

Just as Gordon Wisley entered the meeting room to give his evidence, Dottie was having tea at the hotel overlooking the square just as she had the day before.

And just as on the previous day, she was joined by Mary Holcombe, although this time, not by arrangement. Coming in and without even pausing to greet her, Mary said:

'I hoped I'd find you here. It's not going well. According to Jean Vardry, the chief constable's secretary, one of the witnesses has been refused by Parfitt and his toy soldiers on the grounds that any evidence he gave would be to avenge himself for being dismissed by Parfitt.'

'That would be Mr Michaels. Gervase dismissed him and his wife yesterday,' Dottie said. A sense of dismay began to well up inside her.

Mary indicated the vacant chair. 'Poor Mr Michaels. His mother taught me in Sunday school when I was a girl. A nice lady. May I?'

'Of course.'

Mary sat down, then began to remove her hat and coat. And her gloves, which she placed in the top of her bag. She darted Dottie a worried look.

'Does he have anyone else to call?'

'Well, there's Major Sedgworth,' Dottie offered.

Mary shook her head again. 'He's already been seen. I'm afraid he didn't give a good impression. Contradicted himself then went to pieces. The inspector was given a short break to decide how to proceed. But with Michaels, and the major, and then the old woman who withdrew her evidence, it's looking a bit thin. I'm sorry to say it, but it doesn't look very hopeful.'

Dottie said, rather more directly than she intended, 'You've got to tell what you know. Inspector Hardy is going to need all the help he can get. Please, Mary, we need your help.'

Mary had clearly been thinking about this already. She said, without needing to think, 'Yes I know you do. It's all right, I'll do it, of course, if he wants me to. But don't blame me if it's not enough.'

'Oh thank you!'

They quickly finished their tea and Dottie called for the bill. She said, 'If only Mrs Parkes hadn't changed her mind. She was so willing to help yesterday. What can have happened to make her change her mind?'

'Obviously something fairly big,' Mary said. 'I'm not at all familiar with the case, but she supposedly said Inspector Hardy had bullied her into promising to tell a pack of lies.'

'He'd never do such a thing.' Dottie quickly told Mary about the Parkes case. She opened her bag to get out the newspaper cutting with the photograph of George Parkes to show her.

'Handsome young fellow,' Mary remarked after looking at it for a moment. She handed the cutting back to Dottie. 'He does rather look the type to always be in some trouble or other.'

'Possibly,' Dottie admitted. 'But he was all she had. Part of the case against Gervase was that he persuaded Parkes to confess...' And as she said that, it all began to fall into place. She fell silent, looking at the slip of paper in her hand.

'What is it?' demanded Mary. 'Have you thought of something?'

'Yes, I think... I think I have.' Dottie's eyes shone with excitement. 'In fact, two things.'

'Are you going to tell me?' Mary was amused.

Dottie was so clearly itching for action, jiggling in her seat.

'How long will this hearing go on for?' Dottie asked.

Mary was surprised at the change of topic. 'Until they've heard all the evidence. Until six o'clock? Perhaps a little later.'

'Will you do me a huge favour, please?'

'Of course, dear.' Mary was in earnest. She wanted to help.

'Could you drive me to see Mrs Parkes in your car, and then, if she agrees, drive Mrs Parkes to the hearing? That way you and she can both give your evidence. Also, do you know where the Garside Street Wesleyan Chapel is?'

'That's easy. It's just around the corner.' Mary pointed to the right.

'Right, let's go.' Dottie was on her feet, pulling on her coat, grabbing her hat and bag.

Mary, taken completely by surprise, had to hurry to snatch up her belongings and follow Dottie. 'What have you remembered? Or realised?'

'I can't tell you just yet. I may be wrong. In fact, I probably am wrong. Surely it can't be that simple? Mary, where's your car?'

'This way.'

They were on their way directly, and Dottie was hoping she could remember the way to Mrs Parkes's.

The old woman opened the door just a crack and peered at them suspiciously.

'It's me, Mrs Parkes,' Dottie said. 'Dottie Manderson. Mrs Parkes, I know you don't want to give evidence, but I've something terribly important to tell you. If you could just trust me... If you don't want to change your mind, that's up to you. But, please, I really need you to come with us to the police headquarters right now. It's urgent.'

She held her breath. What if Mrs Parkes said no? What if her new idea was completely false? And oh, they were running out of time!

When Dottie arrived at the Wesleyan chapel, she was feeling exhausted and depressed. She was rather desperately clutching at straws. Even now she knew in the back of her mind that it was likely to already be too late, and she was angry with herself for being so slow.

She opened the front door of the church building and went inside, still convinced she was doing the wrong thing. If she had wanted to do something useful she should have been on hand for when the hearing was over and William needed her to comfort him.

'Good afternoon, miss. Can I help you?' The woman was in her mid-sixties, Dottie guessed, and wearing an apron over a plain grey day-dress. She held a duster in one hand and a vase of wilted flowers in the other.

'I wasn't sure if the chapel was open,' Dottie began. 'I haven't been here before and I'm looking for some help.'

'Well you've come to the right place, dear,' the woman said. She beckoned Dottie in. 'You can either talk to me, or to my husband. He's the Reverend. He'll be here shortly. I'm just tidying up a bit before the prayer meeting later. Now then, why don't we sit down here and you can tell me your troubles. Is it a man, dear?'

Dottie smiled. 'You're very kind, but I'm not here about my own worries, but about someone else's. In fact, it's about something that happened last year. I'm hoping someone will still remember.'

The minister's wife looked rather perplexed, but said, 'Go on then, I'll help if I can.'

Dottie got out the newspaper cutting. 'Do you remember a Phillip Selly? I believe he may have worshipped here. I don't know whether he was a regular member. But he was planning to marry here.'

'Oh my poor boy!' The older woman sank into a chair, and pressed her fingers to her mouth. Tears swam in her eyes. It was a moment or two before she could say softly, 'Phillip Selly was my son. He died a year ago. He was murdered.'

Dottie nodded. 'I knew about his death, but didn't realise he was your son. I'm so sorry. How awful for you.'

She didn't know what to say. She had no wish to intrude on the poor woman's grief. But seeing her wipe her eyes and blow her nose, then sit up straight, Dottie thought it might be worth a chance.

'I'm so sorry to ask about such a thing, but I'm actually trying to find out something more about your son's fiancée, a Miss Moira Hansom.'

Mrs Selly frowned and said, 'Oh that flighty piece! She would never have married him, I'm certain. We tried to tell him. I've seen it before with earnest young men. They jump in with both feet, not using their heads. Taken in by a bit of bright colour and a smile.' She sighed. 'Poor Phillip, he was under the girl's thumb. His only thought was to make her happy. After his first fiancée Charlotte died four years ago, he was so lonely. Then one day he met Moira and... I'm afraid he was all too vulnerable to a young woman who was prepared to listen to him for the first time in an age. He didn't stand a chance.'

'So he was a member of the congregation here?'

'Oh yes, very loyal, very devout. He loved the Lord. He would do anything he could to help anyone in need. I'm afraid that, like my husband, he was a little too idealistic. It made him vulnerable. He wasn't worldly, and forgot that others might be.'

'And she was? Moira? She was worldly?'

'My goodness, she certainly was. We tried to tell ourselves that she had a good heart, deep down. *Very* deep down. But...' she shook her head sorrowfully. 'After Phillip died, we found he'd made out a will, leaving all that he had to her. Not that we minded, of course. It was his money, it was up to him what he did with it. But until she came along, he'd talked about using the money he inherited from his fiancée to build a youth centre, and a school. In fact that was how he met her. She came along to a public meeting about it with her cousin, who owned the land.'

Dottie was surprised. 'Phillip inherited some money from his first fiancée?'

'Oh yes. Rather a lot. Her father had died and left everything to her just the year before she died. He was a wool baron. And so there was quite a lot of money for Phillip to leave to Moira. But as she had no family, I think Phillip was keen to make sure she was provided for as soon as the engagement was announced. It was because she had no family that he always wanted to please her, to do whatever she wanted. He wanted to make her happy, even if it meant making himself unhappy. He used to take her out to places he didn't really want to go. Restaurants. Dance halls. The theatre and such.'

'The cinema?'

'Oh yes, she loved to go to the picture house. She made him take her practically every week. It wasn't enough for her to go to church meetings, or on walks, or for a quiet dinner with friends. She loved the bright lights and noise of the city, and always wanted to see the latest film. He always said it was because she hadn't been brought up to enjoy quieter, family pursuits. I say she had no family, but in fact she had a cousin she was close to.'

Dottie nodded. 'A cousin? The one with the land?'

Mrs Selly nodded, 'Well we never met him, but Phillip and Moira saw a good deal of him, obviously. He was all she had.'

'What was this cousin's name?' Dottie asked. If it turned out to be that Armstrong chap, the one William had told her the police had been looking into, that might explain a lot.

'His name was Parfitt. Gervase Parfitt. He's the assistant chief constable as a matter of fact. As he was her only family since her parents died, she relied on him a great deal for support, and advice. They spent a lot of time together. He was more like a brother than a cousin.'

Dottie stared. She had not been expecting that. Rather hesitantly she said, 'I think you'll find Parfitt and Moira are not cousins but lovers, and have been for years. They aren't related, and her parents are very much alive and enjoying a comfortable retirement in Chesterfield.'

The other woman clapped her hands to her mouth, horrified. 'But...?'

Dottie began to explain why she was there, and asked for the Sellys' help. At first Mrs Selly was taken aback, unsure whether to do as Dottie asked. But when her husband arrived, a plump, genial older man, Dottie discovered he firmly believed in doing his duty. They solemnly promised to come with Dottie to the police headquarters to make themselves available to the inspector.

She thanked them, her heart feeling lighter than it had for days.

If only they didn't get there too late.

Dottie asked them to wait in the waiting room, leaving them in Mary Holcombe's care. She waved to Mrs Parkes, who looked a little nervous, but was, at least, there. Dottie hurriedly explained to Mary that she had to run across the square on an important errand. It took her just three minutes.

On her return, Dottie went directly to the front desk and told the clerk that she was Inspector Hardy's secretary. She said she was there with the items he had sent her to collect. The clerk looked her over a little suspiciously, seeing that she was carrying nothing, but he let her through, directing her to the meeting room. Dottie conveyed Mr Treadwell to the waiting room first.

Inside the meeting room, William was surprised when the same messenger from earlier entered and came over to him. The messenger said, 'Excuse me, Inspector, your secretary has arrived with the things you wanted.'

All eyes were on Dottie as she entered the room. She felt as red and embarrassed as a schoolgirl.

As if things weren't bad enough, Gervase actually got to his feet and embraced her, as she was about to go straight past his seat.

'Darling, lovely to see you!' He kissed her cheek then

turned to the chief constable and the rest of the panel and said, his voice ringing with confidence, 'May I present my fiancée, Miss Dottie Manderson.' Turning to Dottie, he continued, 'Darling, it's wonderful to see you, but we are a little busy at the moment.' He directed a manly smile towards the stenographers, the secretaries, and finally the magistrates. He rolled his eyes at the magistrates, as if asking them how a woman could possibly be expected to understand business.

One of the magistrates frowned.

Another said, quite loudly, 'I thought Parfitt was seeing the inspector's fiancée? How many 'one true loves' does this man have?'

Parfitt hastily transferred his smile to the chief constable.

This little interlude only served to strengthen Dottie's resolve and calm her nerves. It was nowhere near as nerve-racking as when she had been eight years old and had to stand up on the stage at the parents' open day at school and sing *Frère Jacques*. Nor was it anything like as terrifying as unveiling her first fashion collection a few months ago and waiting to see if her customers would like it.

'Excuse me, Mr Parfitt,' she said, brushing his hand from her shoulder. She stepped around him rather as though he was something nasty on the pavement, and moved towards William. When she reached him, she could see he was happy to see her even though he looked perplexed. She was anxious not to endanger his case in any way. She turned to face the chief constable and the magistrates, and very politely, said:

'Please forgive my intrusion. I'm here to give Inspector Hardy some essential information he requested. But if I may, first, I'd like to clarify something that Mr Parfitt has just said.'

She waited, and the chief constable nodded. 'Carry on, Miss, er...?'

'My name is Dorothy Manderson, Dottie to my close friends and family. I'd like to state that I am *not* Mr

Parfitt's fiancée, no matter what he may say. I *was* his
fiancée, but I gave him back his ring a few days ago after
discovering him in an intimate embrace with the
inspector's fiancée.' She indicated William with her hand.
'As you can see from the mark on my face, Mr Parfitt
didn't care to be questioned about his behaviour. But that
is not the reason for me being here. Please may I give the
inspector some information that is very important to his
case?'

The chief constable rapidly consulted with his
colleagues. He nodded his consent but before he could
speak, the barristers were on their feet once more to
complain.

'Sir, with respect, it's far too late in the day for some
chit of a girl to come in from heaven knows where and
claim to have information for the inspector.' That was the
fellow on Parfitt's left.

Then Turner, the one on the right, said at the same
time: 'Ridiculous! It is completely unjust to have new
evidence handed to the inspector to which we have had no
access.'

There was a further whispered conversation between
the chief constable and the magistrates. Dottie pulled a
worried face at William, and he grinned back at her.

The chief constable said, 'Very well, Miss—er—miss, but
you must give him this information here in front of the
whole hearing. That will be fairer to Mr Parfitt and his—
er—his colleagues.'

Dottie thanked him and said, 'Inspector, the Reverend
and Mrs Selly are here to give their evidence, and if there's
time, Mr Treadwell from the Ripley Gazette and Advertiser
is also here with that information you asked for. And Mrs
Parkes is here too.'

Having said that, she sat down in an empty chair beside
William. Even the stenographer paused in her typing to
stare at Dottie. William, still on his feet, was momentarily
at a loss.

One of the barristers immediately bobbed up to say,
'May I remind the court that Mrs Parkes has withdrawn

her statement.'

'How many times, man? This is not a court. And if Mrs Parkes has come here voluntarily, then we shall hear what she has to say.' The chief constable seemed to be almost at the end of his patience. To William, he said, 'Do proceed, Inspector, for God's sake. I think we would all like to get to our dinner at some point this evening.'

Evening it was. In surprise, William noticed that it was pitch black outside. Streetlamps were lighting up, and the headlamps of the cars gleamed on the windows as they drove by.

'Oh yes, of course, sir. I'm so sorry.' William rummaged through his papers, too flustered to see what he needed next. Dottie calmly selected a page and handed it to him. He tried not to look surprised.

'Ah yes,' he said, reading rapidly. 'If you will allow it, Mr Wisley, I'd like to call Mr Treadwell to the stand. Er—that is, to address the hearing.'

With the glimmer of a smile, the chief constable nodded. Mr Treadwell was summoned. He identified himself and was invited to sit.

Again prompted by Dottie, William said, 'Mr Treadwell, do you work at the Ripley Gazette and Advertiser, based here in the market square of Ripley?'

'Yes sir, I do.' Mr Treadwell was not at all nervous, Dottie thought, which probably made a nice change for the hearing. He spoke clearly and in a genial manner that imbued him with confidence and a certain gentle authority.

'Have you been there long?'

'Forty-four years, sir.'

William nodded in approval. 'Clearly you are very good at your job.'

Mr Treadwell smiled. 'I don't know about that. But I have been there long enough that I can put my hand on most of the items requested very quickly.'

'I'm sure you can, Mr Treadwell. Although when Miss Manderson came to see you yesterday, I understand you could not find any of the items she asked to see?'

Mr Treadwell was in danger of taking that as a personal slight, Dottie felt. He looked rather put out. 'I'm afraid I can't account for that, Inspector.'

'Let me see, your office contains every copy of the Ripley Gazette and Advertiser printed since the newspaper began in, I believe it was 1835, is that not so?'

'1825, sir. The 4th of September, to be precise. And yes, sir, we do have a copy of every printed issue stored in our archives.'

'Except for, let me see, six newspapers, all of which just happened to be the ones Miss Manderson asked for.'

'Well sir. I can't account for it. I looked for each one in turn as this young lady requested them, and all of them were missing.'

'I believe you had a theory about how that came to be?'

'We had a break in about two weeks ago,' Mr Treadwell told them, and his voice was indignant. 'At the time, we couldn't find anything missing, and so it was dismissed as a prank.'

'I see. But it's now your belief that these items were stolen?'

Mr Treadwell nodded.

'What were the items Miss Manderson wanted to see, just out of interest?'

'They were the issues that contained the reports of George Parkes' arrest, conviction and trial. About eight issues in all. But Miss Manderson wasn't completely out of luck,' Mr Treadwell added.

'How so?' William was surprised.

'The engagement announcement she asked for. I found that one for her.'

The room was still, hushed. William was aware of a little frisson of excitement that he knew from previous experiences was a good sign.

'Do you remember the details, off-hand?' William asked pleasantly.

'Yes, of course sir. It was Mr Phillip Selly to Miss Moira Hansom, the wedding was to take place on 9th June 1934. At Garside Street Wesleyan Chapel. The date of the announcement was 7th February 1934.'

Dottie glanced across to see Parfitt looking somewhat dismayed, which gave the lie to the comment from one of his barristers, 'Sirs, this is not at all relevant. I ask that we might get on with things. Has the inspector got any actual evidence? If not, this might be the time to admit he is flogging a dead horse.'

The chief constable and the magistrates ignored him.

William thanked Mr Treadwell for his assistance and told him he could leave. William then asked permission to call the Reverend Selly to come in to make a statement before the hearing.

Mr Turner was on his feet. 'I'm terribly sorry, please excuse me, I've just remembered I have a prior engagement... Quite urgent... So sorry... Do excuse... Did not expect things to...' And before anyone could say anything, he was gone, practically at a run, the door swinging silently closed behind him.

Dottie exchanged a look of astonishment with the chief constable's secretary. William stared at the door, filled with a quiet sense of elation. Gervase Parfitt was already on his feet, furiously demanding that this 'travesty' should be ended now, so that he could get back to his office and get on with his work. 'I've already lost a day on this nonsense, which is hardly the best use of the tax-payers'...'

'Silence, Mr Parfitt.'

Parfitt, however, would not be silent. He rounded on his remaining barrister, shouting at him to do something, ending with, 'God knows, you owe me.'

The man, rearranging his tie, said, 'Mr Wisley, in view of what has just happened, I'd like to ask that this meeting be postponed until such time...'

'No,' said the chief constable. 'You asked for the hearing to be brought forward, at great inconvenience to Inspector Hardy, and now you must live with that.' A little late, he glanced at the magistrates for confirmation, and received it in the form of an almost imperceptible nod from the man seated in the middle. The chief constable turned back to Parfitt's barrister:

'There's your confirmation. Now, let's get on, shall we?'

The Reverend identified himself. A whispered prompt from Dottie led William to say:

'Could you tell us how you know Mr Phillip Selly?'

'He was my son.'

'Did he discuss his engagement with you?'

'Yes indeed. He seemed very much in love with the young lady, and he had planned to be married in the chapel amongst his friends and family here in Ripley.'

'Did you meet your son's fiancée?'

'Yes, many times.'

'Did you feel the couple were well—matched?'

The Reverend hesitated, which gave Parfitt time to comment, with a return to his earlier lazy arrogance, 'How is the Reverend's feelings on the matter relevant to these ridiculous accusations against me?'

The chief constable said to William, 'Please tell me this is relevant? And if so, again, Inspector, please get on with it.'

'I'm sorry sir, I promise this will become clear very soon.' William didn't sound very confident, Dottie thought. She would have liked to pat his arm but thought the chief constable—not to mention everyone else—would disapprove. Mentally she urged him on with all her might.

'Er, can you tell us if in your view the couple were a good match, Reverend?'

'No. I didn't feel they were suited. And my wife agreed with me.'

'Can you tell us why?' There was a slight edge to William's voice that only Dottie heard. She realised that any objections the man had to Moira Hansom could well apply to William's own case.

'Well. Not to malign the lady, as she is not here to defend herself, but we felt that their outlooks were too unalike. Miss Hansom was a somewhat worldly young lady, and enjoyed fine things, and expected to live in comfort, whereas my son was concerned about the plight of the poor and needy, and wanted to use his time, strength and his money to help them. We felt she was taking advantage of his material wealth and eschewing his spiritual aims.'

'Are you saying you believed Miss Hansom was a gold digger, in common parlance?' William sounded politely disbelieving. 'Did you ever witness any example of Miss Hansom taking advantage of your son's trust?'

'Er—no. Not exactly. It was more of a feeling.'

'I see. Anything else?'

Dottie was biting her lip nervously. She hoped he wouldn't allow any personal resentment on Moira's behalf to ruin this moment.

'Miss Hansom had little interest in the church, or in spiritual matters. Both of these were of great importance to Phillip. Also, he hoped to have a family, but Miss Hansom had indicated to friends that she would not welcome children.'

'So they differed in their outlooks. But the marriage was going to go ahead?'

'Er, yes. Phillip was after all, a full-grown man, and he was very much in love with Miss Hansom.'

Dottie scribbled a few words on a piece of paper and placed it in front of William. He read it and immediately asked, 'Reverend, did your son ever drink in a public house? Meeting his friends in the evening for instance, for conversation or just to relax?'

The Reverend looked quite startled at the idea. 'No indeed. Phillip was staunchly teetotal and had never been in a public house.'

'Thank you Reverend, that's all.'

An additional nod from the chief constable, and the Reverend left the room.

Under the cover of this slight distraction, William hissed to Dottie, 'Now what? I don't know what to say next.'

But the chief constable said, 'We'll take another break at this point. Shall we say one hour? We shall therefore reconvene at seven o'clock, and it is my earnest hope we shall get this matter dealt with by midnight. Inspector, a word please if you'd be so kind.'

William went over as everyone else began to get up and stretch. Conversation broke out here and there.

Straight away, the chief constable said, 'Now look here, Hardy. Where is all this going? And why have you got my son mixed up in all this?'

'Sir, I'm sorry. But my hands are tied. With other witnesses denied me, I had to use Mr Wisley. I'm very sorry, but he has been seriously led astray by Parfitt.'

The chief constable nodded gravely, his chin almost resting on his chest. 'That's quite clear, yes.'

William said, 'Sir? Could we set this matter aside and see if the other case is enough to remove Mr Parfitt from office and have him arrested? I'm afraid if the case does come to court, there'll be no protecting your son, although he hasn't committed any major crime, he has taken part in illegal gambling, and concealing a number of crimes.'

The chief constable was silent, thinking. William could see he was torn.

William added, 'Look, it's easy enough for a good-natured lad to be manipulated into doing something foolish. I'm sure we all did things in our youth we regret. But he has shown he has a good heart. An overly harsh judgement now could destroy any chance of a useful future for him.'

The chief constable said, softly, 'I can't be seen to be playing favourites. Just because he's my son...'

'What would you do if it was another man's son brought in on a similar charge?'

The chief constable said with no hesitation, 'Why I'd ask for him to be fined a hundred pounds, bound over for two years, and he'd have to work his socks off to repay the money. I wouldn't want to do the lad lasting damage. After all, he tried to do the right thing. Eventually.'

'Well then...' William shrugged.

The chief constable smiled at William. 'Good point. Very well, confine yourself to the other matter. I'm not quite sure where you are going with any of this, but be quick about it, will you, we all have homes to go to. Now, I'm going to have something to eat. I suggest you do the same. Oh, and Hardy?'

'Yes sir?'

'Thank you.'

'My pleasure, sir.'

William hurried back to Dottie's side, heading off a sneering Parfitt who was shaking off his barrister's restraining hand.

'Dottie, let's go and get something to eat,' William said, and grabbed her hand.

'Good idea.' She picked up her bag and coat and turned to leave. Parfitt came right up to her, and almost snarled in her ear:

'Watch your step, missy. I will not tolerate being humiliated by a chit of a girl.' His lip curled and his eyes blazed. Never had he looked less like a decent man.

Dottie recoiled as his hand came up, but at that moment, William stepped in front of her, whilst Parfitt's remaining barrister bodily hauled Parfitt away, hissing 'Are you insane, man? To carry on like that right here in the meeting room?'

Outside, Dottie clutched William's arm and tried to calm herself. He covered her hand with his warm one.

'Are you all right?'

She nodded. 'Let's go to the waiting room, I want to see who's there.'

'Don't you want to eat first?'

'Afterwards. I suppose we don't have time to go to the hotel for dinner?'

'No. But there's a small café not too far from here, they might be able to feed us.'

She nodded. 'That'll do. I only want a cup of tea. Then we need to work on your argument.'

At seven o'clock that evening, back in the meeting room, William looked at the chief constable and the three magistrates.

'May I ask for your indulgence once more?' he asked the chief constable.

The chief constable almost smiled. Almost. He managed to control his expression and to say with admirable seriousness, 'Inspector, this is a closed panel with a very particular agenda. It is not a free-for-all where anyone, even a police officer, may say or do what they like.'

'Oh yes,' William quickly responded, 'But you see, Mrs Parkes is here in the witnesses' waiting room. As you know, Mrs Parkes withdrew her statement and—well, I'm afraid I *was* rather relying on that evidence. Er—not that I want to bully Mrs Parkes at all, far from it,' he added, seeing that there were about to be objections raised from several quarters.

'Go on,' the chief constable said. His tone held a warning note.

'I'd just like to ask her to come in here. Not to ask her any questions, I don't want that. I just want to tell her something that she will not be aware of. I realise this is an imposition, but it's very important. I swear, I wouldn't ask if it wasn't.'

If the chief constable sensed he was being led up the garden path, and would later regret this decision, he nevertheless nodded and said, wearily, 'Very well, I'll allow it. But be quick, Inspector.'

Gervase was on his feet. 'I must object in the strongest possible terms, Chief Constable. Mrs Parkes is perfectly within her rights to decline to testify. The inspector has already been accused of ruthlessly attempting to coerce this elderly woman.'

Somewhat belatedly his remaining barrister bobbed up and said, 'Exactly my point! Mr Wisley, I emphatically...'

'Do not presume to lecture me on the law, gentlemen. Hardy, this is the last time I indulge you. This had better be both relevant and useful. I assume we were being duped when you introduced this young woman as your secretary? I know the Met have their own way of doing things, but I'm fairly confident that a private secretary for a mere inspector is not one of them.'

'Ah yes,' William admitted. 'I'm afraid Miss Manderson has been assisting me in a purely private capacity as Mr

Parfitt's ex-fiancée.'

The chief constable appeared neither impressed nor surprised. He nodded to the clerk, who looked at Hardy.

Hardy said, 'Would you tell Mrs Parkes that I would be grateful if she could come in here? Tell her I have something very important to tell her, something she needs to know, and that if she still doesn't want to say anything, that's completely all right.'

The clerk nodded and hurried away.

Silence—or near to it—fell on the room. Parfitt was whispering to his barrister. Both men were clearly angry. But everyone else waited in silence. Dottie reached out to pat William's arm and he caught and held her hand for a brief second, smiling at her.

Then they heard the tapping of Mrs Parkes' walking stick and the sound of her boots on the polished wooden floor. The clerk held the door open for her, and the old lady, looking warily about her, came in. The clerk guided her to a chair. How old she looked, Dottie thought with something like fear, how frail. For a moment she wondered if they ought not to do this, better perhaps to let her be.

'Mrs Parkes?' the chief constable said, his tone gentle, polite.

She looked at him and nodded.

'I'm sorry to inconvenience you, madam. This is a rather unusual situation that I admit has got away from me somewhat. However, I'd be grateful if you would be gracious enough to bear with us. I believe you have met Inspector Hardy before?'

She nodded again.

'No one is trying to make you do anything you don't want to, Mrs Parkes, but the inspector has something he would like to say to you.'

'What is it?' Mrs Parkes demanded, gripping her handbag and walking stick tightly in gnarled hands.

'Er—well, I don't know, I'm afraid,' the chief constable admitted. 'But if you do not wish to stay, you may leave. No one can compel you to stay.'

'If I don't know what he's going to say, how do I know if I want to hear it?' Mrs Parkes snapped.

The chief constable kept a straight face. 'Yes, I know what you mean. Perhaps you would allow the Inspector to explain?'

'Oh all right. There's no bus for another forty minutes anyway. At least it's warmer in here than out there.'

'Very true,' said the chief constable with a smile. 'Inspector, continue.'

William glanced at his papers, glanced at Dottie, then straightened himself to look at Mrs Parkes. 'Mrs Parkes, I'm very sorry about all this. But I just wanted you to hear something. I think you will be glad that you agreed to listen.'

'That's as maybe,' she said, shifting in her seat and looking at the floor.

'To briefly summarise for everyone present, Mrs Parkes' only son, George Parkes, was convicted of murder and hanged in December of last year. Gervase Parfitt was at the time of the crime, supervising the officers investigating the killing of Phillip Selly, a customer enjoying a pint of beer with some friends at the Purple Emperor public house, in the village of Blackhall on the evening of 2nd April. It quickly came to light that the perpetrator was George Parkes, who had attempted to rob the pub, and who, on making his escape, struck Mr Selly with a piece of fencing he found close to hand.

'Mr Parkes confessed to the crime, greatly distressed that he had caused the death of a man, and fully believing that a confession would mean a more lenient sentence. However, he was unfortunately sentenced to hang. Just before the sentence was carried out, Mr Parfitt, by then Assistant Chief Constable and no longer involved in that investigation, but he went to visit Mr Parkes in prison and asked him to confess to another murder. After all, Parkes was already facing the full extent of the law, he couldn't make things worse for himself. Am I right so far, Mrs Parkes?'

Mrs Parkes sniffed and grudgingly agreed he was

correct. Hardy continued:

'Mr Parfitt offered George Parkes something in return for the favour—he offered to ensure that a sum of five thousand pounds was given to George's mother, Mrs Enid Parkes, before us today, and George Parkes agreed to do as Parfitt asked, believing it would enable his mother to live in security and comfort in her old age. Naturally,' William said, holding up a hand to stay the protesting Parfitt and his barrister, 'There is no evidence to support this, as Mrs Parkes herself told me that the slip of paper Parfitt signed to confirm the deal he made with Parkes, was not among her son's possessions that were returned to her after his execution. But we do know two things. First of all, Mrs Parkes made—I think it's fair to say—a bit of a nuisance of herself here at the police headquarters, demanding to see Mr Parfitt to discuss the matter with him. And secondly, we do of course, have Mr Parkes' signed statement on record to say that he killed Miss Jeanie Brown of Woodend, on the night of 2nd April.'

There was silence in the room as Hardy paused to take a breath. Dottie thought the silence was an attentive one. No one was fidgeting now. William had them under his spell at last. And his confidence was growing.

He said, 'So now I come to the new information I wanted to give you, Mrs Parkes, and then, if you like, you can go home. It's simply this: Mrs Parkes, your son was innocent.'

Everyone heard Mrs Parkes irritably reply, 'Well I know that, you stupid man. I told *you* that! It was me what told you how that there Parfitt persuaded him to sign his paper to confess to that murder he never done, in exchange for giving me five thousand pounds.'

There was a commotion around the room. Parfitt pounded on the table in fury, and his barrister, trying to hold Parfitt back, shouted.

William smiled at the old woman. He waited for the furore to die down. Then he said, softly, 'No Mrs Parkes, I don't mean the death of Miss Brown. We know that wasn't really George. No, I'm talking about the murder of Mr

Selly. The original murder George was convicted of committing. George didn't kill Phillip Selly.'

Everyone was staring at William. Mrs Parkes' mouth was half-open as she froze on the point of speaking. Parfitt had his face in his hands. The stenographer gaped at William, as did the secretaries, the clerk, the chief constable and all three magistrates, and Dottie too, who was watching him in open admiration.

Mrs Parkes struggled to her feet. 'What? No, that Selly fellow, he was the one my George did kill. My boy did it, he told me so. He told me himself...' She fell heavily back into her seat, her voice dying away.

Dottie watched her anxiously, hoping the shock of this discovery wouldn't kill the old woman.

William shook his head. 'No Mrs Parkes. George bludgeoned a man, that much is true. Your son grabbed a bit of wood—half rotten, according to a statement I have here from the pub's landlord, and taken from a broken fence nearby—and he lashed out at someone standing outside the pub. He caught the man a glancing blow across the left shoulder. The man lost three days' work due to the pain from severe bruising. Three days' work, Mrs Parkes. He didn't die. He didn't even go to the hospital, or need the care of a doctor.' William glanced down at his notes, pausing for effect, aware of the rapt silence that attended his words.

He continued: 'Not that any of that matters, because in fact, it wasn't even Phillip Selly outside the pub that evening, it was another man, a Mr Thomas Perkins. The reason we know this is, that having gone there this morning and spoken with the landlord, he admitted he had been paid by Gervase Parfitt to lie about several things. One of the things he lied about was the identity of the man who was attacked. Another thing both the landlord and Mr Perkins himself admitted having lied about was the severity of the attack. Mr Perkins also gave me his sworn statement this morning,' William said to the chief constable.

The chief constable nodded almost proudly at William.

William continued:

'And of course, in any case, we know that Phillip Selly could not have been at the pub that night. The reason we know this is, as his father has already told us, that Phillip Selly was a very religious man, and a staunch teetotaller who took the pledge of abstinence in his adolescence and who had never touched a drop of alcohol in his life. He had never been to The Purple Emperor or any other public house. In addition, it's almost impossible to be sitting or standing and drinking with friends outside the pub as the front of the pub is directly on the road, and anyone standing there would need to continually watch for traffic and keep out of the way. Not a relaxing place to spend time.

'In fact, on the evening of the attack outside the pub in Blackhall, Mr Selly was at the cinema with his fiancée, Miss Moira Hansom, and I have the ticket stubs here.' William held the two tiny pieces of paper aloft. 'These were found in Gervase Parfitt's desk. We know that Mr Parfitt was not at the cinema himself that night, so he could not have used these tickets. Because we've already heard from Gordon Wisley that Parfitt was at the Wisley family's hunting lodge that night, playing cards, shooting, drinking and procuring prostitutes to entertain his friends, then later, disposing of the dead body of Jeanie Brown following her drug overdose.

'With regard to these ticket stubs, an employee from the Rialto cinema in Nottingham has already identified them from the serial numbers and has told us exactly the date these tickets were issued and even the name of the film that the two ticket holders went to see. The employee from the cinema is ready to give a sworn statement, and can provide the cinema's accounting records regarding the serial numbers, date and so forth.' This was again addressed to the chief constable and the magistrates, all of whom were looking grim-faced and alert. Parfitt's remaining barrister had the look of a man who wished he'd listened to his father and gone into the family business.

'Phillip Selly was, however, the wealthy fiancé of Miss Moira Hansom, long-term lover of Mr Parfitt. Mr Parfitt passed himself off as a relative whenever he met Mr Selly. Mr Selly, believing himself in love and planning to marry the lady, had recently made a will in Miss Hansom's favour, against the advice of his family and his solicitor, and not long after that I can only surmise, Mr Parfitt—known for his jealous temper—had a violent disagreement with Mr Selly and as a result, Mr Selly died. We know no one saw Mr Selly after the 2nd April, and that whatever the circumstances of his death, Gervase Parfitt made use of the robbery at the public house and the attack on Mr Perkins to dispose of Mr Selly's body.

'Just as he did with the corpse of Jeanie Brown, the young woman who died after being given drugs at the house party. We heard from Major Sedgworth at the start of this hearing, to the effect that Gervase Parfitt was extorting money from the major's wife to keep quiet about a car accident. Mrs Sedgworth, we can surmise, was convinced that she had hit and killed someone—a man—on the night of the 31st of March or the 1st of April. In fact, I'm sure that with this information, upon further investigation, we will discover the same story: someone was persuaded to believe they had killed someone, and paid heavily to protect themselves. Mrs Sedgworth didn't kill anyone, but Gervase Parfitt used that incident, and that woman's guilt to again dispose of a corpse. Shame the person who died at the hunting lodge was a female, and Mrs Sedgworth thought she had killed a man, but it's very hard to make everything go your way sometimes.'

'Coming back to the night of the 2nd April, the landlord of the pub has given a sworn statement about what happened on the night Mr Parkes robbed his pub, and is prepared to stand up in court on oath and admit that he and two other men, as well as the man who was the genuine injured party, were all paid by Mr Parfitt who also warned them not to go back on their word under penalty of the law.

'Mrs Parkes, your son, though admittedly rather a bad

lot, was not a murderer. Not twice over, not even once. He was as much Gervase Parfitt's victim as Mr Selly was.'

A hubbub of discussion rose about the room. Parfitt's barrister threw his pencil onto the table and leaned back, arms folded, clearly done with any effort to defend. Everyone else was looking in Parfitt's direction.

Including Mrs Parkes. The old lady took a few moments to digest the information.

Two seconds later she ran at Parfitt with her walking stick. She rained blows on his shoulders and arms as he ducked and tried to protect himself. The old woman was dwarfed by the four men who tried to pull her off, still screaming at Parfitt. She collapsed into Dottie's arms sobbing. 'He took my boy. My only son. My baby. And he killed him! It was all a lie! He killed my son!'

Dottie helped her into a seat, kneeling beside her and offering one of William's handkerchiefs. 'I'm so sorry Mrs Parkes. So, so sorry.'

William rapped on the table and everyone was silent, attentive. 'May I close by saying, I believe there is a clear case to answer for corruption, conspiracy to pervert the course of justice, intimidation of witnesses, extortion etc, and I therefore request that Gervase Parfitt be removed from office with immediate effect and placed under arrest pending charges. Thank you for your time, Chief Constable, Gentlemen.' He nodded to them and sat down.

Silence greeted his words. Outside, in the town square, a woman laughed, and a car horn sounded once, twice. Inside, everyone was watching Gervase Parfitt.

He got slowly to his feet and buttoned his jacket. He stared at William with loathing.

'You jumped up little nobody. I know all about you. Your ludicrous fawning after *her*,' he spoke softly but almost spat the pronoun as he thrust a hand in Dottie's direction. 'Then Moira. You were all over her. And now you're back to your old favourite,' Parfitt sneered, his lip curling in disgust. 'And all this—this ridiculous sideshow is what exactly? To get back at me? Discredit me for taking first one then a second of your women? To punish me? Or is it merely to further your own pathetically ordinary career? Makes you feel better about yourself, does it, bringing me down to your level?'

Parfitt came towards William, taking one then a second measured step, without haste, without hurry.

Behind Parfitt, his lawyer was saying something nobody heeded. It was all pointless bluster at this point, nothing more, and served no purpose at all. All eyes were still fixed on Parfitt.

He turned his head slightly to look at Dottie. 'Still bearing my mark, I see. Shame things didn't work out. If only you'd been a bit more sporting. I do like 'em young. Though you're a bit too idealistic and strait-laced for me I'm afraid, my dear.'

Her voice barely above a whisper, Dottie said, 'Oh Gervase. How could you have done all those terrible things? You lied and cheated your way to the top of your profession.'

'Very nearly to the top, anyway,' he admitted, his pride ringing clear in his voice. 'Oh so nearly. It was worth it. Anything rather than be some nondescript little pen-pusher waiting for the day I'd finally get my gold watch and handshake. That's all he'll ever give you,' he jerked his head at William. 'Too afraid of breaking the rules to make things go his own way, too scared to be brilliant. He'll never be able to give you the lifestyle I could have offered.'

Dottie retorted, 'You stole it, it was never yours to offer. Your success has been built on the destruction and misery of others. What you said about George Parkes after his arrest, that he was opportunistic and utterly ruthless, the type of man who would cut down anyone who stood between himself and his objective. You were describing yourself, Gervase. I despise you. You are a filthy disgrace to your profession.'

A snarl ripped from his throat as he launched himself forward to lunge at her, his right hand snatching at her neck, missing her by a mere inch as William grabbed Dottie and wrenched her sideways, whilst Parfitt's left hand ripped the shoulder of her dress at the seam.

The clerk and one of the magistrates ran to help haul Parfitt away as William pushed Dottie behind him.

Parfitt shoved the men off him, and with a smile that said he didn't care about any of it, he straightened his tie and pulled his shirt-cuffs neater under his jacket, adjusting the engraved gold cufflinks.

'Well, well. My temper got the better of me, I'm afraid, Chief Constable, esteemed gentlemen. That does happen sometimes when my aims are frustrated.' He sounded calm, his voice low and even.

The chief constable nodded to the clerk of the court, who opened the door and spoke to someone. Two uniformed officers accompanied by a plainclothes man entered.

The plainclothes man approached Parfitt, saying, 'Gervase Parfitt, I am arresting you on the charges of murder and attempted murder, perverting the course of justice, corruption, concealing a crime, tampering with evidence, extortion, conspiracy to...'

Ignoring him, Parfitt said to Dottie, 'You will remember me for the rest of your life, Dottie, my dear. Me, here, today. There will never be anyone like me.'

She glared at him around William's shoulder. 'Hardly. I'm not interested in you, Gervase. After today, I shall never think of you again.'

He smiled broadly, confidence written in every line of his frame. 'Oh, Dottie dearest, I think you will.'

He turned, straightened his jacket once more, then took off at a run across the room, flinging himself with a yell at the window, his body smashing through the glass and out of view, whilst seemingly at the same moment, there came a crashing and splintering sound in the street below.

There were gasps and cries, then nothing. Silence fell on the room once more.

Then outside, a car horn blared and a woman screamed. Inside the room, everyone suddenly came to life. William was one of the first to reach the gaping hole where the glass had been. He stood looking down into the darkness.

On the road, illuminated by the headlamps of a car, the body of Gervase Parfitt lay still and dead on the wet road, blood seeping out around him in a pool. William turned back in time to see Dottie slump to the floor. He ran to her.

From her chair in the middle of the room, still clutching her walking-stick, Mrs Parkes said grimly, 'Well good riddance, that's what I say.'

*

Chapter Twenty

'I'm sorry Moira was arrested, William,' Dottie said, directing an anxious glance at him.

He was concentrating on the road, of course, frowning as he peered out into the rain and tried to avoid a gaggle of cyclists on a bend.

Was he thinking of Moira now, Dottie wondered. When they reached London and he dropped her off, would he be going straight to his office at Scotland Yard to immediately begin working on Moira's case, eager to ensure her freedom? She held her breath, waiting for the road to even out and become clear so that he could relax a little and tell her what he was thinking. It was a long wait, and she had to let out the held breath and draw in two more before he said:

'I'm not too worried. I'm fairly sure that she'll get off. All she's got to do is keep her nerve and keep on saying that it was Parfitt who did it. With him gone, there's no one to refute that. They will have no proof that she was involved in Phillip Selly's death. She really doesn't need to worry about it.'

So he had been giving it some thought, then, Dottie

decided. She longed to really know what was going on in his mind. It was so hard to sit quietly beside him and hold back her barrage of questions.

It felt odd to remember that Gervase was dead. Just that thought alone made her stomach lurch in shock. Yet it was such a typically Gervase action: rash, impulsive, reckless. Impossible to imagine any alternative where he meekly went to prison to serve out his sentence, or worse, to the gallows, to serve the ends of justice. She felt as though this outcome had been set in stone ever since she sat in the restaurant with William and he had said, 'This is a real police investigation. I want you to know that. It's not just me being angry and wanting to lash out and hurt you.' Not that she could ever blame William. Gervase had made his own decisions and had been forced to face up to the consequences.

But time and again the images ran through her brain, like a cinematic film, and he was alive, sneering at them all, telling her she would never forget him, fussing over his jacket and tie. And then... the gaping hole, the jagged spikes of glass. The awful sounds from outside, the frigid evening air pouring into the room. Herself, waking to find herself on the floor, William's jacket over her. Herself, hugging her arms about her shaking body, too shocked for tears. The moment when the clerk had come back upstairs after going out to the street, and she had watched the man approach the chief constable and the magistrates standing together in the middle of the room. The clerk had shaken his head grimly and after a brief conference, the chief constable had come over to shake William's hand and thank him for his work. William had said later that it felt like an empty victory, until, that is, he spoke with Mrs Parkes, who had no words to describe how it felt to know her son was not a killer after all. All she could say was, 'Thank you, thank you, both of you. Thank you.' She had gripped Dottie's arm with her cold hands and held on as if she never wanted to let go. Dottie hoped Mrs Parkes would have some peace at last.

The following day, they'd had a sombre conversation

Caron Allan

with the chief constable, and he had assured William, strictly informally, that Mrs Parkes would be taken care of, that a sum of money in compensation would be paid to her. Not that anything could bring back her son, but perhaps she would be sure of a comfortable old age, and no longer need to take in washing.

Dottie had exchanged addresses with Mary Holcombe, who had promised to write. She had said goodbye to the Sellys, to Major Sedgwick, Mr Treadwell and even Gordon Wisley, looking sheepish but as if a heavy weight had lifted from his shoulders.

At least she would be sleeping in her own bed that evening, and not in a hotel. It would be wonderful to go home. She hoped she wouldn't have to go anywhere else for a very long time. Except to Flora's which she could hopefully do tomorrow. She wanted to see her sister, to tell her everything, and to see the children too of course.

'If you've got nothing better to do tomorrow,' William said suddenly, 'I've been invited to the London Metropolitan Museum. They have something to show me. Us, I should say. I tentatively accepted on your behalf. I hope that's all right? Shall I collect you at two o'clock?'

'Oh yes, of course, thank you,' she said automatically. After a moment's thought, she said, 'Oh! Is it the mantle?'

He nodded. Smiling, though his eyes were fixed on the road ahead.

'Wonderful!' Dottie said.

The next day, with her hand through William's arm, Dottie stood before the glass display case and looked at the ancient clerical garment that had cost so many lives.

The five pieces had been reunited, and the seams that joined them together were almost invisible. The mantle was draped on a dummy rather like a dressmaker's form, to give the full effect of the front and back of the garment.

Dottie had a lump in her throat as she looked at the embroidered scenes: the Garden of Eden and the Expulsion from Paradise on the left front, the baptism of Jesus and the beheading of John the Baptist in his prison cell on the right front, the first miracle at the wedding in Cana on the bottom half of the back panel, and at the top in the centre of the back, the Annunciation: the figure of Mary adorned in pearls and rubies, gold thread and silver, a gleaming halo surrounding her entire form, and the wings of the angel still gloriously bright more than six hundred years after they were created. Tucked away at the top of one sleeve was a green-worked hill and a cross, whilst on the other sleeve, the final piece that had been so carefully reattached, there was a glorious starburst, and beneath it, the tiny manger, filled with gold straw and waiting...

A week later, Dottie opened the door. William was there on the step. His greatcoat collar was pulled up around his neck, but neither his hat nor his coat offered much protection from the rain.

He didn't smile at her, didn't even look at her, his gaze was fixed about halfway down the door jamb. She could feel the tension in him. She took a step back to let him into the house out of the weather, but he didn't move.

'I thought I should come and personally thank you for all your help in Ripley.'

Whatever she'd expected him to say, it hadn't been that. She hadn't seen him since the afternoon he'd taken her to the museum, and she had longed to hear his voice or better yet to see his face, but didn't know whether he would welcome her calling either on the phone or in person. Now, she simply shook her head and stared at him, waiting for him to say something more to the point. Everything hinged on what he said next.

He glanced away to the side, the movement sending a little waterfall of rain off the brim of his hat to splash onto his shoulder. He bit his lip, uncertain.

She took a breath, then said his name softly. He turned to look at her now, his eyes finally meeting hers. His voice cracked as he said, 'Dottie, I'm so very sorry...'

She grabbed his sleeve and pulled him indoors. Cold water splashed on her as he pulled her into his arms and kissed her. She reached up to grab his hat, threw it away, pushed open his coat to reach the man inside it.

He broke the kiss. They took a moment to stare at each other, both wondering.

'Take your coat off, and come and sit down,' she said.

She retrieved his hat and hung it on the hall stand. His coat—wet through—she hung up beside the hat. With a sense of being on the threshold of something life-changing, she led him into the drawing room. Immediately she crossed the room to the drinks cabinet, and poured them each a small tot of brandy.

He took his, clinked her glass with it then drank it down. He grimaced and choked slightly at the heat of it. 'Very nice.'

She smiled and sipped hers.

'You don't usually drink this kind of thing,' he said. How well he knew her, she thought.

'I need it this evening.'

He lifted his eyebrows. 'Why?'

'To calm my nerves. You see, I've two things to tell you,' she said.

He was silent, watching her closely.

'First of all,' Dottie continued, 'I want to tell you that I love you, William.'

A smile began to appear on his face. He was about to speak, his hands reaching out to take her into his arms, but she held him back with a palm placed on his chest. She paused, checking she was sure. Was she? Was this really what she wanted? She took a calming breath. Oh yes, she knew it was. She *was* certain.

'The second thing I wanted to tell you is, my parents are away visiting my aunt and uncle. We're quite alone, William. Please say you'll stay the night?'

She smiled finally, nervously, and leaned into his arms. His lips were warm and urgent on hers, his heart pounding against hers, beat for beat, breath for breath.

Together.

At last.

*

THE END

Caron Allan

About the author

Caron Allan writes cosy murder mysteries, both contemporary and also set in the 1920s and 1930s. Caron lives in Derby, England with her husband and two grown-up children and an endlessly varying quantity of cats and sparrows.

Caron Allan can be found on these social media channels and would love to hear from you:

Instagram:
https://www.instagram.com/caronsbooks/

Twitter:
https://twitter.com/caron_allan

Also, if you're interested in news, snippets, Caron's weird quirky take on life or just want some sneak previews, please sign up to Caron's blog! The web address is shown below:

Blog: http://caronallanfiction.com/

Also by Caron Allan:

Criss Cross – Friendship Can Be Murder: book 1
Cross Check – Friendship Can Be Murder: book 2
Check Mate – Friendship Can Be Murder: book 3

Night and Day: Dottie Manderson mysteries book 1
The Mantle of God: Dottie Manderson mysteries book 2
Scotch Mist: Dottie Manderson mysteries book 3 a novella
The Last Perfect Summer of Richard Dawlish: Dottie
Manderson mysteries book 4
The Thief of St Martins: Dottie Manderson mysteries book 5
The Spy Within: Dottie Manderson mysteries book 6

Easy Living: a story about life after death, after death, after death

Coming Soon

Rose Petals and White Lace: Dottie Manderson mysteries book 7

NEW SERIES: A Meeting With Murder: Miss Gascoigne mysteries: book 1

New series announcement:

Introducing a new murder mystery series set in the 1960s and featuring a new heroine for a new era: The Miss Gascoigne mysteries, set in the Swinging 60s.

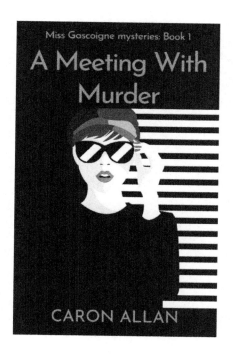

See caronallan.com for details!